HOT
PAINT

Forge Books by Robert S. Levinson

A
Tom Doherty
Associates Book
New York

HOT
PAINT

A
Neil Gulliver
and
Stevie Marriner
Novel

Robert S. Levinson

HOT PAINT: A NEIL GULLIVER AND
STEVIE MARRINER NOVEL

Copyright © 2002 by Robert S. Levinson

A Forge Book
Published by Tom Doherty Associates, LLC
175 Fifth Avenue
New York, NY 10010

www.tor.com

Forge® is a registered trademark of
Tom Doherty Associates, LLC.

Library of Congress Cataloging-in-Publication Data

Levinson, Robert S.
    Hot paint : a Neil Gulliver and Stevie Marriner novel /
Robert S. Levinson.—1st ed.
        p.   cm.
    "A Tom Doherty Associates book."
    ISBN 0-765-30231-4 (acid-free paper)
    1. Gulliver, Neil (Fictitious character)—Fiction.
2. Marriner, Stevie (Fictitious character)—Fiction.   3. Los
Angeles (Calif.)—Fiction.   4. Art treasures in war—Fiction.
5. Journalists—Fiction.   6. Art thefts—Fiction.   I. Title.
    PS3562.E9218 H68 2002
    813'.54—dc21
                                                            2002022187

First Edition: August 2002

Printed in the United States of America

0 9 8 7 6 5 4 3 2 1

FOR SANDRA
The Air That I Breathe

and

To the Memory of

HELEN KORN
August 25, 1918–August 24, 1997

and

ABE LEVINSON
April 20, 1914–February 9, 1989

and

RICHARD STEVEN LEVINSON
February 17, 1950–January 20, 2002

HOT
PAINT

SLUG LINE: HOT PAINT

By Neil Gulliver

Clegg spent most of the night getting drunk at Billy Bob's Texas in the Fort Worth stockyards, hardly taking time out from prowling the thirty-two bar stations of the seven-acre "World's Largest Honky-Tonk" to check the action at the indoor bull-riding arena or the Merle Haggard show cutting loose on the main stage, old Hag rousing the crowd to its boot-stomping feet with his defiant anthem, "I'm Proud to be an Okie from Muskogee."

The place smelled like stale smoke and redneck sweat until he found himself a local pretty drenched in cheap cologne, a brunette in a Daisy Mae hairdo who rubbed her chubby body against him while matching him shot for shot on a high-octane concoction they called Sitting Bull's Revenge and near closing time had no trouble in answering him "Yes"—only in pronouncing it—when he invited her back to his motel.

"We gonna skee-rew?" she said, in a thick cigarette-stained voice full of Texas that added a decade to her age, which Clegg figured at early twenties. "We ain't and your Juicy Lucy here is gonna be one disappointed virgin."

Later, in the harsh motel-room light he insisted had to be kept on, he recognized she was a well-preserved forty or forty-five and, for what she was doing to him, proving that age has its virtues, especially among the less virtuous.

Clegg needed somebody to talk to as much as he needed the sexual release, maybe more, and she was a good listener when she wasn't talking herself, telling him exactly how she wanted it next and each time rating his performance, like Clegg was going for Olympic gold.

He wanted her to stay the night, but she said she had to be home in time to feed the bum and get her bumlets onto their school buses, make herself presentable before heading on to her sorry-ass job at the stockyards.

She gave him a suck and a peck on his pecker before going, declining for a second time his offer of money, a thank-you token of appreciation, telling him that would destroy her amateur standing.

He liked Lucy.

She wasn't like some women he'd met over the years, who were prying and nosy, gave him a different kind of pain in the ass by asking him too many questions or studying him too hard, so that finally he had to kill them for an encore.

Lucy was real, down-to-earth honest and could even make him laugh, by itself no mean trick.

Clegg knew he would have felt lousy if he'd've had to leave her behind with the soiled linen.

Not at all like he'd felt after killing Von Harbou.

Plugging Von Harbou, then dumping the damned old Nazi over the side of one of his precious Bavarian Alps hadn't bothered Clegg at all.

Von Harbou wasn't the first badass he'd done and he wouldn't be the last; anyway, not for a while longer.

The memory was as fresh as yesterday's aftershave, how he had traded the letter of credit worth four million in untraceable U.S. dollars for Von Harbou's van Gogh, Vincent contemplating the landscape at sunset, the colors almost like brand-new: vibrant, alive, like on the day Vincent first put them there, and then—

Clegg shot a finger gun at the framed litho passing for fine art on the motel wall—

Ka-pow.

Good riddance to bad rubbish, like the old saying goes.

Damned old Nazi.

Afterward, he left with both the letter of credit and the van Gogh, feeling better than he had since making the trip up the mountain from Dachau, wondering if he'd have felt this fine about doing Von Harbou, cleaner than in years, if he had not stopped at the concentration camp.

It was a place he'd spent years avoiding, never anxious to confront the horrors it represented to him.

Why this time had been different and he'd gone there he wasn't sure.

Maybe because he'd decided on the flight over that seeing Dachau would salve his conscience by showing him the reality of death beyond any he had caused once he took up killing as a way of life.

The phone yanked Clegg from a deep sleep, his first good one since Salzburg, where the fax message from the boss waiting for him when he checked in at the Hotel Bristol on Market Platz advised, *Phone me at once. Any hour day or night. Another Warhol has surfaced.*

He knew it would be the boss on the phone now, even before the receiver reached his ear. It was always him calling at some ungodly hour or inconvenient moment, making certain Clegg was on the case and following instructions, like some watchdog of a mother treating her seventeen-year-old as if he were still seven, something Clegg swore he would never do with his own son.

He grabbed for the receiver and rolled into a sitting position, grumbled a "Yeah" into the mouthpiece. Squinted for focus at the luminous face of the digital clock on the nightstand and was surprised to discover it was almost noon.

"I called last night, Clegg. Several times. You weren't there."

The boss all right.

"I know . . . I was out."

"I left messages. You didn't return any of my calls."

"I was still out."

Clegg cradled the phone between his ear and shoulder and reached for the three oddly shaped, marble-size white-and-gray stones he had deposited in the ashtray on the nightstand.

He'd picked them up on a camp pathway before leaving Dachau.

Souvenirs.

Not exactly a cap with mouse ears.

The stones were as cold as anything he'd ever felt in his whole life. Even colder than the chill he got seeing the brick ovens.

Standing inside the cottage where the death showers were.

The boss said, "Tell me. The package was waiting for you when you arrived? Everything on schedule?"

"Yeah. The package. On schedule. Everything checked and double-checked first thing I got here."

Clegg began rolling the stones in his palm, the way he'd seen Humphrey Bogart do once in some movie.

"You'll let me know how it went immediately afterward?"

"Don't I always?"

"One can never be too careful."

"No argument from me," Clegg said, and after a moment staring at the stones: "You ever go to Dachau?"

"Of course. The Old Pinakothek, the Bavarian National Museum—"

"The camp, I mean."

"The camp? Why on earth would I go to the camp? Clegg, what kind of question is that?"

"I was just wondering," Clegg said, studying the stones for any secrets they might want to share with him.

The boss said, "Are you all right? You don't sound—"

"I'm fine. I was just wondering, that's all."

"I'd be happier knowing your mind is exclusively on your work."

Clegg said, "*Arbeit Macht Frei.*"

Work Brings Freedom, the comforting words of welcome embedded in the diamond design of the roll-away iron gate at the arched entrance to Dachau, where the railroad tracks ended.

"What? Clegg, I didn't hear what you—"

Clegg took his hand off the mouthpiece. "I said it's always on my work. In all this time, I ever let you down?"

"I'd regret a first time."

"Need to go," Clegg said. "I don't want to be late."

Clegg got to the Kimbell Art Museum on Arch Adams off West Lancaster an hour early, his first time there since the show *From Renoir to Picasso: Masterpieces from the Musée de l'Orangerie*, was hanging, works from the collection of Paul Guillaume that the Musée purchased from his widow, Juliette, after the Paris art dealer died in 1934.

The exhibit had featured artists Guillaume championed at his gallery at 59 Rue de la Boétie, and did he ever have an eye for fine art: Utrillo. Modigliani. Soutine. Rousseau. De Chirico. Derain. Delaunay.

This time Clegg toured through parts of the permanent collection he had missed before, lingering over oils by some of the artists he was especially fond of and would never be able to afford outside a show catalog or an Abrams art book. Jacques-Louis David. Cézanne. James Ensor. Frans Hals. Peter Paul Rubens. Gauguin. Edvard Munch. Matisse, of course, and Picasso. Goya. Ah, Goya.

His taste was as much eclectic as discriminating, why he could never get enough of the Modern in New York.

He didn't need a formal education to know that when it came to art the eye was the best teacher and the keeper of the soul.

More time today and he might have made it over to the Amon Carter to take in the museum's stockpile of Charles M. Russells and Frederic Remingtons, unquestionably two of the greatest interpreters ever of the Old West.

Precisely at three o'clock, Clegg was standing at ease in front of Picasso's *Nude Combing Her Hair* when he heard the echo of heels with taps on the hardwood floor and after another moment felt someone stop alongside and maybe half a foot away.

"Mr. Patterson?"

Patterson, the name Clegg was using this time.

The voice was deep, flat and unfamiliar; had a side-of-the-mouth quality. Turning, Clegg saw nobody he recognized, definitely not the face he knew from the society-page clips as R. Mead Richardson.

This guy was somewhere in his thirties and about twenty years too young. Twenty pounds too heavy. Looked like he did his clothes shopping during post-holiday discount sales at a Salvation Army thrift shop.

Clegg played along.

"Mr. Richardson?"

"Mr. Douglas, Mr. Richardson's secretary. He sent me to apologize and explain he won't be keeping his appointment."

"Oh?"

"He directed me to tell you that he's changed his mind and has chosen not to go through with your arrangement. Mr. Richardson wanted to call and tell you this personally, but he didn't know how to reach you. Mr. Richardson apologizes for any inconvenience and, in fact, is prepared to reimburse you for expenses you may have incurred to now. Your flight? Your hotel?"

Clegg could see by Douglas's put-upon face that it was useless to argue the point or even suggest they meet anyway, to try and persuade Mr. Richardson otherwise. The secretary had his instructions.

That was that.

Period.

Finito.

"Tell Mr. Richardson thank you, but unnecessary. Tell him I understand, Mr. Douglas, but may take the liberty of checking back with him at some future time; on the off-chance he's changed his mind again."

"Yes, you do that," Douglas said, sounding relieved, like he'd been prepared to say Richardson wasn't available or wasn't home, was in a meeting and couldn't be disturbed, but he would be sure to see that Mr. Richardson got the message.

Well, Mr. Richardson was going to get the message.

Sooner than he expected.

However, not the message he expected.

Back at the motel, waiting for nightfall, Clegg reviewed the blueprints and plans to the Richardson Mediterranean-style home in Aledo Estates. Quite a spread sitting on more than eight acres, worth at least a million or so here in Forth Worth and maybe four times that in Beverly Hills. Two stories with a sensational view, from second-story balconies, of a private arbor and the wooded grounds beyond. A private pond stocked with rare species of fish paralleling a stretch of security wall fashioned from imported scenic stone, a waterfall carved into one section.

Inside, the usual amenities of wealthy bachelors: high ceilings and glistening hardwood floors; rooms twice the size of a Vegas suite reserved for the highest of the high rollers; a gourmet kitchen designed to make any master chef's salivary glands overflow; bedrooms and bathrooms also meant for fun and games; an office suite that included a paneled library; a game room equipped with the latest electronic gizmos and gadgets; a gym suitable for a Schwarzenegger and secret doors to secret rooms the twenty-page cover story in *Architectural Digest* only hinted at, but Clegg knew about—

From the blueprints.

The same way they exposed security-system conduits that would be as simple to get by as the security team Richardson had skimped on.

No staff to worry about. Richardson had them on a nine-to-five clock, except for a valet and all-purpose handyman-houseboy named Roy Nemo.

Nemo was a year out of college, a handsome fraternity-type second-team All-America at guard who'd been drafted in a low round by the Cowboys, but didn't make the final cut.

Pretty as a picture.

Easy to understand why Richardson was sweet on him.

When it was time to leave, Clegg double-checked the jet-black beard, mustache and obvious pompon hairpiece he'd worn since arriving in Forth Worth.

As an added precaution, packed his fresh, clean, snub-nosed .38 and a silencer, hopeful he wouldn't need them to finish the job.

Set off with the scuffed, innocent-looking doctor's satchel that held the rest of his tools.

Clegg parked the rental a quarter mile from the wall at the back of the property and checked the time. The security-patrol guys would be finishing their takeout about now and settling down to their evening snooze.

By the time he reached the break spot, he'd decided the Big Mac "Supersize it" guy had lost again to his partner, the Chinese triple-entree junkie.

That seemed to be the pattern, not that the Chinese triple-entree junkie ever made such a great case for the kung pao mandarin chicken. Maybe it was just that the kung pao mandarin chicken sat better than the Big Macs and fries with their nightly pint of Wild Turkey.

Once inside Richardson's house, Clegg headed straight for the office suite.

He located the black box containing the Warhols in the highly polished Flemish carved oak–and–rosewood cabinet—second half seventh century, he figured—that stood about seven feet tall and six feet across, against the wall to the right of the cluttered partners desk, in one of the bottom drawers.

He resisted the temptation to inspect the contents of the box.

Stick to the timetable, he told himself.

He located the Cézanne self-portrait hanging in the secret room behind the bookcase on the south wall of the library. There was belligerence in the way Cézanne stared down at him, commanding his attention.

It reminded Clegg of the artist's grand boast, *"With an apple I will astonish Paris."*

"Shortsighted, maestro," he said. "The whole world came to know your genius."

Clegg flipped the light switch, stowed his flashlight.

The Cézanne, bathed in a key light, had the padded wall all to itself, whereas other oils competed for space, several the equal of the Cézanne in power and beauty, one or two in importance.

Cautiously, he stripped the painting from its ornate frame and rolled it tightly in protective wrapping. Made a choice from among the other oils and wrapped it similarly, then with a mother's care secured both in the soft leather case strapped to his back like a bowman's quiver.

Roy Nemo was waiting for Clegg at the French doors Clegg had entered through, half hidden by shadows out of the moonlight cruising through the glass, just enough illumination to show the double-barrel shotgun he had cradled in the crook of his arm, cocked and ready to fire.

Nemo was the perfect picture of anxiety in his Jockeys, bare-chested and rocking on the balls of his feet.

"I've called nine-one-one, fucker, so you just hold it there," he said, his baritone trembling.

"Sure," Clegg said.

"What's in that bag thing on your back? What you think you were going to get away with?"

"I'll show you," Clegg said.

He bent at the knees, slowly so as not to alarm Nemo any further.

Set the satchel on the antique Kirman carpet.

Kept his eyes fixed on Nemo's eyes as he rose, doing nothing of concern while Nemo traced his movement with the shotgun.

Clegg moved his hands like he was going to undo the case buckle, using his left hand to shield his right hand, which kept going until it had a firm grip on the black-taped handle of the .38 in his snatch holster.

"Not so fast," Nemo said.

"Fast enough," Clegg said, and—

Put a bullet into Nemo that sent him crashing through the French doors like he'd been hit by the entire St. Louis Rams front line.

"Damn," Clegg said. He stepped forward to check Nemo, although he knew he had been too close to miss the score. Paused to audit the brisk night air, heard only the sound of a breeze sailing through the trees. No evidence of the sirens a 911 call would have brought on the double.

More likely Nemo had tried a bluff.

Too early for the security-patrol drive-by.

Nothing to suggest the sound of the gunshot had gone anywhere outside the woods.

He'd have to chance it.

Wondering what happened to rouse Roy Nemo clear of the adage Clegg knew well—*Shit happens*—also knew better than to dwell on, he hurried back inside to the main entry.

Up the circular stairway.

Into the master bedroom.

Richardson was sitting up in bed, shielding his eyes against the glare of Clegg's flashlight.

"What was it, Roy, darling? And that new noise that I just . . . Sounded to me like—"

"None of this had to happen if you kept your damn appointments," Clegg said.

He stopped and put a bullet between Richardson's eyes.

"None of it."

Spent the next fifteen minutes making it look like a burglary gone sour.

Clegg heard it in the boss's voice.

The murders didn't matter to him, only Clegg's reassurance about the Cézanne and, of course, the Warhols.

"When will you have them to me?"

"On schedule," Clegg said.

"And, of course, you'll bring the letter of credit back."

Spoken like he might not trust Clegg to return it. No mistaking. He could be trusted to steal and, if necessary, murder for him, but the money? Something else.

"I thought maybe I'd keep it as a bonus, for services rendered over and above."

A moment's silence, like he didn't hear or understand the sarcasm in Clegg's response.

"I believe I'd like to have it back, Clegg."

Gee, what a surprise.

"You're the boss, boss."

"About the Warhols, you have a look?"

"No. You want me to? Call you back?"

As if he didn't know what the answer would be.

"Thank you."

"Give me five," Clegg said, and hung up.

Let the boss stew for twenty minutes over that.

Watched the news.

The murders of Richardson and Nemo still the big local story. Also headlines on MSNBC and CNN. Police saying they looked to have resulted from a random burglary. Burglars got caught in the act. No count yet on what may have been taken. Investigation still in progress. Et cetera. Et cetera.

"Sorry about the delay, boss. Had to run out and spring for a fresh phone card at the 7-Eleven."

A grunt of acceptance.

"The Warhols . . . Was it there, Clegg? Did you find it?"

"No. Only the same ones as before."

"Christ."

More noise. The boss sounding full of pain, like a jilted lover.

Clegg said, "Maybe we'll catch ourselves a break next time, boss."

Caught himself wishing otherwise.

Not for the first time.

2

There's a little boy inside Neil Gulliver—me—who never grew up.

The little boy clings to his comrade-in-arms, Peter Pan, in the never-never land of his own geography, where there'll always be a Santa Claus, a Tooth Fairy, a moon waiting to hear him say good night, comic-book heroes as sure as a hot-fudge sundae, a mommy and a daddy who will live forever.

Reality is his constant enemy the older and wiser he gets, the truth a beacon that obscures the dreams, but he perseveres, like the little engine that could, even when another myth of his own making proves as false as the promise of a happy ending in a ritual that concludes with words like, *You may now kiss the bride.*

I should know better than to keep him around, this kid that still lets me kid myself after all I've seen and done in my almost forty years, including far too many as a crime reporter with the *Los Angeles Daily* and then as a *Daily* columnist writing seven days a week about people

and events in a city that mixes happiness and horror and often can't
distinguish one from the other.

But I don't.

Won't?

Can't?

Think about it and let me know when you get to know me better,
but I'll tell you now—

You'll have to know me a lot better than I know myself, and even
then it's unlikely I'll agree with you more than I ever agree with my
ex-wife, Stephanie Marriner, who claims to know me better than I
know myself.

Stevie's wrong about that, of course.

I'll grant you that sometimes she knows me as well as I know myself—don't tell her I said so—but most of the time she treats the idea
like it's some kind of a bragging right she got when she divorced me
after seven years of marriage.

The divorce, it was for my own good, Stevie said at the time, like
she knew better than me.

So how come I haven't felt good about it in the eight years since?

It's not exactly a torch I've been carrying; it's more like a beacon,
like a light you'd keep lit for the prodigal bride who married too young
and needs to get a bigger taste of life to appreciate the full-course meal
she left behind.

Stevie has come to understand that.

Trust me on that one.

I know Stevie better than she knows herself.

That's why our divorce has worked out better than our marriage,
because I know that deep down she regrets it ever happened, same as
me.

About this I also kid you not.

Our friendship has deepened in the intervening years, same as our
love, same as our, yeah, need for one another. Honestly? Stevie recognized this part before I did, saw we had to get away from one another
to get closer together, but please don't tell her I said so.

If I deserve credit for anything, it's for spotting the brains that came
with the sixteen-year-old beauty I spied at a rock-and-roll festival and,
after stealing her away for my own, helping her to discover this for
herself, encouraging her to make it work for herself.

Ultimately Stevie used her mind, along with her talent and engaging
personality, to achieve her childhood dream of stardom.

Became Stephanie Marriner, two-time Emmy-winning "Sex Queen

of the Soaps," and last year the toast of London in a West End stage production that had the critics heaping more praise on her than she ever got here in the States.

In between, she overcame the derision of critics prone to talent judgments based on her blonde hair, a stage play that never made it to Broadway, and low-budget movie scripts that came with more fingerprints than the red herrings in an Agatha Christie mystery.

Since returning to Los Angeles three months ago, she'd been weighing offers from all the majors, high-rankers like Spielberg, Scorsese and Cameron, and calls from New York to inquire if she might be interested in new plays by Simon or Mamet, a reworking of Sondheim's *Merrily We Roll Along*, the projected Lincoln Center revival of Miller's *After the Fall*.

Finally, Stevie was being taken seriously, and we were closer than ever.

Figuratively speaking.

Not literally.

Stevie had traded her mansion in trendy Los Feliz for a condo in Empire Towers, the crown jewel of the high-rises on the Wilshire Corridor in Westwood, hardly more than a mile, mile-and-a-half jog from my own modest condo on Veteran, south of the boulevard.

I wanted to believe it was because of some deep-rooted psychological need she had to be closer to me.

She said it was because the three-bedroom place on the top floor of the twenty-story building was a steal, too big a bargain to pass up even though the deal had cost her a cool million-four on top of what she got for the mansion. Lots of pizzazz to go with the prestige address and safety features she still needed for her peace of mind, although it had been almost a year since she and I had run scared of a killer who had us in mind for the eleven o'clock news.

I was teasing her about it while she bustled around the place in the final hour before guests were due to arrive for an open house, adjusting furniture and pictures on the wall and the platters of food arranged by Philippe and Roberto of Oui Two, the caterers Stevie was using for her first social event since moving in and doing a complete renovation to all but the magnificent balcony views of the city and the ocean.

She rearranged the jumbo shrimp after popping one into her mouth, turned to me and said, "Closer to you?" Her high-pitched laugh sent bits of shrimp flying onto the lush olive-green carpeting.

Philippe was there in an instant to survey the damage. Tut-tutted Stevie with an eyebrow and snapped his fingers to get the attention of one of the servers dressed in what looked like an old Playboy Club bunny rig, but without the ears. Pointed out to her the shrimp shards swimming on the pile, then turned and—with another *naughty-naughty* eyebrow for Stevie—put sterling-silver bowls of Swedish meatballs, chicken à la something and stuffed noodles à la something else back where he had originally placed them.

I said, "Admit it, having me so near is as comforting as a baby's security blanket."

"Almost as much as the twenty-four/seven security force that comes with the building."

"Do I detect a note of sarcasm from someone who's never been able to carry a tune?"

"No, it's still me talking to you—but only barely if you don't quit it."

"You can always call security and have me tossed."

"Believe me, I'm tempted."

"And leave yourself unprotected this evening around the two hundred nearest and dearest tax deductions you expect?"

"The word you can't seem to find is *friends*, honey."

"Nobody has two hundred friends."

"Business is business. Besides, who needs two hundred when I have you?"

I clutched my heart. "Did you just slip up and say something nice?

"Only to shut you up," Stevie said.

She switched the stuffed noodles à la something else with a mountainous platter of smoked salmon and crossed to the immense Roy Lichtenstein litho that dominated the wall to the left of the imported marble-faced fireplace.

It was one of the limited-edition, signed and numbered *Peace Through Chemistry* images Lichtenstein had done at Gemini G.E.L. on Melrose. We'd bought the litho while we were married. I was still paying it off a year after our divorce.

Stevie used the frame's glass as a mirror to fluff her hair, smooth out her eyebrows and run a thumb and forefinger out across her upper lip and down and away from the corners of her mouth. Fiddle with the neck and shoulders of a floor-length Chanel cocktail gown she'd found during a run at Saks I made with her earlier in the day, in a shade that brought out the iridescent violet of her showstopping eyes.

A double-loop strand of pearls, a gift from some bogus prince or count she briefly dated three years ago, and that was it for accents.

Except for the one she had picked up in London and would have been better off leaving behind.

Overall, looking as demure as someone who looked like Stevie could look.

I said, "Where is she? What have you done with my Sex Queen of the Soaps?"

"She's all washed up, darling; history," Stevie said, pronouncing it "dah-ling," like she was testing for a revival of Noël Coward's *Private Lives*.

An hour later, the party was in fourth gear, one or two faces familiar to me in a shoulder-to-shoulder crowd sending up a sound storm that competed with the disc jockey spinning a combination of jazz, rock and golden oldies through every room.

Stevie seemed confused by many of the faces pushing into hers with hugs and handshakes, blends of "Welcome backs" and "Congratulations," but nevertheless managed to keep her photogenic smile intact and play the double air-kiss game with everyone, in case the *Vanity Fair* photog had his Nikon aimed and rat-a-tat-tatting in her direction.

Smells from the kitchen meshed badly with perfumes and colognes as Philippe and Roberto's crew navigated the rooms, trying hard to keep up with the elephantine appetites of the guests, some of whom seemed hungry enough to eat the serving trays.

The three bars were as busy, pouring mostly white wines and champagne, passing across bottles of designer water, and splashing combinations of the hard stuff and mix over ice to the unreconstructed drinkers.

I'd settled with a Bud on the patio facing the Pacific with LAPD detective Lieutenant Ned DeSantis and his date. Ned and I had shared some adventures the last couple years, and in the process developed a friendship maybe halfway to the one I'd built from my days on the *Daily*'s crime beat with another of L.A.'s finest, Lieutenant Jimmy Steiger.

Steiger had phoned regrets this afternoon, explaining it was Little League soccer night for the oldest of his and Margie's seven future detectives.

When I told that to DeSantis, he said, "Guy put in as much time taking care of business the way he churns out the babies, the Ramparts thing never would've happened, y'know?"

His date said, "What Ramparts thing, Neddy?"

"Some of our people, that division, they were dirty and they got caught, tried, convicted and shipped off to do the laundry. Good riddance. Made us all look bad." He sailed his butt over the railing, took a sip from his scotch and water, and turned back to me. "Bess here, she's pretty new to town, from New York."

"I do voice-overs," she said. "Like for commercials and animated movies? Cartoons?"

"I know."

"You know Breezy Bubbleworth?" DeSantis said.

"Not personally."

"Saturday mornings on Nickelodeon. She's Mrs. Breezy. Go ahead and do Mrs. Breezy for him, Bessie, okay?"

Bess smiled up at DeSantis and cleared her throat.

She was a coquettish little brunette in her early to mid-thirties with fluttery eyelashes and a butterfly voice that became lighter than gossamer when she pinched her oval face and said, " 'Stacy Bubbleworth, you know better than to cross the street without checking both ways first.' "

DeSantis said, "Great, huh?"

"You watch this Breezy show?"

"I do now, religiously. *The Bubbleworths*. Ever since I met Bessie online at the Love at First Site site. We got to dating and—"

Bess shook her hand like she was waving hello. "Wait, wait," she said. Cleared her throat again and, sounding like someone sharing a quiet confidence, said, " 'You don't have to be named Maxie or Minnie to see and feel the difference in the exclusive safety-first design features of Padorama maxi and mini pads.' "

DeSantis was entranced. It showed like the acne scars on his curiously handsome doughboy face. "Great, ain't she? Got a voice that can go in a million directions."

Bess smiled at DeSantis, looked at me for agreement.

I nodded. "They start teaching them young on *The Bubbleworths*, do they?"

"No, no," Bess said. "That's the national spot that I just did for Padorama Products. TV and radio. Starts running in the next sweeps period."

"I'll be on the lookout."

DeSantis said, "Somebody else on camera, though. Why I wanted Bessie to come and meet Stevie. Thinking your star can give Bessie some acting tips, maybe open some doors for her."

"I had to be her biggest fan when she was on *Bedrooms and Board*

Rooms," Bess said, doing an uncanny impression of how Stevie sounded before London, waiflike innocence trapped inside sexual innuendo. "I miss Stevie on it tremendously. I read in the trades and in *People* how she's not going back."

"On to bigger and better things."

"Also on *Entertainment Tonight*. Tell me, can you? Was it really a contract dispute, what they all were saying was 'irreconcilable differences' ?"

"That was our divorce," I said. Regretted at once leading with my tongue.

Bess gave me a curious look and turned to DeSantis for clarification.

DeSantis started to say something but was interrupted by rapping on the picture window.

Bump-bumpa-bum-bum.

My best friend and mentor, Augie Fowler, was commanding my attention, his head jerking sideways as a signal to join him.

I excused myself and stepped back inside the room.

"What's up?"

"Need you for a minute downstairs, amigo. Tried to get Stevie, but she's holding court like she left the Sex Queen of the Soaps and came back the Queen of England."

"You do have an eye for detail, Augie."

"This one, too," he said, indicating the patch over his blind eye that matched the burgundy color of his cassock.

We rode the elevator down in silence.

A stretch limo with official plates was parked in the circular drive immediately in front of the guarded double glass doors of an entrance lobby that rivaled the set from *Grand Hotel*.

Frank Gordy, the mayor of Palm Springs, was stationed by the passenger door.

He smiled and saluted me as we approached, opened the door and invited us inside the Mercedes with a gesture.

"Maybe move your asses," commanded a voice I recognized immediately. "All night I ain't got, goddamn it."

"Where's the girl?" Aaron Lodger threw the question at Augie after a bare nod of acknowledgment at me. "I thought I told you bring me both of them, Augie. You're so old now you forget by the time the elevator gets where it's going?"

Augie answered with a snarl of his own. "That's you you have me confused with, you decrepit little crook bastard."

Lodger gave him the deathly stare that's hard to forget once you've seen it. Cold brown eye-slits buried inside his forehead and cheeks. Slice of mouth rigid on a small, tight-skinned face the color of chalk.

Maybe why, in Lodger's younger years as an enforcer, before he became the reputed crime boss out here, the law couldn't ever link him to a murder weapon. It was always done with a look that kills.

I suppose I should have bad things to say about Lodger, but Stevie and I are alive because of him and that's worth a lot of Brownie points the way I score the Book of Life.

"A man of God talks the way you do?" he said, hissing like a steam heater.

"To a gangster like you," Augie said.

"Retired gangster, you *momser*. I'm retired. You forget that, too?" His prominent Adam's apple danced to the question.

"You'll be six feet under, you'll still be giving the orders."

"And don't you forget it. I'll be six feet under, you won't still be around to know, you keep talking like that. I've made people disappear on less."

"A regular Mandrake the Magician you are."

Lodger looked at me and said, "You should choose your friends with more care, Neil."

Augie pushed back against the soft leather.

"So, Aaron, as usual we find something we can agree on."

There was a momentary silence before they exploded into a shared belly laugh, Lodger clapping his oversized, blue-veined hands joyously while his face eased back to friendly terrain, Augie patting my thigh, squeezing my shoulder.

Augie and Lodger are about the same age, somewhere in their mid-seventies. Augie was the *Daily*'s crime-beat mug and Lodger was clawing his way up the ranks of the Mickey Cohen mob, when they forged their curious relationship. Augie still owes me the story, beyond a promise to let me read it in one of the journals he keeps under lock and key at the monastery he founded across from Griffith Park after leaving the paper and turning himself into "Brother Kalman" of the Order of the Spiritual Brothers of the Rhyming Heart.

After I got to the paper, he made me a better reporter and to this day thinks he owns me. Maybe he does, but not in the same way Lodger owned Frank Gordy in the front seat, one of his henchmen before he helped Frank get elected the mayor of Palm Springs.

"Look, Augie, I said I got a housewarming gift for the girl, so you shouldn't let me down when I have Frank call up to you and say you should get her and Neil here for me."

"I tried. She's being a good hostess, Aaron."

"Like I wasn't invited?"

I said, "I know Stevie's been looking forward to seeing you, Mr. Lodger. Come upstairs and—"

"I wanted to be upstairs, I'd be upstairs."

He pointed at his hips.

"Ever since last year, I got thrown off that stage at the Lennon memorial concert we did that turned into such a nightmare, into that what's it called, the nosh pit?"

"Mosh pit, Mr. L," Frank Gordy cautiously corrected him through the privacy window.

"I know. The mosh pit. Ever since, walking, it's not the same. Two hip replacements and still some broken bones in my legs don't feel like they healed up right."

I thought about it and said, "I'll be right back."

Pushed open the door and eased out of the limo.

I heard Lodger saying, "You housebroke him real good, Augie," as I headed back inside the Tower to corral my ex.

Stevie settled close to Lodger in the backseat of the limo, leaned in and gave him a light kiss on the cheek.

His eyes shifted left and right.

A hint of a smile came and went.

He looked like he might have been embarrassed by it.

He put a hand to the spot, then slid the hand under the thick cashmere blanket covering his legs.

Stevie adjusted the blanket, did something to the fresh red rose in the lapel of Lodger's brown silk suit jacket and played a bit with the knot on his floral-patterned silk tie.

"You didn't really think that I'd let you leave without seeing you?" she said.

He leaned away and said, "I know what it's like, you got guests to entertain."

"They'll have to wait. How are you? How have you been?"

"It could be worse," Lodger said. "But you, you look like a million dollars. England agreed with you."

"More than I ever hoped."

> >
> >

"Glad to hear, but I miss you from *Bedrooms and Board Rooms*. I stopped watching since you left the show. One word from me again, you're back on, you know?"

"Why I couldn't go last time, Mr. Lodger. One of the reasons. They didn't want me back until you put a gun to their head—"

"Just a friendly word," Lodger said.

"It was kind of you, but it would have been wrong for me. What you did do, though, was help me make up my mind to stop settling for the fame, the comfort, the security that comes after seven years of doing the same old same old. Go chase after my dream again, win or lose, the one I had ever since I was just a little girl."

She looked to him for understanding.

Lodger nodded.

"You got balls, I always said that about you. I always say that about her, Frank?"

"You sure do, Mr. L."

"Hi, Frank. I didn't mean to ignore you."

"Hi, Stevie, sugar. I understand."

"Frankie, talk to her on your own time." Lodger cleared his throat. "Meanwhile, go and get for me from the trunk the housewarming gift I brung."

"You didn't have to—"

"Lots of things I don't have to, but this ain't one of them. I did what I did with them *shtarkers* at *Bedrooms and Board Rooms* because of all you meant to my Richie, God rest his soul. You decided against that, so I still owed you."

"Really, it isn't necessary. Your taking the time to drive in from the desert is enough of a gift."

"From somebody else. Not from me."

The passenger door on Lodger's side opened.

"Here you go, Mr. L," Frank Gordy said.

He settled on top of Lodger's lap a black presentation box about sixteen by twenty or twenty-two inches in size and six or eight inches deep.

The black lettering on the white label in the center of the cover said:

Andy Warhol
P O R t r a I T S

Stevie took in a mouthful of air and gave Lodger a look that said, *You shouldn't have.*

Augie and I traded curious glances.

Lodger didn't try hiding his delight at our reactions.

"Not so big a deal," he said, brushing imaginary dust from the label. "I'll tell you."

3

*S*tevie thought she knew why without the need for Aaron Lodger to explain.

Seeing Andy Warhol's name on the presentation box spiraled her memory back to 1985, her first months as Neil's bride, and to Rick Savage, Lodger's precious "Richie."

It wasn't so long after the second annual Imagine That! music festival on the San Gorgonio Indian Reservation, where she'd gone to cheer Richie, the headliner and rock's number one bad boy, to smoke some pot with her friends and go braless in the arid desert heat; ride some stranger's shoulders and wave the bra like a windmill after Richie and his band took the stage and proceeded to lift the crowd of thousands to a level above frenzy.

That's where Neil found her.

Stevie was sixteen, old and knowing, and maybe too wise for her own good.

Neil was eight years older and glamorous to her, a dude who really seemed to care and see some special qualities in her, something Mama also felt about Neil, so she was as quick as Stevie was to say yes when Neil said he wanted to marry her.

Besides, he was working.

A newspaper reporter.

He had a steady job and a steady income.

That also appealed to Mama, who was raising Stevie single-handedly, struggling at it, but surviving, and trying at the same time to find a different sort of life for herself; for them.

It would be years before Stevie recognized Neil's flaws as well as his virtues, especially the gambling habit eating them out of house and home, and knew she had to do something about it for both their sakes.

"Where did you say we were going?" she asked, back in '85.

"Didn't," he said, driving to L.A. from their itty-bitty home in Arcadia, dangerously close to the Santa Anita track. It was his answer every time she asked, like a nag (her joke), and him repeating, "It's a surprise. How many times do you have to hear me tell you?"

"Will I like it?"

"Would I give you any other kind of surprise?"

"Only if I forgot to take the pill."

Neil reached L.A. and kept going.

After a while they were cruising along Pacific Coast Highway. The traffic thickened and slowed to bumper tag the closer they got to Malibu. Overhead, the incandescent ocean sky was almost as clogged with circling helicopters.

Finally, at a checkpoint off the highway, their clunker reached the head of a line. Neil flashed something out of his jacket pocket at the security cop, who signaled a *Go ahead*, and not long after that they were milling inside a circus tent, among an elite crowd that had been invited to the wedding of Madonna and Sean Penn.

Stevie squealed with delight when she realized what was going to happen.

She hugged and kissed Neil like it would be their own ceremony, like the fast trip to a Vegas wedding chapel was only their practice run for today.

Understood now why he'd insisted she dress up.

He said, "Merry Christmas, babe," and kissed her on the magic place by her ear.

"Honey, you know that won't be until months and months from now."

"I may not be able to do better than today in the gift department."

"I already got the gift I want from you. You, Neil."

She never forgot the look on his face in that moment.

It lingered throughout the day and was still there in their worst of times and their divorce and ever since.

"Here comes the surprise," Neil said fifteen or twenty minutes after they arrived. They'd been plowing through the fancy hors d'oeuvres and glasses of champagne that went down like silk, Stevie trying not to devour the stars she sighted and waved greetings at, like they were supposed to know who she was and wave back. Some of them actually did, like Dolly Parton and Tom Cruise. Emilio Estevez. Diane Keaton, who was about a good foot taller than Stevie'd ever guessed.

He twisted her in the other direction and she saw who Neil meant, the old police-beat reporter who had taken him under his wing, Augie Fowler, strutting toward them like he owned the place.

For all the great and wonderful things Neil was always saying about the guy, she didn't much care for Augie or his bragging, egotistical, holier-than-thou ways—always making sure to let everyone know he was the best thing going at the *Daily*, better than even her man.

Hah! Hardly.

"What kind of surprise is Augie?" she said, letting him hear in her voice that emergency brain surgery would be more welcome.

"Augie got us the invitation," Neil said, "but not him. See who he's bringing over?"

She did now.

Rick Savage.

Rick Savage!

Shaking hands with Neil and saying sure he remembered him from *Imagine That!*

A moment or three later holding both her hands in his and staring into her eyes.

Telling Stevie how good it was to meet her.

Like he meant it.

Like he meant more than just meaning it.

Neil leaning closer to her ear and whispering, "Also Happy Birthday, babe."

Richie saying, "I get from my pal Augie that you're an actress and a pretty damn fine one. I see you in anything?"

She was too frozen to answer, not even after Neil broke the ice telling him, "Not even her bra."

That made her blush, throw a protective arm across her boobs, and give Neil a knock on the arm.

Caused Richie to grin, like he understood what Neil had meant by it, touch her red-hot cheek tenderly with the back of his strumming hand, and suggest, "Work at it, girl, and someday all this could be yours."

"I'll settle for half," she said, finding her voice.

Making them laugh, Richie the loudest.

Next thing she knew, Andy Warhol had joined them.

Andy Warhol, greeting Augie Fowler like an old friend, almost shyly, his manner gentle, apologetic, saying how he hoped he wasn't interrupting.

Saying he wanted to take a picture of Richie, please, if it was all right with them, and showing off his Polaroid.

Richie saying, sure, absolutely, but asking Warhol to please do one of the whole group, keeping Stevie beside him and then asking Warhol to take one more, of just the two of them. Saying he wanted that one for his scrapbook, so Warhol took it twice, just the two of them, one to go with all the others and one just for Richie.

Richie winking at her while he slipped his into a hip pocket of his undersized blue denims.

Neil trying hard not to look jealous, and saying maybe Warhol could do a third one, a souvenir for his wife. Loud on the word "wife," to make sure Richie got it.

Warhol getting a nod from Richie before he snapped the photo, then Richie borrowing a pen from Augie and using his back to scribble something on the Polaroid before passing it to her:

To the prettiest girl at the party from her fan, Rick Savage.

Making her blush again.

Warhol saying how he'd like to do Richie, hurrying to explain when Richie gave him the eye: "Your portrait. Maybe like the one I did of Mick?"

"Yeah, that would groove, man."

Warhol saying, as if Richie might not know, "I've done Elvis and Marilyn, Jackie . . ."

"Elton told me he bought a whole bunch of the Chinese guy you did when he first got into art."

"Mao."

"Elton John. Some place on La Cienega in L.A. Had them shipped back to his castle. We should talk more."

"Liz and Marlon."

"Electric chairs. I saw a bunch of them one time."

Richie excusing Warhol and himself and, an arm across Warhol's back, leading Warhol off explaining, "I can't this trip. Tomorrow I have to go see Dolly about doing her and then I promised to call Cher . . ."

Aaron Lodger tapped Stevie on the shoulder.

"You hear what I said?"

He'd caught her drifting.

"Yes, of course."

"Goes back from when you and my Richie, God bless him, were what they used to call an item, like Johnny S and Lana years before you, when they were an item."

He paused and gave Neil a look and Neil made a face to say he was comfortable with the subject, although she knew he wasn't—that telepathic thing they had going, people on the same wavelength whether they liked it or not, the way some people came to resemble their pet pooches, or maybe it was the other way around.

Augie said, "The year after marriage had put a strain on their wed-ded bliss and a divorce worked like two aspirin and a good night's sleep."

Lodger said, "And you weren't running around like someone out of an Errol Flynn movie, and how often do I have to say 'Don't tell me what I already know'?"

Augie threw a hand at him.

Lodger said, "Good boy, Johnny; a good looker, even as a corpse. So, you and Richie got around to being an item and he goes over to your place the first time and on the wall he spies this Andy Warhol poster."

Neil said, "A print, Mr. Lodger. Silkscreen. A limited edition, signed and numbered."

"Nick Jagger."

"Mick."

"Augie, again with the interruptions."

"Aaron, it's one thing to know. It's another thing to get your facts straight."

Neil said, "She got it as part of our settlement, along with a lot of other art we had on the wall."

"Another country heard from. Just clam up both of you . . . Okay. So, it's there, this Nick Jagger poster, and it reminds Richie all over again, he's telling me years later, about how he saw Stevie at this Madonna girl's wedding when he met this Warhol and after, got his own picture made. Next day, he has sent over to you his own poster by this Warhol, like the one he kept hung in his bedroom, and his poster came to me since he passed on, God rest him. You still got it, I bet." Looking like he already knew better, like it was a bet he'd never make.

Before she could figure out how to explain she had sent it back to Richie after their bitter split, not needing any reminders of a romance gone rancid, Neil told him, "Only the Mick Jagger." Gave her a smug, *I told you so* look.

A rumble drifted out of Aaron Lodger's throat, and for a few moments it was the only sound in the backseat of the limo. Party guests had started drifting out of the building and, waiting for valet-parking delivery of their cars, tried to look casual shifting to see who was inside. She returned the waves and finger-kisses from sweet Patty Paul, Betsy Moore and her latest hunk of the month, and June Wilkinson, out-busting Stevie as usual in a low-cut cleavage-clinger Stevie recalled seeing at Barney's.

Lodger moved on.

"I remembered the Warhol business when this *shmendrick* who's losing to me big-time at hearts—wanders into the club and takes me for the pigeon he turns out to be—confesses he can't cover his debt. A Frenchie, putting on airs until then, and he sees now I am not fooling around when I tell him, 'You got any better ideas than my friend over there taking you to someplace private away from here where he can rip your lungs from your chest?' "

Augie said, "Retired, right? The way Lucky retired when he was shipped back home to Sicily."

Lodger ignored him.

"So this Frenchie tells me about a box of pictures by Andy Warhol he's been keeping under wraps all these years, to pay for his kids' colleges. Worth a mint, he says, lots more than the national debt he's just run up with me. Makes me think of you and Richie, bless his soul, and how I still owe you for how happy you got Richie again last year, after you nixed the deal I put in place for you over at your soap. I send one of my people with this loser to his pad in Rancho Mirage and they come back in about sixty with the box here." He patted the lid. "Eleven inside. I make some calls to some people who would know. Sight unseen it sounds to them like I got the fat end of the stick. Frenchie even have some change coming his way he hadn't played me for a sap. So he gets off with his breath and I got a nice housewarming gift for you."

Stevie didn't have to think about it.

What she'd just heard was enough.

"Mr. Lodger, I appreciate your generosity, but I cannot accept your gift."

It got too quiet again, for as long as it took Lodger to turn and face her, catch her eyes and grip her chin with his thumb and two fingers, so tight she was sure he'd leave bruises.

"Oh yes you can," he said.

4

A week after her open house, Stevie was still angry at me for accepting the Warhols from Aaron Lodger once she'd turned them down, but I turned up my high-kilowatt charm and talked her into joining me when I took the silkscreen prints for some expert opinion.

So maybe it wasn't the charm so much as Stevie was as curious as me to check out the suite's value and possibly pick up some history. I didn't care. It was good to be close to her again, and maybe she felt the same way.

Until now, except for a few telephone battles, she'd ignored me. I knew better than to add to her fury with more than two or three or four calls a day, all of which climaxed with Stevie slamming the phone in my ear.

Hell hath no fury like a woman—
Unreasonable.

She is that, unreasonable, my proud and brainy little monster, who started in proving it again after picking me up at Trevor Thorpe's garage on La Cienega, where I'd taken my acutely aging Jag for emergency repair of an oil leak about twice the size of the Exxon *Valdez* spill off Prince William Sound, Alaska, in March of '89.

Stevie's current transportation of choice was a loaded high-end BMW two-door convertible in an emerald green that caught the color of her eyes when they weren't buried behind her Ray-Ban shades and could do that switchover-from-violet thing that helps make her stare so hypnotically intense on camera.

In person. Anywhere. Anytime.

"Are you ready to admit the mistake you made?" she said, once I'd ducked into the passenger seat and she took off for the New Visions Atelier on Melrose in West Hollywood, about a mile from Trevor's place.

"You're the one asked for the divorce, not me, babe."

"Why did I know the minute I put the question that way that it was a mistake?"

"Like the divorce."

At least I was smiling as I said it, not groveling or whining the way I did in the earliest years. My shrink said it reflected my personal growth and maturity the last time I stretched out on her lumpy couch.

In fact, as I recall, it was my shrink saying it that had made it the last time.

It was also the truth.

Winning back Stevie had become as much a word game as a quest with me.

I'd started dating a little while she was in London doing her play.

It was this speed-dating business where you spend seven minutes getting to know someone up close and personal, then move to the next table in a room full of tables in order to meet the next woman speed-dater up close and personal.

Let her get to know you intensely, intimately.

Fall in love.

Marry.

Have a kid or two.

Live a "Grover's Corner" good life before going on to the next life at the next table.

Meeting up with an ex-fiancée last year and rekindling some sparks that almost turned into a five-alarm blaze may have initiated the turn-around.

Or maybe it was Stevie's reaction to the revelation that Leigh-Leigh Wilder existed.

Something akin to jealousy, although Stevie denied it, called it BS, which I did not translate as "Before Stevie."

Having her jealous may, in my mind, have been a way of proving to myself she was still interested in me, that maybe I still did have a chance with her.

Oh, where's that shrink's lumpy couch when it's needed?

What say?

Who's kidding the kidder?

Stretch out, spill all and find out all over again I'm still a resident in the kind of fantasy land they don't offer at Disneyland?

By the time Stevie got back to town, I was up to full evenings with several of the women I'd met, early mornings with one or two, but I wasn't about to share that news with Stevie.

I insisted on knowing about her various liaisons over the years and she was never reluctant about keeping me informed, not to make me jealous, she said, but as an incentive to go live my own life the way she was trying to live hers.

That none of her boyfriends had panned out didn't seem to quiet her any, certainly no more than it managed to keep hope alive in my heart.

"Why didn't you stick up for me with Lodger?" Stevie was saying as we pulled into the New Visions parking lot. "You were all but drooling when he passed the box over to you, clutching it in your greedy paws instead of giving it back to him."

"Already asked and answered. And asked and answered. And asked and answered. And—"

"Tell me again."

"Because I wanted them? Because I'm smarter than you and know better than to look a gift gangster in the mouth?"

"He practically robbed them off some poor guy who lost to him in some card game and maybe now won't be able to send his children to college."

"He won, the other guy lost. Just like a presidential election. The way it works in gambling as well as politics. You got the good stuff when you left me and it's hanging on your walls. I got to cover the dirt outlines you left behind with museum posters and—"

"You got to keep the *Casablanca* poster, thank you very much."

"—and you're welcome. 'Here's looking at you, kid.' He meant well, Lodger, you heard him. You wouldn't go back on *Bedrooms and*

Board Rooms when he tried to make nice-nice by making that happen, so he still had a need to thank you for being so good for Richie Savage, the same way he'd intended to tell you he wanted you to share the Warhol suite with me. A payback to me for all the help I was to Richie and to him with the Lennon concerts in '80, '85 and last year."

"A payback or a payoff?"

"Rude, Ms. Marriner."

"Lodger said nothing about I and you sharing until he saw how firm I was."

"Me and you."

"What?"

"It's 'me and you' not 'I and you.' How many times in all these years have I had to correct you on that one?"

"Never." She slapped my arm with the back of her hand. "I'm quite capable of correcting myself."

"Yes. Better than you are at understanding an old man and giving him some peace of mind."

"You're not so old," she said.

"You know I meant Aaron Lodger."

"Getting chunkier in the face and losing more hair," she said, "but still able to pass for forty-five, forty-six."

"You know I haven't turned forty yet."

Stevie smiled her sly smile.

"I and you know it," she said. "Don't expect any help from me convincing the rest of the world." She turned the key in the ignition. "We're here."

The New Visions building was an avant-garde combination of brick and glass that stood out among a stretch of antique stores and art galleries. No flashy signs to identify it as a place where many of the world's most distinguished artists come to do some of their most inventive work in lithography and multiples, high-priced contemporary heavyweights such as Johns, Rauschenberg, Stella, Kelly, Lichtenstein, Oldenburg, that whole New York crowd that came along in the sixties and seventies, about the time Pop Art was raging; some to share the resonance of the Pop limelight, others to defy it, and—

Andy Warhol—

Who stood mostly alone and often seemed overshadowed by the others, although he had helped invent and define Pop and created it in ways that would outlive his own mortality.

The real collectors knew to stop here for a first look at new issues that often ranked with the adventurous works turned out routinely at Gemini G.E.L. down the street, one of the earliest ateliers to capitalize on the resurgence of printmaking inspired by June Wayne at the Tamarind workshop in L.A. and Tatyana Grossman's Universal Limited Art Editions in West Islip, Long Island.

Over the years, I'd fed my interest in graphics at New Visions, attending exhibit openings for artists whose work I especially relished or whom I'd come to know by hanging out occasionally in the back shop, on days when the Muse and I could not come to terms on a fit eight hundred words for my "On the Go" column.

The pictures on the wall were always an inspiration and Kip Lingle, who owned the place, a gracious host.

Kip was always good for relaxed conversation laced with art-world gossip over a potent mug or two of coffee laced with generous slugs of the vintage brandy he kept in his cramped and cluttered office, a disaster zone of art magazines and art reference books and catalogs, every inch of wall space covered with photographs Kip took of the various artists conspiring with his resident master printers while in the act of creating limited-edition prints that were as out of my price range as Lakers-game floor seats at the Staples Center.

Barely a minute after the receptionist had announced us, Kip charged into the gallery with a toothsome smile as wide as his outstretched arms.

He called out our names with a manic glee, like a child exhibits opening birthday gifts, and pulled us off the impeccable imported marble floor for hugs and air-kisses, first Stevie, then me, with a strength that belied his size.

Kip wasn't tall, maybe an inch or two shorter than Stevie, but at least fifty pounds heavier, with a barrel chest that began under the shaggy red beard that hid the lower half of his face. The balance of his trademark costume consisted of rectangular rose-tinted Gucci specs resting flush on the bridge of a puff-pastry nose and a black cloche hat that hid a shaved head and matched the formless Armani suit and black shirt he wore open at the neck, exposing a mass of hair that couldn't make up its mind between salt and cayenne pepper.

It was a look exclusively Kip's—whom I judged to be in his late forties—one that fueled his celebrity status among the art world's cognoscenti and added, by Kip's own reckoning, twenty percent to everything he put up for sale.

"You two don't come around often enough," Kip said, his voice as distinctive as his appearance, like he sanded his throat every morning after brushing his teeth. "You, so what?" he said, putting me down. "But you—" He turned back to Stevie and bounced his shaggy eyebrows. "I'd marry you in a minute if you were a man."

"Oh, Kip, I bet you say that to all the women."

"Darling, how many times do I have to tell you? Just the young, rich ones with big tits." He pulled Stevie in for a replay of the hug. "The old, rich ones with big tits I beg to adopt me."

"It matches my outfit," Kip said after I handed off the Warhol presentation box. He called across the gallery to the receptionist, "Darling, if anyone comes looking for me, tell them to take a number," then commanded, "Follow the leader."

He guided us down a short, narrow corridor lined with framed examples of limited editions produced by New Visions, through the swinging doors marked AUTHORIZED PERSONNEL ONLY, and into the workshop, an open room about one-third the size of a high-school gym, dominated by a giant flatbed press used to run the mammoth lithographs the atelier was famous for.

The press was a motorized marvel that made it possible to realize the most complex of prints without losing any of the custom precision master printers have been obligated to bring to impressions of any size ever since the process was invented in the late eighteenth century by a Bavarian named Alois Senefelder.

The reproductive techniques of the age were relief and intaglio, which called for cut wood or engraved metal. Both were too expensive for Senefelder, a playwright looking for a cheap way to reproduce copies of his works.

He stumbled into discovering he could print both words and pictures slathered onto a slab of flat-grained limestone from a quarry near his home by using a greasy substance. Senefelder sponged the stone with water and the unused areas on its surface rejected the oily ink he had applied by roller while the grease of the image he'd set down showed an affinity for the ink and easily transferred to paper.

In a way it was a Microsoft of its time. It brought a new dimension to printmaking, was embraced early by artists such as Manet, Géricault, Redon and Fantin-Latour, and over the years led to the concept of the "original print."

These were impressions of a limited number made by the artist in collaboration with master printers, who brought an exactness to every print pulled and numbered, signed by the artist and sometimes the printer. Once the designated number of prints had been struck, the stone's surface was defaced, to guarantee purchasers that no further images could be printed, protecting the value of the investment and a collector's expectation the value would grow with time.

Lithographs ultimately fell into disrepute, especially in America. Their artistic merit and significance drowned in a sea of doubt as new technology moved the method from stone to commercial printing presses.

U.L.A.E., Tamarind, Gemini, New Visions and others brought back respect by giving artists the renewed opportunity to discover firsthand the sensuous spontaneity and creative potential inherent in attacking a stone, something Picasso and other Europeans had known and practiced all along.

And, of course, collectors began to swarm as major names brought their vision to the form at a price below what oils, watercolors and other single works might bring.

And, values escalated.

And escalated. And escalated. And—

As Kip led us through the workshop, I traded waved greetings with a couple of the printers who were working at the smaller hand presses.

We headed past the small room—where artists in current residence experimented with and exercised their imaginations and developed and refined their singular visions, often with their collaborative printing partners locked at their elbow—and entered the larger proofing room.

Here's where the new editions were checked for quality, consistency and conformity, then numbered, before the artist signed his name as the ultimate seal of approval.

The room was several degrees warmer than the workshop and the air felt more antiseptic.

Quality control.

As rigid as in any museum.

"Peter Westcott, new kid on the block, fashionable in New York, touted by *Artforum* as the next big thing, he just finished up an edition," Kip said, setting the presentation box on the proofing table.

He opened a drawer and found a pair of cotton gloves.

"I knew *Artforum* was right the minute I laid eyes on his big thing. Let me tell you, it's good I don't ever mix business with pleasure . . . Well, there was—Never mind."

Kip fluttered a hand, then gave the gloves a last tug or two and proceeded to open the box.

"We may be getting Stella back here, how would that be for a triumph?" he said, carefully removing each Warhol and laying it onto the table, creating two neat rows. "He's been doing most of his recent work with Kenny Tyler, back East at Bedford Village or whatever, wherever that nonexistent town of Kenny's is located, called . . . There now."

Kip leaned over the table just shy of landing his beard on the prints as he inspected one after the other, mumbling a series of "Um-hum"s as he moved down the rows, then back up, nodding approvals and occasionally peering up at Stevie and me and making a grumbling noise.

After about five or six minutes, he stood up and found a safe spot to lean against the table, clasped his arms over his stomach, and with a smile said, "First of all, you know, they're not lithos. Silkscreen. Andy's medium of choice."

I said, "I told you that when I called."

"That's how I know you know," Kip said, and gave Stevie a wink. "You also wanted to know if I was familiar with the images. No, I'm not. Are they genuine Warhols? My vote would be affirmative, except down in Florida, where it'd probably not be counted. The signature looks authentic enough, but it could have been signed by one of Andy's people, like he was always having done back in the old days at the Factory, when men were men and sometimes also women. Unnumbered, and that's not usual, so I'm going to guess small, a suite commissioned by someone prepared to spend a few bucks as a treat for some friends—maybe Christmas gifts? The presentation box is also pointing in that direction . . ."

Kip turned and did a sweep of the prints with his eyes.

"I see eleven different people in as many images, so let's us figure eleven friends in all. I add some artist's proofs to that, maybe the *bon à tirers*, a set for the printer, one for the generous sponsor, unless he is one of the eleven, and—" He closed his eyes and moved his lips to a mental count. "I would guess you beautiful persons are the proud possessors of one in twenty, maybe twenty-five suites max."

Kip adjusted the gloves again and began repackaging the prints, delicately replacing the layer of protective tissue between each, and careful to avoid damaging edges as he laid one after the other back in the black presentation box.

"Neil, did you say you checked reference books and the auction houses?"

"Yeah, Kip. Nothing."

"The Warhol Foundation back in New York? You know it's about to be headed by my favorite city councilman, Joel Wachs, one of our own and soon to be one of their own."

"No one there had a clue. Nothing in their records to match the suite, they said. They want me to mail photos and they'll see what they see, maybe do better, but I thought to try you first."

Kip half-bowed and said, "I'm flattered."

Stevie said, "Kip, you recognize anybody in any of the prints?"

"Can't say that I do, especially beautiful you, but the one standing in front of what looked to be a Toulouse-Lautrec *La Goulue*, he's definitely to my personal taste."

"You are incorrigible . . . The paintings hanging behind each one of the people in the pictures. Also, no two alike."

"Noticed. Makes me think that maybe they're collectors, all of them; maybe some circle of friends. Maybe all of them kicked in to commission Andy. Maybe—"

Kip finger-smacked his forehead and made a *Silly old me* face.

He brought the silkscreen print in his hands closer to his face and fiddled with it.

His broad smile made his beard dance and his cackle leaped from his throat in two octaves.

"There's your doorway to learning how legit these are, Neil, unless you're going to leave entirely satisfied with my expert opinion."

He pointed to an image discreetly embossed in the lower right-hand corner of the print, the "chop mark" printers and ateliers frequently imprint to identify their work.

Here, the Arch of Triumph.

"The chop mark?" I said. "I did a global search on the Web and couldn't find it. The Foundation people didn't know it, either."

"I know it," Kip said. "So well that it passed right by my gorgeous *punim* without me giving it a second thought."

5

The chop mark belonged to Henri Godard.

Godard, a rhyme with *Go far*, was a master printer of high regard and basement repute in the international world of graphics, Kip said; "Hank" to his friends, if there were any left after the angles he played, somebody who tended to burn his bridges before they were built.

It wasn't always that way.

At first, Henri had traded on the reputation of his father, Henri Jean-Jacques Victor Hugo Godard *père*, called "Hugo," a provincial farmer's son apprenticed to a printer in Paris at the age of fifteen shortly after the close of World War Two.

Hugo had demonstrated an eagerness to learn and a natural affinity for printmaking while he was still sweeping floors and sponging stones at the atelier, absorbing knowledge and technique quicker and with greater relish than the lithographic crayons ever had for the lithographic inks.

He graduated to master printer before the age of twenty, and within a year had been stolen away by the grandest of the ateliers, the internationally famed Mourlot, where Hugo quickly was demanded by the most famous and important of the artists working there: Picasso, Dubuffet, Miró, Chevelinski, Chagall.

By the time he'd graduated to his own atelier, followed by artists who said they could not possibly collaborate with anyone else, Hugo was married, to the daughter of a well-to-do attorney who spent a fortune annually on works on paper—as well as oils and sculpture of all periods—and had sired five children, of whom Henri was the oldest.

Henri showed the same unquenchable lust for printmaking as his father and, in time, his skills were ranked superior to the old man's, more so as he expanded his range to include other forms of the graphic art, even screen printing, which in those years was sneered at as a legitimate fine-art form.

Hugo's artistic ego and temperament couldn't contain a growing resentment for his son and the young man's superior talents. Henri matched his father in both departments. They clashed frequently, often loudly and violently, often coming close to blows, as close as the images sat on the paper.

The old man screamed, "Enough!" the day Henri demanded his father retire and he be allowed to take over the atelier, and sent Henri on his way.

Ultimately, he would bequeath the business to his three other surviving children, who had never shown an interest in it and joined to sell it off as quickly as the legal process allowed, retaining only a handful of presentation proofs and *bon à tirer*s they had been told were most assuredly destined to increase in value.

Henri quickly found backers for an atelier, but he was out of business almost as quickly after certain facts were uncovered that made headlines and made his backers, artists and most ardent customers feel violated.

He denied the charges, vowed to fight the slanders and libels in court, but fled the country in front of reports he was to be arrested and tried.

Henri's father paid off the debts and liabilities in the name of family honor and died soon thereafter, everyone certain his unexpected demise had been brought about by the scandal.

Henri came out of hiding in Japan, where he had spent time mastering the woodblock, and found work under assumed names at many of the leading ateliers of Europe, in Hamburg, Frankfurt and Berlin;

Rome and Florence; for a period at the Petersburg Press in London, where he brought advanced techniques to their silk-screen publications; and afterward at the Galerie Beyler in Basel, Switzerland, where Godard collaborated with the likes of Josef Albers, Jean Dubuffet and Marc Chagall, until Chagall realized who it was working under an assumed name and a beard and mustache, and demanded straightaway he be terminated before he disgraced Beyler as he had his own father, for God's sake.

"How he put it, Chagall," Kip Lingle said, " 'for God's sake', like Henri Godard was pure *schmutz* on all twelve of the maestro's magnificent Jerusalem windows." We were back in Kip's office, hearing about Henri Godard over thick coffee laced with generous shots of Rèmy Martin Louis XIII cognac which he pointedly noted had set him back a thousand bucks. "And that was at Costco," Kip said, belly-laughing.

He savored a hearty sip and continued: "Henri made it to the States next, worked freelance around New York for a while, then came out here. He did a turn at Gemini, where he never got a chance to do one of his nasty old games, caught in time by Serge Lozingot, who was more than Henri's equal where it came to printing a litho, and Sidney Felsen cut him loose. Didn't last much longer at Circus Editions, where the gossip mill had it he did some of his patented SOP nasties with some of their important silkscreens and"—flinging away a three-finger kiss—"adieu, Henri."

Stevie said, "Kip, darling, you've been telling I and Neil how facts were uncovered that caused the scandal back in Paris, and saying things like Godard was playing his old games and doing his SOP nasties . . . Can you be a little more specific than that?"

Kip turned to me, amusement dancing on his face, and said, "Like the Sex Queen is the newspaper reporter now?"

"By injection. I was about to ask the same question."

"You know, gossip I love—" Stretching the word "love." "Truth? So dull, like West Hollywood on a Wednesday night. But I'm always one to be a gracious host, so: Running and stashing away prints beyond an edition's size before he canceled a plate. Selling them under-the-counter to a private network of dealers and collectors. Forging images and impressions. Working out private deals with artists, where they'd sign blank sheets of paper and he'd do the rest, passing off a work like that as true collaboration; the latter-day Dalí trick. How is that for the tit of the iceberg? Oh, excuse me, you buxom *shiksa* beauty. I was distracted by the sight of you."

Stevie thumbed her nose at him.

I said, "All that, yet you're so positive the Warhol suite is legit?"

"Yep."

"Why?"

"Henri Godard's chop, the Arch of Triumph. It doesn't appear on any of the crapola he turned out. He'll tell you that himself, probably, you manage to run him down."

"Where?" Stevie said. "Where is he now?"

Kip stared back at Stevie over the lip of his coffee cup, shrugged and said, "Beats the shit out of me."

"The guy who lost at cards to Aaron Lodger and gave up the suite, he was French."

Stevie and I had the memory flash about the same time and shared it in almost the same words, as we were heading back to pick up my Jag at Trevor's garage. I emphasized the idea by slapping the dashboard, Stevie by jabbing her nails into my thigh.

"Maybe Henri Godard?"

"Maybe Henri Godard?"

Lodger had given me a special number to call if I ever needed him, scribbled it on a slip of paper that I'd stashed in my wallet. I dug it out, fished Stevie's cell phone from her handbag, and dialed.

Got a recording, no ID, a man's flat and bored voice telling me to leave a message at the beep.

Later, back home, I made calls to Sidney Felsen at Gemini G.E.L. and Tom Bakersfield at Circus. Neither knew where Godard might be or had anything kind to say about him.

I tried a few of the smaller ateliers and got the same type of response.

I left a second message for Aaron Lodger.

The next day, I moved on to some graphics dealers who dealt in Warhol here, in New York, San Francisco, elsewhere around the country, even some overseas, hoping one or another might know the suite and be able to give me a ballpark on its worth. That's what it was about right now, actually, getting a handle on the value of the Warhols, not tracking Godard, who'd have been a shortcut to the answer, nothing more.

No luck.

> >
> >
> >

Except for a call about a week later, the Warhol suite became recent history left to Stevie's safekeeping over her objections, until I convinced her it had nothing to do with ownership. She had storage room at her place or she could put the suite in the condo's security vault, where it would sit on a shelf alongside valuables deposited by other unit owners. ("What I really should do is tell you where you can put it," she said, grudgingly accepting the black box.)

The caller had e-mailed me through the *Daily*'s Web site, identifying himself as Theodore Rosenstock, a dealer in rare and contemporary fine art.

I heard it on the grapevine that you have come into an Andy Warhol portraits suite, Rosenstock wrote, *and I would be interested in discussing this with you towards making you an offer to purchase it for one of my valued customers.*

The phone number he included was in New York.

Rosenstock answered with his name, got mine in return.

"Mr. Gulliver, how good it is of you to get back to me so promptly." His voice as glowing as a Southern California sunset, an accent not quite New York, but noplace else that I immediately recognized. "It's correct, then, about you having the Warhol suite? The Warhol *portraits* suite?"

"Yes. How did you say you heard?"

"We dealers talk among ourselves, of course. It came up in conversation and I immediately tracked after you. There's a customer of mine who is positively a raving fanatic on the subject of Warhol. He has absolutely every suite Warhol ever did, except that one, the portraits suite, and it's been on his wish list almost forever. Forever and a day."

"How much?"

"Once authenticated—" He paused about the length of a drum roll. "My client is prepared to go one hundred thousand dollars once the suite is authenticated. How does that sound to you? A fair price? I would say so."

It's moments like this I'm grateful I inherited strong bladder genes from my parents.

Rosenstock misunderstood the silence.

"I could probably induce him to go a little bit higher, maybe a hundred and twenty-five thousand dollars, but no more than that, Mr. Gulliver. What do you say? That, if you do the math, is more than ten thousand dollars for each one and well above fair market, I understand."

"You understand?"

"To tell you the truth, I'm not into Warhol myself. I never have been. The man was always better at publicity for himself than for his art, I thought. But I'm in business to sell, not to judge, and this customer wants and is prepared to pay, so I want and am prepared to offer. Frankly, I will not make much money on the deal, but I will make it up other ways, if you recognize what I mean."

"I recognize. Who told you fair market? One of the dealers I contacted, or—?"

"Yes, one who shares my distaste for Warhol, but I plan to give him a generous finder's fee, cutting more into my laughable profit margin. Such shows of appreciation will often produce greater rewards down the road, you see?"

"You don't know Warhols, how will you know you know—"

"The authenticity of the suite? I will dispatch to you an associate who picks up this slack for me, who would know better than me. A Warhol man through and through. There is no accounting for taste, so I do not make a judgment there, either. He will view the suite at your convenience and, if it passes inspection, promptly hand over a certified or cashier's check to you in the amount of one hundred thousand dollars—"

"You were telling me a hundred twenty-five thousand a minute ago."

A little laugh trickled into my ear.

"I see I still have your attention. Yes. Present you with a certified or cashier's check in the amount of one hundred twenty-five thousand dollars. Now that that's out of the way, can we set a date for his visit, perhaps, Mr. Gulliver?"

Rosenstock sounded too self-satisfied, too matter-of-fact, in my ear and to my gut.

My ear is fallible.

My gut rarely misleads me.

Something was off-base here.

I said, "I'll have to think about it."

There was momentary silence before Rosenstock spoke again, as if he hadn't heard me. "I will have him fly there, should we say tomorrow? How does that strike you? You would make the time available for a profitable meeting such as this meeting would turn out for you."

"I said I'll have to think about it, Mr. Rosenstock."

A purring noise like a cat, then more silence, then, "I give in. You drive a hard bargain, I see, so I'll not waste any time telling you I'm authorized by my client to go up to one hundred and fifty thousand dollars, but not another cent more, Mr. Gulliver. Not one, but look— you just got yourself twenty-five thousand dollars more and you don't even have to think. Tonight, when you climb into your warm, comfortable bed, you can dream about the wishes that might have been out of your reach and now are within your reach. What's better?"

I gave it a long pause and, keeping my voice as calm as when I was going for the pot on a pair of deuces, said, "Kick it up to two hundred thousand dollars and we have a deal."

The noise he made this time sounded like Rosenstock had swallowed his phone.

I didn't expect him to agree to the fifty-g boost.

I was buying time.

Three reasons:

The suite had been a gift to Stevie and me from Aaron Lodger. He told us he'd checked out their worth, but maybe he didn't know the true total value of the Warhols. In all probability, he didn't. I felt obligated to let him know. Offer him the suite back. It was the honorable thing to do.

Reason two:

Whether Stevie agreed or not with my having accepted the Warhols from Lodger, her personal feelings aside, she owned half the suite. She was entitled to half of any sale money. She also was entitled to have her say on any deal. It was an offer she could refuse, probably would, but I had to make it anyway.

The third reason:

Rosenstock had been too quick to kick the offer up to a hundred-fifty thousand. My gambling instinct told me he had climbed up to the eighth floor of a building that had nine, maybe ten floors. Maybe more. His response to the fifty g I added on top of that would give me a better sense of the Warhol suite's full worth.

"You must be more handsomely compensated for your work with a newspaper than I could ever imagine," the art dealer decided. He made a clucking noise. "Or—Mr. Gulliver, are you under the mistaken impression that I don't tell you the truth about my client?"

I didn't respond.

Rosenstock did some calisthenic breathing into the phone and said, "I will tell my client your answer either after this or tomorrow and then I will call you again and let you know. Yes?"

"Sure. Do that."

The last time I heard myself sounding like that, I had a head full of sweat, waiting for some table shark to decide if he was going to see my clear-out-the-cowards raise. He did. I was holding a ten-high straight, clubs, against his squint-eyed bluff, only—he wasn't bluffing. He held a jack-high straight, diamonds. So much for making the rent on time that month.

"Good day, then, Mr. Gulliver. I thank you for your time and courtesy with utmost sincerity and, if you don't already know it without my saying it, I admire your bravado. So very macho, Mr. Gulliver. So very, very macho. Until tomorrow."

Tomorrow came.

Rosenstock's call never did.

When the phone rang, it was my private line.

"Hold on a minute, Gulliver. I got Mr. L here."

First I asked Aaron Lodger about the Frenchman who'd paid his card debt with the Andy Warhol suite, describing what I had learned about Henri Godard.

"Certainly it could be him, but not by that name," he snapped back. "Around the casino he's known as Mr. France. Hold on."

His voice became muffled, like he'd put his hand over the mouthpiece, but sounded like Lodger was giving someone instructions.

After another minute he said, "Nobody's seen him around lately. I'll get back to you with a name and number. So, you don't think they might be genuine, what it's all about?"

I wasn't going to tall-story Lodger.

It had never been a wise practice for anyone who dealt with the old mobster, a throwback to the Bugsy Siegel School of Settling Disputes. I was on solid ground with Lodger, where anybody who tried a trick on him was a prime candidate for six feet under—or so the story went, although the cops were never able to tie him to a chargeable offense.

"You or Stevie, you want to sell the pictures I gave as a gift, yeah, so go ahead," he said. "I did what I wanted to do and now they're yours and you can go do the same you want and it won't hurt my feelings."

Next, I told Lodger about Theodore Rosenstock.

Lodger said, "A hundred and fifty smackers? It's chump change. Two hundred smackers, the same. Chump change. Even at my age, retired, I can make that in a day standing on my head. You make the deal, the bread is yours to keep. I know our Richie, God rest his soul, would say exactly the same, if he was with us right now."

His voice had shifted in tone, going from a simmer to almost a boil, sounding to me like he didn't entirely mean what he was saying. I wondered if the thought of our selling a gift given in Richie Savage's memory hurt him more than he was prepared to admit, but it wasn't the type of question ever to put to Aaron Lodger. It was too personal. Too prying. A none-of-your-business–type question.

He said, "What else?"

"That's it."

"Anything else, you call me right away. Meanwhile, you'll be hearing back about Mr. France," he said. "You ever make a sale, you keep the bread and I don't have to know the amount."

And disconnected us without a goodbye.

Heads turned and eyes stayed with her as Stevie bopped out of her emerald-green BMW convertible and moved with long-legged, posture-perfect celebrity assurance from the parking drive to Le Dôme, stopping briefly outside the restaurant to sign autographs for the collectors and strike a few poses for the tabloid paparazzi, who always seemed to hover there, before she swept past the enclosed patio.

Stevie was dressed to impress, naturally, although the several conversations she'd had with Anthony B. Anthony before he invited her to lunch made her certain she already was the director's top choice to play the title role in a remake of the Garbo classic, *Ninotchka.*

Earlier in the week, she'd made a special trip to Saks and found a Chanel outfit that served the character, a Russian government official in the days when communism was the rage and the rule, who goes to Paris and is corrupted by love. It was a long-sleeved black wool tweed jacket with a lambskin trim worn over a matching cashmere-and-silk blouse and leather skirt; stretch black suede–and–patent leather boots with three-and-a-half-inch heels that quit just below her knees.

She had pulled her hair back into a braided knot, tight so that it gave her as much of that mannish look that Garbo had been able to achieve while putting her unmatched sexual allure on full display.

Stevie had even spent half a day with Rugby Reynolds, Hollywood's preeminent "voice coach to the stars," who gave her just enough of a Moscow Russian accent to show Tony B. Tony—the director's pet nickname—what she was capable of achieving. It had cost sixteen hundred bucks for the four hours. She considered it a savvy investment. Besides, it was tax-deductible.

Eddie Kerkhofs at the maître d's station took a step back when he spotted her, broadened his face into the warm, wide-eyed smile he had for all his long-standing regulars, and threw open his arms as he rushed forward to greet her.

She ended their embrace with a kiss on his cheek, not hard enough to damage her lip gloss, an aggravated scarlet as bright as the brilliantly lit blue sky that had joined a warm sun in defying predictions of rain, and accepted his compliments as Eddie led her to her table.

It was just past what she called the runway room—the lane separating tables for two and four filled by those who could see and be seen with their meal—the dining area off the main room, where Eddie sat regulars and other favorites who had a stronger grasp on who they were, and usually higher up the status totem pole.

"You're the first," Eddie said, pulling out a chair for Stevie that faced into the room and put her on display, even for those wandering to and from the restrooms downstairs. It was across from the table for six at which producers Arnold and Anne Kopelson were holding court and next to two men who looked like teens in their Eminem T-shirts and tight jeans and were trading record-business jargon.

Eddie complimented her outfit again and left.

A solicitous waiter was there in an instant, inquiring about her drink order. She gave consideration for a moment or two to a gin and tonic, to steady her nerves, but settled instead for an iced tea.

She didn't want to chance any drink that might get in the way of her composure or wits in what she was thinking of as a non-audition audition with Anthony B. Anthony.

Stevie knew better than to take anything for granted.

She'd been around too long for that, and if she needed another lesson it had come when the network and the producers at *Bedrooms and Board Rooms* began dumping on her, demeaning any further value to them of their "Sex Queen of the Soaps."

In the end, they did her a favor.

They gave her the incentive and the guts to quit.

That had led to London and a stage performance that won her rave reviews, validation as a serious actress, and—shock of shocks—an Olivier Award over the likes of Vanessa Redgrave and Dame Maggie Smith, for God's sake.

London begat Broadway.

Another personal triumph.

A loss this time, the Tony going to the *très* brilliant Dame Judi Dench, but—it sounded cliché, which of course it was—to even be in the company of Dame Judi and the three other nominees . . .

A humbling experience.

A reminder that good things come with hope and belief in one's self and determination and timing and luck, and—

What was it Neil has always said, whether quietly or loudly encouraging her?

We make our own luck babe.

And Mama before Neil, precious, protective Juliet, her guiding light and guardian angel?

Nobody's ever gonna do it for you, honey. But there'll always be somebody around who's trying to grab it away from you. Keep your feet planted on the ground and your head out of the clouds, give as good as you get, better than you get, but always be yourself. Self-respect. Keep it the one thing nobody can ever snatch.

Pretty wise, Juliet, for a woman who never got past the ninth grade.

The Tony loss on Broadway, a reminder.

Now, in Hollywood, the chance for a different kind of Tony award.

A Tony B. Tony award.

The title role in *Ninotchka.*

She turned around the concept in her mind, even there incorporating her newfound Russian accent.

Tony B. Tony, sounding like he wanted her, but she knew not to take the offer for granted, so, if she was wrong, she wouldn't have as far to fall.

The director was fifteen minutes late, adding another sixty seconds of rudeness by pausing for a loud, laughing exchange with the Kopelsons and handshakes all around their table. Stevie was prepared for it. It was the old Hollywood game of *Who's Got the Power?*

Being late or last to a meeting was a signal of power, not of rudeness or, at best, bad planning.

When it came to making movies, directors ultimately had the power, just as, when it came to giving a production the green light, the power belonged to the studios or the indie producers. Here the game was referred to as "the Golden Rule." As in, *He who's got the gold, rules.*

Anthony B. Anthony had a wave for the personal manager Jay Bernstein, who answered with a two-finger forehead salute, before slipping into the chair opposite Stevie.

He adjusted position so that he had as good a view of everyone as they would have of him. Everything about him was medium. Medium height. Medium weight. Medium build.

He was in his forties—she'd checked—but looked older, which she saw as the result of his trying to look younger. His face looked entirely reconstructed, his alabaster skin as tight as a drum. No glasses, but a glint in his black eyes that said *laser surgery* to her. High cheekbones, a slight sag to the cheek on his left, like he had missed a payment. A manufactured nose; too precise to be otherwise.

She figured the work came after he had survived a run off Mulholland late one night about three years ago. Gossip in the studio makeup room passed on rumors that it came about because of one snort too many, but that part of the accident was never substantiated, not in the real press or the tabloids.

Anthony B. Anthony said, "Jeez, Stevie, I can't even begin to explain how fucking sorry I am about running late on you."

He put on a forlorn look for her benefit.

Stevie nodded understanding. She could have recited the words before him if he'd asked. She'd been through worse in the old days. In the old Sex Queen days, most of the heavy hitters on *Premiere* magazine's annual list that agreed to a meeting or a lunch with her didn't bother with any excuses, like she should value their presence as a gift from on high.

She'd walked out on more than one of them.

Most of them, in fact.

Not today, however.

That's how badly she wanted the movie.

Swallow hard and smile, Stevie, she commanded herself.

"You know the Kopelsons? A hit factory since they came West from the Big Apple. Big, big stuff. *The Fugitive,* great shit like that? Big, big numbers. *Platoon*. Won the Big O for that one. Mr. Oscar, his glorious golden self." Anthony B. Anthony, the exaggerated exaggerated smile on his face unable to cloak the sound of envy as his speech charged to some finish line, his eyes huge and blazing with more than a caffeine high.

He had on a windbreaker and a baseball cap adorned with the logo of his new movie, *Amos Behaving*, which had had a gross of over thirty-five million its opening weekend. Not a major star in the cast, so everyone who mattered was crediting his name above the title with pulling in the box office, making Anthony B. Anthony hotter than ever.

"Jay the Bernstein there. One great personal manager. Makes the biggies biggies, one after another. Farrah Fawcett? From the original *Charlie's Angels*. The other blondie, the one from that other old TV series—?"

"*Three's Company*."

"Three's, yeah. Sells skinny-thigh stuff now on cable. He's also done some TV producing, Jay. The old *Mike Hammer* series and one of his people—Keach, Stacy—as Hammer. Gave me one a my first writing gigs, long before I broke big-big. I even got to meet Spillane—you know him? Mickey? You ever in the market for a personal manager, I can put you together with Jay for a little huddle and confab."

Before Stevie could respond, Anthony B. Anthony tapped the *Amos Behaving* logo on his cap.

"You seen it yet?"

"Seen it." She could have added, *Hated it.*

"What'chu think?"

Stevie made a show of contemplation before telling him, "Let's just say I know where you'll be Oscar night." Smiled, leaving him to wonder if she meant it. His ego wouldn't let him believe otherwise, Stevie knew, or he'd have to finish the sentence the way she had mentally: *Home, turning bloody blue with envy.*

Anthony B. Anthony seemed to be clutching Oscar in his hands as he said, trying for humble, "I thank you, Stevie," like she was all the members of the Motion Picture Academy rolled into one. "By the way, please call me Tony B. Tony."

"Dank you, Tony B. Tony," she said, trying out her Russian accent.

He caught it, understood, nodded approvingly.

He said, "Anticipation. I like that in a girl."

"It's better in a woman," Stevie said, almost without thinking, hoping she hadn't flashed her irritation at being referred to as a girl.

If Tony B. Tony noticed, he didn't let on.

He said, "Show you something."

Dug out his wallet and found what he was looking for. A photo. She took it from him, thinking Tony B. Tony was about to show off the wife and kids.

It was a picture of Tony B. Tony proudly clutching his DGA trophy.

"Got that for beating out the field with *Two Lips in the Garden.* You remember?"

"Who could forget?" she said, forging a smile.

"Lost the Oscar, though, to I'll never forget what's his name." Making a face. He remembered, all right. "Y'know, though, Stevie? That put me in pretty select company. Y'know how many directors have copped the DGA award, then lost out for the Big O? Less than a handful. Francis. Steven. One or two others. That puts me in pretty goddamned great fucking company to date, doesn't it?"

"Abba-so-lutely, Tony B. Tony," Stevie said, shaking a determined fist to the same rhythm as her words.

He showed he liked that, as she knew he would.

He gave her a resolute nod to go with a thumbs-up.

"Dammit fucking damn," he said. "I knew I was right on the money when I woke up that morning knowing you were the only one to be my Ninotchka. Called all my troops together at the Morris office and said, 'Stevie Marriner. Her's who I got to have, so do it, and don't any of you fucking try selling me on anyone else who's on your client roster. The name of this game is Stevie Marriner.' "

He nodded aggressively.

Stevie's heart thumped loud enough to keep time for a rock-and-roll band.

The waiter showed up and set a drink in front of Tony B. Tony. Vodka martini. Maybe gin. No olive or onion. Three cherries on the toothpick.

"Your usual, Mr. Tony B. Tony," the waiter said.

"Thank you, my good man," Tony B. Tony said. He raised the glass and said, "A toast."

Stevie, raising her iced tea, noticed there was dirt under his otherwise perfect manicure.

"To my Ninotchka," he said.

"I'll drink to that," Stevie said, not believing it was going to be this easy, waiting for the catch.

She took a healthy sip.

Tony B. Tony finished half the martini. He put down the glass on the table, moved the toothpick to his mouth, taking all three cherries on a single pull.

"The first version they done at Metro, back in nineteen and . . . nineteen and something?" he said. "All that publicity talk about 'Garbo Laughs' and 'The Lubitsch Touch.' Well, baby, they ain't seen nothing, not until they see it with 'the Tony B. Tony touch.' And Stevie Marriner laughing. Stevie Marriner laughing and crying and reducing the audiences to laughter and tears. Already, Stevie, I can feel the Big O written all over it for both of us, you and me, baby. I would almost bet my dick on it."

He gave her a look she'd seen a million times before.

In that moment, Stevie knew where the catch was.

Before she could respond, the waiter arrived wondering if they were ready to order.

"The usual, Carl," Tony B. Tony said without opening the menu. He pushed it aside, telling Stevie, "For me it's always a cup of gazpacho for starters, then the warm duck salad." Threw a thumb-and-fingers kiss into the air with a loud smacking sound. "Nobody does duck better than here at the Dôme. You hafta try it. Carl, put down the same for the lady."

The waiter turned to Stevie, soliciting confirmation with a tilt of the head and elevated eyebrows to go with an expectant smile. She shook her head. It was obvious to her that Tony B. Tony was used to giving orders, a gifted director spoiled by the wiles and ways of Hollywood. The director as dictator. Ruler of all he surveyed, but—

Wherever he believed, "the Tony B. Tony touch" could take him, it definitely was not going to take him into her pants.

She wasn't about to let him get his dick or, for that matter, his duck into her.

"Carl, the lady thinks not," Stevie said, and, also not bothering with the menu: "My usual, as usual."

Carl stole a wary look at Tony B. Tony and said, "That would be the cold poached salmon, yes, Ms. Marriner?"

She nodded. "Maybe I'll be naughty later and go for the apple *tarte tartin.* You ever have that here at the Dôme, Tony B. Tony? I have never had a better *tarte tartin* anywhere in the world, not even in Paris." The Russian accent back before she got to Paris.

"I'm a flan man myself," Tony B. Tony said, his voice as flat as one of David E. Kelley's leading ladies. His circus smile had faded and his eyes had become tiny slits, like he was trying to read Stevie's mind.

The waiter finished scribbling on his pad and wheeled off.

Tony B. Tony eased out of the expression and said, "So, where were we?"

"You were betting your dick," Stevie said.

"Oh, yeah." His smile as big as before, but forced.

Stevie settled her arms and clasped hands and on the table, leaned in closer to him and dropped her voice to a conspiratorial level.

"I don't suppose you do that very often, do you?"

"Wuzzat?" he said, working over his martini. "You mean the duck? Duck's too fatty for my shitty cholesterol level, so I save it for when I come to the Dôme. Other places, like the Ivy, the Grill, I got other favorites for them."

"Your dick. I don't suppose you lose it very often when you bet it." Hand gestures to go with the Russian accent.

Confusion returning on Tony B. Tony's face.

"Where you leading up to with this, Stevie?"

Stevie said, "The year Mr. Lubitsch's movie came out was 1930. Besides Garbo as Nana Ivanovna Yakusnova, there was Melvyn Douglas as Count Leon D'Algout, her leading man, the role Gig Young had opposite Maria Schell in the 1960 TV version. I won't bother you with Silk Stockings, the musical version on Broadway, and"—dropping the Russian—"you think anything you ever read in the gossip rags or anywhere else about me always falling for my directors is going to put us between the sheets, you can take your Big O predictions and, for all I care, go shove them where the sun don't shine, up your own Big O, dah-ling Tony B. Tony."

She leaned back in her chair and crossed her arms.

Tony B. Tony stared at her incredulously.

The tension in his face began to ease up and he cracked a smug, jubilant smile, like he'd just become the last one left on Survivor.

"Exactly the quality I wanted and knew you could bring to my Ninotchka," he said. "Y'know, we do decent shekels at the box office, I think a remake of something Lombard, maybe To Be or Not to Be or Nothing Sacred would be just the thing for us. Jeez! You and Mel or you and Tom. Dynamite! Dyn-o-mite-ski! I'm gonna turn my people on to it right away, see if we can steal some options."

Later, back at the condo after lunch, among the messages waiting for Stevie on the answering machine, was one about the Warhol suite she'd reluctantly let Neil talk her into keeping there last week.

Some guy.

A voice she didn't recognize.
No explanation how he got her unlisted number.
Leaving an 800 number, but no name.
His message brief, curious, intriguing.

Alarming.

"We must talk about this," he said. "The Andy Warhol suite of portraits you have is more important than you can imagine, Miss Mar-riner. More valuable. More dangerous."

7

Every time he came to Boston, Clegg's thoughts turned to the heist at the Isabella Stewart Gardner Museum in 1990 and how he wished he had been in on it with the two burglars who'd never been caught. What a haul that was, ten or eleven paintings, mostly masterpieces, with an estimated value high above the three-hundred-million-dollar mark.

A reward for their safe return still standing at five million dollars.

With or without the burglars. No questions asked.

What he could have done with that kind of money.

A windfall, the kind of killing that might have saved his marriage and his life from drop-dead falling apart. Kept his son with him. Kept him from turning to a different kind of killing.

His share of the three hundred million, he meant, after the artworks were sold in the underground marketplace to all those gluttonous, greedy bastards who get off on owning the unattainable, even when it's something they have to hide from sight.

Especially if, with the worst of them.

Possession as an aphrodisiac.

Ownership as a disease.

The five million in reward money was a temptation he'd struggled to resist when he was suffocating under a mountain of debt and despair, though even then it was a fantasy more than a reality he'd given any serious consideration.

Even after the Rembrandts surfaced here and there, that fantastic Vermeer, *The Concert*, over there, those works by Degas in that vault below the—

Even when he'd learned who the thieves were and etched their faces and names in his memory, in case he was ever in the kind of fix that—

No.

Roll over on them? Out of the question, then and now.

To do with that old saw about "honor among thieves"? Hardly.

He'd recognized if there were a price on his head or if they needed bargaining power in a plea bargain, his ass'd be grass where that pair of thieves was concerned. It was out of the question, as a means of holding true to his personal moral code, although the world had never seen fit to return the favor.

Clegg stole a quick look in the rearview and gave himself a wink and a nod of confirmation that he was simply amusing himself with the concept, playing a mind game on the drive to Chestnut Hill.

It was all he could do to see the road through the windshield as the wiper blades slashed against a rain that had been pummeling Boston nonstop since before he'd arrived three days ago. More to come, the weathermen predicted, and be prepared for snow if the temperature continued dropping.

How he hated the East Coast.

The rotten weather, but not only that.

The East Coast always brought back nightmarish memories of home and her, what she'd pulled on him before he stopped it from happening anymore, and of his having to abandon the kid for the kid's own sake, they convinced him, and—

William F. McClellan Highway took Clegg into the Sumner Tunnel and out again.

He reached over and retrieved from the passenger seat of his rented

Honda Civic the sheet of paper on which he'd jotted down her address and directions, giving it a quick scan to be sure he caught the right exit.

A series of turns got him past Boston College and onto Hammond Street after about a mile. Swerving to avoid hitting a woebegone dog in the roadway caused him to miss the Shore Road street sign, and he had to double back.

Her home was as she'd described it to him, a lumbering two-story brick Colonial with a series of elegantly sloped, expensive slate roofs, that dominated the block.

It was in flawless condition, with a lush lawn equally impeccable. Artistically placed flower beds drowning in the rain, but beautiful even so. Smoke channeling from a chimney like a commercial for the warmth and comfort of a fireplace.

Clegg parked on the street and dashed in a half crouch for the front door.

It opened even before he made it up the steps and onto the landing in a slip-and-slide that brought him close to losing his legs out from under him.

She urged Clegg to hurry in before he caught his death of, stepped aside, checking her watch as Clegg moved past her and into a tastefully decorated vestibule filled with a half dozen oils that could as easily have hung in the Boston Museum of Fine Art, where they had met yesterday.

Clegg was examining the Zanobi Machiavelli *Virgin and Child Enthroned with Saints Sebastian, Andrew, Bernardino, Paul, Lawrence and Augustine* when he became aware of the woman seated on the nearby viewing bench, who seemed to be studying him more than any of the paintings in the gallery while he jotted notations in his thick two-ring binder.

Close to him in age, maybe a few years younger, dressed tastefully and expensively. Her hair and makeup just so. Not a bad looker, although he could not be certain how much the tailored suit hid. What it did show appealed to him, but he put her out of his mind and went about his work until he got to the gallery where the Domenico Fetti *Parable of the Good Samaritan* hung.

Maybe it was the rich scent of her perfume that caught his attention first, but there she was again. And again after Clegg had moved on to the Herri met de Bles *Landscape with Burning City.*

Clegg's first thought was that she was some kind of a federal cop or maybe even Interpol and that something sloppy he'd done and wasn't aware of was finally about to trip him up. He knew better than to try a run for it.

If they had him this far, they'd have him all the way.

There'd be others waiting for him no matter what exit he chose.

Nonsense, he decided, he was far too careful for that to ever happen. Only his nerves playing tricks on him again, like they had started doing a month or two ago, for no reason he'd been able to discern.

He went back to inspecting the Bles, making his notes, until the perfume scent snapped at his nostrils like a line of snow in the old days.

And her voice, husky and almost as close as the scent, said, "I was told you're the museum's appraiser."

He turned to face her. At close range, she was older, but prettier. Something to do with narrow-gauge blue eyes that held on to him like a person drowning clings to a life preserver.

"Independent contractor. I also authenticate works of art. The museum has me in two or three times a year to spot-check the collections. You?"

"My husband and I are major contributors and I'm also a docent. Some of the works here are gifts from our collection or they were purchased with funds from our family trust."

"Very generous of you," Clegg said, not certain if he should believe her.

"I was wondering, then, if you might be free tomorrow to come out to our place? We need to have several of our newer acquisitions appraised. For insurance purposes."

"I'm really tied up here with—"

"We're not far from here, and it wouldn't take you more than an hour or an hour and a half at the most. Maybe around the lunch hour? Certainly they won't begrudge you lunch, and I promise you will be paid as well as or better than the museum pays you. A minimum fifteen hundred dollars against five percent of the valuation you come up with. How's that?"

"Very generous, but I really—"

She threw a palm at his face.

"Then, there. It's settled."

"I was beginning to believe you might have changed your mind about coming," she said. "Would not have blamed you one iota if you'd called, this rotten weather."

"No, I'm a man of my word, Mrs. Kohner, rain or shine. I missed a turn past Glenoe Road or I would have been right on time."

"I so admire that quality in a man. My husband used to have it." Before he could even think about asking what she meant by that, she volunteered, "I mean, back in the days when he had time for me." Added a *That's the way it is* shrug and grimace. "Enough about that. Listening to me about my problems isn't why I asked you over. Come, let's get you in front of the fireplace and give you the chance to dry off before you start your work. We're agreed on fifteen hundred, correct?"

"Yes, against a percentage."

"I want to add the drying time to that, over and above. I think five hundred dollars should be adequate, don't you? The absolute least I can do to show my thanks for your thoughtfulness in coming out on a day like today."

"Very thoughtful, but you don't have to do that. I told you—"

"Hush. Not another word."

She took him by the hand and led him through a door on the left into the living room, past the living room through another set of doors into the den.

Pointing Clegg to the leather sofa facing an immense wood-burning fireplace that filled the room with a welcome warmth, she crossed to the drapes and drew them, then moved over to the entertainment center.

She had on blazing red silk lounging pajamas that clung to her form just enough to validate her well-preserved body and wiggled her tight, well-rounded ass like a football cheerleader pandering to the TV cameraman on the sidelines.

Sandals revealed toenails the same flaming red color as her inch-long fingernails. Pearl drop earrings matched the pearl choker around her neck.

The soft rock music drifting out of invisible speakers turned into a softer, lush, almost symphonic sound.

She turned back to face him with a huge smile.

"There, that's better, isn't it?" she said. "While I excuse myself for five, you can start drying off. The bar's over there, with fresh sandwiches from our local deli in the fridge. Potato salad, slaw and other goodies to check out, so help yourself. Also to anything else you see around that you take a liking to."

Even in the dim light, Clegg was certain she had given him a salacious wink.

The woman was definitely propositioning him.

A cheat, like his wife was.

"They'll be expecting to see me back at the museum, so maybe we should begin your review right away, Mrs. Kohner, and not waste any time?"

"Not yet."

"We waiting for Mr. Kohner, that it?" he said, giving her the benefit of the doubt, although he had no doubt she wanted him. What was that extra five hundred? A down payment on special services? "Didn't you say yesterday that he'd also be here?"

"I lied."

Another wink.

Definitely propositioning him.

A liar as well as a cheat, like his wife was.

"If he was, it would be the first time in a month I've seen the rat bastard," she said. "He's off somewhere in Los Angeles, making his big important business deals by day and his floozies by night."

The woman crossed back and, legs astride, struck a pose in front of him. Arms wrapped tightly across her body in a way that pushed in and raised her breasts. Her nipples were like bullets against the silk.

She said, "To be frank with you, my husband has no idea what's going on here. I'm about to start divorce proceedings against the rat, and my lawyer told me to find out the value of the newest pieces in the collection before the papers are filed and served. Nobody else knows, not the kids or anyone. Otherwise I would have gone and worked this out through the museum instead of going straight to you after I learned what you were doing there."

"That's it?"

She gave him a curious look. "Why? What else?"

"To be honest, I thought maybe you wanted to make love with me, Mrs. Kohner."

She gave the room an amazed look to go with her laugh, then turned back to Clegg.

"Hell no," she said. "But a little fuck wouldn't be bad."

A liar and a cheat and a whore, like his wife was.

He forced himself to return her smile, patted the seat next to him.

She shook her head and said, "Not in here. His office. The desk. I want you to fuck me on his desk."

Heading from the room, she called back at him, "By the way, I don't even know your name. Mine's Phyllis. My friends call me Phyl."

Phyl was much, much more than kinky.

She had the endurance of a martyred saint. She was like a Joan of Arc on fire.

After the desk in the office, Phyl invited him to take her in the kitchen, bent over the chopping block. The fire in her raged next on the cold ceramic tile of the bathroom floor. Then, competing with the two rows of clothing hanging in her husband's walk-in closet, she gave him a new definition for the word *hung*.

Her imagination late into the afternoon brought him to places and positions past anything Clegg had ever tested or heard about.

She had a different name and noise for him every time, took to comparing his endurance and technique to other men and grading him on a scale of one to ten. Whenever he scored higher than a six on her fuck-o-meter, she let the roof know she was adding another hundred to Clegg's bonus money.

She wasn't that good herself, merely insatiable, and he grew increasingly disturbed by her sluttish behavior and his own contributions. In his mind that combination made Phyl worse than his slut whore of a wife had ever been, except that the slut whore had brought their son into her games and that made her worse than worse, causing a mental destruction to the boy that was yet to be repaired.

Phyl was also starting to probe too much and too deeply in between her demands on him, motorized, he guessed, by whatever she was taking whenever she excused herself and went off for five or ten minutes, never once offering to share it with him, which made her greedy, too.

Even before she came at him with the handcuffs and the leather belts and the silk handkerchiefs from her husband's closet, begging Clegg to bind her to a chair or anywhere and do his worst with her, Clegg was at the point of anger where he was only too happy to oblige.

Clegg had had his fill of Phyl.

He tied her spread-eagled on her husband's bed—that got him a yowl of approval—and shut her up by shoving a used Brillo pad in her mouth.

Then Clegg wandered back to the kitchen and found what he was looking for in one of the utility drawers, a plastic trash-container bag.

Returning to her, he watched the drug-dulled twinkle in her eyes turn to curiosity, then into a hint of terror while he raised her head and fit it inside the green bag, which he tied at the neck using her pearl choker.

He settled by her side on the bed in a sitting position with his feet on the floor and stroked her breasts while he watched her exhaust-puffs pop the bag, first fast, then not at all.

He checked her pulse to make sure she was dead, cursed her for what she was and what she had made him into before saying a prayer over her, blaming her for reminding him far too damned much of his late wife, then went about the task of cleaning up after himself.

There was nothing much he could do about the fingerprints or the DNA.

So be it.

On the way out, he took a mink-lined overcoat from her husband's closet that he had particularly admired. It would serve him in inclement weather like today a lot better than anything he owned.

He used it to wrap the single work of art he'd decided to take after making a full tour of the house, an Eglon van der Neer oil portrait on panel that the Kohners had hung in an obscure corner of the bedroom.

He remembered it from his last time at the museum, but didn't remember it was on loan and certainly didn't expect to stumble across it when he agreed to come here and do the valuations.

Without any doubt, the Kohners had shown exceptional taste as collectors.

Clegg wondered if it was just him, the husband, or if Phyl was an equal partner in the selections and purchases. He felt like kicking himself for not asking her.

Outside, the rains had downsized to a drizzle, but the dark clouds had leaked and were turning the sky the color of ink. The street was as empty as when he arrived.

He drove off comfortable in the belief he was leaving as quietly and unseen as he had arrived.

His first call after returning to his hotel room was to the museum. He apologized for his absence with an elaborately detailed account of his lunchtime accident on Boston's rain-slicked roads.

The apology went unchallenged by the department head, who told him to take the next day off if he didn't feel up to coming in and finishing his assignment.

Clegg said aspirin and a good night's sleep would take care of any problems and he'd be in first thing, punctual as always.

His next call was to the boss, to tell him he expected to have the work done by tomorrow, day after the latest.

"How's it going?"

"Well, I'll have interesting things to tell you, but not over the phone."

He didn't mean about Phyllis Kohner or the Eglon van der Neer, either.

"Of course not, but meanwhile I have something to tell you. Are you ready for some sunshine after all that rain down there?"

"The change would be wonderful."

"Well, get ready. I have people for you to see over in Southern California. Los Angeles."

"The Warhols?"

"The Warhols."

8

Augie Fowler phoned me, skipping his usual morning grunt of a greeting, to say, "You have no idea the can of worms you've opened with those Warhols, kiddo. They're crawling all over you, you know that? Can't you feel them?"

"I feel something, Augie, but I think it's just your overwrought hyperbole."

"Contrary to a thought becoming more and more evident in your simplistic excuse for a *Daily* column, big words do not a big thinker make, Mr. Gulliver. Can you be over here for a meeting this afternoon? One o'clock?"

"I have a lunch date."

"Bring him. We'll park him with Brother Saul. Saul will feed him in the kitchen and regale him with the usual stories about Saul's good old days at the Friars Club with Uncle Miltie, Sid Caesar, Red Buttons, Chick Rainbow, that whole crew from the golden age of comedy, back when the four-letter word you heard most often onstage was 'joke.' "

"It's a her, and I don't think so."

Silence on his end of the phone, followed by a mulling noise that always sounded to me like one of the Heathcliffe Arms' cleaning women lamenting a new and irreversible carpet stain in my unit.

"Do not bring her," Augie said finally. "Whether it's business or pleasure you have in mind. Especially if it's pleasure."

"I won't, as well as not me, either."

He overrode my answer. "Stevie's going to be here. Other reasons, but that one should be enough for you. Mixing an orange with the apple of your eye. Not wise."

Stevie's presence was a good enough reason for me, but I was too curious not to ask, "What other reasons?"

"Didn't I say the Warhols? The Warhol suite the two of you inherited from Aaron Lodger. Nothing sweet about the trouble it could cause you. Is *already* causing you, amigo. You and Stevie. You can even say it's a matter of life and death."

Augie was never one to kid about trouble.

"I'll see you at one," I said.

My date's name was Maryam Zokaei.

Maryam had awakened more than my interest when I met her, under the most curious, unlikely and unpredictable of circumstances when she unintentionally, quite literally, strolled into my life.

It was verging on three A.M. I was in bed enjoying a dream inspired by a movie on the Turner Classic Movies channel that had kept me awake until two, *The Magnificent Seven*. This time, instead of "Chris," the Yul Brynner leader of the pack, I was "Vin," the quite *muy macho* antihero played to steely blue-eyed perfection by Steve McQueen.

I'd been Vin before, even before people began comparing my sly side-mouthed twitch of a smile to McQueen's, but most of the time I was Chris, the boss man; once in a while James Coburn's knife-wielding "Britt."

I thought the doorbell at that hour was my imagination or some derelict sound effect until it became insistent and partner to knocking that grew increasingly louder.

Most unusual.

My one-bedroom unit at the Heathcliffe in Westwood is down an

out-of-the-way corridor in one of five six-story buildings comprising the
condominium complex facing Veteran south of Wilshire and built
around a central courtyard back at the beginning of the 70's.

There are 256 units in all. I got mine after Stevie dumped me from
our marriage and our place near the Santa Anita racetrack, but was
kind enough to pay the down on the place, twenty thousand. It was
either that or a supermarket shopping cart on the street for me, as I
was broke as well as brokenhearted at the time.

Stevie called it a loan, advanced from the great money she had
begun earning as the newly proclaimed "Sex Queen of the Soaps" on
Bedrooms and Board Rooms. I knew even then she had no intention of
ever calling it due, but I paid her back anyway once I was back on my
feet and my life.

Accepting anybody's charity has never been the kind of habit I
wanted to acquire. I was brought up believing it was always better to
give than to receive, unless—as one of my brothers once observed—
you were a wide receiver at UCLA and a candidate for the NFL
draft.

Ringa-ringa-ringa.

Banga-banga-banga.

Damna-damna-damna.

I threw a robe over my pajamas and shuffled barefoot to the front
door. Put an eye close to the spyhole and saw who it was signaling for
the wrath of Vin to rain down upon them—

No one I knew, but I thought I recognized her from around the
building.

I'd seen her at the pool a number of times last summer and once
or twice working out on the treadmill in the gym. She was the type
that's hard not to notice, who radiates an accessible childlike innocence
inside the type of tanned, ripe young mid-twenties body Hugh Hefner
would relish having at the Playboy Mansion.

A Stevie Marriner type.

Out in the hallway, I saw she had traded in one of her fantasy string
bikinis for a pink silk teddy decorated with hundreds of miniature
hearts. Like me, she was barefoot.

Her thick, lustrous hair sat high on top of her head like a black
helmet, tumbled like a waterfall down her back almost to her waist,
fell indifferently past her shoulders on both sides of her moon pie
face.

Her face was masked in a heavy layer of night cream that gave
added prominence to the shoeshine-black, almond-shaped eyes staring

expectantly at the door above a sharp, perfect nose and large, inflated lips pulled tight into a half grin of girlish delight.

I undid the locks and opened the door.

Before I could say anything, she said, "Hi," and swept past me down the short corridor.

She made a right turn, me trailing behind her, and headed around the living room and the service counter into the kitchen.

She attacked the service drawers and storage shelves like she'd been in my place before, which wasn't the case—anyway, not to my knowledge—and within fifteen minutes had two trays of chocolate-chip cookies baking in the oven.

All the while, while I watched in confusion, trying to psych out what this was all about, she carried on a running, congenial conversation with me.

Sometimes, only with herself.

She knew who I was, calling me Neil almost like we had gone through this exercise in baking many times before, and told me how much she had enjoyed my column a couple days ago. It was the one demanding more laughs in funny movies and more tears from the tearjerkers to justify the latest infuriating price hike at the box office.

She brought up the bus placards the *Daily* uses to promote the column and insisted the photo didn't do me justice and that I should have the paper substitute a new photo that would present my best features to better advantage, although she didn't bother describing what those might be.

Her chatterbox nature didn't leave much room for any of the questions I had for her, beginning with, *Lady, what the hell are you doing in my place at three in the morning?*

Not that I didn't try.

She didn't evade or deflect answering so much as she didn't seem to hear the questions.

After she took the chocolate-chip cookies out of the oven, she cleaned up after herself while they cooled off, hand-washing and drying the cookware and utensils.

Decided the kitchen linoleum could use a fresher look and located the sponge mop.

Told me to move to a counter stool or into the living room until the floor was dry.

Shortly, came around to my side of the counter with one of the cookies and invited me to test it.

It was delicious, and I told her so.

You could have lit the entire Heathcliffe with the electricity generated by her smile. She went back into the kitchen and moved the dinner platter from on top of the stove to the counter, admonishing me, "Be a good boy and don't gobble them all down at once."

She surveyed the kitchen and, satisfied with what she saw, returned to my side of the counter.

Moving in close, she said, "It's been fun." Gave me a little kiss on the cheek and called back as she headed for the front door, "Don't forget you should lock up after me, Neil. It's a safe building, but you never know."

Curiosity sent me scampering after her.

I got the door open in time to see her pass into a unit three up from me, across the hallway, on the side facing the main courtyard, whereas mine looks out on Veteran Avenue.

Later, at a more reasonable hour of the morning, I learned her name from the com directory at the main entrance when I slogged downstairs to pick up the two copies of the *Daily* an editorial delivery guy drops off for me every day. I phoned downtown and got her number from the reverse phone book kept by the paper's main editorial switchboard and debated calling Maryam Zokaei, to ask exactly what the drill was she'd put us through.

It was a no-brainer. There was no chance of my curiosity losing out.

Besides, I'd found both her looks and her manner appealing.

Maryam Zokaei struck me somehow as a cross between Stevie and Leigh Wilder, the girl who had been my fiancée when we were both barely more than kids who hadn't yet learned better. Elements I found that compared favorably were tastier in my mind than her very tasty chocolate chips, a third of which disappeared after my morning jog and my pit stop for breakfast in a Westwood Village greasy-spoon diner, with a can of vitamin-and-mineral-intense chocolate NuBasics Plus, a 375-calorie energy boost.

The bad stuff in these *Me man, you woman* entanglements might come with time, it usually does, but for now—

She answered with her first name on the second ring and knew who I was when I identified myself with both of mine.

"The newspaper guy who lives down the hall from me," she said, and recited my unit number. "Hi, Neil Gulliver. I'm a fan of your column. Read it like devotedly every morning. Whazzup? I don't suppose they have you soliciting subscriptions, too, or do they?"

"I was calling about earlier this morning."

"Earlier this—? Oh, I fell asleep with the stereo on surrender-or-else. But don't tell me the sound blasted all the way to your place? Tell you what. You don't turn me in to the Heathcliffe brownshirts and I promise to watch it next time, which probably will be tonight." When I didn't answer her immediately, she said, "Whaddaya say, Neil? You have a problem with that?"

"Actually, I was calling about your nocturnal visit."

"My—"

"Your unexpected drop-in here at my place? The batch of chocolate-chip cookies you baked for me? Tidying up in my kitchen, not that it couldn't use it?"

There was only the slightest hesitation on her part and then she said, "Oh me, oh me, oh my. My parasomnias. I'm at it again, I guess. What's a body to do?"

"Your—?"

"Parasomnias," she said, and burst into an infectious laugh. "I can't tell you how sorry, how embarrassed, how—Well, I just am. Look, I have to get through some things I have to get through, yadda-yadda. If this can wait until noon, lunch will be on me while I explain. Least I can do."

"Lunch and the explanation accepted, but the tab is on me."

"You have an expense account?"

"I do."

"In that case, I now pronounce you man and lunch date."

I got Maryam's machine when I called to tell her I had to cancel out on our lunch, but I promised her it was definitely on for soon.

I closed my message with, "Parasomnias or bust!"—hoping it sounded as humorous to her as it did to me—and not long after was on my way crosstown to Augie Fowler's safe haven for religious misfits, the Order of the Spiritual Brothers of the Rhyming Heart.

It wasn't just Stevie Augie had waiting there for me.

The Order of the Spiritual Brothers of the Rhyming Heart, a convent before Augie quit the *Daily*'s deadlines for what he always spoke of as "God's guidelines" and bought the property, overlooks Griffith Park on a hillside rising south above the heavy traffic hum of Los Feliz Boulevard.

It's a restored Spanish hacienda of hand-fired brick, stucco and red-wood beams and balconies that dominates the almost acre of pricey land that includes strolling gardens, which became Augie's special joy after he converted himself into "Brother Kalman" and enticed the first followers there for his brand of self-realization, through small ads placed under the heading "Salvation" in the *Daily* classifieds.

The number of resident disciples he's hooked like heroin addicts desperate for a fix has grown over the years to where it's now around forty or fifty, more if you accept Augie's count. His always smacks me as about as real as the number of communists in government that Senator Joe McCarthy was constantly quoting in the frightening "Red Scare" days of the Eisenhower era—

Never the same number twice.

Not even in the same breath, according to the history books.

Where Augie came into enough cash to make the deal fly with the archdiocese is information he's always refused to share with me. I've asked often. He's explained never, unless you count a finger to his lips and his head switching left and right.

I identified myself into a voice box and the tall iron security gate at the base of the Order's private driveway creaked back. Ground up the narrow, curving driveway in second gear. Ignored the RESERVED signs and glided into a spot outside the main entry, between Augie's fire engine–red Rolls-Royce and a Pontiac rental.

A recent rainstorm and accompanying winds had cleared away the smog layer and the luxuriant landscape was as visibly inspiring as the air smelled breath-mint fresh for a welcome change, however brief, in this city of the expected unexpected.

The view was stunning, even looking east, where the mountain is dominated by the imposing cross raised on its crest by the Forest Lawn Memorial Park people.

Brother Elston was dancing impatiently at the hand-carved front door.

"You're late, Mr. Gulliver," he said, his reedy voice indignant as he thumbed me inside like he was ordering me to the principal's office.

Brother Elston is a retired schoolteacher who had a drinking problem before Augie permitted him to trade in his pension on permanent residence at the Order. He's since lost the problem, as well as the dandruff problem that had Elston dropping as many flakes as a New England snowstorm. He still has his left-shoulder twitch. It was twitching now.

"Five minutes going on six," I said, checking my watch.

"Late is late," Brother Elston said, his left shoulder shifting into overdrive. "Brother Kalman does not like to be kept waiting. You of all people should know that."

"Next time I'll bring a note from home."

He studied my expression and said, "That was supposed to be funny, I expect," making sure I saw his disapproval.

"Only because I'm late and in a hurry, I'll try to do better next time," I said and, moving past him, headed down the main hall.

After my usual pause to admire the Charlie Russell oil that was a special gem among other old west paintings Augie had on the walls, I reached the main conference room and stepped inside making a *ta-ta-ta-ta-ta-ta* trumpeting sound.

Augie was sitting at the head of a long handmade bench table that stretched the length of the room, facing me, his concentration focused on sifting through a pile of documents in front of him.

Stevie sat to his right.

On his left were two men I didn't recognize, sitting with their hands clasped and their eyes trained on the picture window looking out onto the park.

All of them looked up in my direction at the sound of the trumpet.

Augie scowled and said, "You're late, kiddo."

"I know how much you hate being kept waiting," I said, aiming for the bench seat alongside Stevie.

Like Augie, she showed absolutely no appreciation for my light-heartedness.

For sure, something was troubling her.

The two men had solemn faces but appeared unbothered by my tardiness. Both pushed back their seats and stood up as I approached, each giving me business smiles that fit them as well as the matching brown rack suits they wore with shirts open at the collar.

They also shared intense stares, set in brooding, no-nonsense eyes that sucked me in like quicksand and rows of uneven teeth stained by too many years of too much coffee and too many cigarettes. Cigarettes were burning now in the ashtrays in front of their places, sending up strings of off-white smoke to go with the darker smoke from the lit Cuban cigar parked in the ashtray in front of Augie.

A cloud of tobacco hung overhead and I could see that Stevie's eyes were red and smarting from the acrid tobacco smell, an allergic reaction that had led me to quit the habit in the long, long ago. She sensed I was about to say something about it, tell these guys to butt out, and stopped me with a nod and a tight squeeze on my bicep.

"Mr. Gulliver," said the older of the pair, whom I put in his early to mid-fifties, extending his hand. "I'm Ariel Landau—Ari—and this is my colleague, Zev Neumann."

Next I accepted Neumann's hand. He looked to be in his late twenties or early thirties, but had less hair than Landau, who had let his grow long enough to be worn pulled back into a ponytail.

Both handshakes were firm, tight, Neumann's grip almost bone-crushing in intensity. He had a weight lifter's demeanor and hands big enough to palm a basketball. Ari's hands were slender, long-fingered, more suited to a piano bench than a pressing bench, and he seemed almost fragile in spite of his extremely broad shoulders inside the suit.

Augie ordered us to sit.

"Now that everyone's cozy and friendly, let's get down to business," he said. He patted the top of the document pile. "Amazing, what's here. Amazing."

Ari and Zev nodded agreement.

Stevie gave me a *Don't have a clue* glance.

"Do we get let in on the secret?" I asked. "Is it still a matter of life and death, why you got me and, I'm assuming, Stevie here, Augie, or has life and death been marked down to your basic 'amazing'?"

"Kiddo, should you need reminding—I say what I mean and I mean what I say," Augie said.

"Like Horton the elephant," I said.

Stevie signaled me to knock it off by bringing her fist down on my thigh.

"Ari, please," Augie said, inviting him to begin with a hand in his direction, palm turned up to the redwood-beamed ceiling, "before my errant protégé decides to regale us with the full measure of his knowledge about my late friend, Theodor. Dear Dr. Seuss. He can save it for later, over a marvelous meal I have our Brother Liam working on in the galley."

Ari Landau gave him a nod and said, "We're lawyers, Mr. Gulliver, Miss Marriner; Zev and me."

He saw the doubt stream across my face.

"Honest," he said.

"Honest lawyers. Isn't that a contradiction in—"

Stevie slugged my thigh again.

A wisp of a smile played briefly at the edges of Ari's mouth, where Zev's eyes narrowed and his jaw began twitching with obvious irritation. Ari sensed it and calmed Zev with a grip on his wrist.

"We are not corporate and not criminal, in a manner of speaking, Mr. Gulliver, although maybe partners in crime. A good look at us should show that to a man of your inquiring nature and obvious intelligence or I'm no judge of character myself. We're public interest."

"The American Civil Liberties Union? ADL?"

"Private practice, but you could say that, in a manner of speaking, yes. Human rights. Putting a different way, correcting human wrongs."

"Civil rights," Zev said, in a tone not quite civil. He caught himself and, putting a more pleasant spin on his reed-thin voice, told me, "It doesn't pay much, Mr. Gulliver, but you feel a lot better about yourself every morning when you get up."

"I'd also feel a whole lot better if you put out those smokes. Ms. Marriner's too polite to tell you she's allergic, but I'm not."

This time I got her elbow in my ribs, but they doused their cigarettes immediately and threw her apologetic looks. Augie reminded me who was in charge by taking a deep drag on his Cuban before dousing it, but he was careful to send the smoke to a wall away from Stevie.

She thanked them.

Ari rested his arms on the table, his hands locked, and leaned forward. His tobacco-gutted voice dropped to almost a whisper.

"The wrongs that have engaged us for a number of years now, and which we're on the brink of bringing to a resolution for dozens upon dozens of people around the world after more than half a century, Mr. Gulliver."

Augie hit the top of the file stack a few times.

Ari nodded and continued: "It came to involve the Andy Warhol suite of silkscreen prints that's recently come into your possession. In a way, these silkscreen prints represent millions upon millions upon millions of dollars, and that's the reason we could call and tell her"—indicating Stevie—"that they were dangerous as well as being valuable, why Augie was correct when he spoke to you of this matter as a matter of life and death."

Augie said, "Ari, you are one long-winded bag of words, amigo. Get to the point. I'm getting starved already. Tell them what you told me before Brother Liam's lunch goes cold on us."

"Yes, of course," Ari said. "May we have the Warhols we requested of you, Miss Marriner?"

Stevie leaned over to the side opposite me and retrieved the black box containing the Warhol suite from beside the Louis Vuitton shoulder bag also stashed on the highly polished hardwood floor.

I hadn't noticed it until then.

She settled the box in front of her on the table, then pushed it toward Ari Landau and Zev Neumann.

"Excellent," Ari said, his head bobbing energetically. "Excellent. And believe you me what a story they will help me to tell you."

9

Ari Landau made a production of opening the Warhol box while Zev Neumann slipped his hands into the pair of white cotton gloves he had pulled from a jacket pocket, then rose and began pacing the room while he spoke.

"You know anything at all about what the Nazis were doing about art owned by Jews around the time of the Second World War?" Ari asked. "Not you, Augie. I know how you know everything. Mr. Gulliver? Miss Marriner?"

Stevie directed a blank look at Ari, then me.

"Some," I said. "There's been a lot in the papers and magazines the last few years."

Ari nodded.

"Not enough about it and not so always accurate, Mr. Gulliver." He paused by the picture window and nodded approvingly at the view then, turning to us again, he said, "So, I'll tell you a little background to help you understand better about the Warhol suite."

Augie said, "Why do I suddenly get the feeling lunch is about to get colder than a Siberian winter?"

"A Siberian summer is nothing to shout about, either," Ari said. Then, "Once the madman Hitler went on his rampage, there began a systemic plundering and looting of the artworks that were owned by Jewish-owned galleries and the prominent, well-to-do Jewish families. Germany, France, Switzerland. Everywhere in western Europe. You name it. Holland. Belgium . . .

"It went on from 1939 until the end of the war in 1944, and it started at the top with Hitler himself, who was a collector back in the twenties, and his fat evil henchman, Goering, whose greed when it came to art was a masterpiece by itself. Bad enough that other high-ranking Nazi scum joined in and there was collusion with many gallery owners, some even Jewish themselves."

"Greedy bastards," Zev said. "They turned on their own people to save their skins or just to make a buck before they found out their skins also would be good for lampshades, like their bones would be good for a soap dish."

Ari signaled Zev not to interrupt.

He said, "Let me tell you how bad it got. By the time it was over, the war, more than one hundred thousand great artworks, including many by some of our greatest artists, had been pillaged one way or another. They had been snapped off the walls. Rolled up. Packaged. Marked 'Property of the Third Reich.' Photographed, cataloged and shipped away by transport train to Germany. The Führer and his pets got the best, the pick of the litters, naturally, and the others got the rest.

"Just taken from families in Paris, only Paris, between April of 1941 and July of 1944? I won't ask either of you to try and guess. Twenty-nine substantial shipments to Germany were made from Paris alone in that time. From France—forget the other countries—twenty-one thousand objects went to the Nazis and their avaricious collaborators. Great paintings of all periods. Great drawings. Great engravings. You name it. Stolen away from more than two hundred collectors, including names you would probably know, I mentioned them to you. It doesn't take a Quiz Kid to recognize the name of Rothschild, you know?"

Ari nodded in agreement with himself and turned to Zev for acknowledgment.

"Bernheim-Jeune, David-Weill, Rosenberg, Schloss," Zev began, using his fingers to count them off. "My great-great-grandfather had a gallery on the Rue de la Boétie, built up in the years after he went over from Slovakia, and he had a fine eye for masterworks. The gallery walls and the walls of his stately home were full of the finest of Rousseau, Pissarro, Picasso, Courbet, Braque, Cézanne, Degas, Manet, Modigliani, Renoir, Matisse."

"On and on and on," Ari said, taking over again. "My family's story is almost the same, you could say. In came the Nazis and the walls were stripped bare even before they all were marched off, excepting for my grandfather and those he could convince to escape from the country and certain death by using oils and heirlooms as bartering tools. I'm here today because . . . Well, you have to know that part already."

This last had taken the snap out of him. He stared at the bare floor and shook his head. His eyes glistened with the moisture of hurtful memory.

Meanwhile, it had begun to play to me like a scene the two lawyers had acted out many times before today.

The Ari and Zev Show.

In the brief time it took Ari to regain his composure, I said, "I don't mean to sound indifferent about your story, Ari, but I don't understand what any of this has to do with our suite of Warhols."

Stevie put a hand over my mouth.

"Take all the time you need," she said. "Neil is nicer and more understanding than he sounds sometimes, Ari. Take it from the voice of experience. I'm learning things here I never knew before."

Ari rewarded her with a smile.

He stiffened his back to his full height of about five-five or -six and took in a deep breath.

"I'm almost there," he said. Took another breath. "Now, when the war is over, the job of recovery begins. Find these artworks and return them to their rightful owners. I'll tell you, it's not so easy as it sounds. Greed is like being in a cemetery. Once greed gets buried, it's not always that easy digging it up again.

"The French located around sixty thousand stolen works in Germany and returned all but around fifteen thousand to their rightful owners. Maybe twelve or thirteen thousand of these went unclaimed and were of marginal consideration and sold off. The best of the rest were placed in French museums designated as National Museums of Recuperation, but just you or anyone today claim one as your own and attempt to have it returned. No easy task, that. And not just with the French. As bad as the Nazis were, a lot of stolen works began appearing on the walls of museums in other countries. It's a matter sometimes of not knowing. A donated work. A work acquired at auction or from a dealer. Sometimes it's a matter of knowing and not caring. Like Swiss dealers I could tell you about.

"What we began hearing and reading more and more about was descendants of the original owners recognizing what was rightfully theirs and making a claim. An ongoing process to this day.

"Sometimes the claim comes with proof and it happens. But a far more common occurrence after half a century is that somebody has to go to court and hope a judge sides with them. The right party does not always come out the winner. Zev and me, we got dozens of stories we can tell like that. People come to us to represent them. They know we understand, because we have been victims ourselves. We also recognize not just birthright and justice is at stake in these cases. There are millions upon millions of dollars' worth of great art at stake. You asked where the Warhol suite comes into the picture, Mr. Gulliver. It comes in here."

Ari Landau's explanation began ordinarily enough, how sometime in the mid-1980s Andy Warhol accepted a highly lucrative commission to create a small suite of prints under unusual terms and conditions.

The suite would be based on a series of portraits of wealthy collectors who had bonded through their passion for fine art and desired to memorialize this friendship.

Each portrait was to incorporate a painting chosen from among the many in their private collections.

The work had to be done at an obscure atelier outside Paris in an exceptionally limited period of time, while all of them were gathered for their annual social get-together.

The size of the edition would be limited to the number of collectors represented. There were not to be any presentation sets for the artisans working with the artist or for Warhol himself, who was required to sign a confidentiality agreement that committed him to absolute silence about the suite. Any breach of the agreement would oblige Warhol to pay back twice the contractual total agreed upon, as well as an additional financial penalty and any and all attorney's fees and costs of collection.

In sum, a pretty straightforward deal.

"Only, it didn't work out that way," Ari Landau said.

Zev Neumann emphatically nodded agreement.

"Bad for Andy Warhol, but good for us," Zev said.

Zev, who'd been removing the prints from the presentation box and laying them out in a neat row along the length of the table, took over the story, using his lilting baritone to add dramatic nuances Ari hadn't bothered with, along with a broad range of hand gestures and facial expressions whenever he wanted to emphasize a point.

He spoke faster and with far less precision than Ari, adding to my impression of a performance.

More *Ari and Zev Show*.

"You know anything at all about Warhol, you know that at the same time he was turning his own fifteen minutes of fame into a lifetime of notoriety, he was making the bucks hand over fist," Zev said. "He was amassing a fortune with his art and movies and books. His personal appearances. The *Interview* magazine he started. And he was never one to turn down a payday. He jumped like a Superman at the deal when it was offered.

"But Warhol was also a notorious gossip, like a lot of his famous friends. He was always on the phone or at some gala opening, a cocktail party, a dinner party, sharing the news of the day before it ever got into the papers or those tell-all television programs.

"So, listen to this, the way we got it finally, Ari and me. It's a year, a couple of years later, and Andy is at some swanky event, some gallery opening, and some other big-timer artist or dealer or critic or collector, somebody like that, begins ragging on him about how so-and-so just picked up for himself a commission for a suite of prints that's probably a record for that sort of thing. Two million dollars. 'Can you believe it, Andy?' this person says. 'Don't you wish something like that would fall into your lap?'

"Andy is this sweet, gentle, naive soul, mild-mannered and soft-spoken, horribly polite in an almost frightened-doe kind of way, but Andy also has an ego to go with his stature as an innovator, especially when it comes to what came to be known as Pop Art.

" 'Well, I know someone who made more than that for less work than you're telling me,' he tells this person. 'How does three million dollars sound to you?' This person says, 'Who's that?' Andy gives him a blank smile that at the same time is a tell-all answer and walks away.

"Next thing, it's like Sears telling Roebuck or Lord telling Taylor, Abercrombie telling Fitch. You hear what I mean? Word travels fast in this small circle of insiders, like the bread basket at a banquet table. It's big news at Elaine's and it's big news at Le Cirque. No details to go with Andy Warhol's claim, but someone hears it who knows or who tells someone who knows. By mentioning how he got three million dollars for a commissioned suite, Andy has bordered on breaching his contract.

"He breached it, not a border, was certainly a claim that could be asserted in a court of law and might hold up, costing Warhol a bundle of money, so understandably Andy gets very, very nervous and breaks out in a rash when the gossip he started in the first place gets back to him.

"By this time, it seems it's also gotten back to the party who made the deal with Andy. He gets nervous for his own reasons. It's not a contract or a court of law that he is interested in. He decides Andy has to be shut up before Andy drops public any more of the story and gets the news media checking any deeper into it. That happens, it would be a black day for all the collectors and all the other parties involved.

"Not long after, Andy starts complaining he's got pains in his gallbladder. How or where or why he got them, he doesn't have the slightest idea, but they proceed to get even worse, the pains. So bad, so painful, Andy decides he has to check into a hospital to get the gallbladder removed. Mind you, I'm talking about a man who all his life has been so afraid of hospitals and operations, he cannot even bring himself to say the words.

"In he goes, and the gallbladder operation is textbook, or so it seems. The next day Andy is back on the phone calling his friends. He's watching the TV. He's seemingly fit as a fiddle." Zev played an imaginary violin, like a fiddler on the roof. "Early on the day after that, Andy is dead, and the last we heard, Ari and me, the cause of his death was still being argued."

Zev lifted his eyebrows and turned his palms toward the ceiling.

I said, "Are you suggesting—?"

He shook his head emphatically.

"I'm only saying Warhol was dead before he could spill any more beans about the suite of prints I'm here looking at now."

Stevie had moved around the table and was standing next to Zev, studying the silkscreens. She latched on to Zev's arm and said, "They identify the owners of artworks that were looted by the Nazis. The artworks they're so puffed up about in these Warhols."

"Yes to that, Miss Marriner," Ari said, joining them.

I followed her lead.

Augie also.

He evaluated the silkscreen prints with a swift but careful metronomic sweep before returning to the head of the table, adjusting his cassock—today a citrus orange in color with the usual matching eye patch—and resuming his seat. He put on his half-moon reading glasses with their single corrective lens for the good eye, opened the file folder on top of the stack in front of him, and began comparing something inside with the prints as Ari launched Act Three of *The Ari and Zev Show.*

"These are the collectors who met in France and spent time being immortalized by Warhol in the prints now before us," Ari Landau said. "Only, some proved to be less mortal than some others. Him in the screen print second from the left and him two over from that. The attractive middle-aged woman with the ugly facial mole in the next print. All three dead, or missing and presumed dead, and all under criminal circumstances.

"This fine-looking gentleman to my immediate right was the latest that we know about. Richardson by name, a wealthy Texan. Oil and gas. More government connections in Washington than an outcall-service madam—you should please excuse the expression, Miss Marriner. An astoundingly remarkable Cézanne, wouldn't you say?

"Back there, the old man with all the medals his chest can handle, he went right before Richardson. The mayor of a picture-book village in the Bavarian Alps. His name was Von Harbou. A Nazi disguised as a human being, from a long line of Nazis. The van Gogh self-portrait in a landscape? Nowhere we looked after the authorities were finished with all their poking around. Gone. Missing. Like it had never even existed in the first place."

Stevie said, "The others? Same story?"

"Same story, Miss Marriner. The other man, he appears to have been the first. In Bologna. Lizzani, Cesare Lizanni. His grandfather was tight with Il Duce, Mussolini, in those years when that was the smart thing to be." Ari put a finger into his mouth. "Boom! *Arrivederci*, Cesare Lizzani, and also the astounding Goya that dominates the screenprint."

"The woman?"

"She was a newcomer to their ranks. The Countess Mole, we call her, with a lavish chalet near Gstaad, not far from the chalet in Rossinière of the last to go of the pre–World War Two School of Paris greats, Count Balthasar Klossowski de Rola."

"Balthus," I said.

"Yes, of course," Ari said, and gave me a look to say he was impressed I knew. "The Countess Mole showed up unannounced at the gathering in widow's weeds. Her husband dead after being bitten by a rabid squirrel during a spirited game of lawn croquet, or so her death certificate stated. The painting she's with, you can see it's an early Picasso nude. Still missing, like all the other paintings."

Stevie said, "They're using the Warhols as a roadmap to the collectors and their art treasures, that's it, isn't it? The same as you're trying to do."

"Yes and no, Miss Marriner. They seem to know who and what they're after. We'd only heard rumors about the Warhol suite. Today's the first time Zev and me are actually seeing it for ourselves."

Stevie gave him a doubting look. "Then how do you know so much about who these people in the prints are?" she said.

"A grapevine is a grapevine. You hear names, you check them out. Important people. Rich people. Rich people who collect fine art. Collectors who die suddenly and mysteriously." He inched up an eyebrow. "You build a dossier. Files like our friend Augie is looking at now. You follow up on leads. You dig, dig, dig, and you keep on digging, and hope eventually you turn up more than piles of dirt."

I said, "If only one suite was made for each of the collectors and that was all, no more, not even a set of prints for Warhol, it makes me wonder if the murders and thefts aren't the work of one of the collectors. Someone whose greed got the better of him?"

I noticed Ari split a long glance with Zev.

It said I was close to their reasoning, but not entirely, so I tried something else. "Possibly the collector in cahoots with a printer at the atelier?"

This time they seemed to nod in agreement with me, or maybe just with each other.

Ari said, "You have any special printer in mind?"

Stevie didn't need the sixth sense we've always shared to know my answer.

She answered for me: "Henri Godard."

"The master printer whose Arch of Triumph chop mark is right there, embossed on all the prints," I said.

Without bothering to follow my pointing finger, Ari said, "Very good, very, very good indeed, Miss Marriner, Mr. Gulliver." He applauded in appreciation. "Clearly you have been doing some homework."

"And something else," I said, deciding a gamble on the suspicion that had been building in my mind since I'd met Ari and Zev was overdue.

Both men scrunched their faces in curiosity, waiting for the rest. So did Stevie, while a little smile of expectation began to form at the creviced corners of Augie's lips.

"You're not just lawyers, if that, are you?"

Now, Ari smeared his face in disbelief and said, "Oh? What, then?"

"Interpol agents would be a good guess. A branch that specializes in international art heists?"

He and Zev laughed.

Too heartily.

"I don't think so," Zev said, throwing an *Oh, go away!* hand at me.

Ari said, "Come now, Mr. Gulliver. Come, come, come. Do we truly *look* to you like some kind of secret agents?"

"No, but why would you? How you look would be part of the secret. So—if you're not Interpol, that leaves me with my better guess . . . Mossad."

Mossad.

Israel's *ha-Mossad le-Modiin ule-Tafkidim Meyuhadim*—The Institute for Intelligence and Special Tasks. Set up fifty years ago, in April of 1951, by Prime Minister David Ben Gurion.

Somewhere around one to two thousand people working in near-anonymity from Tel Aviv in clandestine operations that include covert action, counterterrorism and the collection of intelligence that supports the strongest possible defense of Israel against the country's enemies.

And now, I was guessing, it was going after the return of art treasures looted from Jewish families by the Nazis with the same zeal and determination that over the years led Mossad agents to Eichmann, Mordechai Vanunu, the "Black September" terrorists, and Abu Jihad, the PLO's chief of military and terrorist operations against Israel.

It made sense and helped explain what we were doing at Augie's place.

Augie had written several series of articles about the Mossad before quitting the *Daily* to start up his spiritual sanctuary, one of them a runner-up for the Pulitzer. In the process, he became chummy with some of the agents, because he had laid in excuses for some of the Mossad's misadventures, like the killing in 1974 of an Algerian waiter mistaken for PLO security head Ali Ahmad Salameh.

Years later, some of his not-so-subtle references led me to wonder if Augie had called in a favor with them after the county courthouse bombing that killed his protégé, Wimpy Angelman, and almost got Augie.

All the alleged bombers who walked for lack of evidence later turned up dead or missing and are missing to this day, everywhere but on A&E and Discovery Channel historical crime specials.

I've never been able to pin Augie down on it.

Mossad.

Landau and Neumann turned as solemn as gravediggers when I said the word.

It became Augie's turn to laugh.

"I told you he'd figure it out," he called at them. "I'm only surprised it took you as long as it did, amigo."

"Just wanted to hear enough, Augie. Now I'd like to hear the rest."

"Over lunch or after lunch," Augie said, slapping the top of the file pile and stowing his half-moon glasses in a pocket of his cassock. "That explosion you hear's my belly, not some space shuttle setting down in the Mojave Desert." He was up from his seat and halfway to the door before he'd finished the thought.

10

Brother Liam had prepared a sumptuous meal of crab-and-lobster bisque, which he served with a small green salad, thick slices of crusty French bread he'd lavished with fresh creamery butter, and a Napa Valley chardonnay. He grumbled a little after Ari and Zev praised the bisque without sampling it, wondering if he might bring them some fresh vegetables and fruits instead.

It wasn't until we returned to the conference room and they saw the Warhol prints laid out exactly as we had left them that Ari and Zev dropped the nervous edge they'd not been able to disguise throughout lunch, where they sat feigning interest while Augie solved all the world's problems without missing a mouthful of bisque or chardonnay rinse.

The closest they came to conversation was telling Stevie that their wives were fans of *Bedrooms and Board Rooms*, wondering if they might trouble her for autographed photos. She accepted their flattery graciously and asked for mailing addresses.

In return, they handed over cheaply embossed business cards with their names and a postal-box address in Manhattan.

A pair of cards for her, a pair for me.

Their names, the P.O. address, and an 800 phone number.

No other information.

Stevie found a pen in her tote bag and said, "Who would you like me to sign the photos to?"

Ari and Zev traded stares before Ari answered, " 'To Mrs. Landau' and 'To Mrs. Neumann' will do just fine, thank you."

Zev spelled the last names.

Stevie shot me a look.

"I can remember that," she told them, and dropped the pen and the cards into the bag.

They smiled appreciatively and excused themselves to the bathroom, rejoining us ten or twelve minutes later reeking of tobacco.

Back in the conference room, Augie fidgeted to a comfortable position in his seat at the head of the table and pulled one of his Cubans from a cassock pocket, thought better of the idea and returned it. Stevie and I took our seats, as Ari did his. Zev remained standing.

"So, where were we?" Augie said, pushing his half-moon frames tighter against the bridge of his booze-beribboned nose and clasping his hands on top of the pile of folders.

He reminded me of a poker-faced pawnbroker waiting out an answer to his offer.

Ari said, "I believe we were going to hear what you know about the master printer, Henri Godard," directing the comment to me.

"Yes, Godard," I said. "Right after you answer some of our questions."

Ari thought about it. "Some, yes," he said. "Certainly."

"But maybe not all," Zev said.

"And, you being a newspaperman, it has to be off the record, as you newspapermen put it," Ari said. "Even Augie here, in spite of some positive history we share, it also went for him, before we asked him to follow up and explain our call to Miss Marriner, then call you, for you to come to this meeting."

I turned to Augie, who said, "It's okay, amigo. For as long as I've been out of the byline racket, I got asked and gave Mr. Trust No One here my word."

"Then you have mine," I told Ari, without hesitation.

Before Ari could ask her or, worse, ignore her, Stevie said, "My word, too."

Shot him one of her keyboard smiles.

Then, played it for Augie and me.

She knew the philosophy Augie had ingrained in me after the *Daily* hired me away from my job running a small paper's news bureau in the desert two counties removed from L.A. and I fell under his influence on the old crime beat: *Your word is something you give. It's a promise you keep.*

I said, "This matter of life and death you say we're facing, because we have the Warhol suite—"

"Yes," Ari said, while Zev nodded.

"Because of the suite's value or because we might learn the significance behind the collectors and the paintings and tie the murders together?"

"Possible, yes, both," Zev said, making it Ari's turn to nod.

Stevie said, "Because it might get sold to someone who might—a dealer, another collector, or to someone like you?"

Ari said, "Also reasonable to assume, except we're not in the market for them ourselves, Miss Marriner. Our budgets go to other, more practical uses. We will want to take some photographs before we go. Add them to our files and elsewhere."

Years of working at them turns interviews from a craft into another form of art, and I'd done them long enough to know when the truth wasn't the whole truth and nothing but.

Like now.

Law schools teach lawyers not to ask a witness the question without knowing the answer ahead of time, where practice teaches a reporter to ask anyway, to play people like a piñata to get at the good stuff.

Like now.

I said, "Possibilities and assumptions aside, where are you guys coming from? And I don't mean a street address."

A long, loud silence before Ari, with a gesture, turned the floor over to Zev.

"What you don't see on the table," Zev said. "What we were hoping to find in your Warhol suite and unfortunately didn't find."

He sucked in a deep breath and exhaled a deeper sigh of exasperation.

Looked at Ari, who said, "Tell."

"The twelfth silkscreen print," Zev said. "The *Y*-damned twelfth silkscreen print that completed the set."

He stepped farther from us and began to pace, found his pack of cigarettes and jammed one into his mouth.

Remembered about Stevie and stowed it behind his ear.

Came back and sat down, began a nervous fingernail dance on the table.

"You go, Ari," Zev said. "*Y*-damned twelfth print."

Ari consoled him with several pats on the arm and said, "We've known from the beginning, from our intelligence sources, how the commission was for twelve prints, not the eleven you got as a gift from a certain friend of yours. We were hoping for better when the trail finally led to you.

"Not to be, so okay already. Not to be. But this set of prints should not have been, either. Not a surprise when we came to know more history. About Henri Godard and his reputation for bootlegging, printing and spiriting away extra sets that he could turn into his own profit. Yours and maybe more that we are yet to come across.

"We're convinced the twelfth print shows the party who conceived and sold the other eleven on the idea of a suite. One of their own or an outsider, that is the part we do not know. Yet.

"We're convinced, when he got wind we were finally on his trail, he began to cover his tracks. Go after the others and retrieve their sets. While at it, help himself to the art for his own collection or to quietly put out for sale on the underground market.

"We're convinced he is not alone in this work, that he is employing the services of a professional killer. What we have seen so far of the murders bespeaks of that, all being too well done to be the work of an amateur."

Zev interrupted him:

"And something else—this son of a bitch may also be a key to locating many more of the great treasures stolen from our people by the Nazis."

Ari turned a palm to the ceiling and nodded agreement.

"That's the long and the short of it, Mr. Gulliver," he said. "So, if we know about you, chances are good he may or could find out soon, then turn his dog on you, in order to protect his identity. So, you see, it's absolutely a life-and-death matter, our connecting with you. Better you should know the danger of what you have accidentally become a party to than be unprepared and fall into somebody's trap."

Zev said, "Like the phone call you say you got. From some dealer offering you big money for the set, sight unseen?"

"Rosenstock," I said. "Theodore Rosenstock."

"Not a name in our files," Ari said. "Zev, please make a note."

Zev drew a slim spiral pad and ballpoint from an inside jacket pocket and wrote down the name.

"What else about him?"

I gave them the entire conversation.

Zev kept making notes. A few times, Ari prompted him with a finger baton. A few times, I was asked to repeat something, like the phone number Rosenstock had given me. Ari wanted to know if I was sure of it. I was, I said, describing my photographic memory as the equivalent of twenty-twenty vision.

"Just you remember," he cautioned me, "what you don't forget, you don't repeat to anyone else, either. We'll look into this Rosenstock first thing and, should he contact you again, you let us know at once. The eight-hundred number on the cards we gave to Miss Marriner. Don't you call him. If he is part of any of this, he is nobody you want to monkey with."

"Against a monkey, this Rosenstock would be one of those eight-hundred-pound gorillas," Zev said.

Ari said, "Meanwhile, Mr. Gulliver, if your memory is so twenty-twenty, you remember you are yet to tell us what you can about Henri Godard."

I told them about Stevie and me going to see Kip Lingle at New Visions Gallery, what we'd learned there, and how Aaron Lodger was checking Godard out for me against the "Mr. France" he got the Warhol suite from.

"Yes," Ari said, like I had answered another game-show question correctly. "Your good friend in Palm Springs, he told us as much when we contacted him. How Mr. France has seemingly disappeared . . . So, you have nothing else to tell about Godard, otherwise or since?"

"Nothing . . . You?"

"The man is always one step ahead of us. We think, if we ever find him, he'll be able to tell about the twelfth print. If not everything, enough to move us from where we are now, which is almost at a standstill."

"Do you think he's Mr. France?"

"Something else we won't know, not until we locate Mr. France. Something else you're best advised to leave to us. You as well, Miss Marriner."

"Of course," I said.

"Of course," Stevie said.

I knew one of us was lying.

This story was growing far too good, too important, for me to stay an outsider.

When Stevie began stroking my thigh under the table, I knew both of us were lying.

The deadpan look Augie was giving us with his one good eye said he also knew.

It said: *Don't either of you think about doing anything stupid.*

I supposed he also saw the stupid possibilities turning over in my mind.

Ari Landau and Zev Neumann left within the hour, leaving Stevie and me to linger with Augie over coffee and dessert, a mixed-fruit compote topped with a generous dollop of fresh cream the Mossad agents had declined with feigned regret, checking their watches and claiming a need to race to catch a flight at LAX.

We were reflecting on the meeting when Stevie finally converted the puzzled look that had been playing on her face to a question. "Why Andy Warhol?" she said. "All those collectors seemed to be into everything but contemporary art. I'd've thought they'd pick a more traditional artist."

"Based on what I saw in the files the Mossad boys came in with, yes," Augie said. "Very little late twentieth century, and that may be why. Somebody more traditional may have been more likely to recognize the artworks they were being asked to copy for what they were. The collectors probably felt safer with a Warhol. Or, maybe, figured Andy was a better investment, somebody who could give them more fiscal bang for their bucks."

"You think? Hadn't he turned himself into something of a laughingstock in the art world by then?" She looked to me for confirmation.

I shook my head and told Stevie, "Not to the people who truly understood where he was coming from and what, from the beginning, Andy Warhol represented to art."

"Well put, amigo, well put," Augie said, surprising me with a compliment where I might have expected a put-down. In an instant I knew why. I'd given Augie a fresh launch pad for his chronic need to brag.

"I was one of the first to understand and report that," he said. "Cover piece I did for the old *Coast* magazine in—" He muffled the date, like an old woman hiding her age. "Was a commission I took on gladly. I was going on back to New York anyway for that exposé I was researching on that mafia boss who got erased a year later, his face down in a bowl of pasta, the extra red sauce streaming from a major crater in his skull caused by a well-served shotgun à la double. Down in Little Italy, the Blue Grotto, I'm almost certain. Ferrarro's Bakery was right across the street. It was one of those *La Cosa Nostra* family hangouts. He gave me an hour and a half of self-serving nonsense dialogue while he sopped up the splashed minestrone on the napkin tucked into the pointed collar of his custom-made two-hundred-and-fifty-dollar silk shirt."

Augie put down his coffee cup, commanded, "Wait," and left the conference room, returning in a few minutes with a slender black ledger, the kind he'd used over the years for recording what he said would one day form the basis for his memoirs.

He was using his thumb as a bookmark.

He flipped open the ledger and, still on his feet, waited until certain he had our complete attention.

He adjusted his glasses, cleared his throat, and began reciting, his spoiled voice rumbling out, " 'However Measured or Far Away.' " Slowly. A year between the words. "The piece's title," Augie said. " 'Waiting for Andy, waiting for Andy, waiting for Andy, waiting for Andy . . .' The rest of the title. My idea. A multiple-word image, consistent with the artist I was putting under a microscope in the year"—an *Oh, what the hell* expression—"nineteen hundred and sixty-nine . . ."

He cleared his throat.

" 'By A. K. Fowler.' "

A modest bow before he continued the one-man show:

" 'The building overlooks Union Square, between other buildings, and itself is easy to overlook. Warhol, Andy Films, Inc., Sixth Floor, is not alone responsible for the pervading notoriety at Number Thirty-three. The Communist Party of New York State is also a tenant, and who knows what secrets H. Millman, the building manager, might share about Levi Berman, Walker and Hodgetts, Architects, the folks from Eagle Jewelry Case Company, or other occupants, were he to manage a guest appearance on *The Johnny Carson Show*.

" 'He might also have a few tidbits to spill about Warhol, who in 1962 gave the art world a more definable supermarket complex by unveiling his first series of thirty-two canvases of Campbell's Soup cans, painted by hand and all as identical as he could make them, excepting the labels, which identified the contents of each canvas . . .' "

Augie paused.
His good eye followed his finger gliding down the page.
He resumed:

" 'Unlike artists who lack the ingredients for securing broad public notice, Warhol was suddenly in the thick of attention, among the Cream of Pop Art, sharing the warm, full-bodied aroma of celebrity with Jasper Johns, Robert Rauschenberg, Roy Lichtenstein, Claes Oldenburg, George Segal, Marisol.

" 'Some dismissed, and still do, his art as gimmickry, while others acknowledge it as a major contribution to the art of the redundant. Serial Imagery. Echo Art. Marcel Duchamp, the master, whose nude descended a staircase out of the 1913 Armory Show and into legend, history, new planes of creative enterprise, said, "If a man takes fifty Campbell Soup cans and puts them on a canvas, it is not the retinal image which concerns us. What interests us is the concept that wants to put fifty Campbell Soup cans on canvas."

" 'Warhol deals with the everyday, the commonplace, the vulgar, the banal, the values of life and the propaganda of living. He doesn't question the right of anyone or any thing to be coveted, popular, sought after or even ignored by contemporary society. He endorses the idols and idiosyncrasies of our time. He isolates them. He enlarges them. He repeats them time and again, a god in his kingdom, over and over and over and over and over and over and over and over, forcing us to look, to see, sometimes for the first time . . .' "

Another finger-skim, then:

" 'Warhol enobles through isolation and enlargement as well as repetition, turning cans into castles and stars into saints, in the process raising a question: Why? Why a soup can? Why a photograph of a movie actress? Why an electric chair? Why a president's widow? Why? Why? Why? Why? Have our eyes opened a bit wider? Are things as they seem?

" 'What is it we see and is what we see worth seeing?

" 'Would these questions be raised by Johnny Carson and Ed McMahon in conversation with H. Millman?' "

Augie stopped abruptly.

Brother Saul had burst into the room after knocking loudly on the door.

He had an anxious look on his face.

He held out his arm and tapped hard on the face of his wristwatch.

Augie answered with a whispered growl. Closing the ledger, he explained, "Time for our first midafternoon devotionals. Something I'm not empowered to miss, Lord's will be done. The brothers count on my presence for their daily inspiration, especially at this time of the day."

He handed over the ledger to me and, as he turned to go, said, "Take your time, amigo, and you, Miss Beautiful. When you leave, leave the Warhols. They're safer here with me than with either of you."

Stevie showed she didn't appear to like the idea any more than me, but Augie wasn't buying any argument, acting like it was his decision alone to make.

He said, "They'll go into my private office safe. It's a freestanding, top-of-the-line Braswell MegaLock with the patented time-based Drop Click Rotator. Guaranteed to defy the most skilled Jimmy Valentine. None better. That correct, Brother Saul?"

"Yes, Brother Kalman, but please—" Brother Saul said, holding up his wristwatch.

Augie said, "If anyone seriously dangerous tracks the Warhols to us, they'll be hard-pressed to get in to crack that mother of a safe or, that failing, make their getaway without being noticed and stopped. Several brothers here big enough to put the fear of the Lord into anyone."

With that he raised the hem of his cassock ankle-high and scurried toward the door, unnecessarily assuring Brother Saul, "I'm coming, I'm coming."

11

That evening, Maryam Zokaei and I consummated our date. We took in the new Tom Hanks movie at the Bruin Theater in Westwood Village, her choice, and followed with dinner at a small storefront bistro down the boulevard across Wilshire, about halfway between the movie theater and the Heathcliffe, my choice.

The restaurant, Europa, had room for less than a dozen tables between three cramped booths on both side walls, most of them occupied now with other couples after a late supper priced more reasonably than the food and candy treats at any movie house in L.A., where a small tub of popcorn costs what it took to make *Titanic*, the movie and the ship combined. The decor consisted of travel posters and a mock crystal chandelier that provided a romantic glow to complement the piped-in music and also helped to hide the stains on the paper tablecloths.

The words *Continental Cuisine* on the menu translated into a chef who couldn't make up his mind, but I've always found whatever I ordered to be tasty and the portions large, to go with speedy service and a *Linger as long as you like* attitude.

I ordered the "spaghetti *Suprisa*," the pasta equivalent of soup of the day at Europa. Maryam went for a small dinner salad, oil-and-vinegar dressing on the side, only picking at the mixed greens and dwarf tomatoes over our carafe of house red and irresistible baskets of assorted breads swimming in garlic.

"There goes the diet," she said every time she took a mouthful, doing this little entrancing dance with her head and erotically hypnotic stormcloud eyes.

"Not that you really have anything to worry about," I'd answer every time, mainly because she'd respond with a smile and a thank-you that took the form of her warm hand reaching across the table for mine. Every time, she sent over enough of an electric charge to light me up like the City of Los Angeles before the power crisis that engulfed California.

How to explain it?

You don't.

You run with it and hope you're both heading for the same finish line, but—

At the same time, with Maryam, I was warning myself, *Slow down, pal. You hardly know this woman, who's almost young enough to be your—*

Ugh!

Ouch!

I couldn't bring myself to even think the word.

But the company was easy, the conversation easier, damn it. The more she talked the more I convinced myself there was something un-usually intelligent, sophisticated and worldly-wise about her that went beyond her twenty-four years and an enticing physical presence that currently beggared the imagination in a loose-fitting cowl-necked gray wool sweater, sloppy jeans and Nikes as scuffed as mine.

Once again I had been drawn to a woman younger than me, like Leigh was, like Stevie had been, and no way for me to explain it away, like it or not, as passing fancy or typical male midlife crisis.

Maryam had dozens of questions for me, mostly about my work, always asked with the enthusiasm an archaeologist shows around freshly discovered digs, in a kittenish voice working in overdrive, and often prefaced with an apology for getting too personal, which I just as often assured her was not the case.

She was equally forthcoming about herself whenever I got in a question, but I couldn't tell what she thought about me by anything Maryam said or did. There were no real clues outside my imagination, and I wasn't going to ask her that question this early in the—

Relationship?

Too strong a word, really.

Maryam was of Persian descent, one of the reasons she chose to settle in Westwood after her divorce. She had the need to be among "her people," she said of the area, known as "Tehrangeles," because of its immense expatriate Iranian population, the biggest outside Iran. The main streets here are lined with myriad stores whose signs are in both English and cursive Farsi script.

Her other reason was having UCLA in the neighborhood.

She'd been anxious to return to college and her English Lit studies once she had freed herself from a husband twenty years her senior, who'd been imposed upon her by a family obligation stretching back to when she was eight years old.

"It caught up with them and with me when I was nineteen and was too horrible for words, even now," she said, the one time her eyes defied gaiety. "It got me out of my youth, my naiveté, my education, my life, and made me the mom of two sweet, wonderful children. A girl and a boy, in that order, stolen away from me after—"

She stopped.

Wiped at her eyes.

Stole a hoax of a smile from somewhere.

"I'm sorry," she said. "I didn't mean to . . . Can we talk about something else?"

In this moment, I wanted to take her in my arms, give her comfort, but it would have been presumptive of me. For as much as I wanted to know more, this was not the time to impose on her scarred memories or emotions.

I sensed she read my concerns and understanding before her eyes wandered down to the paper tablecloth and she began rubbing at a grease stain with two fingers.

"You said you'd tell all about the beyond-curious way we met, your parsimonious, persimmons, however you say it," I said, making a joke of the word.

Maryam looked up at me appreciatively and said, "Parasomnia."

I mispronounced it intentionally and won a laugh. "*Para*, as in paramedics. *Somnia*, as in insomnia."

"Parasomnia."

" 'By Jove, I think I've got it, I think I've got it,' " I said, doing my best impression of Henry Higgins.

Parasomnias are sleeping disorders.

They include somnambulism—sleepwalking—which affects about twenty percent of the population, and other disorders that intrude on the sleeping process. They occur when a person is in a mixed state of being asleep and awake at the same time, awake enough to act out complex behaviors, yet—

Still asleep and not at all aware of these actions or, afterward, to even remember them.

There's great difficulty in arousing the sleepwalker, who in severe cases might demonstrate violent behavior that results in serious injuries, sometimes death.

When one of these episodes is described afterward to the sleep-walker, the usual reaction is a cocktail mix of confusion, anxiety, embarrassment, shame and guilt.

I had checked out parasomnias on the Web before strolling up the corridor to collect my date, but let Maryam give me a detailed explanation.

By the time she finished, the upsetting moments talking about her ex and her two kids were history and she was urging me to tell her everything I remembered about her nocturnal visit.

She blushed and laughed nervously through most of the report, which I treated like a part of Jerry Seinfeld's act. Shook her head in knowing disbelief. Randomly cruised her hair with her fingers. Looked around to see who might be eavesdropping on us. Balanced her hands against her thumbs and did this silent applause thing with her fingertips. Rolled those wondrous eyes and clucked her dismay.

"No apologies necessary," I said, whenever she tried. "The chocolate-chip cookies were to die for. Otherwise, I might not be so forgiving."

She reached over for my hand and said, "I've heard the same about my oatmeal-raisin cookies. The same for my cakes and pies."

"So I'm not the first beneficiary."

"And probably not the last one. I've also been known to dust and vacuum. Clean windows. Wash dishes. Wash and wax floors and, every so often, cars down in the garage or out on the street. Call up friends and carry on a conversation for hours. Drive over to the twenty-four-hour market and do my shopping for the week—and don't think that's not scary, the idea of sleep-driving . . ." Her eyes went around the track a few times. "The experts have tried all kinds of behavioral modification tricks on me, but nothing's ever worked. Drugs. Hypnosis. Relaxation imagery before I go to bed. They think it's something to do with genetics in my case, because I've been walking the walk and strolling the stroll ever since I was eleven or twelve.

"Lately, some of them have been asking me about willing my body to medical science. I tell them, I am only ready to leave it to Tom Cruise or Johnny Depp, and that, only before I go. When I'm dead, all I'll need or want is a good night's sleep, thank you very much.' "

"How do I get on your list?" I said, the words flying out uncontrollably because of my own chronic disorder—*big-time big-mouthitis*—and now I was the one blushing.

Time seemed to fall asleep at our table. For an eternity after she trapped me with her eyes and I found myself powerless to turn away.

Finally, her head inching up and down, as serenely as an angel granting miracles, Maryam whispered, "All you have to do is ask me, Neil."

Back at my apartment, we made love like kids let loose in a candy store. Urgently in the beginning, desperate for those first mouthwatering tastes. Slower and more relaxed as the hours passed, neither of us satisfied with enough when so much more was so readily available.

Fumbling gave way to precision as we learned what the other liked, giving and getting in equal measure, resisting nothing rather than risk the other's disappointment, making no pretense at love, sharing the unspoken need to first rid ourselves of need and lust.

Nothing contradicted the original sensation Maryam had vested in me since that three A.M. sleepwalker's knock on my door, but a moment came tonight around the same hour when I feared that maybe I had put a destructive wedge in our relationship before it had an opportunity to grow beyond our mutual sense of body-and-soul compatibility.

She rolled over in the bed, fit herself tightly against my back, and invested it with a warmth that grew as her hand strolled down my chest and settled between my thighs.

She kissed my shoulder and said, "Awake?"

"Awake."

"Got a question for you. You mind?"

"Ask and ye shall receive."

Maryam said, "Who's Stevie? We were making love last time, you called me Stevie."

I froze, went limp in her hand, and stared out at the darkness wishing it would start flashing in neon an answer, any answer, better than the truth.

But, if this relationship was going anywhere, I didn't want it traveling on a lie.

I cleared the sleep out of my throat and said, finally, "My ex-wife. Stevie is my ex-wife."

I extricated myself from her and rolled into a sitting position.

"If that's your way of telling me you're gay, it's not going to compute, big fella. I already know better. Same way you know I'm no guy."

"Stevie. Stephanie. Stephanie Marriner."

"The actress?"

"The actress."

"Until then, you never said her name."

"I didn't think it mattered."

"Maybe it does, Neil, more than you think. Anyway, to you if not to me." Maryam was quiet for a moment. "Do you still love her, Neil?"

Again, the darkness offered me no escape.

"I'd be lying if I told you I didn't, Maryam."

She thought some more.

She said, "I'd be lying if I told you I cared."

She pulled me back onto the bed. Straddled me. Leaned over and kissed my forehead. Kissed my eyes. Ran her tongue down my nose and burrowed it into mouth.

Withdrawing, she found my ear and whispered into it, "Call me anything you like, but call me, okay?"

"Okay," I said, struggling to find my voice and barely managing to get out the word before her mouth was all over mine again.

Maryam was gone when the alarm woke me at six.

I struggled across to the bathroom, where I found she had decorated the cabinet mirror with a lipstick heart and, underneath the heart, her name in bold capital letters.

After following the smell of freshly brewed coffee into the kitchen, I found a second heart drawn on a scrap of note paper taped to the door of the fridge.

Underneath this heart, Maryam had written in a delicate script, *Room inside for me?*

I hoped she meant the heart, not the fridge.

I snatched up my portable phone and tried her first on her building com line.

On her phone when I got no answer.

This time I got her machine.

"You invited me to call, so I am calling," I said, and quickly hung up, fearful that she might pick up at the sound of my voice and not trusting myself to get out whatever else I'd planned to say; not really certain what the words would be. I was sounding to myself like the shy Neil Gulliver who never had an easy time of calling girls while in junior high and high school, even when he was strutting around as one of those macho BMOC campus jocks and had lots of them tagging after him, his shyness and a severe lack of confidence in the dating department dogging and defeating him while his hormones raged out of control.

I threw myself into my jogging outfit for my usual morning run into Westwood Village and back, rerouting myself and slowing down to smile and remember as I passed the Bruin Theater and Europa. In between, I stopped at my greasy spoon café of choice for a toasted water bagel, heavy on the cream cheese, and bran muffin, heavy on the butter, to go. I would have had my breakfast there, part of the daily A.M. routine, but this morning I wanted to test the bagel and muffin with more of Maryam's coffee, a way to find out if the coffee was as marvelous and magnificent as she was, or if this was only more carryover from the best night and the best woman I'd stumbled into since—

Okay—

Since Stevie.

Wait.

Not okay.

"Okay," was what Maryam said.

Call me anything you like, but call me, okay?

"Okay," that's what she said to call her.

No, of course that's not what she'd meant.

What she meant was—

Can you believe this?

I was babbling to myself. Making no sense.

Sounding like I was back in the tenth grade.

The ninth grade.

Eighth.

The coffee took the edge off a virtually sleepless night, the toasted bagel and bran muffin off an appetite stimulated by Maryam and visions of our getting together again more sooner than later.

I checked out the two editions of the *Daily* the messenger had dropped off.

Next, my e-mail and the answering machine, in that order, as always.

After all, what would a creature of habit be without order?

Somebody else, of course.

E-mail was the usual combination of spam and more spam, including offers less provocative than anything I'd found to be so with my Okay woman.

I caught myself playing with the old Merle Haggard hit, "Okie from Muskogee," "Okay from Muskogee" in my fabricated lyrics, as I moved through the usual fifty-fifty combination of compliments and complaints I receive via the *Daily* address that tags my column, then on to messages from my section editors and management.

There's one every day from my nemesis, the boss lady upstairs in the executive suite, the Spider Woman herself, Veronica Langtry, who would have rid herself of me a long time ago, except that I'm one of her boss the publisher's favorite sons. Wonder of wonders, the Spider Woman was extending some of her rare Southern hospitality, praise for today's column, a rant against the violence stalking our school system.

In the column, I had challenged the conventional wisdom that blames everything on unhinged kiddie killers and their home environment.

I had moved a chunk of responsibility to their fellow students, who thoughtlessly create the monsters among them by treating them as nerdy nothings, misfits marching to the beat of a drummer out of sync with everybody else. And, as well, to a school curriculum that doesn't consider behavioral counseling as a reasonable part of the educational process, except after the fact, when the psychologists are dispatched to the campus to deal with student survivor trauma.

Today's piece, not the usual shallow you, said the Spider Woman in her e-mail. She went on to ask, *Have you started using a ghost writer, Gulliver?*

From Langtry that rated as praise, like two thumbs up, way up, from Ebert and Roeper.

A bigger surprise was among the two or three machine messages.

"Theodore Rosenstock again, Mr. Gulliver. About your Warhols, you remember? Sorry for calling you at this hour. I'm sometimes forgetting about the time difference between the two coasts. Anyway, I got my man who is on his way out there and he also will be calling you. About an appointment? To arrange about his viewing the suite and confirming these are true Warhols and the portraits suite. Also, I wanted you to know how the two hundred thousand dollars that my client was prepared to pay you before—? If that amount is unsatisfactory to you for any reason, you should not be worried. My client says more is not out of the question."

I played Rosenstock's message again while I tracked the business cards from Ari Landau and Zev Neumann.

Halfway through dialing their 800 number, I quit, unsure this was how I wanted to handle the situation.

I'd have to think about it.

I headed for the bedroom and the storage box under the bed where I stash my weapon of choice, a Beretta 92f that's come in handy on more than one occasion.

12

Clegg had been at the Circus Gallery a couple years ago to authenticate a group of Kathe Kollwitz woodcuts the owner, Tom Bakersfield, was anxious to buy for his private collection. The images were legitimate, he remembered, overpowering in their depiction of deprivation and death.

The more he thought about them, the more they started to mix in Clegg's mind with the horrors he had seen on display at Dachau, although the woodcuts related more to "The War to End All Wars," the First World War, predating by a decade or longer Hitler and his Nazi butchers.

Even earlier were examples from Kollwitz's Peasants' War series. He had never been able to entirely shake off his memory of *Whetting the Scythe* or *The Prisoners*.

Another Kollwitz series dealing with war had scarred his memory with images of the dead and the dying. Wives and children mourning the loss of fathers and husbands. A dead mother clutching her dead baby to her bosom. Another mother, naked and all ribs, empty breasts, her dead infant on her lap, hiding her eyes from hunger, moans of despair Clegg could hear now stalking her mouth.

In another woodcut Bakersfield was considering, *Death Seizes a Woman*, he had always imagined himself as the hand of death summoning an old woman with a gentle touch on her shoulder, even as Clegg could transform the old woman into anybody else he wanted without batting an eye or burdening his conscious.

That was him all right, Death's surrogate.

One of them.

How many altogether, he had no idea.

They weren't organized.

There was no union or fraternal society.

Just ordinary people, many like him, killers by design and circumstance, trying to make a living out of dying.

Clegg remembered the Kollwitz woodcuts better than he remembered the route to Bakersfield's atelier, a few miles south past Union Station on Alameda. He managed to get lost the same way he had last time, once he had navigated the Dodge rental past the Civic Center, down behind Little Tokyo to the disordered industrial area where streets seemed to stop and go and often quit in dead ends the *Thomas Guide* didn't entirely show.

The trick he fell for again came at East First, where Alameda led you astray, onto Central, if you weren't paying attention to the street signs.

Clegg was ready for it, but by the time he got to First the heavy rains that had been drowning the city since before he landed at LAX late last night had become the unrelenting storm promised in all the forecasts he'd checked.

That was his excuse, the damned storm, so thick it hid the sky and was pounding the asphalt hard enough to open new road ruts as round as oil drums, some deep enough to clobber the Dodge's axles as he bounced ahead half-blind, the windshield wipers close to useless.

He was amazed he ever found Miguelito Place, a runt of a block between Miguel Road and Miguel Drive, full of empty lots overgrown with weeds and abandoned bags of refuse, and the Circus Gallery sitting like a two-story brick-and-mortar monument to the illegal dump sites in what had once been a building-supply warehouse.

The security gate rolled back to let him enter after he identified himself into the voice box and, by the time Clegg covered the twenty or so yards to the building, a steel wall gate had climbed up, letting him continue straight inside to a set of white-striped parking spaces.

It closed behind him as he gave the wipers a chance to clear the windows before pulling into a spot between a late-model cocoa-brown Mercedes and a newer Rolls-Royce.

The years had obviously been good to Tom Bakersfield.

Across the way, the safety door dividing two expanses of intermingled open storage bins and horizontal cabinets opened with a resonant click. Bakersfield took a step out and waved a greeting, then signaled for Clegg to join him.

Clegg retrieved his portfolio satchel from the trunk and crossed over.

Bakersfield embraced him like a long-lost brother and steered him past the door, all the while assuring Clegg how fantastic it was to have him visit.

"Fantastic" was Bakersfield's catchword, where last time it had been "neat-o" this and "neat-o" that. Everything was "fantastic," except the stinking weather, Bakersfield allowed; so bad, in fact, he had phoned his staff first thing this morning and told them not to bother coming in.

"But, you, fantastic you should pick this day of days to ring me up, and I absolutely could not let something like the lousy rain keep me from having you over long as you were brave enough," he said.

Clegg allowed, "Duck soup compared to what's going on in the Midwest and back East."

"I swear, it's because of the stuff we keep sending up into outer space," Bakersfield said. "We change things up there, it changes things down here. That or it's the Martians or moon-people's way of warning us to quit turning their turf into Greyhound bus depots."

He shot a finger at the ceiling and gave Clegg a smug, all-knowing nod.

"Watch the skies," Bakersfield said, his tenor taking on a stentorian overtone, like little green men could land here any minute to make certain Planet Earth understood they meant business.

He was of average height and build, in his mid-to late forties, with an oversized face he'd designed to be noticed: a greased ruby-red mustache that extended an inch or so past his sunken cheeks and matching frizzball hair that reminded Clegg of one of the Three Stooges.

Bakersfield had on a rumpled jumpsuit, sleeves torn off and revealing muscles built up and hardened over decades of pulling prints; stained with a full palette of colored inks that might be the envy of a circus clown.

Matching fur-lined leather bedroom slippers.

Status symbols kept to a minimum by what Clegg regarded as Hollywood standards: Gucci neck chain to match a Gucci gold bracelet watch. Gold pinky ring encrusted with diamonds, resembling a Tiffany design by Elsa Peretti. Gold ringlet of uncertain pedigree dangling from his left lobe.

"Walk this way," Bakersfield said. He waddled through the door in exaggerated fashion—the old joke—somehow not as funny as it might be if he weren't pigeon-toed and Clegg didn't have the sense Bakersfield might tip over onto his face with any next step.

The other side of the downstairs area was as open as a loft in Soho and mainly given over to the editions produced at Circus. The largest area presented on portable walls the most recent works, mural-size silkscreens by someone named Spencer Berland that borrowed from both Roy Lichtenstein and Jackson Pollock, combining panels reproduced from superhero comic books with primary colors that seemed blasted onto the surface of the prints with a shotgun.

Auxiliary sections showed examples of earlier editions turned out here, including a lot of West Coast names Clegg recognized; some who'd gone on to national and international reputations; others, lost in the backwater of the business.

At the rear was an inviting sitting area, white leather sofas and chairs, where customers could unhurriedly consider their purchases over complimentary finger snacks, coffee, tea and desserts from the nearby kitchenette, along with any high-end wines or the harder stuff on the portable bar.

"Coffee or maybe something tougher?" Bakersfield said, pointing to the bar.

"Thank you, no. Never when I'm working."

Bakersfield moved past the area, aiming for the metal door marked PRIVATE. It boasted a series of locks and a code pad, but glided open to his push.

They passed into his office and Bakersfield shut the door and threw down a gate bar.

"Can't be too careful lately. Neighborhood's turned to shit. Shit turned to manure, and more shit has been growing ever since, but I have too much invested here. Counting on the eventual real-estate market turnaround that'll let me get out from under and move on to a decent address someplace west. Probably the beach. Santa Monica."

"You look like you've been doing good," Clegg said, dropping into a guest chair as Bakersfield headed for the executive chair behind his eccentrically shaped glass-top desk, settled down and leaned back with his hands locked behind his head.

"Not bad at all here with the atelier, including the secondary market that keeps growing around graphics, but I made my real killing on dot-coms. Got in early and got out before the collapse."

"But more stock certificates up on your walls, and far prettier," Clegg said, a throwaway gesture taking in all the prints on display from Bakersfield's personal collection.

He recognized most of the Kollwitz images from the last visit, including those he'd recommended most strongly, along with other early Germans favored by Bakersfield: Grosz. Dix. Beckmann.

Noticing an early Kollwitz he didn't remember, he rose and went over to it for a closer look. It was a final state of *You Bleed*, from Many Wounds, O People, and signed by the celebrated printer Felsing as well as the artist.

Clegg returned to his chair.

They discussed the print for a few minutes, some of the others, before Bakersfield adjusted his position—leaning up against the table, shoulders hunched, one hand on top of the other—smiled like a bank loan officer, and said, "So, tell me exactly what brought you here. When you called, you said something about Hank Godard."

Bakersfield didn't look happy about the subject.

"Henri Godard, yes," Clegg said. "Let me show you."

He asked Bakersfield to clear space on the desk, while he reached over for the portfolio satchel. He moved it onto the desk, unzipped it, pulled out and put on exhibit a print by Jay Lowy—one of Jay Lowy's infamous sachets—twenty-four inches high by nineteen inches across.

It had been sent FedEx and was waiting for him at the hotel when he arrived last night.

Clegg let Tom Bakersfield take a good, long look before explaining: "An important and well-respected client of ours recently bought it from Godard, paying quite a handsome sum, but still a bargain for a Lowy. He acted on impulse, without coming to us first, as he usually does. Godard had told him he printed it while in your employ. Your chop is there, and so is Godard's, but something about it—it didn't feel right to me. So, our client said, 'Get yourself to L.A. on the first plane out and check it out.' "

Bakersfield settled back in his chair again, shook his head, and said, "I could have saved you the trip if you made the call first, my friend."

"How's that?" Clegg said, although he already knew the answer.

Bakersfield's look of displeasure turned angrier and he began to fiddle with his mustache, first one curled end and then the other. He clenched his teeth so hard Clegg wouldn't have been surprised if Bakersfield's jawbone came crashing through his cheeks.

"First off, the son of a bitch was fired before we were halfway done with the edition," Bakersfield said. "I canned his ass when I caught him ripping us off. He was hanging in here after-hours, running bootlegs for himself, the kind of shit Godard was notorious for a long time before he sneaked onto my payroll. And, if that doesn't do it for you, let me remind you of something . . . The only chop mark that's embossed on a print from here is the Circus Atelier chop. The Godard Arch of Triumph chop gives it away as a copycat."

Clegg slapped his forehead with his palm.

"That's what I was forgetting to remember. Of course. His chop. It didn't belong there . . ."

He let Bakersfield observe his anger, hoping he wasn't overdoing it, before he asked, "Maybe you can tell me where he's gone to? You have some sort of record, maybe you heard it from somebody else he cheated. I'd like to confront the damned crook and get back the money he literally stole from our client."

Bakersfield made a remorseful face.

"I did, I'd have had the son of a bitch already behind bars for grand theft. This isn't the first time someone has come to me with a story like yours, damn it."

Clegg masked his disappointment. He'd been hoping Bakersfield might be able to provide a live connection to Godard, unlike earlier leads that quickly burned out like bad book matches.

Bakersfield's expression changed again to one that was more uplifting.

"One of those coincidences, but you're not the only one who's come asking about Godard lately."

"Don't tell me another Jay Lowy."

"A Warhol suite. Nothing he did here, but these people had fallen into it and were wondering about its value. Knew Godard's name, knew he'd worked here, and wondered if I had a current bead on him."

Clegg said, "I don't suppose you remember the names or kept a phone number."

"The names, sure. Hard to forget. He's a newspaper guy, writes a daily column, a few times even some stuff about me, and she's a hot actress. In fact, I did write down a number, maybe also an address. Give me a minute . . ."

Bakersfield began shuffling the papers on his desk.

Clegg had hoped for something better.

Someone new, names that might become the missing link to Godard.

He didn't let it show.

Tom Bakersfield didn't have to know Clegg already had Neil Gulliver and Stephanie Marriner on his list.

Clegg saw the rain had stopped, as the wall gate lifted and he drove out from the warehouse. Brooding clouds as fat as dairy cows had moved in from somewhere and filled the sky with dark warnings of more rains to come.

Turning onto Miguelito Place, two lots away from Circus Gallery, he noticed a homeless man about forty yards in from the street, trying to reconstruct his cardboard-box shelter in the tall weeds.

The sight saddened Clegg.

Nobody was meant to live like that.

Ever.

He had had his fill of it growing up, never as bad, he knew now, but at the time, as a kid, it felt worse, and the pain he suffered had never left him.

Clegg pulled over and parked and locked the Dodge.

Headed for the homeless man.

The stench of layered filth and cheap booze reaching him before he reached the man. There were some things that not even a harsh rain could wash away.

The homeless man turned at the sound of Clegg's shoes mashing muddied dirt and refuse in the slime of the lot.

Alarm swept across the man's torn face.

His puff-red eyes seemed afraid by habit.

"I didn't fucking do nothing," he said, his voice as ragged as his clothing. "Just trying to live and let live. Can't you cops ever appreciate that?"

"Not a cop," Clegg said, and he gave the man a smile he hoped was signaling friendship.

He was reaching for his billfold, planning to give the man one or two twenties—his to do with as he pleased—when he felt the sledge-hammers of hell come crashing against the back of his head.

Clegg had the impression he was falling forward into a swamp deeper than the mud hole he glimpsed before a blackness richer than oil consumed him, and—

Then—

Nothing.

13

Two days after his call, Theodore Rosenstock called me again, sounding like a favorite uncle, his voice filled with an infomercial pitchman's enthusiasm to mask the explanation he was sharing with me.

"There's been a sorry delay getting my person there to see you," he said. "The weather we got here. Atrocious. Also horrible. Planes not getting off the ground. I hear it's not been so good there, either. Pouring cats and dogs?"

"Not enough to float Noah's Ark down the L.A. River, but the inches are adding up," I said, with enough amiability to give Rosenstock a sense I had become more open to selling the Warhols.

What had raised my interest beyond curiosity about the authenticity of the suite and its value, of course, was the possibility of breaking a news story that had *front page* written all over it.

The Henri Godard connection made it a good story that could get better yet if I were able to locate the chiseler and pin him down to the truth.

What made it a great story was its historical ties to Nazi Germany and those Jewish families whose art treasures were stolen off the walls of their homes, disappeared into the secret museums of greedy collectors, and now appeared—some of them—to be represented in the Warhol silkscreens.

To be able to verify what Stevie and I'd heard from Ari Landau and Zev Neumann, put names to faces in the portraits, help root out their hidden caches, identify the collector in the missing twelfth print, who was possibly the mastermind holding together this lousy art-world underground—

Now, that was a story.

International in scope.

Historically significant.

Morally righteous.

And—

The more I thought about it, the less I began to care about the story.

I began to care more about the role I might play in helping to retrieve the stolen artworks for their rightful owners—

Maybe, help widen the trail to other art treasures not seen for sixty or more years.

Somehow, that goal seemed to lessen the possibility of personal danger for me, although I wasn't about to put away my Beretta, and I knew Stevie had the advantage of building security to go with the .32 she'd started carrying again.

There's nothing like an extra measure of security in a city where pedestrians and innocent bystanders are always as vulnerable as shooting-gallery ducks—which could be any city in the country.

Rosenstock said, "So, my man will call you and you will arrange something about your meeting and him inspecting the Warhol suite."

"The portraits."

"Yes, good, very good, excellent. And you remember we can talk about the money after."

"I remember."

"Nothing my man has to know."

"I understand."

"You have a good idea how much you really want yet?"

"No."

"I don't blame you, either," Rosenstock said, a brass band of enthusiasm as he repeated earlier assurances about the money before hanging up with a final caution, telling me to be sure and get a flu shot. "Lousy weather, a simple cold turns into pneumonia just like so," he said. "I got friends who'd swear to it, only the pneumonia went and killed them, so you should take my word for it."

"Absolutely," I said, taking nothing from him or this conversation but the same lurking sense of suspicion I had before.

Ari Landau also called, responding to the message I left on his 800 number. I'd told him I wanted to write about art treasures stolen from the Jews of Europe and wondered if he could put me together with one or two of the victims.

"The best I've been able to get for you on short notice is down San Diego," he said. "That do?"

"Do fine," I said, and logged into my computer the name and number Ari diligently recited into the phone. He spelled out the last name and made me read it back, to be certain I had it right.

"It's hard to go wrong with Kline," I said.

"Sure, it is," Ari said. "There's Klein"—he spelled it—"which is closer to the truth. There's also Clein and there's Cline"—spelling it both ways—"and I even know a few Clynes"—spelling it—"up in Winnipeg, Canada. I even know Klines you would never want to know . . . You need anything else, you know how to reach me."

It was a day before Maurice Kline and I connected.

He was expecting the call and we arranged to meet, at his suggestion on Sunday in Balboa Park outside the Globe Theatre, where he was appearing in a musical version of *The Catcher in the Rye*.

"You'd like, I can leave tickets at the box office for you, for the matinee. Evening's sold out." I thanked him and accepted the offer. "One or two—you're bringing somebody?"

"A pair would be fine," I said, on spec.

Maryam and I had been spending a lot of time together since she sleepwalked into my life, and that night I asked if she would like to make it a weekend with me, explaining it was for a column.

She rolled onto her side and, stroking my chest, said, "I wouldn't be in your way?"

I reassured her.

"I would have said yes anyway," she said, and bit my ear, then drove her tongue into it.

I held off letting Stevie know until shortly before we left for San Diego on Saturday morning.

"Interviewing some guy for the column," I said.

I left it at that.

If Stevie knew the rest, no doubt she'd have insisted on coming along.

Demanded it.

"Drive carefully," Stevie said, adding to the guilt by omission I already felt.

I carried the guilt with me on the two-and-a-half-hour drive down, but also an air of expectation and exhilaration, not entirely believing I had finally met—was with—someone who could spring me from my yoke of obsession.

For years I had endured Stevie's dating others. She had urged me to follow suit, but it never made as much sense to me as following her.

Until now.

Until Maryam Zokaei.

This was my Jag's first real open road test since I'd retrieved it from the shop, and it glided south down the 5 as smoothly as Maryam's frequent caresses on my cheek. The traffic was unusually light, so I was able to keep a steady 65 mph beat most of the way, once in a while cranking it up to 80.

We had left a drip-dry sky back in Los Angeles, but the sun was breaking through the cloudbanks by the time we hit Camp Pendleton and pretending it belonged to summer by the time we got to the exit that wrapped us into the Hillcrest area of San Diego, about ten minutes away from Balboa Park.

We one-stopped at a neighborhood 7-Eleven, stockpiling enough frozen and junk foods to last us the weekend before I followed directions I'd pulled from the Internet to the rustic, out-of-the-way motel where I had reserved a room with a kitchen.

I registered and, ten minutes later, Maryam and I were under the covers gorging on our favorite snacks, each other. The TV was turned on, but so were we, and we spent the rest of the day watching ourselves make love.

Sometime during the night, over the humming dialogue of an HBO movie, Maryam shook me awake—

Surprised me by saying, "I think I'm in love with you, Neil."

Sitting on the edge of the bed, she looked angelic in the flickering light. The expression on her face was sheer heaven, but—

I felt momentary panic.

I wasn't sure how to respond.

Finally I settled on, "Maybe you shouldn't be saying that. Deciding that. So fast. So soon. So—"

She put a fingertip to my lips to quiet me.

She said, "You can't run away from your emotions, Neil. I tried that once and they just followed me. I know now I should have run faster, but—not this time . . ."

She pulled her finger away and said, "Tell me how you feel."

I rolled out of bed and crossed the room to the window, parted the curtain, and looked up at the three-quarter moon like it might hold the answer.

I heard the bed creak as she lifted off and strolled across to join me. She gently massaged the back of my neck, and then clamped her hand onto my shoulder.

"Tell me how you feel, Neil," she said again. "I don't even care if you lie."

"I wouldn't do that. I—"

"I wouldn't care, really. I'd just like to know that there's maybe something there, between us, that's for real, not what I had to put up with from my"—close to choking on the word—"husband."

"More than maybe," I said, after another moment.

Meaning it.

I didn't have to see Maryam's smile to feel it.

She said, "Let me know when 'more than maybe' is more than Stevie, will you?"

Before I could answer, she'd kissed me on the shoulder and retreated back to the bed.

I spent a few minutes wondering if the moon could see my concerns, my confusion, then joined her there.

She was already asleep, half out of the covers.

I crawled in beside her, pulled up the covers, tucked them under her chin.

Studied her face.

Listened to the steady rhythm of her breathing.

Smelled the natural perfume of her body.

"I think I do," I said, before clicking off the TV, at once glad she wasn't awake to hear me, half wishing I hadn't heard myself say it, although it wasn't a lie.

Only doubt.

Sometimes a worse enemy than a lie—

When doubt is a partner to the truth.

The following morning we made love, then climbed into the shower after a breakfast of packaged chocolate, sugar and crumbcake doughnuts and room-brewed coffee. I'd sensed something was on Maryam's mind, distracting her, and now risked asking.

She said, "Just me wondering—was I talking in my sleep last night?"

"What?"

"Ever since I woke up, I've been thinking you and I had this absolutely unreal conversation last night, where I went and asked you if you thought—Oh, never mind . . ."

Our conversation.

Had it taken place during one of Maryam's attacks of parasomnia? I quickly decided not to ask.

Maryam looked up, brushed suds off my chin, and kissed me there. She hugged me tightly against her wet body, with one side of her face pressed hard against my chest, and turned the letter *m* into a word.

"You are my Mr. Wonderful, Mr. Wonderful," she said with impish grandeur.

I shook my head modestly and said, "I don't know what makes you say that."

Maryam flicked my nipple with her tongue and said, "I think you do."

We got to Balboa Park early and found parking off El Prado Way, within strolling distance of the Globe Theatre. The weather was as friendly as yesterday, although the sun was only a warm rumor behind a panoply of motionless gray clouds, as Maryam and I set off for the art museums.

The San Diego Museum of Art has something for everyone, like those old Sears and Montgomery Ward catalogs—American and European paintings and sculpture, a trove of California artists, a similar treasure in Indian paintings—but we hit it like a respectful Texas tornado, to get it out of the way before rushing over to the Timken and its exquisite blend of works spanning five centuries, from early Renaissance to the nineteenth century.

Maryam had expressed her passion for art on the drive down yesterday, but her wealth of knowledge as we wandered what's correctly called San Diego's "Jewel Box for the Arts" came as a surprise. I thought I'd learned a little about art over the years, but it was nowhere near the depth Maryam showed.

She used the little explanatory cards posted by each of the paintings as her launch pad, contributing facts, figures and historical asides like a docent on speed, whether it was a master such as Veronese, Breugel, Rembrandt, David or one more recent, like Copley.

Finally unable to contain myself, I asked her about it.

She tweaked my nose and gave me a non-answer.

"I like what you like, big fella," she said. "Shouldn't that be enough?"

No, but I could see in Maryam's face that it would have to do for now, as she took me by the elbow and maneuvered me to another wall, commenting, "That Claude, it's new to me."

The Globe Theatre, like the Timken Museum, was a jewel box, in the tradition of Shakespeare's own playground.

No one was a peasant or commoner here, however. There were plush seats for everyone, about six hundred of them in a stadium semi-circle running down from ground level to the proscenium, every one of them occupied by patrons who filled the air with the typical, unintelligible babble of audiences anxious for a payoff to their investment of time and tickets in the show.

The pair of tickets Maurice Kline had left put Maryam and me into seats off the aisle of the sixth row, center section. We settled into them and in unspoken syncopation buried ourselves in the program.

The eight-page booklet that described *Pencey Prep*—the title they'd given this musical version of *The Catcher in the Rye*—called it "a work-in-progress."

There was a slip-sheet insert that made reference to songs no longer in the show or repositioned, songs added, scenes added and subtracted, actors added to the cast in parts that the booklet still attributed to others.

Maurice Kline was barely affected.

He was sixth-billed, playing "Mr. Antolini," described as Holden Caufield's teacher at Elkton Hills, and two other roles. He had one solo number, "Teaching Isn't Everything, (My Boy, My Boy)," and a duet on a song titled "It's Never Too Soon to Fart."

The date on the slip-sheet suggested all the changes had come about since last night's performance, making me fear the curtain would soon be rising on "a disaster-in-progress."

I wasn't far off the mark.

It didn't take "It's Never Too Soon to Fart" to inform me early in the show that the smell emanating from the stage was from well-meaning people tampering with genius.

After the performance, I outraced a couple arguing the merits of *Pencey Prep* for a bench in the forecourt that gave us a view of the stage door. Maurice Kline walked out a half hour later, stationed himself by the door, and looked around anxiously.

He was out of costume, wearing street clothes, an open-collared, short-sleeved shirt outside a pair of blue denims, sandals, no socks, a leather pouch dangling from a shoulder, but I could tell it was him by his small stature, potbelly, and random clusters of snow-white hair that from where I had sat in the Globe looked like a fright wig.

He saw me waving and hurried over, weaving through the crowd with the same dancer's grace he'd exhibited onstage. Gave me an energetic handshake, then Maryam after I introduced them. Apologized for taking so long to join us.

This close, underneath his stage makeup, Kline looked to be in his late sixties or early seventies, older than any of the characters he had played.

"Notes," he said. "Anybody from this afternoon who goes tonight won't know it's the same show." He shrugged, showed his palms to clouds oppressively darker than they'd been two and a half hours ago. "That might not be so bad. What do you think?"

I fished my mind for a polite way to say nothing.

"It was quite a show," I said.

Kline wasn't fooled.

"A stinker is right," he said; then, to Maryam, "You can always tell it by how much coughing goes on in the audience. There was enough of it today you would have thought we had a whooping-cough epidemic in the making."

Maryam said, "You, however, were wonderful, Mr. Kline."

Kline turned to me and said, "I don't know who she is to you, this beautiful woman, but she's got wonderful taste. You should never let go of her." He sat down in the middle of the bench and beckoned us to join him.

"At my age, you take what you can get, whatever parts come along," Kline said. "Even a debacle like this, already it beats talking and singing the words that come at me all the time in the mail from the HMOs and the cemeteries, but I'm not sick and when I die it's going to be on some stage, in the middle of some business, maybe hearing people laughing and applauding, the same way that wonderful Dick Shawn got to go."

He knew he had a respectful audience that wasn't going anywhere, and he played to the two of us like he was center stage at halftime in the Pro Bowl, his voice layering poetry and clarity on every word, like Sinatra treated his lyrics.

"I started in the business back East, New York, in the Yiddish theater," he said. "A young man, but I could play at being any age. Anybody. The ones who were old enough to know said I was another Adler; some of them, another Muni, even. I took that praise as my calling card to Broadway.

"Broadway listened, but not as loud as I ever wanted. I never got the big break, but I worked, I did okay, well, but my pop needed better weather for his health and all Pop ever had was me, so finally I brought us out West, somehow ending up in San Diego, where life is more than the zoo and sailors on shore leave.

"It's got the Globe and the Globe does a dozen or more productions every year, so I work enough, between the Globe and some radio and television commercials I manage to pick up. I manage to keep my instrument tuned. But, Neil, you put any of this in the newspaper column you're writing, I would not be upset in the least if you mention how Fyvush Finkel is not the only one around who can do great by a role in a television series." Kline rolled his eyes and turned them to the clouds. "My lips to your newspaper column to . . . So, Neil, where do you want me to begin? This business about the art."

Germany proved harder for Kline to talk about than New York and his career, after a while almost impossible. He had begun easily enough, with a certain swagger to his voice and manner as he described early memories in Munich, a residence that to a little child was castle-grand, immense in size and filled with art.

"I remember being a happy child, well loved and looked after," he said. "I remember long corridors, the walls full of paintings large and small, my nanny always cautioning me to stop running, lest I trip and accidentally push over one of the statues or splendid busts sitting on their pedestals.

"I remember the men in black uniforms, the first time they arrived at our door and demanded to come in, snarling at us like all of us were beasts in need of a good tanning.

"I remember how the next time they came they took away all the paintings and all the sculptures and all the busts, and all I had to see after that were narrow rims of clotted dust and the bright wallpaper that had been hidden for years by the fine paintings.

"I remember soon after, hearing my father tell my mother we had to leave our home. It would not be until years later that I came to understand exactly what that meant. By then I had survived the camps and was on a boat with what was left of my pop. Heading to America and crying out at night for my mama, my three sisters and my two brothers, who were not so lucky as me and Pop to have lived through the horrors.

"Did I say lucky? Maybe they were truly the lucky ones, Neil. To this day, every day and every night, I feel pains from what I can't remember at all. Pains that are supposed to go away from the memory? For me, the reverse. Remember?" Kline gave his shrug and palms-up gesture. "My memory's a blank screen. The pains? You cannot hear me screaming now, but—believe me—I am screaming now . . . It goes on every day and every night inside of me."

Kline gripped his hands and leaned forward, dropped his arms between his legs, almost to the concrete, and examined a glob of chewing gum cemented to the ground. After three or four minutes, he sat erect again and faked a smile.

"I don't ever talk about this," Kline said, his voice cracking, "but Landau said it could be important to getting back, finally, maybe, some of the art plundered by the Nazi shits. Is that possible?"

"People read my column. Maybe something I describe will mean something to someone and they'll get in touch with the newspaper."

"Sure. It's better than nothing, although it's a story that's been told before, in the years since a lot of us got together and started searching to get back what's rightfully ours, in my case works from the famous collection of Dr. and Mrs. Josef Kleinschmick."

He sucked in air and let it out slowly, started to say something more, but froze after his gaze moved from me over to Maryam.

She said, "Would you be more comfortable if I left the two of you alone for a while?"

Kline shook his head.

He said, "Only that for a second I thought I was seeing my mama."

Maryam's eyes started to cloud.

She rose and said, "I think I'll go check out the gift shop anyway."

Fled across the theater courtyard.

We watched her disappear into the gift shop, then Kline turned to me and with a tilt of his nodding head, a nudge of his elbow, advised me like a village wise man, "She's got a heart, that one. What else you do, you definitely shouldn't let her get away from you."

Kline dug into his leather pouch and extracted an eyeglass case and a thick manila envelope. He held it up for me to see and settled it on his lap. Adjusted the eyeglasses on his face and said, patting the envelope, "Inside is what's left of the Kleinschmick family fortune, so to speak.

"We finally got to some cousins in New York, my pop and me, whatever riches we had in Germany were gone—*kaput!*—and we were the poor relations living off charity, and don't you think we weren't always being reminded of that.

"My pop, a fine doctor, a surgeon, Pop was never going to work again. I never went past eighth grade, but by then I had found the Yiddish theater. I got started there pushing a mop and soon I was learning how to act and dance and sing from the best. You happen to remember the actor David Opatoshu?"

I said, "*The Naked City, The Brothers Karamazov, Torn Curtain, Exodus, Enter Laughing, Silk Stockings*," and named some other movies.

Kline was impressed. "A regular walking encyclopedia you are, Neil. Opatoshu was from the tradition. David was my mentor before he changed his name and went to Hollywood."

"Changed his name?"

"Yeah, back then he was David Opatoshevsky, before he figured out it wouldn't look good, was too big to put on a theater marquee." Kline saw my doubt and reassured me. "How later, for Broadway, I became Kline, and not a Kleinschmick anymore . . . But David's not what today is about." He tapped on the envelope and began playing with the clasp.

"It happens a few years ago, Ari Landau visits me here. I'm starring in *Fiddler* at the time. Wonderful reviews I can show you another time. Ari makes sure first we're the family he's been looking for, then he shows me some old photographs I remember, but haven't seen since I was a boy. Ari explains how a lot of other families that lost their art collections during the war had got together and were scouring the world to find them and get them returned. He asked, Did Pop and me want to join them? Tell me, did King Solomon know what to do with seven hundred wives and three hundred concubines?"

He handed over the manila envelope.

"Look. See what we're talking about."

The envelope contained four photographs, eight-by-tens browned and cracked by age. Crisp images that may have been taken for insurance purposes. Different views of rooms in what Kline identified as the Kleinschmick family home, but just as easily could have been a museum.

The walls were full of masterworks as fine, finer, than what Maryam and I had seen earlier on display at the Timken: Rembrandt, van Eyck, Vermeer, Goya, Degas, van Gogh, Braque, Cézanne, Monet, Matisse, Picasso, Morisot, Bonnard.

Kline said, "Ari's people located these in files taken from the Nazi archives that were buried behind the Wall even for years after the Wall came down. That one?" He showed me the one he meant. "Hitler himself kept that one. Those two? Goering kept those for himself almost up until the very end. All three, like the others you're seeing? Right up to today, no sight of any of them."

Kline read the excitement on my face.

"You see something, Neil?"

I pointed. "This painting. This one here."

"Yeah, so?"

"I think it's a painting I've seen."

"You know where to find it?"

"Not exactly," I said, and told Kline about the Warhol suite, one silk screen in particular.

Stevie's weekend had not gone entirely as planned.

Saturday was fine.

A lot of lounging around.

A few hours watching tapes from the Television Academy, sent earlier in the year to members by the networks and others promoting nominations, programs she'd missed and still had interest in checking out. *The West Wing. The Practice. Will and Grace. Ally McBeal,* and an opportunity to confirm that Robert Downey Jr. more than deserved his Emmy.

A catch-up conversation with her mother, Juliet, who was somewhere between Alaska and San Pedro, the return leg of a cruise with her latest boyfriend, described by Juliet, as she was prone to doing, as "someone you're really gonna like, honey, if it ever gets that far."

Later, the Lakers.

Ugh!

Shaq and Kobe still stalking each other in print more than they were attacking the competition on the floor of the Staples Center. No repeat championship this year. Not the way things were going so far.

Except for his calling about San Diego, she might have invited Neil to come on over and join her, ordered in some pizza, and made a night of it. There were times like these, she didn't know why, that she missed him. Maybe to do with Juliet and her new boyfriends, a reminder of how the two of them were alike, her and Mama, both of them too-too good at picking rotten apples in the bunch, and—

Maybe, for all the faults that led up to their divorce, and there were trillions, Neil was still the best man she'd ever scored.

Late morning Sunday, Stevie began primping for another lunch with Anthony B. Anthony.

Stevie thought she'd successfully blown him off—in the figurative sense, of course—at Le Dome. However, the director had persistently pursued her ever since, calling up and leaving messages with her service ten and fifteen times a day, sending her lavish bouquets of flowers— usually roses that set her hay fever spiraling, which she wound up giving to one of the service crews—and ultra-extravagant boxes of candies and caviar.

Finally, an exquisite Cartier Panthère watch in gold that must have set him back at least as much as *People* magazine had once speculated Anthony B. Anthony spent weekly on what the writer euphemistically described as "the kind of recreational snow one doesn't find on the lusty down slopes near his Aspen hideaway."

The accompanying note, in penmanship too elegant to be his, more likely his secretary or a sales clerk, said, *It is time for you to give me the time of day and watch how I make my big hand give a little hand to your fabulous career.*

Too, too cute for words, his note, escalation in his pursuit of her in keeping with Anthony B. Anthony's infamous *Take no prisoners* approach to business.

Stevie called his office.

He leaped onto the phone and slathered appreciation on her like a starving cat attacking the feed trough, the cat in this case the King of Beasts. He suggested the Ivy, lunch, and how did Sunday at one sit with her?

Stevie made it sound like she had to check her calendar before agreeing.

"Inside, just tell them you're meeting me," Anthony B. Anthony said. "I think you're going to be fucking surprised by what I got to lay on you, Ms. Superstar."

"I can hardly fucking wait," Stevie answered, giving no indication she had her own little surprise in store for him.

She intended to return the Cartier Panthère, thank Tony B. Tony for his interest in her, and tell him to please bug off.

Yes, it could have been done on the phone, or she could have had her agent make the call, but she wanted to do it in person. She knew the type all too well. He was one of those Y chromosomes who'd never get the message without seeing and feeling the weight behind the words. If he ever had to pull into a gas station and ask for directions, he would never be found.

Stevie worked out in the condo gym, the treadmill and just enough weights to help her keep her muscle tone without inching over the line toward the world of the beefy-biceps broads. A lingering sauna took care of her sweat, opened her pores, and began the skin-care process she dutifully finished back upstairs in the apartment.

Not too much makeup today, just enough to look good for any paparazzi who'd be lurking outside the Ivy. Nothing special with her hair, which she'd bundled snugly under a rainproof bucket hat. Under her Burberry raincoat, a Dolce & Gabbana outfit that would leap onto the rolls of color film, a red silk shantung blouse and tropical-print pants. Donna Karan aviator sunglasses that picked up the blue in the pants. A comfortable pair of cotton canvas sneakers. A simple gold bracelet and matching earrings, and as a preview of what was coming—

Her gold–and–stainless steel Raymond Weil "Parsifal" wristwatch with the mother-of-pearl dial and diamonds.

There'd be a point where Anthony B. Anthony's curiosity got the best of him. He'd have to inquire about the Cartier Panthère, opening the way for her to pull it out of her bag and gently, persuasively, close the door on him, letting him know dead cert her life was out of room for any more Anthony B. Anthonys.

Definitely, she told herself. *Whatever you think you're going to lay, Tony B. Tony, it still won't be me.*

This time, Anthony B. Anthony was the first one to arrive.

He was sitting at the center table in the back of the small room.

Back to the wall, with a twenty-twenty view of everyone entering and leaving, as well as outside on the rain-drenched empty patio.

Sunday had filled the tables with show-business VIPs and celebrities. Heads turned to watch Stevie and see who she was meeting. She answered several silent greetings in kind as she moved inside, caught a smattering of gossipy sounds as Anthony B. Anthony rose to greet her and signaled her to come around the table and take the seat beside him.

They traded air kisses, and Stevie had to fight not to recoil from the stench of a sweet cologne that fit perfectly with his flawlessly tailored blue jeans and a polished silk body shirt open halfway down to his waist and giving display to a mass of faded scarlet-and bone-colored scar tissue that centered around his hairless chest. Same windbreaker and *Amos Behaving* baseball cap as before.

A vodka martini, three cherries on the toothpick, was in front of him, alongside a martini glass empty except for the toothpick.

An iced tea awaited Stevie in front of her place.

"I took the liberty," Anthony B. Anthony said, pointing at it. "Got here early myself. Chance to do some meeting and greeting, and who the hell knows who you ever bump into here on a Sunday? Some of the biggest fucking deals I know happen that way. Actually, I should have made it champagne seeing's how we got a lot to celebrate today. Look under your plate, darling."

"I win the door prize, Tony B. Tony?"

"Manner of fucking speaking, yes."

Stevie lifted the plate.

Under it was a set of papers folded in thirds inside a blue cover. It could have been a legal subpoena.

It wasn't.

She didn't have to read past the second paragraph to understand that Anthony B. Anthony DBA Tony Productions had acquired the film remake rights to *Nothing Sacred.*

Tony B. Tony couldn't be more pleased with himself as he searched her face for reaction.

"Bet you thought I was fucking off my balls when I said I saw you for the next Lombard. Forget Garbo for the now. We got us a bigger winner here, across-the-board appeal with a potential for a hundred-mil gate with you in the lead.

"Not an easy score, I want you to know that, so you can believe how I believe in you supersized. Ran up my lawyers' hours legit enough for him to stop padding the out-of-pocket invoices, and that was just on chopping through the rights thicket and getting down to the brass ring. The Goldwyn Estate. The Hecht Estate. You don't want to know."

Tony B. Tony waited for her to say something.

She would have, if she knew what to say.

He said, "Tony B. Tony promises. Tony B. Tony delivers. And, I also got another surprise for you, making it a Sunday one-two puncharoonie I'm going to spring—"

Something had caught his notice and he stopped talking.

He lifted her left hand by the wrist, and brought it closer to his face. He was checking out her wristwatch, her Raymond Weil "Parsifal," not the Cartier Panthère he had sent her as a gift.

His head went up and down like the pump on an oil rig, accompanied by sound effects and a look that dissolved into something less serious as he said, "That is one damn fucking fine timepiece, darling. Before we split, you got to tell me where you got it. First thing tomorrow, got to send over for one for the missus, one for myself if they got it in men's."

A cell phone chimed from somewhere.

It seemed to Stevie that half the people in the small room immediately began checking, including Tony B. Tony.

He pulled one cell the size of a sugar wafer from his shirt pocket and another mini from a pants pocket while she went digging into her bag for hers.

She found the cell in the clutter of her everyday as it gasped its last, but the message readout screen was showing somebody's initials and a 213 number she didn't recognize.

Stevie started to put the cell away, figuring the call was a misdial, until she realized the initials didn't belong to some*body*, but some*thing*: LAPD.

Why were the cops calling her?

Her instant answer brought panic to her breath.

Neil.

Something had happened to Neil.

An accident on the freeway coming back from San Diego.

This weather.

He was a lousy driver in the best of weather.

Stevie waved off the look of confusion and concern on Tony B. Tony's face, responding to what must be showing on hers, as she tapped the recall button.

She turned away from him and stared down at the table, rubbed her knee and thigh nervously, waiting for the call to connect.

A pickup into the fourth ring.

"Officer DeCarlo here."

A woman.

Stevie identified herself.

The lady cop recited Stevie's phone number.

"No. That's my home. I'm on the cell. Your call was automatically forwarded to my cell. This anything to do—about . . . Is it concerning my ex-husband? Neil Gulliver? His name is Neil Gulliver."

"We were hoping you'll be able to tell us that, ma'am," Officer DeCarlo said.

Fifteen minutes later, Stevie was barreling east across Wilshire in her BMW, heading for USC–County General. Tony B. Tony in the passenger seat, patiently explaining into his cell, "No, dream girl, I swear on my mother's father. It's a genuine emergency this time, a hospital thingaroo, or I wouldn't be fucking standing you up this way."

He'd insisted on going along.

Outside, while one of the red-jacketed valet-parking guys was getting her car, he'd slipped Donnie the valet captain two twenties and given him a number to call, instructing Donnie, "You tell my shlep to drag his sorry Sunday ass over here and pick up my Rolls, I said so, okay? I take good care of you, you take good care of me."

The entrance to the indigent ward at USC–County General was a right off the main elevator bank and down a long corridor, policed at the nurses' station immediately inside the double swinging doors by two thick-bodied nurses who looked at them like they might be armed and dangerous as Stevie hurried in, Tony B. Tony two steps behind her.

Before she could identify herself, a voice called her by name.

Stevie did a half turn and looked over her shoulder.

A lady cop was rising from one of the half dozen wicker chairs lined up along the painted ruins of a back wall, the single decorative item a large real-estate company calendar with this month's illustration, a photo of dazzling sunlight exploding through the redwood giants of Yosemite National Park.

"Officer DeCarlo," the lady cop said.

She stepped forward and extended a hand.

"I truly appreciate you giving up this time on a Sunday to come down and maybe help us out, Miss Marriner," Officer DeCarlo said, giving Tony B. Tony a once-over.

Stevie saw Tony B. Tony was doing his own survey, more than likely for less professional reasons than the lady cop, and no wonder.

The lady cop was an attractive, physically fit package inside her uniform. Early forties, Stevie guessed, with dark hair framing a tanned oval face highlighted by her searching creamy-green eyes and a full, resolute mouth; laugh lines at the corners of her eyes to go with the apostrophes formed on both sides of her lips. Ruby-red polish on her manicure that matched her lipstick. A subtle perfume Stevie wouldn't have expected a lady cop to choose over one that was more macho.

Stevie introduced him and released the lady cop's hand, whereupon Tony B. Tony grabbed for it and engulfed it in his palms, pumped it vigorously, and said, "Pleasure's mine. You probably seen some of my movies? Like my dick flick with Bob Redford, I bet. *Layton's Paradise.* Bobby doing Layton. From the book by that big writer I didn't use on the screenplay. Big, big box office, even without counting in the grosses from overseas. Don't be surprised to read soon about my sequel in the works, soon's Bobby decides if he'll commit. If he won't I already got Brucie W on tap for reading the treatment."

Sounding to Stevie like a caricature of a caricature, the mold for the cliché.

Officer DeCarlo looked at Tony B. Tony like he'd been speaking a foreign language and said, "Pleased to meet you, sir." Her voice continued to be pleasant and straightforward.

She turned back to Stevie, who said, "Is it my ex, Mr. Gulliver, Neil Gulliver, who's here, and what are we doing in this kind of ward? Can I please see him, Officer DeCarlo?" Trying to rein in her emotions against possible answers she did not want to hear.

"Like I told you on the phone, we need you to tell us, Miss Marriner."

Neil . . . Was he so badly disfigured that—?

She couldn't bring herself to ask the question.

"Some car crasheroo or what?" Tony B. Tony said. "You have a fucking obligation, you know, to tell her. She's not no ordinary person to be kept waiting. She is a star, but I bet you know that already. Who in the world doesn't know by now Stephanie Marriner?"

The two nurses looked up and over at them, then back at one another, and nodded accord.

Officer DeCarlo ignored Tony B. Tony. "If you'll just follow me," she said, and signaled the nurses to pass them through the waist-high security gate.

The gate lock clicked free. Officer DeCarlo pushed it open and led the way forward down a long corridor lined with beds bunched within a few feet of each other, with only draw curtains for privacy.

Every bed seemed occupied where the curtains were open, and

Stevie saw it was the same with the bed row on the other side of the immense rectangle that was divided at intervals by med stations and supply shelters.

County General was doing a big business in the homeless and the helpless, other outcasts of society benefiting from free care; probably carfare, when they were fit to get back to their shopping carts and back-alley homes and hideaways.

The floors were spotless linoleum and the smell in the air was sterile, astringent enough to mask the whiffs Stevie was getting from fresh puke and the acrid body smell that no amount of scrubbing ever completely peels off somebody who's lived too long on the street, Neil had once explained, telling her about his older brother, who'd disappeared among the walking wounded for four years, only to reemerge and then disappear again.

He was still missing, Neil's brother.

Like her father.

Stevie rubbed some perfume off her neck and cupped her hand over her nose, trying to drown the odor. She wasn't entirely successful.

Nothing she could do about the hacking coughs, the disparate moans and groans floating through the ward, or the mumbled or shouted begging for painkillers or fixes or booze emanating from some of the beds. A symphony of need, Neil had called it, played by people with habits too hard to break: Drugs. Alcohol. Unemployment.

Poverty.

Breathing.

And some who were just never any damn good in the first place, Neil had said, like he believed it, only Stevie knew he didn't, same as she never could bring herself to believe it.

Leave it to Mama to have put it best, a long time ago, when she said, *Honey, it's some higher power putting us to a test and lots of times the best people are chosen for the toughest tests, otherwise the results wouldn't really add up to much.*

Well, she and Juliet, they had had their fair share of tough tests over the years, so what did that make them? How well she knew the answer:

Survivors.

And then some.

People who knew getting knocked down would never matter as long as you remembered to get up again—

The worst bringing out the best in people.

Mama knew that.

Her Stevie knew that.

So did Neil, despite the veneer of disallowance he came to put on through his years spent on the *Daily*'s crime beat, dealing with the kinds of evil that sometimes made him come home too drunk or stressed out to take any consolation in telling her. Maybe they'd fight about it, until she saw the story in the paper under his byline.

Then, she could understand and she could tell Neil she understood, and he would say, "Thanks," but not much more, and maybe take her in his arms, too, and they'd go to bed for a kind of gently violent lovemaking that helped flush out his psyche.

Seven years living with him and going on eight years living without him qualified her to make that judgment about Neil, who'd been through some tough tests of his own, and—

"So, here we are, Miss Marriner," Officer DeCarlo said, pulling Stevie back into the ward, stopping so quickly she almost bumped into the lady cop as Tony B. Tony bumped into her, offering an "Oops" as an apology.

Stevie hesitated before looking past the foot of the bed to the man asleep on his side, the thin woolen blanket drawn over his shoulder. His head above the brow line was heavily bandaged.

She would have to move around to get a better look at his face and did so after momentary hesitation, not daring to breathe from fear of who she'd see.

It wasn't Neil.

She cleared her lungs of air in one rush and told the lady cop, her emotions tangling relief with curiosity over who this person was and how she'd become involved in trying to identify him.

The lady cop was standing beside her and so was Tony B. Tony, who was agreeing with Stevie, telling Officer DeCarlo, "This guy don't look fucking nothing like Gulliver. You know that from those posters of Gulliver's kisser they put on the sides of the RTD buses."

Officer DeCarlo was still ignoring him.

She asked Stevie, "Any idea who he might be, then?"

"No."

"Maybe somebody you saw recently but wouldn't have any reason to remember?"

"I have a better memory than that, officer."

"No offense meant, ma'am. It's just that—"

She pulled a slip of paper from the clipboard she was carrying under her arm and handed it to Stevie.

It was in a clear plastic baggie.

Officer DeCarlo said, "On patrol late yesterday, down the old industrial district off of Almeda, my partner and I happened to spot this John Doe in a vacant lot, too clean to belong there, so probably some mugger got him. He was out of it. Bloody, back of the head. Clothes on his back and nothing else, not even shoes, excepting for this note in a pocket we found. Names, addresses, and telephone numbers. You and Mr. Gulliver—" The lady cop aimed a frown at Tony B. Tony. "We tried to get him first, Mr. Gulliver, doing our follow-ups today. Best I got was his machine, but better luck with you, after I tracked you to your current number. I didn't mean to frighten you, though, so my sincere apologies for—"

Stevie wagged a *That's all right* hand at Officer DeCarlo.

She said, "Why would the John Doe have our numbers? Who would have given them to him?"

"Part of the puzzle, ma'am. Lots of missing answers. He has been out since the paramedics got him to County. Serious concussion. Hit hard on the head with some heavy instrument. Maybe lucky to still be breathing, but expected to pull out of it. Too clean to be one of the bums, but no confirmations on what he might have been doing around there."

Tony B. Tony had moved in to take a closer look at the victim. He shook his head and decided, "He's cleaned up, but he still looks like a run-of-the-mill rummy bummed-out freak to me."

The victim seemed to stir under the covers, only for a fraction of a second, and Stevie thought she could hear some sounds dribbling out of him and breaking the constant rhythm of his breathing. It didn't last long enough for her to be sure.

She asked the lady cop, "No car?"

"No, ma'am. We're guessing whoever it was slammed him may also have gone off in his vehicle, unless tomorrow we locate the vehicle parked at some company or 'nother he'd been visiting and decided to take a stroll in those parts, although that seems unlikely. My partner and I can't check that until tomorrow. Area's closed up tight on weekends."

"Bobby Redford would have this solved by now," Tony B. Tony told himself, loud enough under his breath to be heard, like he was disturbed by the lack of attention.

He grabbed one of his cells and tapped in a call.

"Listen, hey, going over budget here, but I'll let you know when I let you know. Meanwhile, in *Layton's Paradise 2*, the treatment. Did your coverage say something about Layton meeting up and teaming up with a female traffic cop? I got me an idea brewing here. Big. Big-fucking-big-big-big."

It wasn't until they were on the Golden State heading back that Stevie flashed on something the lady cop had said, about the location of the lot where they found the John Doe, in the industrial district off Alameda.

The only time she'd been around there was with Neil, when he took her down to tour the Circus Gallery. The owner had taken down their addresses and phone numbers, saying he wanted to add them to his special mailing list.

Stevie had moved soon after, which would explain why the note had an old number for her, if that was where the John Doe had been, at the Circus Gallery.

It wouldn't explain why or how he'd walked off with their addresses and numbers, but—

Something to do with the Warhols?

She hammered the possibility with a fist on the dash.

She got on her cell and tried all her numbers for Neil.

No more luck than Officer DeCarlo had had.

She tapped in the *Daily*'s number.

Ada on the editorial switchboard only knew Neil was off tracking a column in San Diego.

Stevie had better luck on her next call, to the Order of the Spiritual Brothers of the Rhyming Heart. Brother Gerald said Brother Kalman was in the garden conducting flower prayers and couldn't be disturbed, but—

Yes.

Mr. Gulliver had phoned here about two hours ago to say he was returning from San Diego and intended to stop at the Order. Mr. Gulliver sounded extremely hyper, Brother Gerald volunteered, wondering if Stevie might do well to suggest to Mr. Gulliver that he see to a general physical.

"Better safe than sorry," Brother Gerald cautioned.

Stevie agreed and thanked him.

She clicked the cell shut, and told Tony B. Tony, "Change in plans."

He studied her expression and raised a smile.

"You think you're on to something, don't you?" Tony B. Tony said.

"Where we're heading, not far. Los Feliz. When we get there, they'll call you a cab, and—"

"Thanks, but my sniffer is sniffing at my sixth sense and telling me you're on to something has to do with that bum in the bed. I think I'm gonna go with the fucking flow."

Stevie swiveled her head left and right.

She said, "Nothing that concerns you."

Tony B. Tony was already on his cell.

"Listen, stand by," he ordered. "A new change in plans. Don't know what it is yet, only that it is."

He dropped the cell back into his shirt pocket and told Stevie, "You know, after we're done shooting *Nothing Sacred*, no reason Layton couldn't be a chick. A chick dick teams up with a chick in uniform. You remember the box office turned in by the *Charlie's Angels* retread? Fucking crimebusters."

15

Brother Gerald came outside to greet her as Stevie was pulling her BMW into a space by the front entrance doors of the Order of the Spiritual Brothers of the Rhyming Heart.

"I did not know you were bringing along—company," he said, looking over her shoulder as he took her embrace, his tone a combination of curiosity and suspicion.

She introduced Brother Gerald to Tony B. Tony.

"A friend of Neil Gulliver's, are you, Mr. Anthony?"

"Not that I know about," Tony B. Tony said, sucking in the surroundings through his Ferragamo shades.

Taking back his hand from Brother Gerald, he framed a rectangle with his thumb and fingers and peered through it at the building side to the north, which dissolved into a stunning panoramic view of Griffith Park across the way, a landscape bathed in the orange-and-gold Technicolor glow of a late-afternoon sun that had finally burst through the dark rain clouds.

"Nice angle." Tony B. Tony said. "Has the makings of a good location shoot up here. We can negotiate a good price on use for a day or three. You the one I talk to?"

"That would be Brother Kalman or, in his absence, the task would fall to Brother Saul."

"What does that make you, Brother Doorman?"

Tony B. Tony made a *bada-boom* rimshot noise and tried stretching his smile to his ears.

Brother Gerald let him see he did not appreciate what Tony B. Tony was passing off as humor.

Stevie thought she detected more than disapproval in his expression, although it could have been nothing more than the black circles that made Brother Gerald look like a raccoon. The circles were new, and so was the way the edges of his mouth seemed to sag, drawing his flaccid cheeks down to his wattles.

As he took Stevie by the elbow and headed her inside, leaving Tony B. Tony to tag along, she said, "Are you okay, Brother Gerald?"

"Of course," Brother Gerald said, "but thank you very much for asking."

His voice wasn't as certain as his words.

"Actually, no. Possibly not," Brother Gerald decided.

Strolling toward Augie's sanctuary, he leaned in and lowered his voice, making what he was about to say their secret.

"It is the heart thing of mine that originally drove me here from the brokerage," Brother Gerald said. "It disappeared after I began my meditations, but now, these years later, it seems to have returned in the form of an atrial flutter the doctor thinks he can eliminate with an electrically charged wire inserted into my heart to zap the circuit causing the flutter, but—" He shrugged his sagging shoulders. "If the flutter does not go away, I go back to my pills and they give me a pacemaker to make my heart beat faster. I am going into the hospital on Wednesday next, and—"

Another shrug, joined by a deep sigh.

Stevie gave his soft, blue-veined hand a solid squeeze and said, "I'll say a prayer for you."

He caught his breath.

"As you are ever in my prayers," Brother Gerald said. He surprised her by leaning over and kissing her on the temple. "Bless you," he said, and knocked on Augie's door.

Augie stood as they entered, leaned forward with his palms locked to the surface of the desk. He had the same first look for Tony B. Tony that Brother Gerald had had, but it dissolved into a knowing chuckle before they were halfway to him.

"The Wonder Boy himself, is it?" he said, sending away Brother Gerald with a shooing gesture. "Anthony B. Anthony, as I live and breathe."

Tony B. Tony gave Augie close study.

"Take away the Eugene Pallette dress, the John Ford eye patch, and about fifteen years and I think I got me fucking A. K. Fowler," he said. "Fowler, I thought you died and went to heaven, not Griffith Park."

"I died and came to heaven," Augie said, and drilled him with his wide good eye. "Here on earth."

Turning to Stevie, Tony B. Tony said, "One a my first flicks, *Precious Evil*, based on the stuff Fowler wrote for the *Daily* when he was still alive. Paid Fowler more than he probably made all year from the newspaper."

Augie threw his hands at Tony B. Tony and told Stevie, "Absolutely. Enough to keep myself in rolls of toilet paper for a month. Generosity wasn't your long suit, friend."

He gestured for them to take the guest chairs, sat down again, and then asked Stevie, "Do I guess correctly that the reason you're here and Neil is on his way has to do with the Warhols?"

" 'Do with the Warhols?' " Tony B. Tony said. "What's this about The Warhols?" Putting capitals on both words.

He looked from Augie to Stevie and stuck there.

Stevie had her own question forming on her face.

"I didn't know Neil was coming over about the Warhols," she said.

Augie looked away, raised his chin, aimed his eye at a corner of the ceiling, and arched his eyebrow to go with the "Hummmm" sound of an unanswered question.

"Maybe he's not," Augie said, trying to recapture the last thirty seconds.

"What's about some cockamamie Warhols?" Tony B. Tony asked again, insistently this time, clearly not happy at being shut out. "This some movie thing you-all have going with somebody else?"

Stevie flagged Augie's attention with a desperate look.

Augie understood.

He said, "Fact of the matter is, Aging Wonder Boy, not a movie or, for that matter, television. He, Neil, is doing some research here for a series he's writing on Warhol, and A. K. Fowler, as he's proven time and again, is important to his adoring crime-beat acolytes forever and always."

Tony B. Tony looked at him skeptically.

Finally he said, "My ass."

"Or is that a hole in the ground you're looking at?" Augie said, maneuvering around the desk and crossing the room to his bank of filing cabinets.

He twirled the combination on the drawer he wanted and waded through it until he found what he was searching for—

Sauntered back to the desk with the slim black ledger Stevie remembered from before.

Thumbed through to the section he wanted.

Pushed the ledger across the desk at Tony B. Tony and invited, "Here you go. Have a look for yourself. Some of my best early stuff, I say so myself, and indeed I do."

" 'However Measured or Far Away,' huh?" Tony B. Tony said. "Interesting title."

He began speed-reading, his lips moving faster than his fingers could turn the pages.

"Yeah," he'd say occasionally, agreeing with himself. "Yeah, uh-huh. Uh-huh."

Something got a different reaction.

Tony B. Tony arched his head back and glanced left and right like he feared spies might be honing in on his secret.

"Who woulda thought," he said, then tossed Augie a look and said, "You gotta fucking hear this, Fowler," like Augie didn't already know what he had written years ago.

Tony B. Tony rose to his feet and started pacing as he read aloud in a monotone, stumbling over some of the words:

" 'The narrow-gauge elevator opened onto a pair of matched funhouse mirrors. I moved to the half-open Dutch doors and buzzed for attention and admission.

" 'The young man who admitted me was glum and dour-lipped. The Indian: Joe Dallesandro, I wondered to myself, the star of Warhol's *Lonesome Cowboys* and the new one, *Flesh*, the Warhol film directed by Paul Morrissey?

" 'He wore pimples and an Indian headband and, after I in-troduced myself, settled at a desk near the door, next to a mas-sive, stuffed dog of mixed origin, a sentry on duty. On the wall above the Indian's head, a framed photo of himself.

" 'I moved inside the main room to a nearby white wicker settee that offered a full-scale view of the Factory. It was like a movie set. A spacious emptiness and not a lot to see. Furnish-ings to the mood. The Indian's desk and, to my left, across from one another, two more desks. At the farthest desk was another young man, somber, self-involved, engulfed in silent immobility. Gerard Malanga, one of Andy's original Superstars. Closer, Frankie Freddie Frook, the oafish, tap-dancing cockroach-eating boy from Warhol's infamous *Bug Men and Boys*.

" 'A lot of white, a room full of white walls; wooden flooring, a full-size mirror straight ahead and lots of white. A towering metal sculpture and toward the rear, a series of framed, colored vintage photographs of classic movie stars. At the back, a pro-jector running, feeding through a glass partition into the room beyond, its pale darkness visible through the open doors, as well as what looked like a couple in the act of congress . . .' "

Augie had had enough after about ten minutes that felt to Stevie like ten months and demanded Tony B. Tony stop.

Tony B. Tony slapped the ledger shut.

He shook it at Augie like he was rattling a cage.

He said, "A column? Fowler, you got a fucking movie in here. For-get Gulliver and his writing some newspaper series on any of this here. Would be a waste, my man."

Augie looked at Tony B. Tony like he was measuring him for a straightjacket.

"First thing in the *mañana*, and you can take what I'm telling you to the bank, I'm gonna have my people call your people," Tony B. Tony said.

"I am my people," Augie said.

Tony B. Tony's turn to make a crazy eye.

He said, "What's that from, the Bible?"

"You're serious, aren't you, Wonder Boy?"

"Fowler, believe you me when I swear on a stack of hotcakes that all the elements are here. The young, nuts Warhol. Those kooks he surrounds himself with at this Factory a his. That business about the topless dame who wears a dog collar, the crazy fat dame knocking out

Warhol's art for him and the part where she's copping the stud's joint under the desk, and the other fruitcake, the dame who uses Warhol's chest for a target—" Tony B. Tony fired a finger gun at Augie. "Scenes to die for. You see what Eddie Harris did with that art guy who dripped paint on the floor?"

"Jackson Pollock," Stevie said.

"Him," Tony B. Tony said, and gave her a thumbs-up. "I got better gold than him, Pollock, in this. Why nobody saw it before in Warhol I don't know, I don't care, because it was fate. It was meant for"—thumb-thumping his chest—"is why. So, what say, Fowler? Are we good to go?"

Half bemused and half in surrender, Augie said, "Have your people call"—thumb-thumping his chest—"my person."

Tony B. Tony turned to Stevie and said, "Like I would've left here with any answer but." Addressing Augie again: "I need to take the book here with me."

"No you don't," Augie said. No hesitation. Emphasizing his answer with a gesture. "The only place my ledger goes is back in the file, under lock and key."

"It's combination locks you got; no key," Tony B. Tony said; then to Stevie, pointing to an eye: "It's the details can make or break a movie . . ." Once again to Augie: "C'mon, awreddy, Fowler. Give it up."

Augie was adamant.

Tony B. Tony kept at him until they hit a compromise.

Tony B. Tony agreed to leave with photocopies.

"Three sets," he said. "For my overpriced lawyers. For a writer I got in mind for the treatment. One for our friend here. Yeah, Stevie-reno. You read it, and lemme know you see there's somebody hits home with you. Like maybe the stripper dame. We can build that part up, then, or some other part you like even better. Maybe even sit you down on your sweet patoot with the writer."

Inwardly, Stevie was laughing.

So far, Tony B. Tony had demoted her from Garbo to Lombard to a "stripper dame." Maybe, if she put on some poundage, she could do the crazy fat dame giving the stud head.

"Why not," she said.

Later, she'd tell Tony B. Tony what she really thought.

Augie got on the phone com and, after a minute or two, they were joined by Brother Gerald, who listened to Augie's directions solemnly before wrestling the black ledger from Tony B. Tony under assurance that he would have the number of copies specified waiting for him.

"Am I interrupting something?" Neil said.

Stevie's head snapped in the direction of his voice.

Neil was addressing Stevie, but his eyes had landed on Tony B. Tony with the same combination of curiosity and concern she knew she was displaying about the woman at his side. A green-robed novice brother hovered behind Neil, dancing nervously from sandal to sandal.

"I can wait," Neil said, that old familiar jealousy in his voice. "Go out and come back again when—"

"No, that's all right," Stevie said.

Stevie wasn't about to tell Neil about USC–County General, the mugging victim, the note with their names and numbers, in front of a stranger, whoever the hell she was. Bad enough all this time she'd been trying to figure how to get Tony B. Tony out of here.

What she had to tell Neil would have to wait.

"We were just leaving, ourselves," she said.

She leaped from her seat at Tony B. Tony, just as he was announcing, "You're Neil Gulliver, and I'm—" Trapped him in her arms and planted a kiss on his mouth before he could launch what she knew would be his latest credits and something about the Warhol story.

Tony B. Tony looked astonished, pleased, as she pulled away, then started to say, "We met once, twice before—" She jailed his mouth again, longer this time, and didn't try to resist his tongue.

When she was sure she had him under control, she quit, wheeled around behind him, calling out thanks to Augie, and, "Sorry to rush off like this, but we're late already. Let's move it, Brother Gerald."

Gave the woman the same once-over she was getting while she propelled Tony B. Tony to the door, with Neil—like the Lakers playing defense—pulling the woman closer to him and draping an arm across her back.

As she and Tony B. Tony charged up the hallway ahead of Brother Gerald and the novice, he said, "Don't know exactly what all that was about, but what you say I call over to the Peninsula for a suite and a bottle or two of Cristal waiting on ice for us? Or maybe you'd rather I score a bungalow over at the Beverly Hills?" He clamped a hand onto her ass. "I'm partial myself to the old Howard Hughes suite."

Stevie pulled off his hand and said, "It wasn't about that." Stern enough for Tony B. Tony to understand and not try the move again.

He had called ahead to his shlep, so Tony B. Tony's Rolls was waiting for him in a place of prominence on the circular drive by the time she pulled up to the Empire Towers. A valet had her door open in seconds, and she was out of the BMW in time to dodge Tony B. Tony's latest grab attempt. If he was disappointed, his expression didn't show it. He was cheery and enthusiastic, but not beyond one last try.

"Maybe upstairs?"

"For me, yes," she said. "For you—bye-bye time."

"We could talk some more about the Warhol deal."

She angled him toward the Rolls and dismissed him with a conciliatory peck on the check.

"So I still got some hope, huh?"

"None whatsoever, Tony B. Tony."

He laughed into the air.

"That's what they all think," he said, insisting upon giving the parking attendant a fifty and telling him, "Remember my face, kid. As Big Arnie always useta say, 'I'll be back.' "

Stevie was out of her clothes and into the tub within minutes, washing off the weekend, thinking about Neil and—No, actually thinking about the woman. Pretty. A knockout, in fact. About time Neil fell into something like that.

For how many years had she pushed him to find someone else to get serious about?

The woman. That look in her eyes. *She knew who I was*, Stevie thought. It showed.

More defined than the uncertainty Neil was showing, that look.

More like a competitor studying her competition.

Reading Stevie for what she thought she was and really wasn't, so—

Why had she reacted the way she had upon seeing the woman for the first time?

Felt a momentary knot in her stomach when Neil made a display of the woman with that arm-around-her business?

The woman. She must have a name.

It had to be a better one than any of those Stevie was laying on her now.

No, no, no, not jealousy, Stevie decided.

Protectiveness.

Protecting Neil.

Neil was too good a catch for just *anybody.*

Okay, all right already. So maybe a little jealousy, too.

〉
〉
〉

Stevie settled at the counter in her bathrobe, over a frozen diet dinner, tonight a chicken breast in basil cream sauce with angel-hair pasta, and a can of caffeine-free Diet Coke, and read her set of the Warhol pages photocopied from Augie's ledger by Brother Gerald.

She skimmed over the parts Augie and Tony B. Tony had read aloud, then slowed, giving the story more attention. She wanted to see for herself if Tony B. Tony was right about this being a movie worth making. Whatever else, he was a gifted filmmaker. He actually could be on to something.

Augie had written all those years ago:

Suddenly, without announcement, Warhol stepped from the black room to tinker with the projector. The familiar dark glasses were missing but there was another trademark, the long blond hair, gone white in front. He adjusted a film reel, then stepped back inside the darkened room, where congress had not yet adjourned.

Paul Morrissey arrived a few minutes later, apologizing for Warhol, explaining that Andy was preoccupied unreeling new footage he was seeing for the first time. He'd be out to see me shortly, Paul promised.

While we waited for Andy's return, Paul would push me into conversation with others and disappear, return at appropriate moments to resume the part of cordial host. As Paul talked, often at a rapid clip, it became clear that he was the Factory's main interlocutor, the businessman, the overseer of image, Andy's link between the Warhol world and everyone else's world.

"If you want to talk about Andy's art, talk to Brigid Polk. She does it all anyway," Paul said, pointing to the newly arrived, massive female structure. She was large and loud. Hard-looking and hard-talking. A Mama Crass.

I walked over to her and said, "You do Andy's art?"

"Who the shit you think does it? Andy?"

Blonde, boisterous Brigid, later to explain how she made film history by playing a dyke in *Chelsea Girls*, peddling pills and poking a hypodermic needle through her jeans.

"I've been doing it all for the last year and a half, two years," she declared. "Andy doesn't do art anymore. He's bored with

it. I did all his new soup cans. I did his new portfolio of seven
Marilyns. Tell the people not to cash Andy's checks if they get
any; they'll be worth more."

I said, "You do all of Andy's art, but he signs it, of course."

Brigid responded by taking a piece of paper and forging:
Andy Warhol. Then she added, *Chamberlain, R. Rauschenberg,
Miró, Tallulah Bankhead, Claire Booth Luce, Edward, Wallis
Windsor, Dwight D. Eisenhower,* only she spelled it *Eizenhower.*

Andy was in the room again, again bothering with the pro-
jector, an attractive girl by his side.

I picked up the paper and headed over, but Andy was faster
and had already disappeared back inside the dark room, its only
light emanating from images flashing on a movie screen, and
settled on a white couch.

The girl had stayed at the projector and said as I encroached,
"Andy says to talk to me because I'm a great piece and I'm
going to be a big star." She was tiny, but assembled like a pornographic jigsaw puzzle.

Stevie looked up from the photocopied text.
So this was the role Tony B. Tony instantly had her in mind for?
A pornographic jigsaw puzzle?
She stopped reading long enough to move with what was left of
her Diet Coke into the living room. Switched on the FM to a cool jazz
station. Stretched out on the couch with a pillow propped under her
head, her bare feet crossed at the ankles. Picked up where she'd left
off:

"I'm in *Flesh*," Geri Miller said, and introduced herself. "I
play myself and show my bust and then I blow Joe, don't I,
Joe?" Asking the Indian at the desk.

"Not really," said Joe Dallesandro.

"I did so," Geri went on in her hoarse whisper of a voice.

"Hey, show them your tits, Geri!" Brigid had lunged over.
"Go ahead, show them. She's got the biggest set you've ever
seen."

"Oh, Brigid."

"You wouldn't recognize her if you saw her when she first
started coming here. Nothing. Now look at her, just look. You
ever see a set like that?"

"I have a little-girl look and a woman's body," Geri said apologetically; then, after a pause; "Who do I remind you of?"

"Who?"

"Guess."

"I give up."

"Judy Holliday. Don't I remind you of Judy Holliday? Huh? That's who I'd like to be like. My ambition is to make people laugh and make people happy.

"See this dog collar I wear around my neck? That's because I make out like an animal."

"How did Andy discover you?"

"He knew me from seeing me dance," Geri explained. "I dance topless. He saw me dancing when I fell off the swing at the Rolling Stone. He noticed me, and he invited me to come here.

"I didn't come at first, though, not until Andy was shot. Then I figured I'd better, because he might not be around too long. Now he's making me a star."

Suddenly, Warhol was in our midst.

Paul Morrissey said, "Andy, he'd like to ask you some questions about your art."

It was suddenly quite quiet in the Factory.

I confronted Warhol shoulder-close and got my first real look at him. He looked frightened. There was a look in his brown eyes that I first translated as nervousness, but then I wondered if the look had been there before the night Valerie Solanis used his chest for target practice and came close to ending Brigid Polk's career.

Andy looked afraid. He looked afraid of something. His Beatles-styled moptop seemed more fright-white than silver. And I wondered, too, what he looked like before he became Andy Warhol, a fine artist to some critics, a Barnum in Babylon to others.

As Warhol began stepping back and away from me, not so much impatiently as nervously, I kept pace and posed the matter of Brigid Polk.

"She does my work," he said, softly.

"All of it?"

ANDY WARHOL: "Yes."

Did he plan to ever again work in oil?

ANDY WARHOL: "No."

Could we conclude, then, that he has left the art of the museums for the art of motion-picture theaters?

ANDY WARHOL: "Yes."

Was he at least selecting the pictures or the things that would be reproduced as Warhol's work?"

ANDY WARHOL: "No, nothing."

He let a thought germinate, then said, "Why don't you get undressed and I'll take your picture."

"Thanks, but no," I laughed. "I'm not quite ready for that."

Brigid's head emerged from under Gerard Malanga's desk, flushed; she was being of service to the former Superstar. Then, having had her fill of Gerard, she moved off to cool off by removing her sweatshirt.

Andy kept pace. I trailed along and handed him the sheet of Brigid Polk signatures. Andy looked confused, lost for a reaction.

"Brigid did this," I said. "I'd like you to sign it."

He gave me a silent *Huh?*

I said, "If Brigid does all your art, that makes this an original Warhol, and I'd like to have it signed."

Brigid flapped over, displeased by the request.

"Wait a minute," she said. "Andy doesn't sign any of his work anymore."

By now he was writing his name. It was barely more than an illegible scrawl, implemented by a few stroke lines with the ball pen.

Brigid stalked off, upset by Andy's audacity, while Warhol, past the terrors of confrontation, walked into the dark room and shut the door.

By now, Geri was gone. Brigid shortly packed up her things and left. Geri had invited me to see her perform at the Metropole, but not so much as an adieu from Brigid. Joe, Gerard, even Paul. Gone, leaving me alone in the room. And after a few minutes, when it became obvious no encores were planned, I scribbled a note of thanks and left it on a desk, took one last look around and the elevator down.

En route back to the hotel, from Warhol to the Warwick, I juggled impressions of my time at the Factory. It had been funny and fun, sinful but sincere, and even Brigid, who was tested and found wanton, couldn't be faulted. It is a self-contained society, Andy's phalanges, drawn by his light, yet in fact more needed by him.

About the film, talk to Paul. About the art, talk to Brigid. The past, see Gerard; the present, petulant Joe; the future, possibly someone in the next room or about to strut into the funhouse mirrors.

Can it be that Andy Warhol has advanced his love affair with reproduction to the ultimate? Has he in fact reproduced himself to all sizes, sexes and specifications?

I wondered about the music Andy Warhol hears—however measured or far away—the rat-a-tat-tat of the drummer; better certainly than the shot of a gun, Valerie Solanis, who came closest to finding Andy's heart.

Bang, you're immortal.

The telephone ringing startled Stevie into a sitting position. She had fallen asleep sometime between finishing Augie's Warhol story and thinking about it, trying to catch a message, a nuance, so clear she couldn't see it—

Only sense that it was there.

She reached for the portable on the coffee table, saw it was coming in on the private number.

Figured, *Probably Neil.*

Her "Hello" was answered by silence.

Stevie repeated herself.

More silence before the caller disconnected them.

Some fan who'd somehow found the number, she decided.

Happening more and more lately. That reminded her she'd been meaning to call the phone company and have the number changed again.

Tomorrow.

Tomorrow for sure.

Stevie put down the phone and stretched out again, too tired to even think about heading for the bedroom.

Within seconds she felt herself drifting off.

16

Augie didn't volunteer what Stevie had been doing there. I played the wise lawyer who knows not to ask questions where he doesn't know the answers, because of Maryam. There had to be a better time and way to introduce her, show her off to my ex with more diplomacy than Stevie has shown slobbering all over what I presumed was her latest and far, far from most attractive boy toy ever.

Anthony B. Anthony.

I recognized him as fast as he'd recognized me.

Big time director-producer. A golden hyphenate in the Hollywood spectrum I'd met on a junket a few years ago and later backstage at the Oscars.

Both times, he'd come after me for a column, insinuating himself and his credits, with the added suggestion of special rewards that could be mine for a favorable piece.

He'd struck out both times and to his credit hadn't turned into one of those showbiz hounds from hell who get even for my indifference by dropping me from their preview and party lists.

Anthony B. Anthony, aka "Call me Tony B. Tony, buddy."

Ladies' man. A generally held reputation for needing his platinum credit cards to snag a woman when the opportunities offered through his casting couch weren't sufficient.

All I could do was hope that Stevie was doing a better job of using him than Tony B. Tony was doing on her. *On her.* I seem to have a spontaneously Freudian way with words where men and my ex are concerned.

And, by the way, why was I also feeling some kind of a disloyalty to Maryam?

Like I was dishonoring Maryam and how I'd come to feel about her, intensified certainly during the weekend we'd spent together in San Diego.

Just some of the thoughts competing for attention with street traffic as I aimed my Jag for home from Augie's place an hour or so after Stevie had hustled the hyphenate out of our presence, leaving me free to tell Augie about my meeting with Maurice Kline after I'd introduced him to Maryam.

She charmed him immediately, turning a handshake into a hug, and saying, "Neil has been telling me all about you and how much you mean to him, and just by seeing you I can sense why."

Augie blustered and flustered a thank-you and eased out of her hold, shooting me a look that combined an embarrassed flush with a modicum of appreciation, but whatever he was thinking he didn't let show.

His reaction was different when I told him I was certain I had seen the painting from the Kleinschmick family collection in one of the Warhol silkscreens, growing from mere attention to a rocket ready to explode.

He punched onto his com line and barked out instructions.

Ten minutes later he guided us from the sanctuary to the conference room. The Warhol suite waiting on the table, a pair of white cotton gloves next to the presentation case.

Augie carefully lifted out one print after another and made a single row the same way Zev Neumann had, stopping when he got to a print that matched my description.

I leaned in for a closer look and at once knew that I'd been mistaken. The Warhol showed a Berthe Morisot portrait of a woman, but not the portrait of a woman I'd seen in Maurice Kline's photograph.

"Lose that hangdog look," Augie said, and continued with the process of removing silkscreens from the case. "I thought I'd taught him better than to jump to conclusions," he advised Maryam.

He made a trumpeting sound upon laying down the next silkscreen.

"You apparently forgot there were two Morisots in the suite, amigo," he said; then, to Maryam, "Interesting woman, Berthe Morisot. You see her in a lot of portraits painted by Manet. Married Manet's brother. Maybe her way of paying him for the work?"

"Maybe they were in love," Maryam said, angling a look at me.

Augie said, "Your notion's more romantic than mine, but mine's more intriguing. So, amigo, tell me. This one any better?"

I hovered over the print he pointed to and squeezed my memory to be certain, and—

It was.

The woman preparing for bed or, perhaps, her lover, a demure expression on her face contradicting the diaphanous peignoir falling off her shoulders, or was it a caught half-smile imagining the magic she would bring to him, offset by the virginal white of the dressing gown and the white hiding her image in the mirror, hiding the wall behind her, clues other than two vases to suggest where she was or who she was with.

"It is," I said.

Maryam, who'd seen Maurice Kline's photograph and was now standing behind me, her hands locked around my waist and examining the print for herself, agreed.

"From the way you described it, I remembered seeing it before, and also in one of the files Ari Landau brought with him," Augie said.

"So, he knew what I was going to see when he sent me to talk to Kline."

"Good a guess as any."

"He could have told me that."

"You know these *lawyers*," Augie said, making a farce of the word and rolling his eyes.

I said, "Did Landau's file also ID the collector?"

"That part I don't remember, but if Ari and Zev knew, I think by this time they'd be on their way to recovering the painting for Kline and Kline would've said something about it to you, don't you suppose?"

"Kline didn't. Maybe I should call Ari and ask him the question?"

Augie walked over to the head of the conference table, picked up his portable, and tapped in a couple numbers.

"I put him on speed-dial," he said. After a few moments he aimed a thumb down and said into the mouthpiece, "Hello, Ari's voice mail, this is Brother Kalman, absolutely live in person . . ."

Maryam had sat quietly through the drive home to the Heathcliffe, and I sensed she understood the mind tricks I was playing on myself. She confirmed it when we got to our floor and I asked her if she wanted to cap the weekend with a freezer delectable or, better, a delivery call for pizza.

Or better yet, Chinese.

Or better even than yet—

Her head was already switching left and right.

She pleaded heavy homework before classes tomorrow.

That's not what I was reading on her face or hearing in her voice and told her so.

"Caught," she said, elevating her hands captive-style. She angled around and leaned against the corridor wall with her arms crossed defensively and said, "Would be a different answer if I were a prisoner of love, Neil."

"What's that supposed to mean?" I said, fooling no one.

"One guess."

Maybe I should have waited a few beats before I said, "Stevie."

Not that it would have made a difference.

A smile nowhere close to the one in the Berthe Morisot painting tickled the corners of her mouth, and her eyes took a detour from me to the wallpaper across the way.

She converted her feelings to words gently, softly, careful not to inflict unnecessary pain with them, telling me, "Whatever it is we have or think we have or might be catching, it's a common cold compared to the flu the two of you still have going between you. I felt it from the first minute, from the moment we walked into your friend Augie's office. From what was said and especially what was not said, and before that from the way you pulled me to you—only to send a message to Stevie.

"Her, doing that kissing routine, and that's what it was. The old *I'll show him*. You are over her the way Humpty Dumpty sits on walls, no matter what you think. Stevie, she probably knows how much she still cares, but isn't going to admit it to you or to anybody until she's able to admit it to herself. If hanging in there, waiting for her to say she wants you back, is what you're really all about, Neil, you need a life preserver, not someone like me to hang on to."

She stopped as Mrs. Shepard from down the hall stepped out of
her apartment and headed our way, breathing in heavy grunts from the
burden of carrying a second person she disguised as excess poundage.
In passing, gave us a telling look, not the least obliging, like she'd caught
two dogs in heat.

We watched her round the corner and pass out of sight, whereupon—

Maryam resumed her soliloquy, like it was the rest of a script she'd
started writing and rehearsing at Augie's.

"Before, I didn't care. I told you that. I believed it was true. But I
do care, Neil. That's what I found out this weekend, first in San Diego,
and then meeting Stevie, or not meeting Stevie, because that's precisely
what happened, what didn't happen. If you'd said to her, 'Stevie, this
is Maryam Zokaei. I have something going with her,' then—"

A shrug.

She nailed me with her eyes.

I felt the hurt in them.

Not knowing how to respond, but certain whatever truth I might
share now would not help the situation, I started to reach out, touch
her cheek, in the hope that contact would help let her understand we
weren't a lost cause.

She stopped me with her hand before it got that far and pushed
mine down to my side.

Eased sideways from me.

Turned and headed for her apartment, and when she got there—

Blew me a kiss ahead of a smile that hurt more than a million
goodbyes.

Maryam's scent lingered long afterward, while I dragged through what
was left of the evening thinking about what she had said and how on
the money she was about the parts to do with my frame of mind.

I couldn't speak for my ex, of course, any more than I could call
her and ask her, say: *Babe, this is what someone thinks you think about
us. Right or wrong?*

Not "Babe." *Stevie.*

Stevie, this is what someone thinks you think about us . . .

Yeah, sure, and get any answer different from any I had heard before from her, always adding up to No Sale.

Cap *N.* Cap *S.*

But the bigger question was, bottom line, did I care as much as I thought I did or was it really a game I'd played so long I didn't know any other games anymore?

Even that thought begged the truth.

There *was* a new game and I was playing it and it went by the name *Maryam and Me.*

And I was pretty good at it.

Damn good.

For a beginner.

Because I wanted to be.

Shaq and Kobe together, some Derek Fisher thrown in for good measure, playing to win, and—

I had an urge to pick up the phone and call Stevie, do it now, right now, and say: *Stevie, that was Maryam Zokaei I didn't introduce you to today. She and I, we, Maryam and me, we have something going.*

And mean it.

Mean it, damn it.

I knew Stevie would understand.

Thought so.

Understand better than me.

Maybe.

When was the last time I spoke for her or really knew her mind beyond this little telepathy thing that's always been there between us, until lately—

When Maryam sleepwalked into the picture?

Not for a long while and not now, but I'd call her, and then—

And then I would call Maryam and tell her and commit to getting our relationship back on track.

Yes.

Up and charging like the old Super Chief.

I popped the top on the Bud I had just pulled from the fridge and beelined it over to the desk, hooked the phone, and punched in Stevie's number, and—

Disconnected before any ringing.

I wasn't ready for this.

Get an answer I hoped to hear, wanted to hear, that'd free me (maybe) and (maybe) let me get on with my life, and Stevie—

Stevie. Stevie what? Stevie, so what?

Sleep on it, Neil, I told myself.

I stopped breathing, like I was doing it on a learner's permit, settled at the desk and ran my messages.

There was nothing urgent, nothing important, nothing that couldn't wait. (Nothing from Stevie.) No Augie telling me he'd heard from Ari Landau or Zev Neumann, or a call from them direct.

I brought over the remains of a turkey sandwich and a few more Buds from the fridge, lining the cans within reach, and after a fast check of e-mail full of the usual usual, zeroed in on writing my column about Kline. After about ten minutes, I saved and stored some graphs I'd done about the Kleinschmick family collection, the Nazis and the missing Morisot, deciding it would be better to first get some answers out of Ari and Zev. I ripped into a new lead about Kline's career and was filtering in some of the anecdotes he'd shared, like the one about David Opatoshu, and some polite, noncommittal remarks about *Pencey Prep*, where *"the farts are smarter than the stu-dents / A gang of whom get to sleep at night with lewd-ents,"* I think the lyrics went.

No ghost of Larry Hart walking the halls of the Globe.

As an act of generosity and all due respect for Maurice Kline, I didn't call the show a stinker.

The column a wrap, I uploaded it to the *Daily*, eased up from the computer with a firm grip on my last live brew, and padded over to my *Casablanca* poster, an original I've had for years; Paul Henried still listed above the title, an equal with Bogie and Bergman.

Lifting the can in toast to the enduringly irresistible object of his affection, I said—what else?—

" 'Here's looking at you, kid.' "

My drowsy eyes played nasty tricks on me, transforming the beauty in the slouch-brimmed hat into Stevie, then into Maryam; maybe it was Maryam first, then Stevie, as if my confusion wasn't already on par with a duffer unable to dig out of a sand trap.

I moved over to the couch and stretched out, snapped on the TV, and found myself in the middle of *A Place in the Sun* on AMC, the one movie where Liz Taylor wasn't more beautiful than her leading man.

Good thing I know how the George Stevens classic ends, because I was a goner long before Monty Clift sent Shelley Winters to sleep with the fishes; totally disoriented when the phone rang, waking me; surprised to see the time when I managed to find it on the desk.

Almost noon.

"Yeah?" My voice in need of a good gargle.

Nothing coming back at me.

I figured it for one of those boiler-room pitchmen who had misplaced his finger on the sucker list and didn't know who'd answered, until—

After another moment—

"Mr. Gulliver?"

Not a voice I knew.

"Says who?"

"Mr. Neil Gulliver?"

"You go first, but I already have enough of whatever it is you're selling."

Only line noise for a moment or two.

"Mr. Rosenstock said you'd be expecting this call? To hear from me? Mr. Theodore Rosenstock? I'm to review and authenticate a Warhol suite you have an interest in selling, on behalf of Mr. Theodore Rosenstock and a certain client of his, yes?"

That pulled me out of my lethargy.

We arranged to meet.

Augie said, "You lose your mind, kiddo?" Nothing in his tone to suggest the question was rhetorical. "Fortunately, I have the time today to help you find it again."

"I can handle the situation, Augie. I'll be packing," I said.

He made a noise that sounded like a water main bursting in my ear.

"Packing to leave town—that, I wouldn't mind as much as you getting ready to take on this bad guy."

I said, "If he is a bad guy."

"And if he is a bad guy, maybe he'll also be packing? And bad guys are known to get off the first bang, especially if the other guy doesn't know for sure he's the bad guy. For example, this guy on his way over to your place?"

"He won't be coming upstairs. Guard at the front desk will know to point him to the conference room and have him wait there. Too public for any funny tricks. Besides, if he is a bad guy, he'll want his hands on the Warhols before he makes a move."

"And, of course, I have the Warhols here."

"Where I'll be bringing him. Safety in numbers, Augie. The reason I got off the horn with him and on the horn with you. So you can be prepared."

"Thank you. Spoken like a true Boy Scout, one who's got a lousy memory. I'll remind you what you heard from Ari and Zev, about the danger you and Stevie are in because—"

"They said they didn't know a Theodore Rosenstock, not that he posed a threat."

"If your life's in danger the way they described, everyone poses a threat, kiddo. You said he's due there how soon?"

"I told him to make it an hour and a half. Time for me to jog, shower and dress."

"Don't forget to put on a clean pair of shorts. Nobody should ever get shot in dirty underwear. I'll be over in an hour."

"Augie, no. That's not—"

"An hour, Braveheart. I'll have the Warhol portfolio with me. Ari and Zev, I can get hold of them."

"Augie, damn it!"

"You'll find me waiting in the conference room. I'll also be packing."

Augie was right about me playing Boy Scout.

I trooped downstairs to the conference room early, to prepare for the possibility that Theodore Rosenstock's man might be a threat.

Be prepared—the Scout motto.

Words to live by.

The room is at the north end of the lobby and accessed from the lobby or through a door off the corridor that leads past ground-floor apartments to one of the building garages. It's L-shaped and small, room for a meeting table that seats ten and a study round for four. The board of directors meets here, and Heathcliffe tenants can reserve it for a small fee or try for it on a nonexclusive, potluck basis.

It was vacant.

There hadn't been enough time for Augie to make the drive cross-town.

I'd brought with me two hastily hand-printed *Reserved* signs and a roll of tape and posted them on both entrances. Next, set myself up in a seat that put my back to the wall, with sightlines to the doors and a window view to the patio and pool; a few meaningless files for show; jacket draped over the chair.

My Beretta in a pocket, easy to get at.

I'd be planting Augie in the end seat to my left, for a clear view of the two doors and my guest, whom I'd invite to take the seat directly across from me.

If Augie was packing, it would likely be the pocket-sized Colt Bisley six-shooter with the rubber handle and three-inch barrel he always swore was the one carried by Bat Masterson up to the day in 1921 the old lawman slumped over dead from a heart attack in the sports department of the New York *Morning Telegraph*, pen in hand, halfway into his next column.

If Rosenstock's man was less than legitimate—

My Plan A: First false move the guy makes, we have him covered.

My Plan B: The guy jumps to his feet, does a fast turn, and makes a run out the door—

Okay, so he could do that.

He did that, there was a chance of his getting away.

Okay, so maybe it would be better to sit Augie and his Bisley Colt next to the guy, so he could jam the six-shooter in the guy's ribs if the guy jumped or tried any other funny business.

Maybe lock the corridor door, so the guy couldn't use that for his getaway.

Maybe, instead of my sitting and waiting in here, take a lookout-post lobby seat, size up the guy as he goes by me, and have him covered front and back from the get-go.

Or, I'm in the conference room and Augie is out in the lobby, or—

Where's a Plan C when you really need one?

I walked over to the window and worked over scenarios while studying the UCLA student bodies lounging around the pool in swimsuits inspired by nudity, under a sky once more torn between sunshine and showers, although the temperature seemed to have settled in the comfortable mid-sixties. They didn't look like that in my year as a Bruin, especially the coed in the water who seemed to be doing a breast stroke without moving her arms.

"Excuse me."

The words jarred me around.

The guy standing just inside the doorway was a Brooks Brothers type in a rich blue pinstripe with timeless lapels, a dignified tie, luminous black patent leather Oxfords and a mustache to match. His left shoulder slightly tilted from the weight of his satchel, the kind doctors carried when they still made house calls.

"I'm here for our meeting?" he said, putting a question mark to it.

"Yes, come in," I said, forcing a smile and trying not to let him see me structuring a new plan, and—

Where the hell was Augie?

He settled the satchel on the table and checked his watch.

"I'm a little early," he said.

I walked over to him and threw out my hand.

He took it. Thick hand. Strong grip.

"Neil Gulliver," I said.

"Yes, you are," he said, like he was making a little joke. The edge of a grin tilting at his mustache. "Donald Whittemore, but please, not Don." He released my hand. "How is this one?" he said, pointing to the seat I also had chosen for him.

"Run of the table," I said.

He sat down, arms resting on the table, fingers laced, and said, "You brought it?" looking doubtfully at my files.

"My associate. He's on his way with it." I checked my watch. "He should be here any minute."

Not Don's expression turned fleetingly sour.

"I understood it would just be two of us."

I gave him a look and gestures that added up to *It's news to me*, moved around the table and settled down on my chair.

"Well, let's get started, if you don't mind," he said, like I had no choice.

He snapped the locks on his case and dug a hand blindly into it, like he knew where to find what he was reaching for.

I tried to hide the panic starting to build as I dipped into my jacket pocket and eased the Beretta onto my lap, aimed at Not Don out of sight under the table.

Be prepared.

Something to say for the Scouting movement.

"Mr. Rosenstock spoke highly of you," I said. "He said you're quite an authority on Warhol."

Not Don gave me a strange look.

"Who?"

"Mr. Rosenstock."

"Who's Mr. Rosenstock?"

What kind of game was Not Don playing here?

Before I had a chance to answer, Augie appeared like a genie, stepped up to Not Don, and pressed his Colt Bisley against the back of Not Don's head.

"Keep that hand where I can't see it," he said. "Don't do anything stupid or you'll learn how the pop-top on a can feels."

Not Don's eyes became the size of headlamps.

He shouted at me, "Jesus Christ! This is supposed to be a friendly pre-divorce conference, your client and mine! Get him away from me!"

"What?"

I brought my hand up from under the table, exposing the Beretta as the corridor door opened and a woman stepped into the room.

Attractive, rail-thin, the haggard look that comes from the wrong kind of dieting. I recognized her as a homeowner who was always showing up at the annual meeting with complaints, usually about some area that needed painting, re-roofing, fresh carpeting, but always voting with the group against assessments that would make that kind of work more possible.

She saw the Beretta and gasped.

Saw Augie's Colt Bisley denting Not Don's head.

Raised her open hands in front of her face, palms out, and screamed, "My god! What he gone and put somebody up to! A killer! A hired assassin!"

Swooned and sank to the carpet.

Her alarm blew onto Not Don's face. He fell forward, his head hitting the table with a thud and a crunch that sounded like his nose breaking, confirmed in a few seconds when blood started leaking onto the walnut.

Augie, who had been momentarily frozen by the confusion, dropped his gun hand, stepped to one side, and leaned over to assess the status of Not Don, at which point—

Earlier Bogus, the security guard on duty, dashed into the room and captured Augie from behind in a wrestling grip. Earlier is a large man in his mid-thirties. He lifted Augie off the floor effortlessly, wheeled him around, and slammed him against the wall, causing Augie to drop the Colt Bisley.

Earlier released Augie, swooped after the six-shooter, calling, "Don't you worry none, Mr. Gulliver. All's gonna be safe and under control!" Rose and pointed it at Augie, whom he's seen hundreds of times and now recognized. Froze in bewilderment as—

Ari Landau and Zev Neumann bounced into the room, one from each doorway, both with weapons drawn, matching Glocks, aiming them at Earlier and the unconscious Not Don, warning both against any false moves.

Zev almost tripping over the homeowner.

Ari looking at Augie for an answer of some kind.

Augie turning and doing the same with me.

Me, shrugging, and a confession: "I didn't know the room was already reserved."

"Hello?"

A half-familiar voice to go with the stranger who was half in and

half out of the conference room—his concerned eyes going in several
directions at once-asking in a voice short of alarm, "Mr. Gulliver? Mr.
Neil Gulliver? Or maybe this is the wrong place?"

Some guy materializing behind him, wondering, "You Mrs. Stork's
lawyer, the one I'm meeting here?"

17

By the time everything and everyone was sorted out, all egos appeased, all threats of litigation erased, Mrs. Stork and her lawyer revived and mollified, the lawyer's nose set by a Fire Department team of paramedics summoned by Earlier Bogus, Mr. Stork's lawyer gone off to find his client, and Augie through reassuring everyone that prayer and meditation would see them through this day and all other troubled times, Ari and Zev had spirited off Rosenstock's man, who was still in a modest state of confusion, upstairs to my apartment, with my blessing and my spare key.

The three of them were in the living room, engaged in conspiratorial conversation, when Augie and I got there. I had to cough to get their attention.

Ari looked over his shoulder and said, "Come in, come in, come in," like this was his place. "Come meet and shake hands with Bernie

Berkelly and hear what the gentleman knows about Andy Warhol . . . Everything."

He turned to Zev, who agreed. "Everything."

Ari said, "Not just about Warhol's art. Those movies. Warhol's magazine. Warhol's people, those that mattered and all the hangers-on."

"Everything," Zev said.

"Like he wrote the book," Ari said, pumping his head.

"Matter of fact, I did," Berkelly said. "The definitive study. *The World According to Andy—Ours and Others*. It's in all the libraries, and they're always running out of copies at MOMA."

He got up from the couch, looking ready to take a bow.

"You ever want to check my reviews on the Internet, it's Berkelly with two *l*'s"—spelling out his last name—"although it's pronounced same as the famous old dance guy from movies."

"Busby Berkeley," I said.

"Yes. Berkeley spelled it B-e-r-k-e-l-e-y. With three *e*'s, but only one *l*."

Augie said, "I already know you. From somewhere. We've met before."

Berkelly's face said he wasn't as certain.

He tugged at a tie as conservative as his black suit.

Ari shifted in his side chair and said, "A book we came to know, Zev and I, as our own interest in Mr. Warhol's work developed. The best of its kind."

"None better," Zev said.

Berkelly beamed.

"Only, nowhere in its pages a mention of the portraits suite, not even in the current twelfth edition," Ari said, lathering his words and a hand gesture with astonishment.

"Which is pretty amazing, don't you think?" Zev said.

Ari agreed, and he turned and gave Bernie Berkelly a hopeful look.

"A reason for that," Berkelly said anxiously, like he feared having his credentials revoked.

I said, "That reason being?"

"I'm an historian, sir. I deal in authenticated facts, not rumors—all the portraits suite has been to me up until now, rumor, and still a rumor until I can see it and verify the prints with my own eyes. Once that's in place, if the suite's in fact genuine, it will most certainly be given its deserved due in the next, revised edition of *The World According to Andy*."

"The dealer who sent you, Rosenstock, he and his client were treating the suite as more than a rumor," I said. "They offered me enough money for it, Rosenstock saying it had been on his client's wish list for years."

"While Mr. Rosenstock is a most private art dealer, along the lines of the great Bernhard Berenson, contemporary is not his field. Why he engaged me on behalf of his client. The offer made to you is contingent on authenticity. A client's wishful thinking, no matter how sincere, doesn't make it so."

"Of course. And who is Mr. Rosenstock's client?"

"None of my business, he made that plain. Somebody who fancies Warhol's work, can afford the luxury of indulging in art purchases at today's inflated prices, and also knew of the rumor. And—who's willing to pay the premium for my services. I don't exactly work for poverty wages, I might point out."

Berkelly paused and seemed inclined to take another bow before advising, "I still don't know exactly what your two friends here are all about." Gave once-overs to Ari and Zev. "Your firearms? That frightening scene downstairs?"

"Private security," Ari said, improvising. "Specialists in fine-art security. We were called in by Mr. Gulliver this morning to stand guard over the Warhols while they're out in public. Even inside a secure building like this one, one cannot be too safe or too careful, can one?"

"Anywhere in the fifty United," Berkelly said, giving the ceiling a wide-eyed grimace. Turning his attention to Augie. "You? Also security?"

Augie, who had been studying Bernie Berkelly all this time, said, "I give the young man here spiritual security. He also entrusted the care and feeding of the Warhol suite to me."

"I'm born-again, myself," Berkelly said. "So—about the Warhols? You can see how anxious I am to get my first look at these 'rumors'."

When Berkelly spoke, his squeaky-clean voice hardly rose above a whisper—almost as if he were afraid of being heard—certainly never as high as he was tall. He was six, six and a half feet tall, gangly, and half the time seemed to be missing elbow and knee locks; the Scarecrow on leave from the Tin Man and the Cowardly Lion.

I figured him to be in his early to mid-fifties, although he had a youthful cast to his face, from good genes or a great plastic surgeon. There were no wrinkles or laugh lines on his tightly drawn pale skin. Horn-rimmed specs and a blond rug made him look a bit like Warhol.

"The box is locked in the trunk of my car," Augie said. "Would you like me to get them now?"

Augie feigning saintly innocence, like he needed somebody's permission.

Ari said, "Zev, you go ahead with him while I'm holding down the fort here."

"Your dining table over there should do me just fine," Berkelly said, leaning over for his attaché case. He got up and headed for it, suggesting, "Let's just double-check the surface to be certain it's clean and neat, shall we?"

The latest white-gloved inspection of the Warhol suite didn't take long.

Berkelly roamed the dining table like a border guard, stopping long enough at each of the silk-screen prints to warrant something was to his satisfaction with a "Yuh," sometimes a "Yuh, yuh," but otherwise sharing no clue to his thoughts. After the first three or four passes he began moving more quickly.

After about a half hour, he put aside the Sherlock-sized magnifying glass with its built-in light that he had pulled from his attaché case. He straightened up and arched his back, a palm against his lower spine, and worked out a kink before turning to face us.

"My understanding was there might be twelve prints, not the eleven here," Berkelly said, directing the comment at me.

"What you see is what I got."

"Not holding back, then?"

I shook my head.

"From the sound of it, I take it they're legitimate Warhols," I said.

"Reminiscent taken part by part of other print works in Andy's oeuvre. Taken as a whole, distinctively original in design and intent. Are they legitimate Warhols?" He held on to the answer like a miser hording gold. Finally, letting a smile tease his mouth, "That's my expert belief, and you can go to the bank on it. In fact—"

Berkelly nursed the prints back into the presentation box.

He tossed his cotton gloves into his attaché case and took out two sealed envelopes. They both had my name typed on the face, one followed by the numeral 11, the other by a 12.

He double-checked the numerals, returned the one with the twelve to his case.

"Mr. Rosenstock instructed me to hand this over to you if I determined the suite to be authentic. I'm to tell you that it contains the purchase amount he discussed with you. A certified check. Payment in full."

"What's in the other envelope?"

"Also a certified check. A pro rata higher amount. I was told to give it over if there were twelve prints, not eleven, and for you to consider it a bonus."

"I get the check and you leave with the suite."

"Yes. Of course."

Something didn't feel right about this.

The transaction sounded too easy.

That, but also something I didn't have a handle on.

Not yet, anyway.

Chalk up my reaction to a newspaperman's instinct built on twenty years of understanding that anytime a silent siren goes off it means the lyrics being sung don't match the tune being played.

I said, "If I want to think it over again? Let Rosenstock know in a day or two?"

Berkelly recoiled from the question.

"Why would you want to do that? I was led to believe either amount was more than generous. More than what you might expect to realize at auction."

"How much would that be?"

He averted his eyes while he thought about it.

I said, "If the prints in the suite are what you say—'distinctively original in design and intent'—I would guess they're worth more than the hundred thousand dollars in the envelope."

"Two hundred thousand," Berkelly said, at once looking at me like he wanted to withdraw the correction.

I'd caught him.

I'd remembered Rosenstock saying dollar figures were nothing his man had to know about. Always the possibility, of course, Berkelly had played peekaboo with the envelopes.

"Oh, right." I tapped my temple. "Not one, but two hundred thou."

Berkelly seized on my response with a smile about as real as a hooker's orgasm.

"I have them, too, those moments, so I absolutely know what you mean," he said. "But take my word for it, the two hundred thousand is a fair price, especially considering it comes without deductions. No auction-house commission, what you'd be losing going to a Christie's or a Parke-Bernet. And, moreover, the check is made out to you personally. How you cash it, what you do afterward with the money, is up to you alone. Mr. Rosenstock has no reason to tell tales out of school to the IRS, nor does his client."

"Who is?"

"I already told you I don't know, but I've run into my share of these collectors who know their way around the tax bites far better than us, Mr. Gulliver. I doubt he would have a desire to call undue government attention to himself or his cash-flow sources."

"Five hundred thousand," I said.

"What?"

"Five hundred thousand to me and you take the Warhols out the door."

I turned my back on him and looked over to Augie, Ari and Zev.

They were out of hearing range in the living room, so didn't quite know what to make of my wink.

After another moment, Berkelly said, "Even if I had any authority to negotiate or permission from Mr. Rosenstock to hand over both checks, there would be a shortfall of half what you're now asking." He threw up his hands.

"Cash and carry, Mr. Berkelly. Name of the game. Let's call Mr. Rosenstock and see what he says, how about that?"

Berkelly slowly grew a foot taller and began to seethe with indignation.

"I'm not a bank, sir. No matter what his answer would be, that's not my role here. Make your call or do what you have to do, and good luck to you."

Berkelly was out of my place in another minute, like the Scarecrow flopping along the Yellow Brick Road, barely pausing to grumble a brusque, insincere "Thank you" to me, an equally brisk nod goodbye to Augie, Ari and Zev.

Zev and Ari exchanged glances.

Zev rose from his chair and followed after Berkelly.

I headed over to explain what had happened between us.

When I'd finished, Ari said, "Your instincts served you well here, Neil. Berkelly's reaction, absolutely no surprise under the circumstances and all things considered."

"And they're also serving me now . . . What do you know that you haven't told me yet, Ari?"

"Very, very sharp," Ari said to Augie; then, to me: "The real reason he may not have been so anxious to call Theodore Rosenstock is because Mr. Rosenstock's dead. The police fished him out of the East River on Saturday."

My heart qualified for the Olympics in the long jump.

"Therefore," Ari continued, "it stands to reason the man calling himself Bernie Berkelly was not Bernie Berkelly, or he wouldn't have gotten on a plane yesterday and flown to L.A., unless he had an ulterior motive. The story was on all the local news. He would know his client was dead."

"Who is he, then?" I said.

Augie, quiet until now, said, "Whoever he is, I know I knew him from somewhere. Trust me, I'll figure it out."

Ari gave him a *Why not?* gesture.

"My guess, I had to guess? Rosenstock's mysterious collector and maybe the reason Rosenstock's no longer with us. Maybe also the man in the missing twelfth print. Any luck, Zev'll be coming back to us with the answer. Until then, the danger I spoke to you about, Neil—it seems to have come closer to you than ever."

Already, my concern wasn't for me.

"Stevie," I said.

Ari understood. "I don't think so. This person knows the Warhol suite is with you, so, if anywhere, he is more likely to return here." He looked past me, motioned me to turn. "In fact, here he is now."

Bernie Berkelly was back, Zev Neumann alongside him, giving Berkelly directions with his Glock.

Zev marched Berkelly back into my apartment and pushed him onto a counter stool. We joined him, and at once he and Ari began making out like badass actors in an RKO film noir classic. The two Bobs, Mitchum and Ryan, playing NYPD detectives in from the Big Apple specifically to find Berkelly.

Berkelly stuck to his story until Ari and Zev wore him down through innuendo and outright threats, playing the good-guy–bad-guy game about what he could expect by his complicity in what was clearly a case of first-degree murder.

Ari and Zev invented scenarios about life in prison that had Berkelly ticking fear like a time bomb until, finally—

It reached the point where he began boiling with fear, bubbling over with answers that convinced all of us Berkelly was who and what he claimed and had innocently fallen into a sour situation beyond his full understanding.

Yes, Berkelly said, he knew Rosenstock was dead.

Yes, he said, he knew who Rosenstock's buyer was.

Yes, he knew how much the certified checks were for, he said, his voice a whine on the verge of a breakdown.

How? Ari and Zev asked when Berkelly stopped to catch his galloping breath, making a finger canopy over his heart, as if to prevent it from leaping out of his chest.

The buyer had told him, he said, his mouth twitching to a rhythm set by his eyes and their Saint Vitus's dance.

"He called," Berkelly said. "The phone rang and I heard this voice I didn't know asking to speak with me and I said I was me. He said, 'The one who is employed by Mr. Theodore Rosenstock?' 'Yes,' I said, 'that Bernard Berkelly.' I could tell he already knew, though, because he'd called me on my private, unlisted number."

"When was this?" I asked quietly, after Berkelly landed his beggar's expression on me.

"Sometime Sunday morning is what I remember. After mass. I don't remember if it was before or after I turned on *Meet the Press*. I was already reading the Sunday *Times*, the 'Arts' section. I always devour the 'Arts' section first."

I gave him a friendly, *Doesn't everyone?* look and said, "Did you know by then that Mr. Rosenstock was dead?"

He pulled his face into a pained expression and said, "I don't think so. I think he asked me the same question, and I thought he was joking at first. It hadn't been too long before that I'd visited with Mr. Rosenstock, only the day before. I collected the envelopes with the checks from him, and we talked about me flying here to Los Angeles the next day, on Sunday, if the weather cleared up. So, all of that was set and I was already packed to go. I always pack the night before. Saves a lot of last-minute racing around."

I said, "Who is he?"

The concept of answering seemed to frighten him until Zev raised a growl in his throat.

"His name is Rudy Feather."

Ari and Zev exchanged split-second glances and shrugs to match. Ari said, "From?"

"South Carolina," Berkelly said. "Myrtle Beach, South Carolina."

Ari glanced at Zev, who nodded and retreated from the room, a cell phone materializing in his hand before he passed out of sight.

Ari continued his interrogation, asking, "What else do you know about this Rudy Feather?"

Berkelly's head began twisting like a drive chain had broken. "Nothing. Not a thing. Not before then."

"And after 'then'?" This from Augie.

"After, he asked me if it was correct I had the checks from Mr. Rosenstock. Et cetera. Et cetera. He asked me to go to Los Angeles anyway. To meet here with Mr. Gulliver. See the Warhols and, if I determined they were authentic, make the offer to his specifications. Fly the suite to him in Myrtle Beach."

"And if I rejected the offer?"

"Mr. Feather doubted that you would. In fact, he was quite confident you'd jump at either figure."

"He say why?"

"He said you had a gambling habit and probably owed a lot of money. That you'd jump at the chance to pay off your debts."

Ari gave me a questioning look.

"Years ago," I said, throwing a hand at the air. Then, to Berkelly, "And you didn't think twice about obliging his request, this Rudy Feather? That maybe he wasn't all he was making himself out to be?"

"Mr. Feather offered to double what Mr. Rosenstock was paying me," Berkelly said. "Hard to turn down, wouldn't you say so? In fact, impossible."

"And no doubt in your mind that Feather meant it, that it was a sincere offer?"

"First of all, Mr. Gulliver, I had in my possession two checks which were made out to cash. Even if you got one, that still left one for me as a good-faith deposit."

Zev had returned.

He called us into a huddle in the hallway, outside Berkelly's hearing.

"Feather checks out," Zev said. "A collector, and richer than milk that comes straight from the cow. Wealthy enough to buy all the Warhol suits and probably all the paintings in them."

Ari said, "One of the eleven collectors in the suite we haven't put a name to yet?"

"Maybe. Maybe even our twelfth man. Only got a phone description so far, so no way of knowing for sure. I think we should head to Myrtle Beach and have a look. What do you say?"

Ari thought about it for a few moments.

"I got a better idea," he said, throwing a thumb at me. "Gulliver here goes to Myrtle Beach, checks him out for us. Fewer suspicions raised than strangers in town, poking around and dropping Feather's name."

"Like Gulliver has to personally deliver the suite?"

"Yes, but only if Feather is ready to raise the ante to half a million. Payment in full and in front."

"If Feather rejects the deal?"

Ari turned to me and said, "Neil, you're a betting man. What's your bet?"

"Once was . . . He's rich enough and he seems to want it bad enough to at least want to negotiate."

"My reasoning exactly," Ari said.

"But he'll want to do it with Berkelly," I said. "His identity's supposed to be kept a secret, remember?"

"So we have Berkelly call and report, tell him that's the deal-breaker for you," Ari said.

Augie said, "Berkelly is falling apart over there. He slips up and then what?"

Ari said, "Don't be so sure, Augie."

He motioned for us to stay where we were and, with Zev, went back to Berkelly, smiled amiably. Said something in his ear and after a minute had Berkelly smiling back at him.

Berkelly dug into his attaché case for a small leather-covered binder and flipped pages until he found what he was looking for.

Pulled over my counter phone and dialed.

Moments later, was deep into a conversation that lasted five or six minutes.

He hung up the phone, clearly pleased with himself, and exchanged a few more words with Ari and Zev before Ari gave Berkelly a generous pat on the shoulder and headed back over to Augie and me.

"Feather told him the half million you're asking is not impossible. And yes, he'll meet with you there to finish up the deal. Berkelly goes, too, to verify that the Warhols are the Warhols and to collect his bonus."

"If I'm going to Myrtle Beach, I'll be more comfortable without Berkelly. He were to do or say the wrong thing, like mention you and Zev, and—"

Ari stopped me with a gesture.

A hint of a smile dug into his cheeks.

"I had Berkelly throw that in. It sounded right that he would ask, but I agree with you, Neil." Turning to Augie, he said, "Augie, you still a good actor, like I remember?"

Augie made a scoffing noise and said, "Better than your memory, Mr. Landau."

Ari said, "Mr. Gulliver, meet Mr. Bernard Berkelly."

18

The hospital ward didn't get many visitors, maybe three or four since the cop and the actress, Stevie Marriner, had made small talk over him on—

What day?

How long ago?

The orderly said it was . . . that was—

Was it on Sunday?

What he said when Clegg finally drifted out of a tunnel that sometimes seemed to have no end to it, no bright light enticing him forward, and managed to stay awake long enough to wonder where he was, how he got there, and take down some warm, clear broth before taking the needle that let him sink again into the welcome black miasma and relief from the kind of ceaseless pounding he imagined lighthouse rocks took from an angry sea.

Sunday, yes.

And, today was—

Monday. (Only Monday?)

And Clegg was hearing the cop again, only this time she wasn't with the actress. He recognized the other voice, too. It belonged to Tom Bakersfield, sounding genuinely dismayed as he told her, "Yes, that's him, all right. Matthew. Matthew Vaughan."

He feigned sleep, trying to catch what they were saying over the incessant chanting going on all day from one of the nearby beds. It was oppressively loud and unintelligible, a kind of foreign-language mumbo jumbo he was powerless to do anything about, except endure it as part of his pain.

"An art appraiser, you said?"

"More of an authenticator," Bakersfield replied. "Mr. Vaughan came by to check out one of the Lowy sachet prints we published. I can't believe this occurred, but it's not a total surprise, given what the area's turned into. Bums all over the place nowadays. One hell of a way to run a city . . ."

"Still, Mr. Vaughan is a lucky one, sir. Whoever it was that struck him from behind, stripped him of his valuables, and drove off in his rented vehicle was no doubt running low on energy and in need of a bag or a bottle. Only a bit more force with the lead pipe he used and Mr. Vaughan would have been a goner or at best a vegetable . . . Other people in some of the beds not as lucky as he is, this being baseball season."

"Baseball season?"

"Fall and spring, the Department thinks of them as 'the baseball seasons,' when most trauma injuries we're called out on result from baseball bats, pipes, pieces of lumber. When it's summer and people are dressing lighter than air we see more stabbings. Winter and more clothing, we know to expect more gunshot wounds . . . Often, during the baseball season, the head battering bloats the head so large that the head won't fit onto the scanner when the docs take the victim down for an MRI."

"Absolutely fantastic," Bakersfield said, loud enough to drown out the mumbo jumbo.

"So, he's lucky, Mr. Vaughan is, really lucky," the cop said; then ended a long pause by asking, "The Lowy whatever-it-was you were telling me about before, sir?"

"One of his sachet prints."

"Valuable?"

"Quite valuable. Grows in value every year. Why?"

"Valuable enough to make Mr. Vaughan want to carry a weapon?"

"To some collectors, I suppose. Was he?"

"Found in the Dodge Mr. Vaughan rented when it was gone through at impound. Other things, too, but not a permit for a concealed weapon. We'll want to talk to him about the gun whenever he pulls out of this. Questions that could use some answers."

"Like what?"

"Police matters, routine, nothing I need to bother you about," she said, making it sound unimportant.

Clegg knew better.

Clegg knew what questions, as well as he knew he had to get away from here before they could be asked, but—

It had become a losing struggle to stay awake.

Clegg fell back asleep.

At once, he caught the tail end of his last nightmare.

Like he was a stranger to himself, Clegg watched as a Nazi in uniform clubbed him from behind, stripped him naked and dragged him unconscious to the ovens. Laughing over his prostrate body and hooting, "A nice shower for you and soon you will be as clean as you can possibly ever want to get."

Clegg thought the screams were his, and maybe some of them were, the noises that accompanied his waking up, still fresh in his mind the picture of him standing naked in the showers and watching the big spigot-heads rain down gaseous white clouds of death instead of the water he felt covering his body like a wet outer layer of flesh.

"Okay, you relax now, Mr. Vaughan," he was being told a minute or two later, by the orderly hanging over his bed and patting his shoulder through the thin blanket. "Just a small problem elsewhere," he said. His voice was as rich as fresh cream, calming against a rush of noises, urgent commands and a cavalry of feet clumping and squeegeeing back and forth at about where the mumbo jumbo had been coming from.

Clegg eased open his eyes and looked up at the orderly, whose benign smile overrode a pebbled olive complexion on a chiseled face that would have looked ominous encountered on some L.A. side street.

The orderly said, "Let's get us some dinner and don't you worry none," and elevated the bed into a half-sitting position. He wheeled the service table into place alongside the bed, settled onto the visitor's chair, and in a moment was spoon-feeding Clegg a clear broth that didn't smell or taste like the last bowl; more of an egg flavor to it this time, laced with what might be noodle particles.

Clegg found his voice and asked, "What was the racket?" Surprised by how whispery he sounded, like helium escaping from a balloon. *Escape*, the right word, reminding him he had to get out of here and soon, preferably before the cop came back with all the wrong questions.

The orderly lowered his voice and, like he was sharing a forbidden secret, said, "Black magic down the way. Haitian as all get-out. Woman been chanting for days to raise up her husband from a head bang far worse than yours is, his having got him on the brink of brain-dead. Think she done it to him the first place, but no way of proving it.

"She's carrying on as usual, words making no sense at all, until she goes on over to the nurses' station and tells them, 'I got to exorcise him, my beloved, before it too late.' She grabs up a scissor and a letter opener and races on back to him. Before anyone can even think to stop her, she stabs the opener into the back of his neck and plunges the scissor in one a his eyes, screaming, 'Devil needs a way of escaping! Devil needs a way of escaping!' Over and over like that. What woke you on up, her screams followed by hell breaking loose, devil or no . . . Ready for another spoonful?"

Clegg opened his mouth and relished the warm broth as it played on his tongue, thinking, *Devil's not the only one needs a way out.*

Hours later, Clegg awoke drowning in sweat.

Still anxious about the cop, who had become one of the Nazis of his nightmare, and—

Desperate to get out of the hospital.

He had a plan.

It had come to him just before he freed himself of the cop's grip, elbowed past her and the other death merchants, and charged through the door held open for him by the ward orderly, who was dressed in puritan white and urging him to "Hurry up before they catch you again."

The cop leaped after him, on top of his back, locking an arm across his chest; swiftly booting aside the orderly before plunging a dagger into Clegg's neck; bringing around and raising a second dagger, aiming it for an eye; swearing at him in German, where the words meant nothing to him, but the depth of her contempt said everything.

The ward was asleep, dimly lit and quiet.

Some snoring.

A few muffled cries from the other side of the room.

No mumbo jumbo.

The aroma of fresh piss and shit blending in with the smell of disinfectant still wet on the linoleum.

Now, if he could marshal his strength and endure the head-splitting pain long enough to . . .

Clegg threw back the cover and willed himself onto his feet, managed two steps forward before the room closed in on him.

He felt himself falling and, reaching out, managed to get a grip on the footboard that swung him around, bounced him off the footboard, and broke his fall. He landed on his knees, hurting and out of breath, and stayed that way for a few minutes.

He recognized that moving too fast had caused the fall. He should have sat for a minute or so on the side of the bed before standing, to equalize the blood flow.

Clegg pulled himself back onto his feet using the footboard for support, worked one leg and then the other before he felt able enough to let go.

He waited another moment, making certain the noise of his fall had not drawn attention, then passed through the sleeper curtain to the aisle.

Most of the light illuminating the ward was centralized down the corridor to his right. The nurses' station. Casting designs of light and shadow on the ceiling. The duty nurse a broad hump of backside, using her arms and the work surface for a pillow.

Clegg moved in the other direction, stealthily, aiming for the supply closet, where the orderly had promised him he would be, waiting with street clothes, prepared to take him home with him, let him hole up there to put in the call that would quickly bring a friend in less than twenty-four hours, and—as the orderly's reward—five thousand dollars.

Cash money.

"Must be a lot of loose wires waiting to be connected in your head," the orderly had said, when Clegg broached him on the subject between spoonfuls of soup. "You here in a pauper bed and making promises like that. Unh-unh. No way."

"Two thousand."

The orderly laughed.

"What if I want five thousand?"

"Five thousand, fair enough. My friend will have five thousand dollars for you when he arrives."

Clegg saw the look imbedding itself in the orderly's eyes: greed pushing its way in front of doubt.

"Cash money?"

"Cash money." He saw doubt winning again. "I'll give you the number. You call him now. Reverse the charges. You tell him what I told you. He'll tell you it's the truth." The doubt dissipating. "What've you got to lose?"

The orderly weakening again. "Well, not like you're some prisoner here."

"Mugging victim. Just need to get out. Away."

"Bad thing to do, your condition."

"Five thousand."

The orderly trying to read through the glaze in Clegg's eyes.

Finding enough, finally, to pluck a ballpoint from his shirt pocket.

Lick the tip and say, "What's that number?"

Write it down on his palm.

The supply closet, where the orderly said it was.

Unlocked, like he said it would be.

Clegg inched the door open, halted nervously when the hinges squealed. Listened for any sense that the duty nurse was aroused. The patient snores had served as a discordant shield against possible discovery.

He stepped inside the closet and pulled the door shut behind him. His hand felt the wall, found the light switch where the orderly said it was. He snapped the lever and was temporarily blinded by the light.

The supply closet was empty. No supplies. No shelves. No clothing. A room empty of everything but the orderly's deception and—

Overhead, jutting from the ceiling—

A shower spigot.

His eyes grew wide and a noise of alarm sounded at the base of his throat.

Proof positive he'd been deceived.

Lied to.

This was no supply closet.

Clegg was back in a death room at Dachau.

And suddenly—

Casting a giant shadow from the corner where she'd been hiding—

The cop.

Smelling of evil, smelling of death, far worse than the piss and the shit smells outside—

A long-bladed dagger in both hands.

Filling the room with hyena's laughter as she leaped at him.

Clegg wanted to move out of the way, but he couldn't.

The orderly had him locked in a power grip, his hands knotted at Clegg's breastbone, Clegg's arms clamped to his sides.

Clegg screamed, felt the blackness rushing him ahead of the cop's blades, and—

Awoke to the somber light of the ward, his hands held out defensively in front of his face, drowning in sweat and fighting to catch his breath.

After a moment, aware of the nurse's presence and the expression of dread painted on her tight-lipped, bug-eyed, motherly face.

Clegg worked the words out of his mouth:

"Thousand dollars," he told her. "A thousand dollars."

When Clegg managed to open his eyes again, instead of the nurse, he saw the boss's face, and—

Fell back asleep.

Woke up again, only—

This time not in the ward.

Clegg didn't have to open his eyes to know that.

The smell, different; dusty; the odor of stale tobacco part of the thick mix being tossed around the room by an air conditioner with a rattle.

The bed, different; the angle of his body supported by pillows propped under his shoulders and neck.

No privacy curtain.

Instead, looking at flocked wallpaper, a Latin motif in pastel shades of blue and rose.

Instead, looking at wall sconces bookending a mahogany door that could be cut crystal, in a floral pattern that was dated by the 1930s.

The door swung open.

Clegg's body convulsed, anticipating a charge at him by the cop, her daggers speeding toward his throat with all the accuracy of a Cruise missile.

"About time," the boss said from the doorway. "Welcome back to the land of the living, Clegg." He put a smile into the words and headed toward him.

"Where am I?" Clegg said.

"In a better place than you were before I got to you," the boss said. He focused on Clegg's turban bandage. "What's your name?"

Clegg understood it wasn't a joke and told him.

"What's my name?"

Clegg told him.

"Sounds like your memory's all it should be," the boss said. "That's the good news . . . The bad news? Somebody else is after the Warhol suite . . . I need you back in business, Clegg, and the sooner the better."

The Casa Mañana was an old hotel behind Sunset Plaza Drive, on one of those half-hidden, circular streets that began and ended below the Strip, on Franklin Avenue.

It was built in the late twenties and quickly became a local overnight resort for movie stars who needed a place to bring the temporary loves of their life.

It kept its well-deserved reputation for discretion and privacy throughout the thirties and forties, fell from vogue sometime in the late fifties, but was discovered by the rock world in the mid-sixties and earned its way back among those who wanted someplace out of the way for their dalliances.

It was where the boss always stayed when he was in Los Angeles. The rockers had no clue to who he was and the Casa was sufficiently removed from the art world to give him the absolute privacy he coveted whenever he was working out one of his deals.

Then and now the place had an unlisted switchboard and a cash-only, pay-in-advance policy that broadened its profit margin and narrowed evidence of residence should the police or other guardians of law and order or contemporary morality come snooping.

Even the parking lot was hard to spot, behind a duplex two lots away that looked like it had been ready for a teardown thirty years ago.

Equally invisible behind three walls of thick shrubbery that disguised the high wall of faded brick and razor wire was the small patio where Clegg listened carefully as the boss started bringing him up-to-date.

Sitting in a shaded corner where he had been wheeled by the full-time male nurse the boss had hired, Clegg tried not to be distracted by the half dozen topless starlet types who were catching sun around the kidney-shaped pool while their potbellied, skinny-legged benefactors lazed on the sundeck mumbling into their cell phones.

It had been only a day since the boss sprang him from the hospital, but just the change in scenery had put Clegg closer to feeling better physically, almost back to normal, enough so that he was experiencing a welcome throb between his thighs as he watched the starlets stroke themselves with sunscreen and bring their nipples to full attention.

How long since he'd been laid?

Too long, longer than his dick, and just recognizing that informed Clegg he needed to get back to work. A fuck, always the reward he allowed himself after taking care of business.

Had it been that way when the wife and kids were around?

He tried not to remember.

Shifted back into listening gear, hearing the boss talk about this Rosenstock, the dealer in New York he had to pop.

"No choice?" Clegg said.

"His decision as much as mine," the boss said. "I found he had a client for the Warhol suite, I called and inquired. He wasn't about to release the name, as if I had any need to steal a client out from under." A derisive laugh. "I went to New York and tried with him once more, in person. Rosenstock was polite, charming, but firm. When I could not find you, I made a call to a freelancer I'd used occasionally, for other things, before we ever hooked up."

"Everett?"

A curious stare. That nervous gesture of his, a forced cough into his hand, like he was firing at an insect trapped in his palm, then using his shirtsleeve to brush it away.

"I never told you who," the boss said.

"An educated guess. He'd be someone you'd be more than likely to connect with."

"Everett managed to persuade the information out of Mr. Rosen-stock and then, as his usual precaution, sent him on a submarine cruise."

One of the starlets caught Clegg mining her mint and responded by rubbing lotion from her belly button—she was an "outie"—to inside her transparent bikini triangle. She was also a shaver, so he had no way of knowing if she was a natural blonde.

He averted his eyes and said, "Everett's MO, the sub. He likes the evidence to sail away. It comes back, whenever it does, clean, especially with him as careful as he is."

"Like you. Careful. A good trait."

"You can never be too careful in that line of work. So it's the client you want me to visit?"

"If you're up to it."

"Another day, maybe, and fine. Before or after I visit with Gulliver and Marriner?"

"Put them aside for now, and I'll tell you why."

"Everett?"

"Lot bigger reason. How I came to locate you at County General." The boss shook his head, took his eyebrows to his widow's peak. "A call comes from a cop, woman, who tells me where you are and how they figured out who you are after a rental turns up in South Central, abandoned, with your bag in the backseat and paperwork that led them to Circus and Ted Bakersfield for a positive ID. Teddy gave her my number. She's nosy about the gun, the Glock the carjackers somehow missed. Asking about the coincidence of Gulliver, Marriner, coming at Teddy about Henri Godard, then you.

"I grab the first plane out. I meet with her, satisfy her questions. The Glock by explaining the value of the art you frequently have with you and did this time on behalf of the gallery. Gulliver, Marriner, as coincidence. Same stories she heard from Teddy. I get the car and your property out of the impound garage, then I get you from the hospital— before she might decide to come at you again with any questions she might have missed with me. In short, we're safer not putting you any-where near those two for the duration."

Clegg recognized the wisdom of the boss's decision.

The boss hadn't confirmed or denied he had Everett on to Gulliver and Marriner. Clegg took it as an affirmative.

He wasn't happy someone like Everett was into it, but he was not up to making that an issue. Everett was careful, for sure, but never as careful as Clegg. If something went wrong, it could lead back to the boss. To him. To the game he'd been playing with the Warhol suite on top of the game they were playing together.

Clegg was certain the leggy one with the nipple, nose and eyebrow rings was spreading them to keep his attention. Maybe she had a thing for men twice her age in wheelchairs, unlike the one stretched next to her and bearing the entire weight of Silicon Valley.

He asked the boss, "If Rosenstock is no more, why are we bothering about his client? No way he's in line anymore for the Warhols Marriner and Gulliver have."

The boss waved him off. "He is, Clegg. Before Everett got to Ro-senstock, he'd sent Bernie Berkelly—you remember him?"

Clegg made a hand-job gesture that said he did.

"He sent Berkelly here with cashier's checks from the client." He told Clegg the amounts. "There's every chance a deal's been done by now and the portfolio is gone. If so, I have that end covered by you while I follow up on this end with Gulliver and Marriner."

Clegg couldn't resist a second time. "Isn't that what you have Everett for?"

"Backup," the boss said. "Just-in-case insurance." He held on to Clegg's eyes, like that was proof of what he was saying. "There's another, more important reason to send you to see Rosenstock's client." Emphasizing the word "you," like he wanted to make certain Clegg understood his value to him.

"What reason?"

"You'll know when you get there and call on Feather," the boss said, adding a superior smile. Raised a hand like he was taking an oath.

Cocksucker, Clegg thought. *Games-playing mind-fucker.*

It was another one of those secrets the boss took joy in springing on him.

He'd hold back, then spring it, if only to remind Clegg who was in charge.

The boss recognized his reaction and seemed amused by it.

What he couldn't see was the rage under Clegg's placid exterior, held in check for now, no clue to the surprises Clegg had in store for the boss one of these days.

Better sooner than later, Clegg reminded himself, *but not before it's the right time.* With any luck, that day was not far off.

19

Nothing about Monday went as Stevie had planned.

By that evening she was seated yoga-style, warming herself in front of the wood-burning fireplace of the historic Kennedy Suite of the San Ysidro Ranch, a sprawling five-hundred-acre paradise buried in the Montecito hills outside Santa Barbara, compliments of Tony B. Tony.

He'd awakened her with his call around noon, out of breath with exuberance over what he kept referring to as his "fucking coup," which he repeatedly mispronounced with a hard *p* like he was talking about a type of car.

"I got good news like you wouldn't fucking believe good news," he said.

"Try me, Tony B. Tony."

"Our screenplay for *Nothing Sacred?*" Almost singing the words.

She laughed to herself about the "our" part, Tony B. Tony working at pulling her deeper into the project.

He said, "What would you say if I told you I got Ossie ripe to do it for us?"

"Who?"

"Ossie. Oswald Parkman. Do not tell me you never heard of Ossie. One Oscar up on me. Everybody after him. Rakes in the big bread just by script-doctoring, a hundred-fifty thou for a day's sweat. I just got Ossie's pump primed to do us a page one rewrite. You miss the big spread on him in last month's *Vanity Fair*? By Nicky Dunne. Headlined 'The Wizardry of Os.' " Tony B. Tony took a deep breath, almost sucking her ear into the phone. "*That* Ossie is who. I paid the piper and got him for you because I don't want you doubting that where Stevie Marriner is concerned I ever mean anything but first-class business all the way for Stevie Marriner. That's the whole *emmis* and nothing but the *emmis!*"

Tony B. Tony went stone quiet after that, waiting for a response.

She knew what else that kind of quiet meant in showbiz-speak.

"What's the catch, Tony B. Tony?"

He gave it a couple beats before answering her.

"Not exactly a catch. Just that if we're gonna fucking close with Ossie, we have to up and do it today."

"How high is 'up'?"

"A few hours' shlep is all. The San Ysidro Ranch. Ossie is up here the rest of the week doctoring some dialogue for something on Jerry Buck's plate at Universal. He can give us tonight and tomorrow before we lose him to some fucking film festival in the Ukraine."

"I'm busy," Stevie said. She wasn't, but she wasn't about to get pushed around or into anything. She'd been pushed enough at *Bedrooms and Board Rooms*.

"Stevie, Stevie, Stevie. Think Lombard. Think an Oscar to go with your Emmy—"

"Two Emmys."

"Two Emmys. Think Ossie Parkman. I hooked him, but its gonna take a Stephanie Marriner to reel him in. Your name was a magic wand when I waved it in his face not ten minutes ago."

"You're there now?"

"Tracked him here and here I be, superstar. Fishing for you and me. Going after the big one you deserve."

Tony B. Tony was playing to her ego and doing a good job of it. He was typical Hollywood, but he had a certain charm about him and, like so many up-from-the-street powerhouses, an endearing quality to go with his gutter language.

"I need you to close our deal, Stevie. We get Ossie in the package, think Bobby De Niro as your co-star or Pacino in the Freddie March role. Both crazy about Ossie. What major's gonna turn its back?"

"Tonight and tomorrow and that's it?"

Hesitation before Tony B. Tony said, "Maybe Wednesday."

"I have to be back here Thursday no matter what. Doing the dais for a charity luncheon at the Beverly Wilshire, for the City of Hope's breast cancer division."

No hesitation before Tony B. Tony said, "Listen, I am already pulling out my checkbook and writing out a check to them for five g."

"Tony B. Tony, you don't—"

"Done! Never let it be said Tony B. Tony doesn't know when to stand up and be counted . . . Tax-deductible, right?"

"Tony B. Tony—"

"Pack for poolside weather, superstar. The stretch'll pick you up in an hour."

Stevie had stayed at the San Ysidro Ranch a number of times, with and without Neil. It had been a favorite haunt of the Hollywood crowd since way back when, people like one of Mama's old favorites, Jean Harlow. It was where Laurence Olivier and Vivien Leigh were married. Where JFK and Jackie spent their honeymoon, here in the eighteen-hundred-dollar-a-night suite Tony B. Tony had reserved for her.

He also had champagne on ice, caviar, a fruit basket and a garden of roses waiting for her. A welcoming note to say he and Ossie Parkman would be waiting for her poolside.

Tony B. Tony, the complete entrepreneurial hustler.

She unpacked in the bedroom of two she chose to believe was the one JFK and Jackie used, slipped into a barely-there bikini and headed out after fifteen minutes on the cottage's sundeck under a cloudless, Technicolor-blue sky; sucking up her panoramic view of the Pacific Ocean and the Channel Islands; marveling at the multicolored majesty of the Santa Ynez Mountains behind her.

There was an outdoor wedding in progress in the central courtyard, everybody dressed like characters from a Jane Austen novel, even the minister, who lost his place joining the heads that turned as Stevie sashayed up a side cement trail to the pool.

Tony B. Tony had the pool to himself.

Rubber-rafting on his back.

Wearing skintight Speedos and a pair of outsized purple shades, bushels of body hair protecting him and his oiled tan from the tiring late-afternoon sun.

He gave her a high sign, then pointed her to the only other person around, a middle-aged, bare barrel-chested man in cutoffs and an Atlanta Heat cap, sitting at an umbrella table with his bare feet crossed at the ankles.

She guessed him to be in his early sixties.

A white beard and a half-drained bottle of Padron Gold at his elbow contributed to the Hemingway look she imagined he was purposely cultivating.

Stevie headed over.

It was a minute or two before he seemed to take note of Stevie's shadow falling across the sheaf of papers in front of him and script pages spread out on the table. They were full of cross-outs, insertions and indecipherable scribbles in the margin.

He looked up and peered at her above his half-moons, a question mark in his sodden red, white and blue eyes before deciding, in a trembling tenor that told her where the rest of the Padron had gone, "The Plow and Angel Bistro club with a double helping of chips, white toast, no mayo, and some of that dark imported beer with the unpronounceable name that you served me last night."

She held her temper.

"Mr. Parkman, I'm Stevie Marriner."

"Yes, yes, of course," he said.

He smiled and nodded.

Stevie smiled back.

He made an arbitrary grab for one of the script pages, turned it over, and reached after one of the thick stubbed pencils he had in a water glass. He wrote, *To Stevie, with all good wishes, Oswald Parkman.* Aimed the page at her and said, "There you are, young lady, and don't forget about the mayo. No mayo."

"No mayo," she said, answering his smile with her own, replacing it with a scowl for Tony B. Tony before she dashed away and back to the cabin.

Tony B. Tony, huffing, and puffing, his face as flaming as her temper, got there before she'd fished the key from her halter.

He bent over with his hands clamped to his knees and told her, "I can explain," the words punctuating one gasp after another.

"You mean about lying to me about Parkman to get me up here, and God knows what else you've been lying to me about? I should have known that anytime you said 'nothing sacred,' it included the truth. I am out of here, Tony B. Tony."

"Okay, so maybe a few little white lies along the way, but Ossie Parkman, not one of them." He looked up, swallowed a lot of sky, and said, "Ossie's that way when he's into his cups and you caught him into fucking everybody's cups. Look at this stuff before you say another word, okay?"

He offered her three or four pages he'd been holding.

"Please, Stevie? They're some pages Ossie worked over before you got here."

"Not interested. I'm packing and taking the limo back to L.A."

"You hate 'em, off you go. You see what I see on those pages, I want you to know there's already more of the same for the three of us to talk about later."

"Too late for later, Tony B. Tony."

Tony B. Tony raised up, shook his head and grinned at her.

"Exactly what I'd expect your character of Hazel Flagg to say in this situation," he said. "Ossie caught on to it, too, without my uttering word one. You'll see when you read the pages."

"And you read this, Tony B. Tony," Stevie said, raising a middle finger like it was the Washington Monument.

She finished unlocking the cabin door, stepped in, and closed and locked it behind her. A moment later she looked down to find the noise she'd heard was Tony B. Tony shuffling the pages under the door.

He called to her through the door, "Tonight at eight, you, me and Ossie, dinner over at the Stonehouse Restaurant. Their lobster's to die for."

Stevie threw some kindling into the fireplace, watched as the fire devoured them and grew. Picked up Oswald Parkman's script pages and read them again. Tony B. Tony had told the truth about them, the only reason she wasn't already in Los Angeles, although she wasn't entirely convinced she wanted to stay here, either.

No denying Parkman was on to Hazel Flagg and on to her. He had seamlessly matched the character to Stephanie Marriner, the same way Ben Hecht had fit Hazel to Lombard for the Selznick production, to a T.

Parkman's notations, the ones Stevie had been able to decipher, caught the private person as well as the Stevie Marriner the public usually got.

〉
〈
〉

Guesswork, or something else?

Stevie checked her watch.

A little past eight.

She hopped in and out of the shower.

Into jeans and a tank top.

Her Lambertson Truex lizard heels.

Did a marathon through her makeup and hair, which she knotted into a tight ponytail, and—

Shortly before nine had made it to the Stonehouse and was being escorted by the maître d' to Tony B. Tony's table in a see-and-be-seen location.

Parkman was with him.

They rose as Stevie approached, Parkman using the table to help elevate himself after taking a last gulp from one of two martini glasses in front of him.

He'd taken both her hands into his before Tony B. Tony introduced them, squeezing them tight, as if they connected him to a rescue rope.

"Too late now for the club sandwich, my dear girl. I've ordered the chateaubriand," he said.

Plumbed her eyes for her soul as he broke into instant laughter.

Announced loud enough for everyone in the restaurant to hear, "The only reason Oswald Parkman is here is because you are here, Stephanie Marriner." Picked up the stack of papers alongside the fine bone-china plate. Offered it to her. "You and Hazel Flagg in perfect constellation, as I knew would be so the moment this wretch dropped your *nom* and shanghaied me into service."

Tony B. Tony beamed.

So did Stevie.

She and Parkman spent the rest of dinner bonding, with Stevie trying not to be overwhelmed by Parkman's insightful remarks, how he somehow seemed to know her better than she knew herself, although they'd only just met. Not even the liquor got in the way of his depth perception.

He seemed especially pleased with the homework she had done on *Nothing Sacred*, her ability to discuss in depth the Broadway musical version from 1953, also a Ben Hecht scenario, music by Jule Styne that didn't begin to compare to most of his other work, maybe a reason the show had folded after 190 performances.

"No *Gypsy*," he said.

"No Sondheim lyrics, either," she said.

"Sondheim told me he wasn't proud of them."

"What's his opinion against the world?"

"What's yours worth, Stephanie Marriner?"

"As much as anyone's."

"Much more, I'm beginning to suspect."

Tony B. Tony said, "Wanna know what I think?"

"No," they answered him, the word locked like Siamese twins, and shared a high five.

Parkman said, "*Living It Up?*"

Tony B. Tony, not one to quit easily, said, "I'll say we are."

Again they told him to shut up, split a high five, and Stevie said, "The Martin and Lewis movie from 1954, Jerry as Homer Flagg."

"A nut, but no Hazel," Parkman said, checking closely to see if she'd caught his pun.

Stevie notched the air with her index finger.

Parkman grinned and said, "Where do you get off knowing so much about Broadway? The movies?"

"My mother. I'm living her dream. Also, my ex. One of the things we had in common when we had more in common, and since."

Parkman used both hands to motion Stevie for more and listened intently as she explained Juliet, but he seemed to drift away when she moved on to Neil. When she was finished, Parkman hid a yawn behind his fist and said, "A writer. How interesting. But, of course, not a writer like Parkman."

Stevie began to defend Neil.

Parkman laughed, allowed himself another swallow from his gin martini, stopped her with a gesture. "Even a humble screen scribe is allowed his ego, but, say, aren't you the loyal one? I like that, Stephanie Marriner. It is so—" A smile as rich as gold sprang from his beard. "So very Hazel Flagg."

She acknowledged the compliment and said, "I also know a little about novels, Ossie. Like yours, for instance."

"I'd heard that someone read one once," Parkman said. "What can you possibly know about them?"

"Before tonight, a little. Now, a little more."

"Share," he said.

Stevie made like she had a problem finding the right words, then: "They're so—so Oswald Parkman."

Parkman roared delightedly, picked up his glass and announced, "I'll drink to that!"

"And just about fucking anything else," Tony B. Tony said, again trying to worm into the conversation.

Again, they ignored him.

For as much as he drank, Parkman seemed to stay curiously sober, attentive, interested, enthusiastic and often ecstatic about some of the ideas she offered for the rewrite, as much as he was into her background, which he mined with the same kinds of subtlety she'd often seen Neil use, enticing secrets during interviews from the most close-mouthed of people.

The process lingered long into the night, took up all the next day and, when Stevie talked about having to return to L.A., an anxiety-ridden Parkman persuaded her to stay.

He stressed the importance of her helping him out—his words, "helping me out"—for at least one more day.

Verged on begging her, but with more dignity than Tony B. Tony showed.

Convinced her it would not be possible for him to flesh out Hazel Flagg's backstory otherwise.

Consequently, it wasn't until Thursday morning that the limo got her back to town, straight to the Beverly Wilshire Hotel and the City of Hope luncheon with barely an hour to spare.

She slipped in through a side entrance and found a ladies' room to straighten her outfit and freshen her makeup, shook her head to get her hair just so, and moved on to the red carpet leading to the ballroom past the media and dozens of clamoring fans begging for attention and autographs.

Took her time running the gauntlet, making certain all the camera crews and civilians were satisfied, talking up the City of Hope and the importance of breast cancer research while dodging questions about her career and the rumor that she and Tony B. Tony had become an item.

Nothing Stevie had told anybody, and nothing she'd put past Tony B. Tony or his high-octane press agents.

Finally back at the apartment, hot, sweaty and sticky, Stevie left a trail of clothing on her way to the bathroom, and within minutes was soaking in a tubful of bubbles, her eyes closed to the world.

A noise past the half-open door pulled her awake after thirty or thirty-five minutes.

It didn't fit her dream about Ossie Parkman out on a date with Hazel Flagg.

It wasn't her imagination, either, more like—

Someone settling on the bed, pushing air out of the mattress.

An intruder? Burglar?

Impossible. Not here in a twenty-four/seven security building.

Had she remembered to throw the door lock, punch in the alarm code, or was she so worn-out that she—

That sound again. Not quite, but definitely a sound.

The portable phone was within easy reach, by her towel and the new issue of *InStyle*.

The line was dead.

Battery, or . . . ?

Her .22 was in her bag, the bag on the floor, somewhere early on the trail from the door.

Shit!

Stevie slipped out of the tub, wrapped her hair in a towel turban, her body in another towel, and approached the door cautiously, edged out of sight while she tried to study the bedroom through the crack.

She saw nothing, heard nothing, only her sigh of relief a moment later, before she moved into the bedroom.

At once someone gripped her tightly from behind with a hand squeezing hard on her right breast. The other hand wielding a knife under her chin.

The man's voice, flat and dull, calmly urged her back into the bathroom, warning her not to "try anything funny," like he was reading for the Elisha Cook Jr. role in some goddamn old gangster flick.

He spun her around and out of the body towel and told her to climb back into the tub.

Stevie felt his eyes chewing on her flesh as she did so and, once she was there, he settled on the edge near enough to run her with the knife, a switchblade.

"I love the water," he said. "How about you? Any kind, but nothing beats a warm bath to sooth the savage beast that rages in all of us."

She said nothing.

He dipped in a hand and pushed a bubble wave at her.

The wave hit her in the face.

Her eyes began stinging.

She wiped at them and heard him chuckling, the kind of laugh that signaled anything but humor.

When Stevie was able to open her eyes again, she saw he was using the switch to pare his fingernails. They were long and dirty. His fingers were long, too, meaty and hairy, and he sported faded blue tattoos on his knuckles. The tattoo on his left hand read GOOD, the one on his right, the one with the knife, BEST.

Stevie averted her eyes to the toilet bowl, not wanting him to think she might be learning him for a lineup.

In the pass, she saw he was dark-haired, thick-bodied and young—maybe her age or a few years younger—and wearing a brown Eisenhower-style jacket with the Southern California Gas Company logo stitched on the pocket.

He'd caught her at it and said, "Places like this with security up the yin-yang, you tell them you're here to read the meters and it's like the keys to the city." Taking pride in his work. "Your door? A powder puff compared to some. I'd a been gone by now, before you got here, if I'd a been able to find what I'm looking for."

He said it like a question.

"See, not a quick piece of ass, if that's what you've been thinking, although yours is really something to behold. To be held . . . Like your boobs, but I suppose you're hearing that all the time."

She didn't answer him.

His words took on a grayer shade, telling her, "I get what I'm here for, I go, my way of saying thanks. You don't help me, I go taking along one of those pretty pink nipples as a souvenir. Maybe an ear. It wouldn't be any use to you anyway after I left."

"What do you want?"

"Not your autograph." He enjoyed his little joke, then turned grimmer. "You have some artwork I'm interested in. A set of prints by Andy Warhol. A gift to you that I'm hoping you'll make a gift to me, so I'll get out of your face."

It was nothing she'd expected to hear.

She couldn't help showing her surprise.

He just looked back at her blankly and said, "Where are they, the Warhols? I poked around before you got here, but I wasn't able to find them."

"Not here," Stevie said arbitrarily, feeling defiant before she recognized the stupidity of her answer.

He floated another breaker at her.

Looked up at the ceiling and shook his head.

He said, "I heard better. You tell me, or—" He leaned over and poked her forearm with the tip of the switchblade, drawing blood.

Stevie winced.

He smiled at the sound and poked her again.

"In the bedroom, where you wouldn't look unless you knew," she said solemnly, acting a truth she knew was a lie.

Step one to safety: Get out of the bathtub.

Step two: Not a clue, except—

Somehow get to the living room.

Find her bag.

The .22.

"Let's go," he said, motioning with the knife for her to get out of the tub.

"A towel."

"Like you just the way you are," he said, and winked.

He put the knife in his *GOOD* hand and ran the *BEST* one along her thigh as she rose and stepped from the tub, made a sound you'd hear from someone overdosing on whipped cream.

Stevie told herself she had nothing to lose.

She wheeled around abruptly and shoved him with both hands into the water.

Dashed through the bedroom with him splashing and screaming behind her.

Looked but couldn't find her bag anywhere, and—

No, there, on the floor by the side table. Where the hallway met the living room. Put down when she stopped to lose her heels.

She darted for the bag, had her hand prowling for the gun, when he pushed through the door into the living room, spotted her, yowled and dove for her.

Stevie tried rolling out of his way.

She wasn't fast enough.

At once he was on top of Stevie, his *BEST* hand poised to slam the switchblade into her, when—

He froze at the voice trumpeting, "Special delivery for Miss Stephanie Marriner."

Coming from behind him, at the open front door.

Stevie could see enough past him to verify it was Tony B. Tony, holding out a script for the world to see.

Tony B. Tony declaring, "And Miss Marriner should know better than leave her door unlocked. You never can—" Tony B. Tony glancing down and suddenly aware of the two of them on the floor. "Jesus fucking Christ! What the hell is going on here?"

Stevie rolled away and went after her bag and the gun again as the bastard pushed himself off her.

He raced toward the door and, when Tony B. Tony stepped in his path, pushed the switchblade deep into Tony B. Tony, who put a disbelieving look on his face as he backed against the wall and slid to the floor.

Stevie charged to the front door, ready to use the .22.

Too late.

He was gone.

She checked Tony B. Tony for a pulse.

Found it.

Told Tony B. Tony to hang on.

Jumped after a phone and dialed 911.

Watching over Tony B. Tony while waiting for help to arrive, Stevie used towels and pressure to dam the wound, careful not to budge the switchblade and possibly cause more damage.

All the while, she worked her mind through the nightmare of the last half hour, trying to figure out how the bastard knew about the Warhol suite, seemed so positive she had it. Where he figured in everything that had happened since Neil accepted the portfolio from Aaron Lodger.

That made her think about calling Neil.

The last time they spoke was Sunday, but—

So what?

She needed comforting, not that she was ready to admit as much to him.

The messages light was flashing.

Stevie hadn't played back the machine since clearing it on her way out the door to the San Ysidro Ranch.

A traffic jam of messages.

One of the last in the stack—

From Neil.

"Fats, me. Listen close. This is important. I'm down in South Carolina. In Myrtle Beach. I need you to take the Warhols and bring them down here. Get on a plane and bring them to me ASAP. It's a matter of life and death, Fats. Mine. Grab a pencil and make some notes, okay?"

20

Augie surprised me when he showed up at LAX on Tuesday looking like he'd just stepped off the eighteenth green at Hillcrest. It had been years since I saw him in anything but a cassock.

"When in Rome," he said, interpreting my look. "I hear Myrtle Beach is full of golf courses, amigo. Therefore, this outfit seemed appropriate to the journey."

He settled his overnighter on the terminal floor and modeled for me, doing a set of dainty quarter turns with his arms extended and flapping, as if he were preparing to take flight on his own, humming hoarsely what may have been "A Pretty Girl Is Like a Melody."

He ignored the stares of other passengers waiting for the gate call, except for a little girl under a mop of red curlicues, who couldn't have been more than five or six and had toddled over to giggle and grin as she awkwardly tried duplicating Augie's steps until her anxious mother swooped over and stole her back.

Augie shifted his good eye to me. It appeared full of wonder that the woman might have considered him dangerous.

I tapped my eye to suggest it probably was his eyepatch that did it. This afternoon the patch was in silly shades of red, green and blue matching the checkerboard pattern of his breeches and short-brimmed tam.

He sank into the seat next to me and said, "This bird suggests we do our talking on the course, I'm ready for him, albeit my game's a little rusty."

"Don't you think Rudy Feather would have said something about it yesterday, when Berkelly phoned him to set up this meeting?"

"Berkelly didn't call Feather to socialize."

"And we're not going to Myrtle Beach to socialize with him, Augie."

"Better start calling me Bernie," Augie said, putting a period on the subject of golf. "You wouldn't want to make a slipup in front of Feather."

Augie placed his wrist under his nose, palm down, and wiggled his fingers at the little girl.

She giggled and did the same thing back at him.

Her mother caught them at it.

Yanked the little girl's hand away.

Hurled daggers at Augie.

In exchange, he thumbed his nose at her and grumbled at me from the side of his mouth. "You see that? How rude some people are? That girl will grow up to be . . ." He had to think about it. "Mark my words, she'll grow up to be a woman."

The Delta 767 set down in Atlanta after four-plus hours of increasingly bumpy weather. The Airtrans Airways connector to Myrtle Beach lounged on the runway for almost an hour before getting an okay to take off.

More and bigger bumps for another hour.

They'd grown to roller-coaster proportions by the time we cracked the rain curtain and were on the ground, where our cabbie confirmed what the sky was already telling us.

"Storm front's building and building," he said. "Signs point to a big one coming in from the sea. Maybe not a big one like the big one they had in 1893, but a mighty big one, plenty big, providing it don't wipe itself out first."

He talked nonstop, like he was auditioning for a taxi job in New York, wheezing and coughing between sentences, wiping his mouth with the back of a hand and swapping one cigarette for another, driving a cautious ten or fifteen miles an hour along South Ocean Boulevard, blindly, window wipers barely useful against the pounding rain.

"You spot a gray man during your stay with us, better you pack your belongings and make a fast getaway," he said. "That gray man, a gray ghost hereabouts. He's sighted, and a hell of a storm for certain. Never fails. A major hurricane. Like in '93. He got seen and the storm hit the Coast the way my dear daddy hit the beach at Normandy. Hard and horrible. Wiped out everyone and everything over at Magnolia Beach, north of Pawleys Island, it did.

"You remember Hurricane Hazel in 1954? Took out most of the buildings and trees along the Grand Strand? How come we got ourselves room to build so many new and larger homes and hotels. Hurricane Hugo in 1989? That also was the Gray Man's doing, although a funny thing—anybody who sees the Gray Man of Pawleys Island firsthand is safe from actual true danger or harm, personal-like, like the Gray Man has cast his magic spell over them."

Augie leaned forward and wondered at him. "You read a lot of Stephen King, my friend?"

"Who?"

"Never mind," Augie said, pushing himself back into a corner of the seat.

The cabbie said, "Then we also got ourselves the legend about Grace Ellen Crane. I don't suppose you know about her, from way back when, her rich daddy owning the Homestead and all?"

I said, "The Homestead?"

He heard my surprise. "Oh, you do know about Grace?"

"No, the Homestead. We're meeting someone there."

"Over to Murrells Inlet?"

"Yes."

"That's the one, like a private kingdom in the middle of a marsh. Been rebuilt and then some since sweet Grace's time, when it was a fancy rice plantation. I suppose you're meeting Rudy Feather."

"Yes. What do you hear about him?"

"Less'n I know about the Gray Man. Keeps to himself, that one. Write-ups in the paper every once in so often, about him giving big bucks to this charity or another, but I don't remember ever even seeing a photograph of him."

The cabbie filled the cab with another blast of smoke and traded in his cigarette for a fresh one.

"Tell you one other thing, though," he said. "If you think you're seeing him today or probably tomorrow, you got yourselves another think coming. Definitely no way in this weather, my friends, especially not out there at Murrells Inlet. A marsh being a marsh, this weather, never no way at all."

Feather had reserved a two-bedroom suite for us at the Grand Strand Sands, an eight-story slab of glass and cement overlooking the Atlantic in the fashionable south end of the Strand. It came with guest cards giving us unrestricted use of the Olympic-size pool and assorted subsidiary pools, the coed health club and the glorified motel's self-proclaimed championship-caliber golf course.

"Gray Man weather," the clerk said while we registered, apologetically, as if it were his fault. He was eighteen or nineteen, tops, and had the eager-to-please face of someone in his first job that called for a jacket and tie.

"We've heard that," I said.

"No, please. Put away your credit cards," he said. "Mr. Feather has taken care of everything, including a VIP booth in our Club Shag Cabaret over there." He pointed to a lounge door about fifteen feet away. The signed mounted on an easel advertised: *Tonight! King Kongg and the Beach Gorillas.*

"It you're into shag dancing, no better band anywhere in the Carolinas," he said, growing more animated, like he planned to illustrate shag dancing for us when he read the puzzlement on our faces.

"Is that anything like the Lindy?" Augie asked.

The clerk said, "The Lindy?"

"Jitterbugging?" Augie said, and got the same reaction.

I advised the clerk, "You'll have to forgive my friend. He's an older person . . . 'The Twist' strike a chord with you?"

He gave me a fake smile and a courteous look that said I had forgotten to include myself in the inventory of old-timers while he handed over our computer-coded card-keys.

The message light was blipping in our suite on the top floor, a South Carolina version of a high roller's paradise in Las Vegas, overdone furniture and furnishings in a motif somewhere between gaudy and garish, with the added bonus of a powerful saltwater smell that had me feeling like a sea bass out of water.

Rudy Feather on voice mail.

Apologizing that the lousy weather made it impossible for him to personally welcome us, and asking Mr. Berkelly to call once we were settled.

I was on the extension when Feather picked up.

The usual pleasantries:

How was the flight?

How's the room?

Apologizing again for not being around.

The rotten weather.

About to get worse, Feather said.

Flights in and out now canceled.

Storm warnings posted in the last half hour.

Him trapped at home and us stranded on the Strand, he said, making a joke of it.

At least for the duration, but—

Not to worry, he said.

We were his guests.

Sign for anything and everything.

Then, almost like a throwaway afterthought, "You did bring the checks with you, Bernie?"

"Of course," Augie said.

"The Warhol portfolio?"

"Of course," Augie said. "Everything exactly as called for, Mr. Feather."

"Perfect," Feather said. The phone briefly went silent. "Are you okay, Bernie? I'm asking because somehow you're not sounding like you."

Augie's panicked stare met mine halfway.

In the same fraction of a moment he said, "Start of a hoarse throat. Felt it on the flight and worse since we got here. The rain. Also puts a hole in my plans for some golf."

"Never took up the sport, myself," Feather said, "but to each his own, I always say."

"To each his own," Augie repeated at Feather, while his good eye fled my smirk.

———

Even if the clock wasn't three hours ahead of our body time, winds rattling the picture windows and the rain trying to crash through the thick plate glass, neither Augie nor I was ready to settle in for the night. We were starving for some real food after two encounters with airline haute cuisine du jour. We flipped a coin and Club Shag Cabaret beat out the Café Eleganté Shag Continental three times out of five. We took it as a sign, rather than trying for five out of seven.

The cabaret was packed, a line behind the ropes waiting to get in that stretched almost as far back as the elevator banks. Mentioning Rudy Feather's name to the guardian of the gatepost bought us an easy welcome, a smiley-smile greeting from the maître d' that usually takes a twenty, and a booth on the first tier overlooking the crowded dance floor, along with reassurances that this was the best booth in the cabaret and the one always made available to friends of Mr. Feather.

The genuine lime-and-chartreuse Naugahyde was stained and squeaked whenever Augie or I moved, our drinks—Brandy Alexander for him, Chivas and water for me—were watered, our prime filets were past their prime by a couple years, but—

The music blasting our eardrums from the five-piece band wailing on the postage stamp–size stage was some kind of get-up-and-shake-your-booty magic that had Augie ready to join the dancers, who were making body and foot moves that could have been choreographed by the Berkeley who'd spelled his name with three *e*'s. It was like I was watching syncopated swimmers floundering en masse on dry land.

No question about the band.

Ripping into one song after another in a way that made the desk clerk telling us there was none finer anywhere in the Carolinas an understatement, along the lines of calling Stephanie Marriner "mildly attractive."

Had to be King Kongg and the Beach Gorillas.

My magic powers of snap analysis not at all impeded by the fact the guy out front on lead guitar, wailing into the mike in his burgundy tuxedo, ruffled lemon shirt, and spit-shined Florsheims, was wearing a gorilla mask. Or because the other musicians also looked like fugitives from *Planet of the Apes*.

The band finished "I Love the Night Life," King Kongg attempting to sound like Alicia Bridges, and burst into an ear-reaming version of "I Love Beach Music," King Kongg and his bass player sharing vocals and both of them sounding like Alicia Bridges.

Augie pitched his voice high enough to be heard over the music and said, "Beach music, huh? Kiddo, it's updated, up-tempo swing with a lot of R&B zing. See them out on the floor? Like I was doing when I was a mere youth, during my brief fling working 'dime a dance' halls." His fingers began drum-rapping on the table. "You watch. They're showing off to a basic six-count pattern."

I looked over the railing at the couples smiling and sweating under the rotating glass ball showering them with glitter. Holding on to one another with both hands, all movement emanating from below the waist. Coming together close, into a closed 360-degree rotation. Breaking apart to perform mirror steps.

No two couples alike, but all traveling forward and back for *Look at me* attention to a one-and-two, three-and-four, five-six count.

The Beach Gorillas played out of "I Love Beach Music" and began ripping into "Up On the Roof," trying their failed best to harmonize on the golden-oldie classic like the legendary Drifters.

Unable to contain himself any longer, Augie slid from the booth and signaled our waitress for another round.

Adjusted the multicolored sport shirt he was wearing over a pair of gray drawstring pants. Hoisted one shoe and then the other onto the seat. Retied his laces. Filled his lungs with air. Puffed out his chest, and headed off to the dance floor, as confident as Ben Affleck leaving for a blind date.

A handsome black woman who looked around forty-five or fifty, her fulsome body wrapped in a ruffle-trimmed floral-patterned dress, sat alone at a tiny table for two perched uncomfortably at the edge of the floor, directly in front of the blaring amps.

She seemed to be dancing in her seat, every bounce an invitation to stare at her. Even in the frenetic lighting, her large eager eyes and a sunshine grin made her impossible to ignore.

Augie paused in front of the woman and said something.

She smiled up at him and, in a moment, was on her feet and being escorted onto the floor by Augie. Another moment and they had disappeared somewhere among the dancers in the middle of the floor.

A few moments more, after the band had segued into the other Drifters Hall-of-Famer, "Under the Boardwalk," Augie and his dance partner became as obvious as Fred and Ginger.

The floor cleared slowly, then faster, until they had it all to themselves.

Their moves became bigger, broader, more expressive.

Augie, astonishingly for a man his age, moving like he was that dancehall kid again, the way I'd once seen him do as a chorus boy for a musical show at the Motion Picture Retirement Estates.

The woman, matching him effortlessly.

Every step like it was a routine they'd practiced for hours.

The other dancers rimmed the floor, studying them like students, some cheering them on, others clapping generously when Augie and his partner executed an especially intricate maneuver.

They had the full attention of the room by the time the song ended.

More applause before they'd finished taking bows, and he led the woman from the dance floor, steering for our booth, but—

Not a lot of applause; at best, polite and brief.

I felt a frostiness in the lounge that hadn't been there up to now and had to be at least as cold as the temperature on the street.

Heard an uncomfortable buzz among the patrons that grew after King Kongg announced a "take ten" and reminded everyone that all the band's CDs and cassettes were available in the lobby.

Our waitress had paused to watch Augie's demonstration after delivering our drinks and now was clucking and shaking her freckled face.

She saw the question on my face and said, "Your friend should have remembered this here is South Carolina and lots of locals are still fighting the War Between the States."

"Somebody should tell them about Appomattox," Augie said, guiding his dance partner into our booth, across from me.

He settled alongside her and asked, "What will you have, Aleta?"

Aleta, eyes shifting nervously and her smile obviously forced, said, "I still really don't think this is such a good idea, Bernie. Easy for any of the people here to take it the wrong way, and it wouldn't be for the first time."

"A celebration of our triumphant performance is what it is, my dear," Augie said, then to the waitress, "A split of your finest bubbly, young miss, and three glasses."

The waitress grimaced and disappeared, replaced almost immediately by a trio of tight-faced kids in their twenties, two in lumberjack shirts and tight denims, the third wearing leather everything. Clutching beer bottles and sharing looks that spelled trouble, possibly better than they could handle the word in a spelling bee.

Rednecks glowing in the semidarkness.

Each one bigger than Augie and me combined.

Their spokesman, the one in leather who looked like he could fit into King Kongg's band without a mask, addressed Augie.

"You must be a first-time visitor our way," he said.

"Why's that?"

"It looks to me like you never heard how down here we mix our liquors, not our whites and the coloreds."

"People or laundry?" Augie said.

The spokesman snickered and said, "You got a smart mouth on you for an old man, old man."

"Like an old whip," Augie said.

"Like you're bustin' for a whippin'."

"Like you've never heard of civil rights."

"Sure," the spokesman said. "That's where smart-mouth old men can take up with some damn nigra bitch whore any ol' damn time they please."

The spokesman showed his buddies the sneer on his face, then took a swipe of beer, and two-fingered his lips dry.

I felt the entire room staring at us and was trying to figure how the three of us could make a fast getaway.

I was already too late.

Augie said, "I think you should apologize to the lady here."

"For what? Calling a spade a spade? Calling you for the sperm reject you sprang from?" the spokesman said. Turned to make sure his buddies appreciated his cleverness.

They grunted approval.

"Really not necessary," Aleta said. "Really. I should maybe—"

"Wait for our champagne to arrive," Augie said.

He pressed his palm on her forearm.

She sent me a look that wrapped experience and wisdom with desperation.

"It's getting late, Bernie," I said, and moved onto my feet.

The spokesman said, "Late for what, dickhead? For you to give your grampa here a bedtime blow job?"

As much as his flowering bigotry, it was that damned smirk of his that got to me.

I said, "You look like you've had plenty of practice on your Kluxers here. Mind taking your smart mouth and teaching me how it's done?"

"I hear you right, nigra-lover?" he said, pushing his face so close to mine I could feel his foul breath staining my skin.

Augie inched out of the booth, any further movement blocked by the other two troublemakers, saying, "On second thought, we have to be up early tomorrow."

I asked the spokesman, "What's the problem? Cocks stuck in your ears? Or maybe is it only the South that can still rise again?"

The spokesman shook his head and half closed his heavy lids, ran a hand through his buzz cut, hauled back with his beer bottle and crashed it against my head before my fist got to him.

I thought I heard Augie saying something, and he seemed to be scrambling with the other two before everything turned silent and invisible as I sensed myself tumbling from up on the roof to under the boardwalk.

Voices in the dark.

Meaningless.

Gray shadows moving in my mind.

Sounds I know and can't identify.

The bliss of nothing at all until—

A splash of light on my face startles me awake.

I track its origin.

Daylight charging through a narrow break in the night blinds of my suite's windows while a drill press eats into my temple, creating a batch of scrambled brains.

How's it go, from *Showboat?* Body hurting. Racked with pain. Something like that. Only worse.

Moaning and groaning, sounds that don't quite make it as words, but—

It's not me.

My eyes, swollen and struggling to focus, hunt down the noises to the couch on my left.

Augie on the couch.

Augie moaning and groaning unintelligible words.

I struggle to my knees and crawl over.

Augie is talking nonsense in his nightmare.

I use the couch and a side table to work onto my feet and pace myself across the room to the light switch.

Brightness explodes.

I momentarily squeeze my eyes closed in self-defense.

A crazy-quilt of color shags inside my eyelids.

I open them after a minute.

Discover the room has been turned upside down, looking like the hurricane made it inside, making me aware that the world-class heavyweight champion of a downpour is still trying to bust through the picture windows.

I stumble across the room to my bedroom, then Augie's.

The hurricane has hit harder in both places.

Drawers dumped.

Pictures ripped off the wall.

Mattresses stripped and slashed.

Clothing turned into piles of cloth rubble.

Somebody looking for something, or—

The advance guard of Ku Klux Klanners from the Club Shag Cabaret, jus' treatin' theyselves to some moh redneck revelry?

A finger pokes me between my shoulder blades.

I wheel around, my fist drawn back and ready to launch.

It's Augie.

He turns his head and dodges on reflex and the right cross slides harmlessly past his bruised, red-splotched and blue-veined alcohol-embalmed puss.

"Where was that punch when we really could have used it?" he says.

"What happened?"

"What do you think happened?" he says. "You got sucker-bottled, so I had to beat those three fugitives from a chain gang silly all by myself."

"You expect me to believe that?"

Augie shrugs and says, "Worth the try, amigo."

"The woman? Aleta?"

He shrugs again.

"How'd we get back up here?"

Another shrug.

After a hefty room-service breakfast that Augie devoured like Jimmy Cagney getting ready to strut his last mile, we wandered down to the lobby, settled in and watched as linemen moonlighting as bellmen struggled to keep the torrential winds from blasting open the doors.

You take your entertainment where you find it. It was a reasonable alternative to watching the same winds batter the Grand Strand on the local channels and a resounding victory for reality over reality TV with us and maybe a half dozen other besieged warriors of the Grand Strand.

We had been sitting for about an hour, counting the rain bullets and occasionally catching sight of palms outside the drive entrance bow to the wind like obedient servants when—without so much as a final whimper or a gracious adieu—the storm front seemed to drop dead of its own boredom.

It took a moment before people understood it wasn't their imagination, and they broke into cheers.

Augie and me, too.

We also split a look that bespoke the same thought—

Use what might only be a brief break in the storm to risk making the trip to Murrells Inlet.

I said, "Find the Homestead. Surprise Feather."

Augie said, "Better to call Feather. Let him come after us."

"By then the glorious Grand Strand could be back to being a candidate for Atlantis. Besides, it would ruin the surprise. How many times did you take me on your knee and tell me surprise can reveal truths you can't get any other way?"

"My surprise now, kiddo, is learning that you actually took heed."

"How else was I able to assume your mantle of greatness on the crime beat?"

"Thievery and deception to go with cunning and guile," Augie said. "Only some of the other sterling qualities you stole from your master."

We crossed over to the concierge's desk.

The concierge was half asleep with boredom, but snapped to attention over the thrill of something to do.

Lost his smile when we asked him to order us a cab or limo and told him why.

"Not possible, gentlemen," he advised, and sniffed at the carnation boutonniere in his rumpled sand-and-surf T-shirt advertising the local House of Blues. "Not even for Mr. Rudy Feather himself in weather like this that turns itself on and off like a lightbulb. The locals know the rain-slick Murrells Inlet roads spell trouble, even for the likes of them, especially where you need to be going. The Murrells marshes?" He gave us a wide-eyed look and slapped a hand on his pimpled forehead. "No sir, no amount of money, times like this."

The concierge went back to sniffing his boutonniere.

Augie turned to me and said, "Plan B."

We moved to the bank of lobby phones, and Augie had the hotel operator dial Rudy Feather's number.

Held the phone enough away from his ear for me to hear.

Feather came on, saying, "You know what they say about great minds, Bernie. I was just getting ready to call you. How's everything, besides being wet as your wildest dreams, I mean?"

Sounding like he already knew the answer.

Augie went into his Bernie Berkelly mode and explained about last night.

What we woke up to.

Feather put distress in his voice, like what happened was his fault, then shifted gears. "A good thing, then, that the storm is napping. Pack your belongings. I have a car on its way over to pick you up."

"And Mr. Gulliver."

"And Mr. Gulliver, of course. The checks, the Warhols and Mr. Gulliver."

Feather's laugh straining too hard to be real, like he had a surprise in mind for us.

We, of course, still had a surprise for him.

We hadn't brought the checks or the suite of Warhol prints with us to Myrtle Beach.

21

Coming upon the Homestead was like arriving at Xanadu, Charles Foster Kane's palace of mind-boggling wonder that'd been modeled after San Simeon, Citizen Hearst's castle of excessive opulence, only in a sprawling plantation motif that also conjured up images of *Gone with the Wind*'s Tara, except—

The Homestead sat in isolated splendor deep in the marshlands of Murrells Inlet, a kingdom unto itself far from Highway 17, somewhere east of the fishing village founded in the late eighteenth century and still a place where fleets of deep-sea fishing boats anchored between daily journeys to the Gulf Stream.

Before detouring onto asphalt roadways that twisted and turned and ultimately became a maze of narrow, unpaved paths barely wide enough for the limo Feather had sent after us, I calculated there were almost as many seafood restaurants as ancient oak trees lining a main drag that probably sees ten times as many tourists in better weather.

The aroma of the tidal and salt marsh creeks we passed was pungent enough to seep through the windows, something not even the light rain that had started up in the last ten minutes of what was already a complex hour's drive could erase. It wasn't just the slow drudge on muddy roads that were suffering an encroaching fog. It was as if the driver were taking us to Murrells Inlet and the Homestead via North Carolina, Tennessee and Georgia.

He was the surly type, inside the kind of face even a mother could learn to hate, someone you'd expect to find in a wrestling ring, not in spotless white livery behind the wheel of a white Bentley suffering bravely through a thickening layer of storm-induced crud. He didn't say more than a dozen words the entire drive.

Augie or I would lower the privacy window and call to him with a question. He'd mumble back something incomprehensible, then raise the window and bump up the radio another notch; a station playing beach music as disrespectful as the roads.

Kliegs mounted on the highest posts exploded as we got to within fifteen feet of gates and fencing that might have been picked up during a garage sale on Alcatraz Island. The beams ate through enough of the miasma to let TV security cameras make certain ID before the driver stepped out of the limo and walked over to the keypad.

As the gates motored noisily aside and he turned back, I caught the flash of a silver gun handle jutting from under his belt. It didn't make me feel any more secure than the snatches of sound outside—

Animals, reptiles and insects competing for attention with the marsh waters that, however deep and dangerous, were running anything but still.

I gave Augie a look he recognized.

He shifted closer from his roost against the door and whispered, "This is an area notorious for its highwaymen."

"Especially when the weather plays blindman's bluff."

"Especially."

"Thank you. I feel better now."

"Never fear when Bernie's here," he said, tapping under his good eye while his blind side stared blankly through the contact he sometimes wore instead of his patch.

The route turned more invisible but smoother after we passed through the gates. The driver accelerated to maybe twelve or fifteen miles an hour and, after another thirty minutes, we pulled up to the Homestead.

It was lit like a movie set.

Looming out of the fog like a miracle of imagination.

A black servant in white tails moved swiftly on bowlegs down from the portico to the car, carrying a white umbrella large enough to shelter Augie and me from the slanted rain as we tread carefully up a dozen wooden steps creaking under our weight.

The limo took off behind us.

"Our gear," I said.

"In your rooms, shortly, waiting for you," the servant said, and smiled reassuringly.

Two other black servants in white magically appeared to help us out of our jackets.

Everything within view smacked and smelled of opulence, from the dominating crystal chandelier that tinkled in tune as result of a light draft leak from somewhere, to the fine embossed off-white silk wallpaper, to the winding stairway I instantly visualized Rhett using to carry Scarlett from here to maternity.

Staring down at us from the first landing was an oil painting of a commanding figure in a white suit and white, wide-brimmed hat, his hands on his hips, legs spread, an amused look that dared us not to admire, possibly envy him.

The portrait was twelve or fifteen feet high and almost reached the ceiling. Could have been painted by a Sargent or Eakins, a Manet, one of the Spanish realists, like Ribera or Velázquez. Was encased in a gilded frame that glittered loud enough under its spotlights to possibly be genuine eighteen-carat, yet incapable of overpowering the image.

"Please to follow me this way," the servant said. "Mr. Feather will be greeting you momentarily in the parlor." He headed to a set of giant doors to our left and spread them aside. "Nice warm fire's burning in the fireplace and please to help yourself to the bar, unless you'd like for me to—"

Augie's gesture told him that wouldn't be necessary.

The servant backed away, turned around and hurried off.

The parlor glittered like gold in its furnishings and oils impeccably framed and artfully dotting the white silk walls like this was a gallery at the Louvre. The works, while eclectic in subject matter, reeked of the collector's flawless taste.

Augie moved to inspect a Renoir, leaning forward with his face inches from the canvas, his hands gripped behind his back. I was drawn to a Gainsborough portrait of a young boy on par with anything at the Huntington Library collection back in Pasadena, except the *Blue Boy* himself.

He had moved on to two Rouaults competing for attention, and I to an amazing van Gogh, when the voice behind us said, "Gentlemen, never let anyone convince you that money cannot buy happiness. It simply isn't true. A canard of the highest order."

We wheeled around to find ourselves staring at the oil on the landing come to life, down to the hat and suit, only lacking the flattery society portraitists customarily put into their commissions, either by their choice or by edict of whoever's footing the bill.

He was still tall, but not as slender and not as young, a difference a decade or two will make in anyone except, of course, Dorian Gray.

A full head of hair now gone silver at the temples.

Bags under his eyes and a chicken pouch under cheeks falling into a lantern jaw.

A sly hairline mustache that went out with Errol Flynn.

Posture straighter than mine, adding to a casual elegance that had to be as much a female-catcher as his bank account, if indeed this was our well-heeled host, Rudy Feather, master of all he surveyed, up to and including the better weather days here in the middle of Swampville, U.S.A.

Altogether a better-preserved, better-conditioned, far-more-than-acceptable package for somebody around forty-five or fifty, maybe fifty-five years of age.

Augie said, "Mr. Feather?"

"If not, it would certainly come as a shock to my dear, departed mother," he said.

An easy sense of humor, too, and—

Something else.

I caught myself thinking like Augie, who lives his life thinking everybody he meets looks familiar, like they've met somewhere before.

Rudy Feather looked that familiar to me, but it would be awhile before his face jelled inside my photographic memory, always faster with words than with pictures.

"You're not at all as I imagined you, Bernie," Feather said. He joined us. Shook Augie's hand, then mine. Forcefully, to communicate sincerity, or whatever those bone-crunchers are meant to suggest. "You're much closer to my image of a Neil Gulliver, Mr. Gulliver."

I could swear I knew his voice, too.

Graceful, to match his sophisticated appearance, but nothing Southern about it, as if he'd worked to erase its point of origin.

I said, "And you look like we've met—"

"Before," Feather said, finishing the thought. His face swiveled left and right. "You wouldn't believe how often I hear that. Must be something in my gene pool."

He turned up his palms, as if to say *What can you do?* but his anemic smile seemed to suggest otherwise.

He said, "A little cruise of my collection before we move on to other things? That something that appeals to you fellows?"

Feather's tour took us through a series of rooms, one more exquisite than the next, each extravagantly furnished with impeccable taste, and all devoted to the glory of fine art. It was akin to walking through the galleries at one of the great museums of the world. The Metropolitan. The Louvre. The Prado. The National Gallery of London.

No, not one of them.

All of them at once, as if we were party to a sampling of the finest works by only the finest artists, brand names from the thirteenth or fourteenth century forward to about the time Realism descended, well past Impressionism and past Marcel Duchamp's nude on the staircase, to about the time "Pop" became a word no longer exclusive to weasels.

Curiously missing were lithographs or silk screens.

Prints of any kind, not so much as a token Rembrandt or Picasso.

No Warhols, prints or otherwise.

An interesting kind of Warhol collector was our Rudy Feather.

After an hour, we were back where we started, in the parlor, high tea set for us by the fireplace. Feather explaining we'd barely seen highlights of his collection. "Less than the tip," he said, "but the eye, like the palate, can only accommodate so much at one time. Perhaps we can resume later, after we've concluded the business at hand."

Okay, maybe that explained the absence of the Warhols.

Feather finished pouring tea and directed us to the scones, gave us time for a few mouthfuls, then gestured expectantly.

"Mr. Feather, I don't have them, not the checks or the portfolio," I said, hoping I sounded convincingly apologetic.

Feather's eyes narrowed into slits and rolled several times between Augie and me.

He said, "You mean you didn't bring them out here with you."

"Didn't have them to bring them," I said.

At once, the only sounds in the parlor were coming from sparks flying off the logs crackling in the fireplace.

A slight tremor overtook Feather's face. His thin mouth went sufficiently taut to make his upper lip disappear.

"I'm sure you have a reasonable explanation," he said, the words coming slowly and barely shy of seething.

He rose, crossed over to the bar, and poured himself a shot of something dark brown from a crystal decanter.

Offered us nothing but time to answer him.

When Ari Landau and Zev Neumann had instructed us on how to handle our meeting with Feather, they'd told Augie and me to keep our eyes open for the paintings Warhol had incorporated into his suite and, if we spotted any, say nothing to him.

"Just bring us back the information," Ari had said. "We'll take it from there with Rudy Feather. Just stick to the game plan. Stick to the story. Don't make waves."

It was your basic game plan:

Get in, have a look and get out.

The story wasn't much more:

Oh, the cashier's checks, Mr. Feather? The Warhols? Lost with the rest of our luggage, somewhere between here and only God knows where. Damn airline. You know how airlines can be with luggage.

"Simple is easy to believe," Zev had said. "You see what you see and you catch the first plane back."

Right.

Wrong.

What had Zev been smoking before he told us that, or didn't he know Augie Fowler as well as he thought he did?

I was about to launch into the airline riff when Augie jabbed an elbow into my ribs and said, "Let me explain what happened to us to Mr. Feather."

From his tone, I knew Augie had no misdirected luggage in mind.

He began, "That business in the lounge last night, that ugly business I told you about on the phone?"

Feather showed he remembered.

"Those redneck bums didn't leave it at that, Mr. Feather. They tracked us back to the suite and forced their way inside. They pounded us some more. They ransacked the place. They found the checks and the Warhol portfolio. They got away clean with all of it. Other valuables . . . Isn't that so, Mr. Gulliver?"

"So," I said, as if I had a choice.

And what had I been smoking to think Augie was good to go on anyone's rules but his own?

"I see," Feather said, nothing else to suggest he did see. "Sounds like you two were lucky to escape with your lives."

"If we'd put up more of a fight, maybe not."

Feather put down his glass and looked at us over his slender nose. "Can I tell you what I think, Bernie . . . You, too, Mr. Gulliver?"

Once sure of our attention, Feather said, "I think you are lying to me, Bernie. I think some lounge employees got you back to the suite and, later, your rednecks did manage to break in.

"I think that while you were asleep to the world they turned the suite upside down searching specifically for my checks and for the Warhols. I think they left empty-handed, because neither the checks nor the Warhol portfolio was there to begin with. So that alone makes you the liar I've made you out to be, Bernie."

Feather made a clucking sound.

Flicked a piece of lint off his jacket.

He said, "If what you said happened happened, I would have put on a very sad, glum face, done my own bit of lying, and seen you off at the airport. But now, unless I get the truth and the Warhols, it's highly unlikely that either of you will be escaping from *here* with your lives."

I hadn't seen Feather press any buttons or do anything, but the parlor door opened as if on some silent signal from him. The rednecks trooped in single file, all now dressed in white T-shirts and tennis pants, and formed a wall of muscle at the door.

"Three of my handymen," Feather said. "Handy at many things." He arched his eyebrows, pasted on a false smile. "So, gentlemen, your thoughts?"

My smile no better than his, I said, "I don't suppose you'd believe me if I told you about the airline, how they lost our luggage?"

Feather said, "That's true, Mr. Gulliver, but you can believe me when I say I haven't been fooled for a minute by A. K. Fowler here pretending to be Bernard Berkelly. You may not remember me, Mr. A. K. Fowler, but I certainly remember you." A beat. "You too, Mr. Gulliver."

"How did Feather know you, Augie?"

"The same way I know him, from someplace somewhere in time."

"Weren't those just my words to you?"

"You'll have to share them for now, amigo. The answer is deposited in my memory bank. It'll come to me and then we'll both know. First, however, we have a bigger problem to deal with, wouldn't you say?"

"I did say, the minute we got dumped in here."

"Here" was a black hole of a room, the size of a two-car garage in a cheap housing development, whose last occupant was probably Edmond Dantès. Windowless. Walls of stone and cement surrounding jagged brick flooring lit by a single bulb dangling by a frayed electrical cord from a ceiling barely ten feet overhead.

Feather's version of the Three Stooges had strong-armed us here, using a small hatch in a corner of the basement that opened up to a narrow, poorly engineered wooden stairway. The steps angled sharply down to a level colder than a spurned lover's glare and on to a central area that fed four massive oaken doors—like a subterranean version of *Let's Make a Deal.*

We wound up behind Door Number One, expecting our prize to be a pounding meant to make us tell Feather why we'd come to Myrtle Beach without the checks or the Warhols. And, of course, where they were.

Instead, the Stooges had forced us inside, pointed to hand-forged steel wrist and ankle irons dangling from the walls, and hinted broadly they'd be slapped on us soon enough. They trooped out, cackling. Rolled the door closed. Turned the key in the lock.

Augie and I chose opposite walls and struggled to find a comfortable position on the floor while we considered our options. It was a brief conversation.

"Let's nap on it," I said. "We'll do better with some rest."

"Even better with a little spoon and a lot of digging," Augie said. He stretched out his legs, settled his clasped hands in his lap, and within a minute was asleep.

Another minute, so was I.

The rusty sound of the door being unlocked and opened startled me awake, I don't know how long afterward.

I threw a forearm against the bolt of light that shot into the room and after a few seconds recognized it was Feather stepping inside.

He wasn't alone. He had the Three Stooges with him, and—

Aleta.

Augie's dancing partner from Club Shag Cabaret.

Her makeup was a mess, her hair unraveled, her clothing ruffled enough to suggest she had been roughed up. A swollen lip and a purple welt underneath one half-shuttered eye were more than a suggestion.

She was quaking.

Pressing her hands hard against her hips to stop their trembling.

One of the Stooges used a .45 at her spine to prod her deeper into the room while another boot-kicked Augie's shoes as a wakeup call. It took Augie a minute or two to rouse and read the situation.

"Leave the lady be, you idiot cowards," Augie said.

He used a wrist iron to help himself onto his feet and joined Aleta in the middle of the room. Threw an arm around her.

"Fuck you," the Stooge with the .45 said. "Not as good or as often as the nigger bitch, but—fuck you!"

Aleta winced and whined and turned away, rolling into Augie's protective custody.

Feather said, "Enough of that, Jackie Boy."

"The nigger-lover there, he called me an idiot coward, Mr. Feather."

Feather delivered an index finger to the Stooge's face. "Jackie Boy, I don't want to have to tell you that again. Do you understand me?"

Jackie Boy lowered his chin and nodded contritely.

Feather struck an at-ease pose, hands locked behind his back.

"Gentlemen, being as I'm never one to waste time, I'll make this brief . . . I asked you politely last night to tell me what I wished to know. You declined. Now, I'm hopeful that a new day has brought with it an attitude more to my liking. If not, I won't waste time seeing how much physical pain you can endure before I find out anyway. Cooperate with me now, or Mr. Fowler's friend will be killed. Summarily shot."

Aleta made a noise and glued herself tighter to Augie.

Feather said, "Alternatively, make it possible for us to conclude our business and you get a handsome check for your time and trouble. You erase me and all this from your memory. Goodbye. Good luck. Safe journey back to Los Angeles. The end."

I said, "Except I don't believe you, Feather. You get what you want and we get to contribute bloodstains and brain splatter on the wall."

"I didn't rise to where I am today negotiating in bad faith, Mr. Gulliver . . . Jackie Boy, shoot the woman."

"You bet, Mr. Feather." He couldn't contain his glee. "Fellers, pull her free from that ugly nigger-lover so's I can get myself a clear shot at his whore bitch."

Aleta screamed at the ceiling.

Jackie Boy steadied the .45 on his forearm, cocked the hammer and took squinting aim, his tongue peeking out from a corner of his mouth.

"Everything's still in Los Angeles," I said.

Did I believe Feather? Of course not. I was buying us time.

Feather commanded, "Hold it, Jackie Boy."

Jackie Boy hesitated before relaxing his grip and raising the .45 to the ceiling, his features sagging with disappointment; mumbling curses under his breath like some good ol' boy at a Klan lynching.

Feather said, "Where in Los Angeles?"

"With my ex-wife."

"Stephanie Marriner."

"Yes."

If he was trying to read my eyes, they were telling him, *Royal flush and no bluff.*

He snapped a nod. "I want you to call her. I want you to have her bring the checks and the Warhols to Myrtle Beach. I want her here with them within twenty-four hours. No excuses. No delays."

"So you can kill her, too?"

"That, Mr. Gulliver, is a gamble you'll have to take."

Aleta was looking at me like I was God.

I said, "Where's a damn phone?"

Four or five few minutes later, I was upstairs talking into Stevie's answering machine, saying:

"Fats, me. Listen close. This is important. I'm down in South Carolina. In Myrtle Beach. I need you to take the Warhols and bring them down here. Get on a plane and bring them to me ASAP. It's a matter of life and death, Fats. Mine. Grab a pencil and make some notes, okay?"

22

hope for your sake she returns the call," Feather said, taking the phone out of my hand and replacing it on the bar counter. "Something to drink before Charlie and Jimmy Ernie take you back to join your friends?"

I shook off the offer.

"Tell me something instead," I said.

"Try me."

"Why the sudden passion for Warhol? That you'd go to all these lengths, the—"

"Sudden? What makes you suggest my passion is *sudden?*"

"You've assembled a remarkable collection of art. To a point. The point comes before Warhol or any of his contemporaries."

"Based on the little tour I gave you."

"Yes."

"I told you there was more to my collection. How do you know it doesn't include Warhol?"

"I don't."

"That's right, you don't. A lot you don't know."

"And you intend to keep it that way."

Feather's smile grew another three inches. He filled a brandy snifter, took a whiff and knocked back a greedy sip, which he used like mouth-wash before swallowing.

He eased off the bar stool and said, "Come."

I stepped in behind Feather as he swaggered toward the door. Charlie and Jimmy Ernie fell in a few steps behind me, like this wasn't a maneuver new to them.

The quantity and the quality of the art in room after room was over-powering.

My eyes grew at the sheer brilliance Feather showed by his choices. My mind rattled at the millions of dollars he had to have invested on them.

In one gallery was an early Picasso the equal of his portrait of an early wife, Olga, auctioned by Christie's not so long ago for upwards of twenty-five million.

Dominating an entire wall next door was a Monet water-lilies oil, as awesome as the largest version at the Museum of Modern Art. Worth fifty to seventy-five mil or more, were it ever to come up at auction.

In his other rooms, other voices of the great artists called out to me. Cubists. German Expressionists. The Post-Impressionists. The Fauves. The Bauhaus bunch. And in the last room, an elite assortment of art from the last decades of the twentieth century, and—

Silk screens on canvas by Andy Warhol.

Not many, but enough to validate his role as one of the most important artists of his generation.

Jackie Kennedy.

Marilyn Monroe.

Elvis.

Mick Jagger.

Rick Savage.

"The Duke," John Wayne.

Icons all.

Every one of these canvases selling today for more than a million.

Cuh-chung. Cuh-chung. Cuh-chung.

I couldn't stop my mental cash register, or delete the question that came up on every receipt:

Where and how had Feather come by this kind of money?

Inheritance?

The market?

Was he one of the dot-com billionaire/zillionaires who had managed to survive after investors wised up and pushed most of them into bankruptcy and dot-comas?

All the artists I knew, but these were works I'd never seen before—

Except for the Warhols.

Was the Feather collection his miser's gold?

Did that explain why he kept these treasures buried out here in the Rudy Feather Museum for One, protected by nature and the elements and his handymen—the three I had met, and who knows how many others guarding the Homestead from the world?

What the hell. I had nothing to lose, so I asked him.

He finished checking the temperature gauge and adjusted the lighting dimmer while he thought about it.

"Is our tour now to become an interview, Mr. Gulliver?"

"It could."

Feather cocked his head, ran a fingertip over his lips a few times before remarking, "An interview that, like you, will be going nowhere."

Oops. I did have something to lose.

Augie was pacing our cell when Charlie and Jimmy Ernie shoved me back inside. He immediately sent me his *About time!* look and eased down onto the cold brick floor.

Aleta stepped quickly to the door and pressed her ear against it, monitoring for sound.

After several moments, she reported in a half-whisper, "They're gone."

We joined Augie on the floor.

"We have a way out of here," he said.

"Body bags don't count," I said.

"Kiddo, our current situation, like your comment, is no laughing matter. Aleta, please explain to Jay Leno what you told me."

"There is a reason for these rooms under the basement," she began, her voice a level lower than we were. "Back when the Homestead was built, it was here the owners brought their slaves fresh-arrived from

Africa or bought on the open block." Indicating the irons on the wall. "They whupped them into shape and hung them up to dry until they were sure they wouldn't think about running away or causing problems out on the rice fields. For those who did, it was back here, for as many times as it took. If it took once too often, well, that's what the marshes were for, and nobody around who mattered to mourn one more missing nigger. Always more where that one came from."

Aleta's eyes began to glisten.

Augie reached over to pat her hand.

She smiled back at him appreciatively.

"Things were different around here when the War Between the States broke out. New owners had taken over the Homestead and they were sympathetic to President Lincoln's belief that all men are created equal. Runaway slaves were welcome here. The Homestead became a stop on the underground railway taking them up North to freedom. Right here on this floor, here in this room and the others, is where they waited until it was safe to sneak them off to the next stop on the railway . . ."

Augie asked me, "See where this is heading us, amigo?"

"North to freedom," I said, "except for several not-so-minor details . . . We are not dealing with sympathetic owners, Augie. The railway doesn't pass through here anymore. If we try walking out, it's straight into a marsh for us. Six feet under and then some."

"Six? We're already at least that," he said.

"Yes and no," Aleta said quietly, picking at her hair. "It hasn't been used in more'n a hundred years, but there's still the railway. It's a tunnel that goes from here to someplace outside, far enough away and secret enough that it kept the Confederates always spying on this place from ever finding or recapturing the runaways."

"You know that for a fact?" I said.

Aleta stiffened and threw me a hard stare.

She said, "I'm a black woman, an African American with roots in these parts. My people passed down history as well as natural rhythm and a supposed taste for watermelon, which I happen to despise."

"And jazz," I said, "the one and only original art form ever invented by Americans, which I happen to love, even if it was invented by *your* people, who I like to think of as *my* people, too."

Augie blew out a lungful of air and said, "Do either of you mind if we continue this civics lesson later? Right now, we need to march for our own freedom."

He gave Aleta a *Go ahead* look.

She said, "We can get out using the tunnel. It still exists in one of these safe rooms. An entrance hidden in one of the walls. Something else I learned from"—Aleta paused and her eyes flashed me a peace sign—"*our* people. The same way, maybe, you learned about jazz, but—" Her tug at pursed lips finished the sentence.

I said, "Not this safe room."

"No. Augie and I checked it out while you were gone."

"One of the other rooms."

"One of the other rooms."

"And you don't know which one."

"A fact I don't have."

"So all we have to do is somehow get ourselves out of this room and get into the other three, one by one, until we locate the secret tunnel."

"Yes."

"No trick to that, right? All we have to do is ask one of Feather's muscleheads politely. He'll be happy to let us go searching. Even wave us on our merry way."

Augie said, "Stow it, amigo. Your sarcasm's starting to rage like a dog in heat."

It was more like I was having a panic attack.

I leaped up from our powwow circle to go hold up a wall with my back and one foot, blanketed my arms across my chest to defend me a little against the rude cold of the stones.

Nobody said anything for two or three minutes.

It was so quiet, I imagined I heard the sound emanating from the cockroach trailing across the room to join buddies holding a convention in the corner near the piss pot.

Augie broke the silence.

"Aleta has a plan that gets us out of here," he said.

Her eyes blinked confirmation.

I said, "And once we're safely out of here, all we have to worry about is getting out of the swamps in lousy weather that's as deadly as anything Feather's dreamed up for us."

"First things first," Augie said.

"It's a plan you may not like," Aleta said.

I said, "Is it anything like jazz?"

She snickered and said, "A lot like jazz."

———

Aleta's plan played out the next morning, when Charlie and Jimmy Ernie arrived with breakfast, calling out the menu while they unlocked the door, the only way I could gauge the time down here, by what we were being served.

Feather wasn't stingy in doling out the meals. Last time it had been a thick cut of grilled pepper-and-garlic-coated filet, grits and four kinds of vegetables, hot buttered biscuits and assorted breads, out-of-the-oven apple cobbler à la mode, and a large sterling-silver pot of rich, cocoa-flavored coffee.

Now we had the two henchmen announcing, like they were auditioning for jobs reporting halftime at a ballgame, that the serve cart was delivering our choice of hot oatmeal and cold cereals, including their favorite, Wheaties, mountains of scrambled eggs, slabs of ham, crisp bacon, country fries, mashed potatoes riddled with butter and onions, grits, crisp rolls, fresh-squeezed orange juice, sugar-and-spice–flavored coffee, assorted French pastries, lemon meringue pie, and—

We'd already stopped paying attention by the time Jimmy Ernie clomped inside ahead of the serve cart, made a gasping sound, and howled, "What in the name of holy shit—?"

Aleta and I were locked on the floor, naked, me on top of her, matching her low moans with low groans.

Like we were engaged in the hump of a lifetime.

Like we were oblivious to the possibility of sightseers.

Augie appeared to be asleep to the left of the door, a buzz saw blowing through his nose, and was half hidden when Jimmy Ernie said, "Charlie, you gotta come see this nigger never-no-mind getting it on."

Then Charlie saying, "Pull that asshole off. Gonna get me my own piece of that poontang. Breakfast of champions."

Jimmy Ernie saying "Me first."

Me smelling his body odor, as foul as a plugged toilet, while his fingers dig ten holes into my shoulder and roll me aside.

Jimmy Ernie straddles Aleta. Unbuckles his belt and drops his baggy stonewashed blue jeans with a flair. He's ready for battle, his crotch-crowding shorts exploiting a bulge under his humongous belly that was bigger than that famous battle in World War Two.

Aleta fires the first shot, a swift kick in the groin that sends his gonads where no gonads like to go.

Jimmy Ernie "Oomps", and now it's his eyes bulging as he bends forward in pain, his hands protecting whatever's left hanging between his side-of-beef thighs.

Aleta lifts into a sitting position and in the same move sends a fist zooming at Jimmy Ernie's face. The blow connects with his nose. At once, blood is raining on her.

Jimmy Ernie steps off Aleta, tottering like he can't decide how to fall, and makes it about one o'clock. Aleta rolls out of the way to give him a clear path to the brick before he can turn her into a flapjack.

Meanwhile, I'm back on my feet and Charlie's charge at me has been slowed by Augie, who's bronco-riding his back, his legs tied around Charlie's thick waist, Charlie's neck trapped inside Augie's elbow.

Augie's other hand is pounding on Charlie's head with the sterling-silver coffeepot from the serve cart.

He calls over to me, "The door keys!"

I check out Jimmy Ernie and his clothing.

No keys.

Hot coffee is raining on Charlie's head and shoulders. Charlie's screams sound like a punk-rock band playing at mach speed as he tries to tear loose from Augie.

Another minute, he's succeeded, but—

Charlie in his new rush to reach me trips over Jimmy Ernie and head-butts the wall.

He bounces back on his heels.

Augie steps over and crashes him with a roundhouse slam to the temple.

I frisk Charlie.

No keys.

Aleta calls, "There!"

She's pointing at the door.

The key ring is hanging from the lock.

Augie goes for it while we gather up our clothing and flee the room. He gets the next door open and throws me the key ring before jumping inside.

I pull our cell door shut and lock it.

One-foot it dressed and advance on the third door.

I find the right key on the fourth try.

Aleta is dressed now, and I toss her the key ring.

She makes a one-handed catch and heads for the fourth door.

Every wall in the third room is solid.

No tunnel.

I dash back into the central area.

Augie is already there, his face announcing that he's had no better luck.

Aleta emerges from the fourth room with the same look of desperation, her head swinging left and right, her palms turned upward.

My eyes do a sweep of the central area.

Maybe one of these walls.

Maybe—

Like the way we were brought here from the basement?

"It's got to be a hatch," I call. "This time check for a hatch in the floor."

We dash back into our rooms. A couple minutes later we emerge wearing new masks of defeat.

We work the walls and stomp the floors out here.

Nothing.

Augie retrieves the key ring from Aleta and, calling for divine intervention with his eyes cast at the ceiling, unlocks our cell door and uses a shoulder to shove it open.

At the top of the stairs from the basement, a voice yells down, "What the fuck's holding up you guys? Feather needs our asses for something."

It's Jackie Boy.

Augie darts into the cell, followed by Aleta.

Jackie Boy calls, "Hey, listen up. I said what's the score there?"

Another few seconds and he's clomping down the stairs.

He recognizes the score and charges after me like he's Shaq and I'm the basket.

Augie and I barely manage to push the cell door half closed and are struggling against his overpowering presence when Aleta steps from the food cart with a fork and uses it like a pitchfork, digging into Jackie Boy's paw, again and again until his hands withdraw.

We manage the door closed and Aleta gets it locked.

Jackie Boy is banging and ranting while we work around the two Sleeping Beauties.

We're on our hands and knees exploring for a trap door.

Jackie Boy stops his racket.

Instead, inside of a blink, we're listening to gunshots pound into the door and assail the lock.

It takes the combined muscle power of Augie and me to shunt Jimmy Ernie aside and check his brick mattress.

Nothing.

Aleta helps us do the same with the beefier Charlie, who may be carrying the weight of the world on his belly.

I probe the bricks, and—

There it is.

Barely visible channels, no more than a sixteenth of an inch wide, forming a rectangle about three by five feet.

The hatch, only—

Time has sealed it tight.

Aleta grabs three butter knives from the cart, and we start chipping away.

The hammering beat from Jackie Boy using the cell door as a shooting gallery begins to work like an alarm clock on Charlie and Jimmy Ernie.

Suddenly, somehow, on the latest try, when Aleta digs her chipped and broken nails into the grooves, she gets the hatch open.

One at a time, we squeezed through the narrow opening, Aleta first, then Augie, then me, descending down a flight of awkward, mismatched steps no wider than a ladder into a darkness made more foreboding by the increasing coldness of four walls of damp earth.

At bottom, I found myself ankle-deep in water, as if I had stumbled into a subterranean sewer. At once I felt my feet going blue from the chill attacking my sneakers in a space barely large enough for the three of us.

"Over here, this way," Aleta called, only her voice to light the darkness. "The tunnel. Here."

I felt around and found it, not so much a tunnel as a hole no higher than my chest. Narrow. We'd have to travel it single file.

Aleta was inside.

I called around, "Augie?"

"Right behind you, amigo."

We locked hands.

I stepped aside and maneuvered him inside ahead of me.

We took it slowly, cautiously, one step at a time, the water up to my calves and shuffling with us, walls sweating against my hunched shoulders, crouched most of the time, and sometimes—where the path made a sharp twist or turn—on all fours.

We weren't the only travelers. Whatever nature of creature routinely used this route floated or raced by, sometimes taking a curious nibble in passing.

A gaseous smell stung my nostrils. It was thick enough to clog my throat, cling there, resisting the hacking coughs that punctuated a journey that seemed to have no end.

Augie's ancient legs gave out a time or two, slowing us down, obliging the three of us to take a welcome minute or two to catch our breath.

"Soon, we'll be there soon," Aleta reassured us more than once, sounding increasingly uncertain whenever she gasped the words.

We'd been at it for a half hour or a half year, it was impossible to be sure which, when I heard sounds echoing in the distance. Others sloshing and coughing, sometimes, the murmur of voices making indistinguishable words, maybe fifteen minutes or three months behind.

After another fifteen or twenty minutes, after we had to dog-paddle a stretch where the water level offered barely any head room, we crawled out into a dead end—

A rectangular well wide enough to accommodate the three of us standing—

The ceiling a foot or so higher than me and reinforced with slats of timber.

Aleta instructed us to push up, hard as we could.

The noises behind us were growing closer.

The hatch refused to budge—like it was being held down by something heavy—then seemed to lift of its own volition.

We pushed it aside. Glimpsed daylight. Felt a rash of fresh air.

I pulled myself out through the scrawny rectangle, then leaned over on my knees to help Aleta and Augie through.

A gray curtain masked a sky heavy with dark, pregnant clouds hanging ominously overhead and a light mist played up from the ground, but the winds were hardly a gentle breeze. Mercifully, no rain.

Aleta got her bearings and said, "We should be outside the estate." Pointing, "We head that direction, about fifty yards through the thicket, we'll be at the main road."

We'd barely traveled five yards when the voice behind us said, "Hold it right there, you shitheads!"

Jackie Boy was standing beside the tunnel exit.

He had an Uzi aimed at us.

Motioned with it for us to raise our arms.

Jimmy Ernie and Charlie emerged from the hole looking like they'd be more at home crawling out from under a rock.

They also were armed, and more agitated than Jackie Boy, urging him to let them drop us where we stood. Jimmy Ernie looked like he was considering the request when—

A gunshot.

It echoed throughout the marsh.

Then two more gunshots.

Jimmy Ernie, Jackie Boy and Charlie hardly had time to show their surprise before they fell over, reflexes setting off their trigger fingers, their bullets killing the air and the weed-matted earth instead of us.

We dropped to the ground and, after a moment, I turned in the direction of the firepower.

I glimpsed a gray shadow, no more than a fleeting image of a man, his shoes snapping at stray twigs while he hastily retreated through the tall grass.

About ten feet to the right, two men were approaching us cautiously, holding Glocks like divining rods.

Ari Landau pulled up, out of breath.

"All thanks to God you're all right and we got here when we did," he said.

Zev Neumann nodded agreement and kept advancing.

Stepping over Charlie, he moved on to the open hatch and pumped a few shots down. Waited a moment or two, then added a few more shots.

"Just to make sure," he called.

Waited again.

Nodded satisfaction and joined us.

Ari said, "Also all thanks to God you were later than you thought, Aleta. We'd still be waiting by the van for our reunion otherwise, instead of heading over to look for you the way we did."

He read my face and smiled.

"Yes, Neil. Aleta's one of us."

I turned and caught Augie with a glance.

He looked back sheepishly and said, "I wanted to tell you, amigo, but—" Shrugging. "A promise is a promise."

23

The weather reports were sour, flights to Myrtle Beach being canceled one after another, so Clegg finally stopped looking for a connection and took Delta's offer of a free room overnight at a hotel near the Atlanta airport. The hot water didn't peter out midway through his shower, like it did at so many of these franchise operations, and afterward he threw on some fresh clothes and headed for the bar.

It was full of attractive flight attendants and other airline personnel waiting out the storm front.

Clegg posted himself on a highboy stool that gave him an overview of the crowd coming and going. Summarizing the women, he found several to his taste, including some he knew instinctively would not find him to their taste.

The one he settled on was a loner who sat studying her flute of champagne like it contained the secrets of the universe. She wasn't the best-looking redhead in the room, just the gaudiest, in an outfit that fit too tight, revealed too much, and screamed *hooker*, same as her excessive makeup and mountain of hair done up in a style about as old as she was, maybe thirty.

What he liked best about her, she somehow reminded him of the one from Billy Bob's in Forth Worth.

Lucy, the sweet mama who smiled pretty and didn't ask any wrong questions.

Not like Lucy in the looks department, though.

Lucy was older, but better looking, and she wore her chubbiness better, so maybe it was the hooker's hairdo.

Or just that, going in, he needed the fantasy of a nice woman.

Clegg hailed his waitress, told her to deliver to the hook another champagne and an invitation to join him.

Five minutes later, the hook was hip-shaking her way over, her bucktoothed smile delivering more promise than Clegg saw past the black mascara curtain of her burned-out cerulean-blue eyes.

She said her name was Shania. It was as phony as the name he gave her, Clegg knew, but names weren't what this was about.

She had an Arkansas twang and trouble translating thoughts into words, like she had been a major contributor to the lost art of conversation, but Shania certainly knew how to punctuate her simple sentences with playful rubs and squeezes that got him big and hard and close to creaming on the spot.

A half hour later, the financial arrangements made, he led her up to his room and, after Shania excused herself to do a prep in the toilet, stripped for action and stretched out on the bed.

He must have drifted off for a couple minutes when he closed his eyes, because she was hovering over him when he opened them to the sound of creaking floorboards under the stained russet carpeting.

She was still dressed, only now her outfit included a pearl-handled .45 aimed at his chest. The man half hidden behind her held a blue steel .38 automatic and wore a *Don't fuck with us* expression on his ferret face like a permanent fixture.

"Got your watch, sweetmeat," Shania said, showing it off in her other hand. "Your billfold, though, not in your jacket pocket no longer. You tell us where, so we can fetch it and be on our way." She made a face. "Oh, cripes. Dix, you see all them ugly scars acrost his body? And I was even like thinking about doing the nasty with him?"

"See them . . . Just tell us, Mr. Ugly, and we'll skip out of your life fast and easy as we come aboard."

Clegg feigned a frightened look while he reviewed his options.

"Not so hard a question to answer, so don't y'all go tempting fate any," Dix said.

Shania's .45 trailed his arm as he raised it to point at his attaché case sitting on top of the all-purpose table.

Dix checked over his shoulder.

"Cripes, shoulda thought to look there before disturbing Sleeping Beauty. Who knows what other buried treasure that's inside, huh, carrot-top?"

Dix pivoted and stepped off.

Before he was halfway into the turn, Clegg had rolled off the bed and onto his feet. He clutched the woman to him like a shield while he wrestled the gun from her.

"Sumna'bitch, sumna'bitch," Dix said, twisting back to Shania's shriek, taking sideways aim at Clegg while dancing a nervous jig from foot to foot. "You let my lady go or you are one dead man, Mr. Ugly."

"Action speaks louder than words," Clegg said, and fired at him through Shania, using her pork belly for a silencer.

He released her and she hit the floor the same time as her boyfriend. She was still alive, moaning softly, her eyes pleading against the pain as he stepped over to check Dix.

Dix was dead.

Clegg got a pillow from the bed.

He kneeled beside Shania and said, "All I wanted was a goddamned friendly fuck," before he shoved the pillow down hard onto her face, holding it there until he felt the rest of her life go away.

Thinking, *I am getting careless. This should not have happened.*

Clegg blamed it on his concussion, but he knew better.

He knew none of this mattered anymore, except getting out of this business on his own terms.

Planes began taking off for Myrtle Beach early the next morning.

Clegg was on the first shuttle, a fresh reservation under a fresh name and ID.

Another name and ID for the Hertz counter.

He headed straight for Murrells Inlet over roads that were slick but manageable, and slowed down navigating his way through the swamp.

Memorized peculiarities along the route that might be useful later, getting back from the Homestead.

About a quarter of a mile from where the boss told him he'd be finding a gated entrance, he spotted a van parked off the road, half hidden in the wild foliage. Two men using the hood for a sofa, smoking and chatting amiably; lots and lots of gestures, like words alone weren't good enough for them.

Clegg figured them for security.

He stopped, backed up about twenty yards to a wide spot in the road. Engineered a turnaround and, twenty or so yards after that, pulled the Jag off the road, to a place where no one would find it unless they knew what they were looking for.

Clegg shaped a new footpath almost up to the gate, on the side of the road across from the van, then proceeded to work around the perimeter, looking for a possible point of easy entry.

There wasn't one.

He hunkered down to consider his options.

Scaling the fence. A possibility, especially if he was able to psych out the TV cameras. No problem taking care of the razor wire with his cutters, but, if the fence was also rigged electrically, goodbye Clegg.

Unless he scouted out the wiring—nothing overhead, so there had to be ground cables—and knocked out the entire electrical system or the phones.

Ding-dong.

Repairman, sir.

No.

Chances were strong that, living out here in the middle of nowhere with Pogo and Albert the Alligator, Feather would have every kind of power backup conceivable. Also, he'd need to go back to town for a uniform, credentials, special gear. Overall, a tough bluff to pull.

Bluff his way inside by passing himself off as this Bernie Berkelly?

A possibility, but everything Clegg knew about Berkelly might not be enough to get him through the gates.

Maybe Feather had worked out a secret code between them that Berkelly never got around to sharing before Everett did him. Something like that.

Feather wouldn't be the first one he'd come across with his kind of bank account who was into screwy stunts like that, and it fit like a Savile Row suit on someone queer enough to think a man's home is his swamp.

Clegg kept at it for a while, frustrating himself and always coming back to the Bernie Berkelly dodge as his best bet among the lousy ideas. That was every idea, all the tricks that had worked for him in the past, under admittedly softer circumstances.

A gunshot startled him.

Two more gunshots.

Clegg advanced cautiously in their direction.

Heard a symphony of bullets.

Saw three men in dirty whites on the ground, their Uzis useless to them now.

Two men and a woman, looking around in wonderment.

The two security guards he'd seen by the van, emerging from the brush with drawn Glocks.

Clegg retreated, hid deeper in the brush as the guards engaged the men and the woman in a brief conversation before leading them away.

He rooted himself to a place where he observed them all pile into the van and drive off. Waited until he was certain they were gone, then headed back to the kill site to see if what else he thought he'd seen he'd seen.

He had.

A grass-masked lid, sized to fit—

The hole in the ground.

Too large for a rabbit, but not too large for people.

Why not?

They had to have come from somewhere.

He leaned over the edge and peered down into unyielding darkness.

What the hell, Clegg decided. *Nothing ventured, nothing ventured.*

Clegg pick up an Uzi and worked himself down into the hole feet first.

For sure it was a shithole, but he followed the tunnel it fed and lost track of time, got wet and filthy and smelly and angrier and angrier until—

A ladder took him up into some kind of torture chamber, he supposed, judging by the irons mounted on the walls, not that it mattered.

What mattered was knowing he was inside the Homestead.

The open hole in the floor, the overturned food cart and other signs were enough to tell Clegg what had probably happened down here. It was an even-money bet that Feather had people outside hunting after the trio who got away in the van. By now Feather must know about the dead guys who'd gone after them through the tunnel.

None of which meant that someone wouldn't be back here sooner or later.

Clegg had to get moving, but—

Stepping from the room, Clegg's head started throbbing and his eyes lost focus. His legs turned against him and he had to grab a door-post to keep from dropping; use a wall for a mattress.

The tunnel crawl on top of last night's business with the hook and her pimp had wiped out his energy. He knew he needed to pack it in, catch twenty, before he tackled Rudy Feather or anybody in between.

Clegg finished giving the area a speed-reading.

He took a heavy dose of air to summon energy and pushed off, aiming for a corner immediately behind the stairs that offered some degree of security.

Settled down with his legs stretched out.

Uzi across his lap.

Finger at the trigger.

Years ago Clegg had trained himself to sleep lightly, with his eyes open. He'd hear and see anyone coming before they had a chance to spot him.

Smell him, that was something else.

He reeked of tunnel filth.

Steps complaining under the weight of feet galumphing down. A guy in white coveralls, close to his size, about a dozen years younger, toting a mop bucket and a bucket full of assorted cleaning utensils, mangling the words to an old Bobby Darin hit.

Clegg checked his watch. He'd slept for four hours.

He felt stiff and his head still ached, but not as much as before. He could function.

The guy reached bottom, paused, took a deep breath and made a foul noise, muttered something about a damn stinking garbage dump heading for the torture chamber. Began singing another golden-oldies hit by either the Four Tops, the Four Seasons or the Four Freshmen.

Clegg waited a few more minutes before gliding over to the chamber and started sneaking up behind him.

The guy had righted the food cart and was loading it up with the mess from the floor.

He stopped, along with his singing, and sniffed loudly.

Brought up a louder ugly growl from his tonsils.

Was turning around when Clegg pressed the Uzi against his heart and answered the question suddenly burning holes in the guy's eye sockets.

"It only goes off if you don't tell me what I want to know. You understand?"

Clegg said it slowly and deliberately, so there was no misunderstanding his intent.

If nods were answers, this guy was the entire *Encyclopædia Britannica*.

"I'll start with an easy one. What's your name?"

"John?" Like he was too nervous to be certain.

"Hello, John. The next ones will be a little harder."

Within a few minutes, Clegg knew most of what he needed to know about the layout of the Homestead, its safety systems, Feather's staff and how only a few of them were around at this hour, and—

Where Clegg was likely to find Feather now.

"John, I hope you're not lying," Clegg said.

John gave him a weak smile and a hopeful look.

"The silkworm can't be too careful or there would never be any butterflies," Clegg said.

He flew the Uzi up and clipped John under the neck with the barrel.

Snapped his head back.

Sent him banging into the wall, then face-forward onto the bricks with some last tuneless whine scoring the blood spilling from his nose.

Crossed over and pushed the chamber door closed.

Swiftly and efficiently, Clegg stripped the coveralls off John. He rolled him over next to the tunnel opening and manipulated the guy into it, arms first. Replaced the cover. Rolled the cart over it. Did a little more tidying up before he stripped and used mop-bucket water to wash himself. Dried off and donned the coveralls.

A minute or two later, Clegg was on his way upstairs to the basement, carrying the Uzi inside the utensil bucket and doing a better job on the old Bobby Darin hit than John had done.

The shark *did* have pearly teeth, and Clegg was on his way to sink them into Rudy Feather.

Feather had no security cameras on the basement level or, if John's truth continued to hold up, anywhere inside the Homestead.

He shared with so many other collectors Clegg had come across the arrogance of the extremely wealthy, who believed a foolproof security system on the outside made protecting the inside an unnecessary expense.

Stupid is as stupid does, Clegg thought, stepping into the first gallery and adjusting the lighting.

He froze, intimidated by the beauty of the oils on the walls.

He whispered to himself the names of the artists and the names of those paintings he recognized at once, but until now knew only from books and often faded photographs.

The next room, the ones after that, drew out of him the same response.

Well before he'd finished his hurried inspection, Clegg was verging on tears, conquered by the beauty and magnitude of Feather's collection.

The collection was as brilliant as Feather was evil.

In the gallery across from the room John had said was off-limits to staff, Clegg settled on the viewing bench for a brief rest and explored a dominating self-portrait by Max Beckmann.

It was easily the equal of the *Selbstbildnis mit Horn*, he'd painted in 1938 that had recently fetched more than twenty-two million at Sotheby's, a new auction record for a work by a German artist.

From Beckmann's appearance, Clegg judged it was from an earlier period, and there was another significant difference, of course:

The Sotheby's *Selbstbildnis* was no secret.

This one had been out of sight since its disappearance more than a half century ago.

Clegg checked for activity before crossing the corridor to the room whose status was verified by a sign plate on the door: NO ADMITTANCE AT ANY TIME WITHOUT PERMISSION.

He put an ear to the door, then tried the knob.

The door didn't resist as he opened it a crack.

The room was dark.

It felt as empty as it had sounded.

Clegg slipped inside quickly. Closed and locked the door behind him. Felt for the light switch.

The room lit up to reveal what instantly put a victory smile on Clegg's face.

Even more than the boss had suggested.

Far more.

The room was a good three times the size of any one of Feather's galleries.

It was dominated by the largest, longest lithographic press utilizing hydraulic bed and hydraulic scraper systems that Clegg had seen outside of Bern, Berlin, and Gemini in Los Angeles.

Secondary hand- and mechanical presses were not as big, but also built to custom specifications and able to create or re-create engravings, lithographs, silkscreens, woodcuts, intaglios, dye transfers—images in any medium.

The evidence was framed and on the wall.

All types of reproductions, a spectrum of artists as broad as art history.

Some of the images were familiar to Clegg, others new to him, but one thing he was prepared to bet on:

Unlike the paintings in Rudy Feather's collection, all of them were counterfeit.

Fakes.

Phonies.

Created here at the Homestead.

To know that, Clegg only had to look past the type of impression, the signatures, the print and edition numbers, the *"a.p."* indication it was an artist's proof, the artist's *bon à tirer*—"good to print"—sign-off image, the remarques, the embossed chops, the printers' co-signatures, the kinds of papers.

On a quick print-by-print scan, those elements were on-the-money accurate in relation to the artist, the historical time frame, the image, but—

The earliest prints lacked antiquity.

They were too pristine.

No evidence of handling, not so much as a single torn, creased or wrinkled corner.

No thin spots in the paper.

No browning, fading, fold marks, margin trims, hinge damage, glue stains, sun stains, repaired breaks or other evidence of restoration.

Not one liver spot, not even on the astonishing Dürer work *The Entombment*, one of Dürer's larger woodcuts.

It hung with all the other prints like a freshly minted bill, like someone's trophy to be admired for the quality of the craftsmanship, someone daring anybody to find any flaws in its creation.

The modern-day prints on display carried similar but less obvious burdens, their authenticity more a matter of guilt by association, but—

Absolutely no doubt in Clegg's mind as he moved to a connecting door and checked for sounds of presence before starting through.

The noise of a doorknob clicking uselessly and a door rattling stopped him.

A muted voice outside in the corridor.

The sound of a key turning in the lock.

Clegg quickly crossed to the mop and utility buckets, hunched over them on his knees, pretending to search after something with one hand while his other firmed its grip on the Uzi.

The voice louder. Momentary pause and then an angry challenge hurled at his backside: "What are you doing in here?"

A French accent.

"Starting to clean, sir," Clegg said, staring into the utility bucket.

"The sign on the door, dammit to hell. *Merde*. Can't you read?"

"Yes, sir." Clegg turned his head slightly to steal a half-glance.

The man standing defiantly at the door with his legs apart and his hands on his hips was older than in any of the photos the boss had given him, but no question it was Godard, master printer, master forger, master of all Clegg had just surveyed.

Clegg rose and gave Henri Godard his first look at the Uzi.

Without having to be told, Godard jerked his arms to the ceiling.

Clegg said quietly, "Please, step inside and close the door. You and me have a lot to talk about, *Monsieur* Godard."

Godard's dome-lidded eyes blinked in puzzlement.

"Who are you that you know me?" he said.

"Maybe your biggest fan," Clegg said, just ahead of a voice sounding through an overhead intercom, telling Godard, "Don't take too long, Hank. Miss Marriner just drove through the gates and will be here in a matter of minutes."

24

You do crazy things when you're in love, Stevie told herself. And she still loved Neil. Otherwise, why would she have disregarded every caution, every reassurance from Ari Landau and Zev Neumann and flown to Myrtle Beach, into the eye of a storm front that had been threatening the Carolina coastline for days?

She'd had no problem deciphering the phone message from Neil. *Take the Warhols and bring them down here,* he said.

A matter of life and death, he said.

But he'd called her "Fats."

Once, twice, then a couple more times laying out her instructions, and—

He knew better than that.

It was his short-lived nickname for her, abandoned years ago, when she was dieting for the cameras, determined to lose the twenty pounds the cameras added. Neil insisting she was already too thin, how dropping twenty, or even ten, would put her in the pencil category, set her up for rumors that rising soap star Stephanie Marriner was plunging fingers down her throat for dessert. Stevie telling Neil to quit it, cut it out, she didn't find "Fats" amusing in the least, and if he persisted, she'd be calling him "Charlie," as in "Goodbye, Charlie."

All right, so maybe she did wind up under a doctor's care. That was after she figured losing five more pounds after the original twenty was also a good idea.

At least Neil didn't gloat.

He stuck by her bedside closer than the bedsheets, at the hospital and when he brought her home, using up his own sick leave and vacation time to take care of her.

The only time he said "Fats" to her afterward, it was about Fats Domino, saying since he—Neil—would never in a million light-years be able to play piano like Bill Evans, he would happily settle for playing like Fats Domino.

So, calling her Fats now had to be a signal.

Same as talking like the Warhol silkscreens were still at her place, not at his.

Red flags.

Neil telling her what to do without telling her.

Telling her the danger was real and he didn't want her to be part of it.

She explained all this to Ari and Zev when she phoned them, unable to hide the panic building on the fear lingering inside her since that bastard broke into her apartment looking for the Warhols. Tried to kill her. Almost succeeded in killing Tony B. Tony.

She told Ari, "I couldn't think where else to turn. He said Augie's also there in Myrtle Beach, so—"

"So you called here, which is exactly what Neil would have been trying to tell you. We already know about Myrtle Beach, you see? Trust me when I say we're already looking after them, Neil and Augie. They'll be fine, so stay calm. Stay home and be safe, the way Neil meant for it to be by his message. Trust Zev and me to take care of the rest."

Stevie wasn't satisfied.

She said, "Who is Rudy Feather?"

"A *ganseh macher* down there. A big deal. Ultra-rich and used to having his way. This could be a big breakthrough for us."

"What kind of breakthrough?"

Ari's end of the line grew quiet.

"Let's just leave it at that for now, can we?"

Stevie thought about it.

"No. What kind of breakthrough? What makes the Warhols so important to him that he's threatening to kill Neil and Augie if I don't deliver them to him?"

A sigh of surrender, then: "Feather could be one of the collectors in the silkscreens that we've been unable to find up until now. Even the one in the mysterious missing twelfth print. Maybe the one behind the whole suite. Someone to lead us to the other collectors."

"If Feather is one of the collectors, he'd already have one of the suites. Why would he want or need another one?"

Ari said, "You stop and think on how Feather, for all his wealth, he's threatening to kill for what he wants? Do that and can you understand how, if we come by that answer, I think we'll have a whole lot more than a breakthrough?"

"A whole lot more of what?"

Silence, then, "I can't tell you that."

"You can't because you don't know or you can't because you won't?"

"What do you think?" he said, trying to put a smile in his voice.

"I think what my mother used to say is true."

"What's that?"

"She'd tell me, 'You can be pretty certain somebody is Jewish if he's answering questions with questions.' "

"How perfectly delightful," Ari said. "So. Tell me. Your mother, is she Jewish?"

They talked a while longer and, when they were through, Stevie gave him her word she'd stay home. The instant she was off the call, she speed-dialed her travel agent and had him book the earliest flight to Myrtle Beach.

Did it make sense?

Of course not, but—

You do crazy things when you're in love.

With Neil, "in love" came down to a case of degrees.

She was in love with him the way she loved to drown her tortillas in DSL's Crazy Sauce, "The World's Hottest Sauce," whose label also bragged it also could remove the oil stains on garage floors and strip the shellac off wood surfaces.

The sauce terrorized her duodenal ulcer, but it was a habit she couldn't break.

Like Neil was a habit.

Even though once or twice he'd come close to breaking her heart.

Never intentionally, any more than the pain she sometimes inflicted on him was meant to last.

She knew she couldn't just sit still, ringing her guts out waiting to hear that Neil was safe.

She had to be where he was.

Do something.

Help.

How?

Hell.

She had the whole trip to think of something.

It was late Friday when Stevie arrived in Myrtle Beach.

Following Neil's instructions, she used a pay phone in the airport lobby, tapped in the number he'd specified.

A pickup after three rings.

She identified herself and was told to hold on.

Another minute, another voice.

"Miss Marriner. Rudy Feather here. Where are you?"

She told him.

"We had almost given up hope of hearing from you," he said, sounding more anxious than she was. "You're alone?"

"That's what I was told."

"You brought the Warhol portfolio with you?"

"Of course."

The truth as far as it went.

"Excellent. If you'll kindly sit tight at the snack counter, I'll send my car after you. A tricky route this time of the day. I wouldn't want you or your precious cargo getting lost on me."

"Let me speak with Neil. Put him on. I want to know that he's okay."

"My telling you so will have to do, Miss Marriner."

"Not good enough, Mr. Feather."

"Beggars can't be choosers, Miss Marriner. I thought I made that excruciatingly plain in the message I had our Mr. Gulliver leave for you."

"I hear it from his lips or I catch the next flight to Atlanta."

"*Bon voyage*, Miss Marriner. I'll say farewell for you to Mr. Gulliver."

If Feather was bluffing, he was pulling a good one.

"Bring Neil to me here at the airport. We'll make the exchange here. I get Neil. You get the Warhols."

"It's my way or the skyway, Miss Marriner."

"How do I know you won't kill Neil, me with him, after you have the Warhols?"

"You don't."

"That's comforting."

"I'm not the Myrtle Beach Chamber of Commerce. But I'm not a murderer, either, Miss Marriner. I'm a man who's used to getting what he wants. Too spoiled that way for too many years to change. So, I get the Warhols. You get Mr. Gulliver and he, as originally agreed, gets an appropriate payment. We all leave winners. That's the best and only bargain I have to offer you."

"You don't think I and Neil would immediately head straight to the police?"

"There's an old saying, Miss Marriner. 'Where the rich can't buy, their lawyers can.' Your word against mine? My word wins. Especially here in Myrtle Beach."

"Big fish in a little pond."

"If that's how you choose to characterize the Atlantic Ocean."

Stevie moved the phone to rest on the booth counter for several moments, then told Feather, "I'll be waiting at the snack counter."

The tall, moss-encrusted trees that leaned at awkward angles after years of windy assault had fallen into shadows, and breezes that seemed to rise from nowhere were playing them like a musical instrument by the time Feather's limo pulled up to the Homestead.

The driver hurried around to open the door. As she stepped outside, Stevie felt a damp cold embracing her body like an anxious lover, a velvet drizzle lavishing kisses on her face, while an array of foul swamp odors overpowered the nasty mothball smell of her politically incorrect, allergy-unfriendly, ankle-length mink.

The mansion entrance appeared to swing open by itself as she went up the stairs, protecting the presentation case against her body.

As she passed through the arch, hands reached out and a voice she recognized as Rudy Feather's said, "Welcome, Miss Marriner. Let me help you with that."

He freed the case from her grip and placed it carefully on the entry-hall table, then turned around again and helped her off with the mink, complimenting her on her choice.

"The true Hollywood Glamour with a capital G," he said. "Like in all those 'What Becomes a Legend Most' ads, only richer. Better. More luxurious."

"Real mink."

"Like I wouldn't know?" Feather hung the mink in the guest closet, retrieved the portfolio and told Stevie to follow him. "Sorry to bring you so far out on a night like this, but you'll be warming yourself in front of a pleasant fire in another minute. Lovely outfit, by the way. It gives you a casual elegance most women can never achieve."

Stevie gave the crystal chandelier a frustrated glance and moved with Feather at her side down the central corridor to a door just past an intersecting corridor that branched out in two directions. The door opened into an elegantly furnished paneled conference room with a fireplace crackling on the wall opposite a giant bay window that had been boarded up from the outside.

Feather noticed her staring and said, "Storm warnings all day long, so I had the staff take care of all the windows before sending most of them off to tend to their own homes and families . . . Please feel free to help yourself to one of the hot toddies on the serving cart. Made them myself just before you arrived. A little brandy bracer goes a long way."

Stevie answered him while crossing to the fireplace, where she began rubbing warmth into her palms and forearms. "I don't think so," she said, nothing gracious in her tone. "Where's Neil?"

Feather struck a tight smile and said, "In time, Miss Marriner. You're aware that all good things come to she who waits. As they also say, 'First things first.' "

He placed the portfolio on the clear glass conference table that dominated the room, gave the black box a loving look before taking a pair of white cotton gloves from a pocket of his brocaded white silk housecoat, whose dramatic collar and hem that hit the top of his pointy-toed white rattlesnake boots furnished him with an especially theatrical air.

Feather did a *Shave and a haircut, two bits* tap step, ending on his left foot, left hand extended.

"Now, let us see what we shall see," he said, leaving Stevie to wonder what there was about the step and, suddenly, about Rudy Feather that struck a familiar chord.

He proceeded to remove the Warhols and their protective tissues from the case, delicately laying them one by one on the table, until—

Feather's head began to switch left and right with the exactness of a grandfather clock's pendulum. He began making unpleasant noises with an equal amount of precision.

Finally he swung around to confront her, the mask of congeniality off. A scowl on his lips and menace leaping at her from eyes that no longer twinkled good-naturedly. Tics sending warnings from his upper lip and every bristling hair of his trim mustache.

"What's your game, Miss Marriner?"

"I don't understand."

"Of course you do."

His breathing had become labored. He couldn't find a place to land his eyes. "I said, 'What's your game?' "

"It's your game and your rules. There are the Warhols. Where's Neil?"

"Not," Feather said. "Not, not, *not!*"

He stepped over to the cart for a cup of hot toddy and flung it across the room. It bounced off a small oil painting and splashed the plush white carpeting on its way down.

"They may be Warhols, Miss Marriner, but we both know they most definitely are not *all* the Warhols."

"There are five."

"I can count."

His next toddy-pitch cracked the frame of a watercolor under glass.

"You and Mr. Gulliver have eleven. Where are the other six?"

"They're near enough." She gave him her best smile.

Feather took off the cotton gloves and cast them aside.

Took an inhaler from his housecoat and gave his throat several blasts.

Probed her maliciously with narrowed blue eyes when she told him, "California is a community-property state, so half the Warhols are his and half belong to me, his ex. Those are his, in exchange for him." She paused to be sure her explanation was sinking in. "Fair is fair, Mr. Feather. Once we have that settled, once I'm satisfied Neil is free to go, we deal for my half."

Feather pushed out an exasperated wheeze and sank into a chair at the head of the conference table.

He planted his elbows and built a finger pyramid.

"You know my price. It was a fair price. For all eleven prints. But"— sending her a smile as real as Mickey Mouse—"I said before through Mr. Berkelly, more than once, that I was open to negotiation and I am. What are you asking?" His anger replaced by the quiet, mindful calculations of someone used to negotiating.

Stevie gave him the kind of deadpan she'd always notice on Neil's face when he held certain winners in 10-and-20 seven-card stud at one of the Gardena poker clubs.

"Six million," she said.

Without pausing Feather said, "Outrageous. Absolutely out of the question."

"Maybe last week."

"What's that supposed to mean?" he said, shifting his eyes away from her to frown at the damaged oil.

"The latest auction at Christie's in New York, a Warhol silkscreen of flowers went for over eight million dollars."

Feather nodded. "That was for one of Warhol's rarer works, an exceptionally large silkscreen oil on canvas; on canvas, Miss Marriner, not from an edition of inks on paper."

"Someone bought one of his Marilyn Monroe's for almost four million dollars, a million more than Christie's sold it for two years ago."

"The orange Marilyn, I know. Also a silkscreened oil on canvas. Far more coveted than Warhol prints."

Stevie pretended to weigh his words, then: "I'm convinced," she said. "Make it five million for the rest of the suite."

Feather's eyes turned to slits and his fingers drummed the table. "You're out of your mind."

"Five million and I'm also out of here with Neil. You get the rest of the silkscreens and we all live happily ever after."

Feather didn't respond at first. He ran his thumb and index finger over his mustache and under his jutting lower lip several times.

He was thinking something, but what?

She prodded him. "That's less than a million a print."

"I know my math."

"And your bargains? We both know they'll be worth more in a year or two. They're already worth more. How much rarer can any Warhol silkscreens be, whether they're oil on canvas or ink on paper?"

She won the staring contest that followed.

"Three million," he said.

"Six million."

Feather gave her an incredulous look, filled the room with broken laughter.

Stevie shrugged.

He fell silent again.

Looked daggers at her.

Stevie used the time to focus hard on Feather and try to pull him from her memory.

Shave and a haircut, two bits.

It had something to do with Warhol, but—

Not here. Not now.

When?

What?

"Four million," Feather said, slapping the table.

Sending her attack on the past into limbo.

Stevie recognized she had pushed Feather as far as he would go.

"Deal," she said.

"Not yet," he said. "I have a partner. He will have to approve before I can write you a check."

She shook her head. "Cashier's check or better."

"Then it will have to wait until tomorrow. Already too late for the banks."

"Neil and I will meet you at the bank tomorrow, finish up there, then take you to the prints."

"You'll stay overnight and then you and I will go to the bank. Once I'm satisfied, Mr. Gulliver will be brought to you. Unharmed. Good as new." He raised his right hand. "Swear."

Stevie saw his ego needed some bargaining victory and said, "I own the deck but you have the cards, Mr. Feather."

After all, what difference did it really make?

None, really, if Feather knew what she knew.

He'd know soon enough, of course.

Feather got up from the conference table, threw back his shoulders and marched to a control panel built into the wall behind an exquisite antique mahogany writing table and matching armchair.

He pressed one of the buttons and shouted across the room, "Hank, you should have been here ages ago. What's keeping you?" Began pacing the room like a soldier on sentry duty.

Stevie's finger painted aimless, invisible doodles on the glass while examining him again for a memory clue.

Shave and a haircut, two bits.

A Warhol connection.

Art.

More than art.

Stevie felt she was closing in on it when—

Feather broke into her thoughts, screaming, "Damn him, damn, damn that man!" He threw up his arms. "Sometimes he makes me think it's Godot I'm waiting for. He does it on purpose. He knows how it angers me. Come!"

Feather led her to the basement, constantly reassuring Stevie she and Neil no longer had anything to fear now that their deal was sealed.

He was being far too amiable, far too condescending and, having experienced how quickly his moods swung from ground zero to the moon, she kept herself steeled for any surprises that might be beyond the door advertising, NO ADMITTANCE AT ANY TIME WITHOUT PERMISSION.

It was locked.

Feather fished a key ring from his pocket and found the one he was looking for, then a second key for the deadbolt.

He steered her inside and relocked the door, calling, "Hank? You still here, Hank?"

Stevie saw at once she could be inside Kip Lingle's New Visions atelier, only this room was grander, better equipped for any kind of printmaking conceivable; framed works on the walls jumping out at her like the definitive textbook on the history of graphics.

"Hank?!"

A connecting door to her right squeaked open.

A glum-looking man in black denims and a black polo shirt under a white, ink-stained printer's apron stepped into view.

Feather said, "About time, Hank," not trying to suppress irritation that evaporated quickly into a giant smile. "Monsieur Henri Godard, this is Mr. Neil Gulliver's friend, Miss Stephanie Marriner. Miss Marriner, Monsieur Godard."

He was in his fifties, stocky, and built close to the ground. An arched back and muscular arms and forearms which Stevie guessed had come from years of pulling handpresses. Thick, curly brown hair pulled back into a taut ponytail on a short face full of exaggerated features and moles that was intriguing in a homely sort of way. Wide-set, oversized brown eyes frozen with worry behind Coke-bottle lenses in wire-rim frames. A day-old growth of gray stubble decorating the five-o'clock shadow on his otherwise sallow complexion.

"I told Miss Marriner I was starting to believe it was Godot and not Godard I was calling for," Feather said, laughing for his own amusement until he stopped short, realizing that Godard wasn't alone.

The workman in white coveralls who'd materialized behind him had an assault weapon and was pointing it at Feather. He used his free hand to shove Godard inside and order him to join them. Godard crossed to a spot several feet opposite Feather, Stevie not quite between them.

Once inside, himself, the workman used the side of a shoe to push the door closed.

He told the two men, "I am now going to read you your rights. You have the right to remain alive if you don't do anything stupid."

Turning to Stevie, he said in the same soft-spoken tone, "What're you doing here?"

He seemed disturbed by her presence.

"I could ask you the same question," she said, certain he was the same person she'd last seen in a bed at USC–County General.

"You might not like the answer," he said.

Stevie said, "Try me."

25

Clegg, expressionless, shook his head and said, "No."

It was none of the Marriner woman's business.

"Let me guess. If you told me you'd have to kill me, too," she said.

Clegg could see she was trying to be funny, the kind of funny lubricated by sudden fear.

Not the first time he'd seen it.

No intention of making it his last time.

He wondered, What did people find funny about death, about killing, about murder?

It was easy to fault the bloodless, beautified, born-again culture of the movies and television, where murder was a clean sport, only a make-believe that people confused with real life, where bullet holes spilled blood and guts and the dead stayed dead.

Clegg had asked himself the question before, numerous times, after his prayers to heaven were answered from the bowels of hell and he made killing a profitable sideline, a necessary evil, but—

Never once had he found anything to laugh about.

No question it was a serious business.

You had to have a head for it and, to be any good at murder, even adequate, no heart.

He'd lost his heart to killing.

Only now, it was coming back, a transplant turning him into a different person, or was the old Clegg returning to life after too many years among the living dead?

Because he was closer to achieving his dream, to make his son whole again, live to see that dear, sweet, precious child as he once was?

That, yes, of course.

And something buried deeper inside him, stirred as he had not expected by his visit to Dachau and his walk among the innocent victims of mass horrors and by the cry he took with him: *Never again.*

Stirred anew today by the roomfuls of art in Feather's collection.

Only, Clegg still had his work to do before it would be *Never again* for him, and bristling with resentment he pushed the image of his son—smiling brightly, hugging him tightly, calling him "Daddy," smothering his cheek with kisses—from his mind before answering Stevie Marriner's question.

The heart transplant, still a work-in-progress.

"Yes, I would have to kill you," he said, and made sure she read the same answer on his face. "There's no guarantee I won't have to kill you anyway, so don't do anything foolish that makes the decision easier."

Feather demanded, "Hank, who in hell is this person?" Arrogantly, trying to act like he was the master of the situation as well as the house.

"What's left of your future if you don't smarten up and shut up," Clegg said, hoping he wouldn't be obliged to kill Feather before he had the answers from him that Godard said he couldn't give him.

Wouldn't give him, maybe?

Feather and Stevie Marriner showed up before he got that far with his interrogation.

A little later and he might have been gone as quietly as he'd arrived, leaving behind the late Henri Godard as a souvenir of his visit.

Stop lying to yourself, Clegg told himself, immediately retracting the notion. Rudy Feather was a dead man long before he'd found his way inside the Homestead through the tunnel. The roomfuls of art only sealed Feather's death warrant.

Stevie Marriner, she would have to go because she could identify him.

The safety of his future meant he could leave nothing to chance.

He would make it fast and clean, not like what Everett would have done to her if he'd found her first.

"In that case," Stevie said, her voice returning him to the room, "why don't I tell you what I think?"

Before Clegg could respond, she pointed at Godard and said, "I think you're more than Henri Godard." Godard just looked at her. "I think you're also Mr. France."

Godard recoiled. His eyes dropped away and swept the floor as she continued.

"That's right," Marriner said. "I know all about you and how you gambled away the Warhol portraits suite that ended up with I and Neil Gulliver, Mr. France." Stretching the name, saying it smugly before she snatched a quick look at Clegg and asked, "You know that, whoever you are?"

So, Clegg thought, *she's just like most other women, a know-it-all full of questions and answers at the same time.* His wife. All those others, who—Why couldn't they be more like Lucy from Fort Worth? Dear Jesus. A time like this, here he was thinking about Lucy again.

Lucy had her own flaws, a talker, but she listened as well as talked. Was square with him, not prying nosy. Didn't ask questions, and best of all, had this obsessive love thing about her kids. He remembered what Lucy called them. Referring to them adoringly as her bumlets. *Bumlets.* She might be a wild party-girl type, but *bumlets* redeemed her in his eyes. So far there was nothing redeeming Stevie Marriner.

Clegg answered Marriner's question with a shrug.

He didn't understand the "Mr. France" reference or think he cared, but she had his attention.

"What else do you think?" he said.

"I think he had no business owning the suite of prints he passed off on my friend Aaron Lodger, the person who won them from him at a card game in a casino out in the Southern California desert. How am I doing, Mr. France?"

Marriner hit Godard with a smug, accusatory look.

Godard seemed about to reply, but not after he inched a glance at Rudy Feather.

Aaron Lodger, Clegg thought. Jesus H. Christ! Aaron the Baron.

Nobody had bothered before now to say Aaron the Baron was involved.

Not Godard. Not the boss, damn him.

He was bad news, that one. Aaron Lodger.

Not someone to fuck with under any circumstances.

Marriner said, "The only ones who were supposed to get a set were the twelve collectors who financed the suite. Not even the master printer who worked with Warhol, Godard here, but Godard's reputation as a thief of prints is well deserved, as well as his reputation as a master forger, maybe the best there ever was. The entire art world knows that about him."

She cocked an eyebrow at Godard.

He failed to suppress a hint of a smile.

"Looking at what's on these walls," Marriner continued. "I'm thinking they're fakes. I'm thinking he and his friend Mr. Rudy Feather have been in cahoots for years. Down here in this fantastic print shop cranking out fakes and making a fortune selling them. Why they were starved to get the suite back. Why Feather was ready to pay a king's ransom for them, whether he got the entire twelve or only eleven.

"Since nobody knew about the suite in the first place, except the twelve collectors, it didn't really matter. They were planning to sell them one at a time or however it made the most sense and the most money."

It was nothing Clegg and Godard had talked about.

Clegg said to him, "Is what she's been saying true?"

"Some of it," Godard said, ignoring Feather's unspoken command to keep quiet.

"You passed off a set of Johnny-come-lately phonies on Aaron Lodger?"

"*Non*. I had not gotten around to working with them yet. They were as real as those I printed for the limited edition and the one more that I struck for myself, before I defaced every one of the screens. It was my entitlement as the master printer, orders *au contraire* be damned.

"I didn't know it was this Aaron Lodger, only some old man who played dimwitted at first, then like he was able to read through the backs of the cards. I lost a huge amount. I did not have that kind of money. I was threatened." Hunching his shoulders. "I thought to pay him off with the Warhols."

Something wasn't ringing true with Clegg.

He said, "If they were legitimate and you were going to forge and duplicate them, what were you doing with the suite in Southern California? Why wasn't it here?"

Godard averted Feather's penetrating stare and said, "I had a falling-out with him. I decided to move on. The Warhol suite I had not dealt with yet, so it had the greatest value for where I had in mind. Los Angeles first. I had great luck over the years in Los Angeles. Nothing possible there, as it turns out, so I thought, On to Japan, where Andy Warhol has a special appreciation and where I have done some of my finest work in past years. Chagall. Dalí. Miró. You've only to look at art books from Abrams and others to see that the quality of their color printing is close to unrivaled. And, there are certain ateliers there where I am still welcome." He licked his lips like he was savoring a feast.

Marriner's expression showed doubt.

"What about the twelfth print?" she said.

"Ask your friend Monsieur Lodger that question. It was there when I turned over the portfolio."

"That's not what he told—"

As far as Marriner got with the thought before her head snapped at an angle and her eyebrows constructed deep ridges in her forehead.

"Of course," she said, her eyes frozen wide by some new comprehension. "I should have seen it before. Not a bootleg. The suite that belonged to the twelfth collector, the one whose print is missing. Rudy Feather."

"Nonsense!" Feather blurted out. "Damned poppycock!"

The suddenness and intensity of Feather's response took Clegg's attention off Marriner and Godard for a fraction of a second too long.

Godard used it to spring forward and get a two-handed grab on an ink roller sitting on an auxiliary service table.

He swung it like a baseball bat.

Caught Clegg on his upper arm.

The pain radiated through Clegg's body and jolted the Uzi from his grip.

It hit the linoleum-covered floor with a thud.

He saw the roller heading at him again, but he couldn't get his reflexes to work.

His legs refused his demands. He was paralyzed in place.

The roller smashed against Clegg on the other arm.

Godard raised the roller above his head. Now using it like an axe, he was intent upon smashing it down on Clegg's head.

Clegg somehow mustered the strength to inch his upper torso sideways, enough to keep the roller from hitting him squarely on top of the head. Instead, it caught him on the shoulder blade. Sent him tottering backward.

He tripped over something and landed hard on his back.

Godard started toward him, cursing him in French, no question ready to finish him off.

It wasn't exactly the way Clegg ever figured the end would come. Not even close. He framed a picture of his son in his mind as he steeled himself for the blow, helpless to do anything else. Asked for forgiveness, although certain it was too late for any higher power to be bothered. Hoping the effort might get the boy consideration his father didn't deserve.

Amen.

Except the blow didn't come and when he opened his eyes he saw Marriner was hanging on to the print roller to prevent Godard from following through.

Heard Marriner shouting for Godard to stop.

Godard shouting her off him and how she was crazy.

How the man had intended to kill them.

Feather settling the dispute with the Uzi, which he now held clumsily and was using to get Marriner's attention.

Feather screaming, "Off him, off, off, or so help me you're a dead woman!"

Godard struggling to rid himself of Marriner, whose grip on the roller is tenacious.

Muscles straining, veins rising, as he tries to swing her away.

Finally letting go of the roller, twisting to confront her as she crashes onto the linoleum, the roller her prize as—

Feather gets off a series of random shots that scatter over the room, hitting walls and doors and the giant press, bullets ricocheting, and—

One bullet catches Godard in the back.

His arms swing out in dismay, and Clegg can only sense the surprise on his face as Godard stumbles forward and collides with Feather, spins around tangled in his legs, and confirms Clegg's imagination before toppling.

Feather equally astonished, his face a pit of disbelief as he flings the Uzi aside and gapes at Godard.

Three more shots. Cutting noisily into the corridor door.

The door breaking open.

People charging in to their employer's rescue.

Clegg knew he was better off than Godard, but for how long? Not long by any reckoning, he knew, as he fought off searing pain and eyes that wanted nothing more than to shut down in search of sleep and any comfort it would bring.

26

Ari and Zev grabbed Feather and pushed him against the wall while Augie moved to the man on the floor, who stared with empty curiosity at the ceiling and tried to form words with a mouth that wasn't co-operating. He settled beside him and began reciting the Brother Kal-man–Order of the Spiritual Brothers of the Rhyming Heart version of last rites.

I kneeled beside Stevie, urging, "Babe, tell me you're okay, just say the words." I stroked her forehead and tried to analyze the vagueness in her eyes. She seemed to be in a trancelike state.

About a minute later, realizing it was me, she offered the printer's roller she'd been clutching like a favorite toy.

"I know who he is, honey, I remembered," she said. She tried a smile. "Why you said he looked familiar to you."

I pressed my fingers over her mouth. "First I need to hear you're all right." Waited a moment before removing them.

"Yes, all right," she said, clearing her throat. "Would have been a whole lot better, you'd gotten here sooner."

I turned my head in the direction of the man Augie was comforting. Stevie tugged at my shirtsleeve.

"No, not him I mean, honey. The other. Feather."

I gave Feather another once-over.

You know how it can be with husbands and wives, others who spend a lot of time and proximity together? They begin looking like one another or they somehow develop an ability to start and finish each other's thoughts?

The answer that'd dogged and dodged my memory was at once as clear as Stevie's announcement.

I also knew where Feather fit in our past.

Under the mask of time was Frankie Freddie Frook, one of Andy Warhol's most ardent disciples.

An older edition by about fifteen years, but no question it was Frook.

Plucking his name from my memory bank had also peeled the years from his face.

Frankie Freddie Frook. Stevie and I had met him less than a year after Madonna and Sean Penn's wedding in '85, in New York. We'd flown back for a Richie Savage concert at Madison Square Garden. It was the capper to the cover piece I was freelancing for *Rolling Stone*. Jann Wenner had cleared it with the *Daily*, and I might have refused after learning Richie had demanded me on condition Stevie come along for the ride to the Big Apple. On Richie's dime, Jann mentioned, mindful of the expense account.

It didn't take a certain Mr. Holmes to deduce that Richie had the hots for my child bride. Stevie and I talked it over and agreed it was *No way, Jose*, for Richie.

Meanwhile, it was a great, expense-paid excuse to give Stevie a taste of Broadway theater. Shows like Neil Simon's *Broadway Bound* and revivals of Coward's *Blithe Spirit* with Geraldine Page and Shaw's *Pygmalion* with Amanda Plummer could serve as lessons for the future she was constantly dreaming about.

Was I practicing corruption of journalistic integrity, or could I write it off as an established perk of the trade? I chose to write it off as corruption in the name of love.

Everything was first-class, including our one-bedroom suite at the

Plaza, across the corridor from Richie's four-bedroom suite, where the
rumble-jumble of sights and sounds correctly identified the constant
party in progress. Friends of the rock star, and a continuous parade of
groupies harvested by his roadies from the hundreds of fans mashed
outside the hotel with crude signs and shouts and sighs of anticipation,
hoping for a glimpse or more of their rock hero.

Early on the day of the concert, the phone rang.

It was Richie, inviting us over to meet an old friend, he said.

The old friend turned out to be Andy Warhol.

Richie said, "Andrew, of course, you remember Neil and Stevie,
from last year at Madonna's wedding gig."

Andy made a shy smile, taking Stevie's hand.

"Of course," he said, his voice as soft and sweet as cotton candy.

The question mark on his face said otherwise and it remained there
through our handshake, until Richie mentioned I was the writer doing
the *Rolling Stone* cover.

Now, the question mark disappeared.

The handshake remained fragile.

The smile shy.

But it now seemed tinted by a degree of cunning.

Andy said, "Oh, how nice. We're doing a cover also, for *Interview*.
Pictures for the portrait I'm doing of Rick. Why don't you come along?"

He took a step back and aimed his Polaroid Big Shot at me, then
Stevie.

Slipped the photographs into a jacket pocket as they whirred out.

Took several shots of Richie and deposited them.

Extra security was in place and a path cleared by the time we got downstairs.

We raced past the hundreds of fans begging, screaming and crying
for attention outside a Plaza side door, Richie looking neither to his left
nor right before bounding into the stretch limo waiting with its motor
humming.

Stevie and I piled in next.

Then Andy, on one of the two seats bordering the bar and entertainment console.

Then, on the other side, someone I'd noticed hovering upstairs in
Andy's shadow, where he'd seemed in a state of constant, anxious alert.

I made him for early thirties. Lean. A face to match. Basketball tall.
Hair ponytailing down his back. Eyes that radiated a few hits or some

other magic dragon. I'd tagged him for one of Richie's crew, incorrectly as it turned out.

"Frankie Freddie Frook," he said, answering before I could ask. Crossing his arms. Using his knees as a counter for his wide chin. "I'm one of Andy's Superstars. Bigger'n all them others one of these days. Even Viva and Ondine."

He glanced at Andy. Andy nodded.

"People who saw it don't ever forget me from *Bug Men and Boys*," he said. "I was just a kid then, sixteen and a half, when Andy took me. Made me a Superstar to remember." Another glance. Another nod from Andy. "The boy who ate the bugs?" I shook my head. He showed disappointment. "You mention me in *Rolling Stone* and you'll be amazed at all the readers who'll be thrilled to learn Andy and me are still a team. You can even tell them the cockroaches were real that I ate. They were, too. So was the raw mouse got skinned for *Mouse Men and Boys*, the sequel."

Another glance at Andy.

Another nod before Andy drilled us with his Polaroid Big Shot.

Frankie Freddie Frook was never more than a dash away from Warhol during the photo session downtown at the studio of Barry McKinley, whose method of flattering attitude out of Richie was to laughingly shout out things like, "Give it to me, motherfucker. Push. Push it out all you can. You on drugs, motherfucker? You on Quaaludes? Come on, push, push, push."

Andy stuck to the sidelines, popping out Polaroids of Richie or anyone else who strayed into his line of vision, Frankie Freddie Frook explaining to me, "Barry's doing the *Interview* shoot, but only Andy shoots for his silkscreens."

Two hours later we piled back into Richie's limo and headed for Madison Square Garden.

Andy reveled at being backstage and meeting rock stars and a collection of VIPs whose faces were enough to get them past security checkpoints to Richie's dressing room. We had to wear special slap-ons marked ALL ACCESS.

Click, whirr. Click, whirr. Click, whirr.

Andy never stopped shooting.

About fifteen minutes before Richie was due onstage, I told him Stevie and I would be watching the show from a spot onstage, behind the giant amps, not in the VIP section. Our IDs permitted that.

I asked, "Would you like to tag along?"

Andy's face lit up like the Rockefeller Center tree at Christmastime.

"Oh, yes, please," he said passionately, generating more emotion than I'd seen from him all day. "I've never been on the stage at Madison Square Garden."

Click, whirr. Click, whirr.

We headed there through the arena. The sound level grew in proportion to the number of people who recognized him, and they were applauding Andy's presence by the time we got to our hiding place behind the amps.

Frankie Freddie Frook was always six paces behind. As the applause increased I glimpsed him from the corner of my eye. Arms raised victoriously, his wave broader than his grin, as if the clamoring were for him. During the concert, tap-dancing to some of the songs and taking bows when Richie did.

Click, whirr. Click, whirr. Click, whirr.

I told Stevie, "Frankie—"

"—Freddie Frook," she cut in, nodding, before I could finish his name.

As I helped her to her feet, Feather shouted, "That rat is getting away! Stop him!"

Using his chin as a pointer.

Trying to bolt from the wall, but Ari and Zev had too tight a hold on him.

I swiveled my head and checked halfway across the room.

The man must have been hiding underneath or behind the press.

He finished using it to steady himself and as a launch toward one of the inner doors.

I confirmed Stevie was okay and charged after him.

He was through the door and snapping the locks before I got there.

I pulled the 9mm automatic Zev had armed me with from its perch at the small of my back, inside the belt.

Fired at the locks.

When that didn't work, made the hinges my target.

That and my shoulder as a battering ram followed by a few heavy kicks worked better. The hinges gave and the door fell down like a boxer with a glass chin.

I jumped the door and immediately moved into a two-handed shooting stance, wagging the gun in all directions.

This room was almost as large as the other, but most of the equipment was for silkscreens, etchings and engravings. Several vintage lithographic handpresses.

Across the way, pinned to the cork proofing wall, was a series of Andy Warhol silkscreens, an image familiar to me from the 1980s in a range of typical Warhol colors, and—

Past an archway leading into a deep alcove, a section of drafting table showing, and—

A glob of shadow budging across and down a row of line drawings on the alcove wall, then disappearing entirely.

I charged across the room, figuring I had my man trapped there.

Entered the alcove weapon-first.

Nobody in sight. Nowhere for anyone to hide.

Realized the shadow must have been thrown from an angle just outside the alcove, but—

Too late to swing around.

A sharp blow, like a judo chop, pounded my back between my shoulders.

The next one caught me somewhere on my neck.

I dropped the gun.

Then, I dropped.

To my knees.

To the floor.

To some black cavern where dreams were being shown.

Stadium seating for one. I floated onto it. My dream had just started: Neil Gulliver and Stephanie Marriner in *What's a Nice Boy Like You Doing Back in a Place Like This?*

I had top billing, of course.

It was my dream movie, not hers.

FADE IN:

Stevie enters the Myrtle Beach airport terminal.

We're waiting for her. Ari, Zev, Augie, Aleta. Me.

It hasn't been that many hours since Ari and Zev pulled us safely away from the Homestead and brought us to a rinky-dink motel on a side road off the Grand Strand, whose bath towels were almost as clean as the motel's mud puddle of a parking lot.

We've cleaned up and are being debriefed when her call to Ari and Zev is patched through to Ari's cell phone.

He greets her by name. Listens briefly before telling her, "Neil's already safe. Yes. Here with us. In one piece. Yes. Augie also." Ari gives Zev a look. I can almost see the wheels of his mind spinning.

"What's that all about?" I say, unhappily. I already have a pretty good suspicion. It's Stevie intent on taking matters into her own hands.

I stick my hand out for the phone.

Ari steps away and signals me off.

He asks the phone, "Do you happen to be bringing the Warhols with you? Yes, like Feather was demanding." A smile. "Too long a story. Neil can tell you at the airport. Tell me the flight number and the time. We'll meet you."

Weaving and bobbing to keep me from snagging the cell before he slaps the lid shut. Repeats the conversation.

I say, "You get her back on the line or give that thing to me. I don't want her here."

Ari says, "Neil, a lot of things we can do. Turning her plane around in midair isn't one of them. Besides, based on what you saw, we need a way back inside the Homestead to see what else there is to see. Stevie and the Warhols can be our ticket in."

He explains what he has in mind.

"Stevie's an actress, she'll act, she'll do fine," Ari says. "We'll never be so far away she won't be safe."

"And Feather's a real sicko. I won't let you expose her to danger."

"Can't that be her decision?"

I shake my head vehemently.

I appeal to Augie for support.

All I get back is an apologetic smile.

Ari, Zev and Augie greet Stevie warmly while Aleta relieves her of her overnighter and the Warhol portfolio.

I'm not so warm.

I say, "What's a nice girl like you doing in a place like this?" More a growl. Not meant to hide how upset I am about her being here, although by now we're locked in a hug and she's checking my face for damage and trying to stop at the few tears already making tracks down her makeup.

I'm on the verge myself.

"I thought I was coming to rescue the flabby ass of a nice boy like you," she says. "What did I miss?"

Looking at me, then Augie, then Ari and Zev.

"Over there, out of the way, let's sit," Ari says.

It takes him five minutes to answer her question.

Another five to tell her his plan.

When he finishes, she doesn't hesitate.

"Of course," Stevie says. "Where's a phone? I'll make the call now."

Following the instructions I'd delivered earlier, she uses a pay phone in the lobby and taps in Feather's number.

A pickup after three rings.

Stevie identifies herself and is told to hold on.

Another minute, another voice.

"Miss Marriner. Rudy Feather here. Where are you?"

Ari reviews the plan with Stevie again and again while waiting for Feather's limo. "You're an actress and you'll be wonderful," he assures her.

She doesn't disagree.

"What we're doing will bring you satisfaction worth far more than any Academy Award ever could," Zev says, placing a hand over his heart.

"Why I'm doing this," she says; then, with a look at me, "Why we're both doing this."

When the limo driver finds her at the snack bar, Stevie excuses herself to the ladies' room. The driver is gone when she returns. Zev is wearing his white livery. "Aleta will be watching over him for the duration," Ari explains on the way to the parking lot.

They locate the car and Zev climbs behind the wheel.

Stevie piles into the back with Ari, Augie and me.

Before they reach the Homestead, there's a brief stop.

I secret myself under a blanket and Ari and Augie make themselves as comfortable as possible in the trunk.

Stevie disappears inside the Homestead.

Zev pulls the limo around to the garage and snaps the trunk. Augie and Ari climb out. A few minutes later, we've found a series of unlocked French windows.

Zev satisfies himself they're not wired and inches one open.

We slip inside, cautiously work toward the entrance to the basement.

I stay behind, in a shadowed corner with a view of the corridors and most of the doors Stevie and Feather could be behind. After what seems like hours, they emerge and I track them at distance, down into the basement. They pass through a door marked NO ADMITTANCE AT ANY TIME WITHOUT PERMISSION.

I peel off a wall and paste myself to the door with an ear, trying unsuccessfully to decipher the muffled exchange of voices.

Then, gunshots.

A gallery door down the hall swings open. Ari, Zev and Augie join me. Ari and Zev shoot the door open and we crash inside to—

"It's okay, honey. Everything's fine now."

I opened my eyes, not sure where I was, only that it wasn't Feather's basement atelier. Verified it was Stevie's breath warming my face. Felt like Shaq had just slam-dunked a two-pointer into my head and was currently squatting on my shoulders.

The room came into focus.

An oak-paneled library that glistened in the recessed lighting.

Three walls of floor-to-ceiling shelves full of elegant leather-bound volumes that smelled musty and sat in perfectly aligned rows, as if they'd never been cracked. One of those culture-by-the-pound libraries drooled over by the priciest of interior decorators who regularly frolic on the pages of *Architectural Digest*.

The fourth wall, however, different.

Dominated by a "blue period" Picasso to swoon over, a standing nude, her arms discreetly crossed over her breasts and staring down at us with an expression that seemed to say, *I dare you to turn your eyes from me.*

I'd never seen the oil before, not in any of the myriad books about Picasso's art I'd pored over, but I knew I'd never forget it.

Stevie got up as I moved into a sitting position on the couch, then sat down again next to me with her legs tucked under her, yoga style.

"How long was I out?" I said.

"A good hour," Ari said.

I shifted my gaze. He was seated at an antique reading table of mahogany, birch and rosewood in the middle of the room. Zev was across from him. Rudy Feather between them.

"The guy who slugged me?"

"Gone before Mr. Feather decided it was in his own best interests to share his special knowledge with us," Ari said.

"Everything we thought and more," Zev said.

"And we're not yet finished," Ari said. "Are we, Mr. Feather?"

Feather grimaced. Nervously laced and unlaced his fingers.

Zev reached over, gave Feather's cheek a pinch and a pull, then several gentle pats. He said, "My partner just asked you a question, Mr. Feather. What're you supposed to do when you're asked a question?"

Feather took a deep breath through his mouth, flushed it out through his nose.

"We're not finished yet," he said.

27

Augie used a shifting hand to turn off Zev and Ari and said to me, "Stevie says you already know who this bird is, amigo."

"Frankie Freddie Frook," I said.

Made reference to Andy and Madison Square Garden.

Augie wagged his hand in my face. "Ancient history. We heard that already from Stevie. I have a topper." He flashed a gratuitous wink at Rudy Feather. "Don't I, Frankie Freddie Freak Frook Feather?"

Feather glowered at him.

Zev elbowed Feather's arm. "Already forget the rule?"

"Yes," Feather said, like the word tasted bad.

Augie stepped away from the bookshelves where he'd been exploring titles and sauntered over to the table.

"Stevie saying the magic name brought it all back to me in a rush," Augie said. "My prescient, prize-winning feature about Warhol in *Coast* magazine in '69. It logged him in the sycophantic pack present the day I visited Andy's Factory.

"The issue appeared and next thing I knew, I had an irate Frankie Freddie Frook bitching over the phone. Telling me how he deserved more of a mention than his name, gigantic Superstar that he was. Even a feature story all his own. *Bug Men and Boys*? I divined at once, *Bugs, definitely*.

"I told Frankie Et Cetera to check back with me after he won his 'best actor' Buggy at the annual Pests 'R' You Awards. I clicked off. He called back. Told me not hang up. There was a better reason to write about him, he said. He told me it wasn't only Brigid Polk who did Andy's art. He, Frankie Freddie Frook, also did Andy's art.

"Alas, too little, too late, I advised the pushy brat," Augie said. "The story was not only in print but that tasty morsel about Brigid had been appropriated like the exclusive revelation it was by *Time* magazine and carried around the world. No reference to me, I hasten to report. A slight I subsequently made them rue."

Augie paused and looked at me like there was something I was missing.

I was. The point of his topper. I told him so.

"Just setting the stage for what we were hearing from Frankie Et Cetera scant moments before you woke up from your nap," he said.

"The topper to your topper?"

"Exactly," Augie said, and with a grand gesture turned the floor back to Ari.

Ari said, "Mr. Feather was just about to tell us how it came to be him and not Andy Warhol who created the portraits suite of prints."

"The topper," I said.

Feather took a deep breath.

His grave appearance dissolved into something short of glee as he told us, "In the end, I outlasted them all. Viva gone. Morrissey gone. Malanga gone from The Factory, from Andy. Dallesandro gone. Holly Woodlawn, Candy Darling, Edie Sedgwick, Penny Arcade, Mario Montez, Francis Francine, Geri Miller." Reciting the names finger by finger. Another deep breath. "All gone. Gone gone gone. Who's to say whose choice? Probably Andy's. Changing his friends like some people change their socks. For others who could do him more good. But—my star always climbing higher and burning brighter alongside him. My choice. I knew how to make my value to him grow. And grow. And grow."

He surveyed the room like it was Madison Square Garden all over again, like the crowd was responding wildly to his performance.

"By the time Brigid Polk was out of there, I was doing her job of doing Andy's art when Andy couldn't be bothered. Better than she ever had, if you must know. When I ran away from home, I arrived at Andy's doorstep with more schooling in art than I'd ever had as an actor. A natural at both, you can believe it, but Andy immediately saw how I could command the silver screen, so first I became Frankie Freddie Frook.

"Meanwhile, I observed him working every chance I got. Brigid working. I sponged up Andy's method. His technique. I did my homework. Practiced, practiced, practiced until I knew I had become better than Brigid and in some ways even better than—"

He threw a hand over his mouth, as if he were stopping a blasphemy.

Feather continued: "With the real work, the celebrities and the big commissions, Andy would use the Big Shot to take fifty or sixty pictures, then whittle them down to four and send them to his silkscreen guy, usually Rupert Smith.

"The silkscreener turned them into eight-by-ten positive images on acetate and sent them back to Andy, who'd choose the one he wanted to use and where to crop it and how to fix up the face so it'd be more attractive, like a plastic surgeon. Noses. Lips. Necks. Whatever it took. The eight-by-ten became a forty-by-forty-inch acetate and the silkscreen was made from that."

It was obvious Feather was showing off for us, equally obvious Augie was growing irritated by the lecture. Ari also noticed and sent Augie a sign not to interrupt.

I was surprised.

Augie had been the one to teach me how the best interviews were the ones where you got your subject talking and let him keep talking. A slip of the tongue in a moment of excited, rambling excess often produced something not even the most exacting Q&A could generate.

The strategy was used by cops during interrogations.

Clearly, also by the Mossad.

"Next, Brigid, me, some assistant, would pre-paint the rolls of canvas into a flesh-toned background, for a man, or a pinker flesh tone for a woman," Feather said. "Andy or one of us would then trace the forty-by-forty image onto the canvas using a carbon transfer under tracing paper.

"Then, the colored areas would be painted in. The hair. The eyes.

The woman's lips. The man's outfit. When that was done and the silk-screen was ready, the image would be lined up with the colored areas and the details of the photograph were silkscreened onto the canvas.

"There were always minor variations in the alignment of the image with the painted colors. Intentional. They made a Warhol a Warhol. Gave his portraits a special distinction a lot of people imitated but could never duplicate." Checking our faces. "Present company excepted, of course."

"Of course," Ari and Zev said in harmony, making twin facial and hand gestures that begged the point. "How else could you have gone on to fool so many collectors with the portraits series that bore his name?"

Feather showed he liked that.

He smiled and said, "I should tell you how that came about." As if he'd forgotten that was what we were waiting to hear.

"Yes, yes, please," Ari said, encouraging him.

"First, understand that Andy was getting twenty-five thousand dollars for his commissioned portraits. The first canvas. Then five thousand dollars for every one after that."

Stevie said, "And what did you get?"

Feather looked at her like the answer was obvious.

"Privilege," Feather said. "The privilege of working alongside a master."

He shook his head in disbelief and continued.

"So, along comes someone who wants him to create a suite of twelve silkscreens, not even oils, in a limited edition. For three million dollars. That's right. You heard. Three million dollars. Under very specific terms and conditions that are not at all the way Andy usually works. Paris, for one thing, where the work has to be done. Some out-of-the-way atelier he's never heard of. But, three million! A windfall for someone who treats money like any day now will carry him back to the poverty of his childhood.

"This wasn't long after the Rick Savage concert at the Garden. It was April in Paris. Andy was enthralled, as usual. And me. We had hardly begun work on the project, though, when Libya or some country got bombed and because of it Andy was cancelled off some live television program.

"He got so rattled, he decided he was leaving early and I would stay behind to do the work. He'd finished the basics, or most of them, not that I needed that to do what there was to do next. Andy knew that, also, or believe you me he would not have chanced doing anything, *anything* that would forfeit his three million dollars."

Ari said enthusiastically, "You were Warhol as much as Warhol was Warhol."

Feather accepted the judgment with a gracious nod. Ari had him glowing at the recognition.

"Given the complexity of the work, more," Feather said.

"Why am I not surprised?" Ari said with a shrug.

"I did things with those portrait silkscreens that went beyond anything he had ever done himself, Andy."

"Yes. Clear to see the minute I saw," Ari said. "And it must have been especially gratifying to have working at your side a master printer like Henri Godard."

Feather pulled in his eyebrows. His eyes narrowed as he furiously smoothed his mustache, like he didn't know how to react to sharing the credit.

"Did I say he was?"

"His chop on the prints?"

"Oh, yes," Feather said, remembering he had no choice. "Yes, yes. But not as helpful to me as you would think. His skills, his artistry were more with artists of the past and those working in the European traditions. There he excelled. The paintings reproduced and collaged into the image before printing, I don't diminish what his value was to me in that department."

Augie, trying not to look bothered by being ignored, waltzed up behind Feather, leaned over and said matter-of-factly, "How the two of you came to know each other. How Godard wound up here. The atelier and all. All the phony prints on the wall."

Feather thought about it.

"Yes and no."

Zev gave a back-of-the-hand slap to Feather's shoulder.

"Start with the 'yes' " he said.

"You don't have to get rude about it," Feather said, so Zev slapped him harder.

Feather's hands started shaking. He pressed his fingers down hard on the table surface to make them stop.

"I didn't see him for years afterward," he said. "Hank was completely out of my mind until the day he came knocking on my door, proposing we go into business together. I looked at him like I didn't know what he meant. I didn't, you see?

"He said, 'Look, Frankie Freddie, the fakes you've been turning out have been flooding the market for years. Warhol. Lichtenstein. Johns.

Lowy. Rauschenberg. Ritzer. Do I have to name all of them?' I denied it. He said, 'Come on, I know your touch from the Warhols we did together. Brilliant, what you do. Undetectable almost, except to a person with my eye, my knowledge and skills. I could go blow the whistle on you, make a bundle, but I know how together we can make even a bigger killing. More money than you can imagine.' It takes a genius to recognize a genius, so Hank now had my attention.

"He didn't have to explain much more before we shook on the deal, and as a show of good faith he handed over one of the portraits suites I'd created. It was the extra set he'd managed to strike for himself and have me sign the Warhol name to unwittingly. A clever one, he was. Shrewd. And, where I'd developed a modest sales market with my silkscreens, Hank knew everybody, *everybody* on the international art scene who dealt regularly in our special kind of fine art and no questions asked."

Feather slipped on a triumphant smile and locked his hands while checking us out for a reaction. I sensed him idling, in need of a question to kick him back into gear.

"Weren't you also the collector in the twelfth print?" I said. "That's what we were all thinking." Ari encouraged me with a nod. "The great oils you have in room after room certainly show you belong in that exalted group."

"What I said to him before about that missing print," Stevie said.

"To which I said to you, 'Poppycock!' " Feather retorted. "I say it again. Now. To you and to you and to you and to you and to you: Poppycock, poppycock, poppycock!"

"But you know the collector who is?"

His head swung left and right.

"Not any of them. They came, bringing the work of their choice with them. Hank and I dealt with them. They left. Not one around longer than necessary. No conversation except for, maybe, the obvious question, 'Where's Andy?' They were as quick to buy an excuse as they were to go."

"So you didn't know any of them."

"No."

"Or the work from their collection."

"Or the work. The artist, yes, of course. The work, no. Nothing, not one looked even vaguely familiar."

Stevie said, "The twelfth print. Could it have been of the collector who arranged for the suite to be made?"

Feather shrugged.

"I was never close enough to the business end, any of Andy's business dealings, to know. My time was devoted to the art, what mattered."

I said, "Henri Godard. You think he would have known?"

Another shrug. "Nothing we ever talked about, so you'd have to ask him." A flash of memory. "Oh. I mean if Hank were still here."

"Could he have known?"

"Same answer," Feather said.

By now he was fidgeting like he couldn't shake a bug out of his slacks. His eyes were blinking wildly. His words telling one story, his body language telling us a different story. He was laying out dots, but they didn't connect.

Feather swallowed and exhaled a gasping breath.

Then he switched subjects.

"The great oils, as you'd put it, came later," he said. "With my art background and great eye for quality, I began collecting from my first day in New York. Early Warhols, at a bargain; what I couldn't take home for nothing. Works by other Pop artists. Very often a spectacular, undervalued find. A steal at auction, where I caught something other collectors missed. Mostly prints. Some oils. Some sculpture. Most of it I picked up for a song or on terms. If necessary, I spent my meager salary from Andy, from odd jobs, on art instead of on food. I won't tell you how often I fell behind in the rent.

"Obsession, a collector's disease, but it was worth it, worth it, worth it. Slowly, I was able to trade up. Up, up, up. Later, when the money began to flow in from my own work, I could purchase outright. My screen prints brought me enough money to purchase the Homestead.

"It was the perfect home for me and my expanding, ever-growing collection. When Hank came to me, after I accepted his proposal and we got cracking, more money flowed in than I ever dreamed possible. With my share I continued to build my collection and turn it into what it is today."

Feather threw his hands to the room and fell silent.

"A museum for one," I said.

"Yes, for now. It's my intention to share it with the world one day. The Rudolph M. Feather Collection. I see it in its own wing at the Smithsonian. All of a piece as some small visual, eternal measure of my time on earth."

Zev made a scoffing sound.

Ari said, "Better it should go to Washington for the Holocaust Museum, Feather, don't you think so?"

Feather froze. His eyes, which had been wild with self-adoration, grew bigger, bothered, almost frightened by Ari's words.

"I don't understand what that means," he said, shaking his head and at the same time trying to control the palsy in his hands.

Ari said casually, as if he hadn't heard Feather, "Only the works where we're unable to locate the rightful owner."

Feather gasped for air.

Slammed his fist down onto the table.

"I told you I don't know what you're talking about. I am the rightful owner. Me! Me! Me!"

Zev backhanded Feather's arm.

"Come off it, Feather. We know what we've been seeing. We know where it comes from. We know what it's all about. We know you're a damned liar."

Feather's gaze filled with poison for Zev.

"Fuck, fuck, fuck you!" he screamed, no longer able to contain himself.

He reached out for Zev, going for his throat.

Zev backed away and brought a hard slap across Feather's cheek, then another one.

"Don't go stupid on us," Zev said.

Augie said to Feather, "There's something they haven't told you yet."

Feather rubbed his cheek, ran his hand across his face to get to the other one, rubbed some more, and waited for Augie to say more.

Augie said, "They know better, Frankie Et Cetera. We all do."

"No way to know better."

Ari said, "We heard better from Henri Godard."

"That cheating liar? What came between us before. Lies lies lies. If he were still alive, if he were here, I would tell him that to his scurvy little face."

Ari looked at Zev, who nodded and, rising, said, "I'll go and get him."

28

have to believe I looked as astounded as Rudy Feather when Zev said that, and no less so a few minutes later, while he led a trussed-up Godard into the library and sat him on a straight-backed antique chair by the reading table. He was a little unsteady on his feet, and bare-chested, his polo shirt and apron serving as a mountainous, makeshift bandage on his back, held in place by the apron strings.

The renegade master printer and the former Bug Boy shot arrows at each other's eyes while Ari quickly explained how Augie had realized he'd acted too hastily administering last rights for Godard when, midway through a melancholic chant Brother Kalman had learned during his soul-searching time among the holy men of India, Godard managed to reach up and clamp his hand to Augie's mouth.

In a voice barely more than a remote washboard rasp, he had commanded, "Stop that moronic singing and help me, you damn fool idiot."

The ricocheted bullet had hit Godard on the back in a noncritical area, with great force but without causing any serious damage.

Ari said, "Before then, we had removed Feather and you to the library. Zev had gone back across to see if he could find how your assailant disappeared. He came for me and we traded off with our questioning of Feather and Godard during your lengthy nap."

"Quite successfully," Zev said.

"But obviously not without contradiction," I said.

"Not without contradiction," Ari repeated, "but getting at the truth is something we have a great deal of experience with, Zev and I."

"Whatever that peasant Feather said, you can't believe a word of it," Godard said. "What you would expect from a person who eats cockroaches and mice and brags about it like he's scaled Mount Everest."

"See, always lies from his mouth," Feather said. "You know what they say about the French? Every breath they take is a lie. He proves it just now, doesn't he? Doesn't he?"

They traded several more insults until Ari gave Zev a high sign. Zev whipped out one of the Glocks he was carrying, a .40-caliber semi-automatic. Waved it in their faces. They got the message and shut up.

At once the noise level reduced to the clamoring of the storm front that seemed to be growing again outside. Banging at the walls like a distant drummer.

Ari said, "Monsieur Godard, you and Mr. Feather seem to differ greatly in your stories."

"About what?"

"About everything."

"I suppose he bragged about how big and important he was in making prints. A competent hack until I came along."

"Liar, liar, liar!"

Zev said, "Shut up, Feather," and made sure Feather saw him slide his finger inside the Glock's trigger guard.

Feather shut up.

"Forget that for the time being, monsieur," Ari said. "Please repeat for everyone to hear what you told us about Mr. Feather's art collection, which he told us results from his Warhol silkscreens and the work you did together."

"Some of it yes, most of it no," Godard said. He gave Feather a look that said he would be taking pleasure from what he was about to reveal. "Frankie was the heir to most of the collection from birth, long before he even heard of Andy Warhol, when all he knew from a can of Campbell's soup was that inside was soup. How he came to own this place and so much greatness on the walls. Why I even came to want him for a partner in the first place. A dishonest rich boy with money to burn."

"Scum of the earth!"

"Feather, I told you to shut your face." Zev moved over and pushed the Glock against Feather's temple.

Feather shut up.

Ari urged Godard to continue.

The story Godard told unhurriedly went back to the thirties and forties in wartime Europe.

"You know how the Nazis stole art from the Jews, from others, during their rise to power, looting and plundering with the same clockwork precision they expected from their railroads," he began. "In Occupied France, the confiscation of the art fell to three special branches of Hitler's Third Reich, especially the *Einsatzstab Reichsleiter Rosenberg fur die Besetzten Gebiete*, called the ERR.

"The ERR inventory of stolen treasures not shipped back to Germany, where castles and once-private homes were turned into warehouses, became so large that it quickly outstripped the capacity of locations in France that were designated as depots. Among them were the German embassy, assorted rooms at the Louvre, and storerooms contributed by collaborating art dealers, auction houses, and private collectors who were not Jews and therefore able to curry favor with the Nazis. The Louvre's Jeu de Paume itself housed more than four hundred crates of paintings and sculptures designated for cataloging before being sent on to their Fatherland.

"In 1944, after the Liberation, the Americans and the British began searching out, gathering, and storing many of the plundered treasures, intent upon returning these works to their rightful owners. They set up warehouses in Germany where found works could be inventoried, just like the Nazis had done at the Jeu de Paume. A great, great many of the missing works were located by the time the search ended, but a number equally as great stayed missing. Right to this day. Only, not all of them are as missing as they seem. Only missing from sight."

Stevie said, "Like the art here?"

Godard nodded and continued.

"Growing up, I heard of this from my late father," he said. "More. I heard how many of the Americans and British soldiers knew the value of what they were looking for. How art would be found, only to pass into their hands and—poof!—disappear again. They had become creatures as greedy as the Germans had been. Some paintings were sold fast into the black market. Others they hid until they could safely be transported back home, to eventually be sold privately for a sizable profit.

"One of the soldiers, an American senior intelligence officer, had a love for fine art greater than his honesty. He kept the best of what he located for himself and hid it away in the cellar of a château outside of Paris. Years later he retrieved the paintings and got them back to America."

"Rudy Feather's father," I guessed.

"Of course," Godard said. "A few of the pieces he sold off, to support his family, to buy the Homestead, to build his underground museum and enjoy his personal spoils of war the way other American soldiers framed or mounted souvenirs taken off the bodies of dead Germans."

Feather made a derisive noise.

"See what I mean about lies? Was Godard even born then? He always takes great pleasure in demeaning me. He is the Thomas Alva Edison of storytellers. One invention after another after another."

"Shall I tell you how I know, then, Frankie?"

"Don't worry about him," Zev said. "Just tell us."

Veins began popping out of Feather's neck and temples, a bluish shade that grew increasingly radiant as what color was left continued to drain from his face.

"First, I request freedom from my constraints," Godard said, fidgeting in his chair. He exhibited his hands, which were bound at the wrists with miles of a thin wrapping cord. To Zev, with a dry smile: "You certainly know how to tie a tight package, monsieur."

Ari signaled approval.

Zev unbound Godard, who expressed his appreciation as he rolled, stretched and flexed circulation back into his hands.

I watched the master printer's forced smile give way to melancholy as his eyes wandered the room like a fly looking for a landing spot. They attached briefly to Picasso's "blue period" nude before settling on a small Matisse lithograph of a reclining nude I'd overlooked earlier, resting at an angle on a bookshelf across from the Picasso and now inch-for-inch its rival for attention.

Godard caught me studying him and said, "My work. One of my

first forgeries and, oh, did it make my papa angry to recognize what his son could achieve that not even the great Henri Jean-Jacques Victor Hugo Godard *père* could achieve."

"The story, man," Zev said impatiently.

"*Oui*, of course. How I would come to know from stolen treasure and Feather's papa? I know it from Hugo, from my own papa, you see? So honest to the outside world that he would disown his own son, yet in truth my sturdy oak was a brigand like all the others who after the war profited and prospered over the graves of thousands. Not just Frankie's father, also my own father, and came the time, they were in it together."

He rose and crossed the room to the Matisse, lifted it lovingly from the bookshelf, and appeared to be tracing the image with his index finger while he spoke.

"After the war, Papa had gone to Paris to apprentice at an atelier," Godard said. "He was a fifteen- or sixteen-year-old farm boy and anxious to learn and experience beyond the poverty he has grown up with, but so far not much good with anything except a broom and trash barrels.

"One day a soldier came into the atelier, where he had been sent by a dealer on the Rue Faubourg Saint-Honoré, whose gallery had been conspicuously open for business throughout the war." Godard sent a nod and a *You know what that means* kind of look over the gilded Matisse frame. "It seems that the dealer was in cahoots with the atelier, and next thing, my father was an errand boy delivering stolen treasures to the château of a prominent lawyer who had coincidentally also prospered throughout the war. Some of these artworks found a place on the walls, but Papa was directed to carry most of them down to the cellar, where they were hidden from sight.

"These errands increased. It wasn't just this soldier who—"

"Rudy Feather's father," I said, interrupting.

"*Oui*. Yes."

Feather hammered the table surface.

Godard ignored him and continued: "Yes, he was the one, the avaricious American senior intelligence officer, but he was not the only one who came to use the dealer, the printer and the lawyer as their means for criminal activities. There were other soldiers as well.

"My papa soon found himself on a treadmill, making more and more trips to the château. Discovering all its secrets. More than that, he discovered one of the lawyer's daughters, who in time became his wife. My mother.

"I suppose you want to ask, Did Hugo come to marry her for love or for greed? I would have to say, as my mama once confided to me, as she confided so much, it was a little of both. After all, their five children speak to some touch of the heart.

"In time, this union financed my papa's own atelier and comfortable lifestyle. How he could afford to buy my way out of certain problems before he disowned me entirely, and this before Grandpapa died and Papa came into possession of the treasures buried in the basement of the château."

Godard returned the Matisse to the shelf and started to wander the library like a shepherd searching for lost sheep, exploring everything and nothing at the same time. It seemed to me that the history he was reciting may have turned into, perhaps surprisingly, something as unpleasant for Godard as he had expected to make it for Feather.

I'd experienced similar reactions before in interview situations and, typical of me, caught myself feeling sorry for the guy, but—

I wasn't about to turn Godard off.

I couldn't let my emotions get in the way of what Ari and Zev, all of us, were on the verge of learning from him.

I sensed we were closing in on it.

Another look at Feather showed me he did, too.

There was still defiance in his demeanor, the way he sat stiff-backed at the table, hands embracing, like some defendant daring his jury to return a guilty verdict, but I also read it as resignation, a condemned prisoner strapped inside the gas chamber and waiting for the cyanide pellets to drop.

I thought, What could Godard possibly reveal that was bad enough to provoke this reaction in him?

What could we learn now that was worse than the wartime crimes his father had committed and, later, visited upon the son?

Faster than a finger-snap, as if he had read my mind, Feather became the poster boy for dejection.

His shoulders sagged, his chin dropped onto his chest, his downcast eyes became desperate to escape his face.

He cried out in a voice filled with despair, "The two of them played me for the fool. All along. A sap was all I ever was to them. All along. A sap, sap, sap."

And I thought, *That's it?*

Sap, sap, sap?

That Godard had held Feather up to ridicule?

Punctured his ego and put it on public display?

I split my attention between Feather and Godard, waiting for one of them to lay some meat on the bones of the Bible's observation about pride going before the fall.

Feather's reaction seemed to reinvigorate Godard, who bared his mouthful of misshapen, tobacco-stained brown-and-yellow teeth and showed off a thumbs-up sign.

"*Oui*. The worst kind of sap," Godard said. "The kind who keeps coming back for more."

Feather fixated on his neatly trimmed, highly glossed thumbnails, unaware or ignoring the tear bubbles bursting by the bridge of his nose and running down his cheeks.

Godard moved to one of the library's ladders on wheels and made himself comfortable on a lower step.

"You think it was coincidence that he and I would meet up making Warhol prints?" he said. "In a fairy tale, maybe. It was calculated, part of a plan." Focusing in on Ari and Zev. "I suppose now you want to know how?"

"All of it, yes," Ari said.

"That's our deal, nothing less," Zev said.

Godard said, "After, I'm free to leave here unharmed?"

"I'll even give you the shirt off my back," Zev said, showing a spark of good-natured humor.

"Better from his closet," the master printer responded, indicating Feather with his chin. "Custom-made of the finest silk. They defy sweat. Frankie, he sweats a lot."

Godard resumed his story. He filled it with grandiose gestures, dramatic pauses and every so often a contemptuous laugh for Feather, who'd pull out of his personal abyss briefly, to respond with the whimpers of an ailing mutt.

"So, at an appropriate time after Grandpapa died, Papa took his place in the business of making a fortune off these well-hidden looted masterpieces," Godard said. "Feather was still in the picture, and so was another partner in crime, a soldier named Porter Havilland. Does that name mean anything to you?"

Ari and Zev sent each other a blank look. Ari took out a small spiral pad and a ballpoint. Wrote down the name. Spelling *Havilland* aloud to be sure he had it right.

"*Oui*. What he's known as to me, but he's used many noms de plume over the years since, like Feather and others with secrets. Something to hide.

"To say my papa cut me adrift and let it go there would be kinder than he deserves from me," Godard continued, "but Mama was always understanding in ways only a mother can be, so at my lowest I could turn to her, as I did when Porter Havilland came to me with an offer. Whenever I could give him the name and location of one of my papa's customers, he would have an appropriate sum of money for me in payment."

"What was that about?" Stevie said.

"I didn't ask, he didn't volunteer," Godard replied. "I didn't care, except for the money. Always a generous amount, I assure you, to someone frequently in need. When I ran out of my own knowledge, I prevailed upon my mama, who never let me down.

"By this time, Porter Havilland and I had built a relationship based on my artful contributions to the world of lithography and other multiple images. I delivered the goods and he paid me a fair price. Sometimes he wanted something in particular and, if it didn't already exist, I was pleased to find a way to add it to my inventory.

Ari said, "And Feather's papa, he was also a partner in this enterprise?"

"*Non.* Never that I knew of, anyway. They'd had a falling-out, you see. At some point Havilland discovered Feather had not lived up to his part of their association. For years he had been selling or siphoning off paintings that belonged to both of them."

" 'Honor among thieves,' " I said.

Godard laughed facetiously.

"Not among any thieves I have ever known, monsieur."

The look he turned on Rudy Feather let us know who led his list.

This time, Godard's taunt drew a different sound out of Feather, whose eyes were drying into something more intense, almost dangerous, like he was rounding the corner that would take him over the edge.

If Godard noticed, he didn't let on, continuing: "I got a call one day out of the blue from Havilland. About what we since have come to know as Andy Warhol's portraits suite. He had invited collectors to take part based mainly on names he had secured from me over the years. Only I could be trusted to do the printing, he said. I said, naturally, that I could do it all. Leave it to me. But Havilland was anxious the prints be authentic, so Warhol had been chosen.

"Warhol seemed like an odd choice, *non?* But it wasn't for me to say. How I come to meet Warhol and Frankie there. Then—*poof!*—Warhol is going, gone, like the traffic at the Arch, and Frankie was doing the work. Always bragging to be sure I knew how important he was, not only to Warhol, but the world as well. I listened, I learned. I never forgot.

"Some time after we finished and went separate ways, I once again had need for financial remedy. I brought my case to Havilland, to no avail this time. I remember Frankie and his claims of secret wealth, riches beyond my wildest dreams that are someday to be his. I reconnected with him and here is what I discovered." A grand gesture with his arms. "This modestly talented man in this *palais fantastique*, printing Andy Warhols and others in a piddling little shop downstairs." A throwaway gesture. "I describe to him what more is possible with us working together. A bottomless pot of gold. This golden goose could not go for it fast enough."

Godard turned his palms to the ceiling.

"And that's the story, gentlemen."

Part of it, maybe, I thought.

For all the dots Godard had connected—some the same as Feather, but with a different egomaniacal twist—there were still too many stranded orphans.

I asked, "Did you ever learn why Porter Havilland wanted Andy Warhol? Because he had linked Frankie Freddie Frook to his missing partner Feather, was that it?"

Godard laughed like he had just heard the funniest joke ever. He let an answer linger as a puzzle momentarily before slapping the mattress of hair on his bare chest with a palm and advising, "It was I myself who saw the truth and brought it to the attention of Porter Havilland."

"And what was that truth?" Ari said, calmly digging as usual.

Godard never got a chance to answer.

An explosion preceded the thump that put a blooming red rose to Godard's chest.

His back hit the library steps.

He looked down in amazement and touched his finger to the hole before pitching forward onto the intricately woven Oriental rug on his side, adding a fresh layer of crimson to the delicate geometric hearts and flowers design.

We'd been so focused on Godard that nobody had been paying attention to Feather, who had pulled a gun from somewhere and was now looking at the master printer with the kind of smile you usually saw on the face of a carnival-midway sharpshooter who had just won a teddy bear for his date.

29

In the frozen moment that follows startled surprise, Feather pushed back his chair, jumped up, and pitched the gun at Godard. It hit Godard's shoulder and bounced onto the rug as Feather swerved and did something to a section of the bookcase. The section swung inward like the secret entrance to Ali Baba's cave.

Feather leaped inside. The section closed behind him with equal swiftness, and I heard a resounding click of locks shifting into place.

Feather was safely lost behind a wall of books.

Zev, past his astonishment, did a 360-degree turn and got off five quick shots, wounding as many leather bindings. He jumped at the bookcase. Pounded everywhere, trying to hit the key that would reopen the secret door.

No luck.

Out of frustration, Zev killed three more bindings.

Ari, who'd been patting down the table surface, went to his knees and began feeling the underside. Made a noise of discovery and moved farther under the table.

Assorted sounds for several moments before Ari backed out and used the table as a catapult onto his feet.

"A buzzer under there, like a doorbell," he said. "I tried it. Anything?"

Zev said, "Nothing." He began checking support panels and underneath shelves.

"Still nothing, dammit!"

He dug his hand behind a row of books and pulled at them angrily.

They crashed to the floor.

Stevie was leaning over Augie, who was on his haunches next to Godard, checking him for a pulse.

Without looking up, he announced, "This time it's for sure," and began reciting his Order's jumble of last rites over the lifeless body of Henri Godard.

I picked up the weapon. A .22-caliber Ruger pistol, a mail-order blue-ribbon choice favored by schoolkid killers and others. Like that fourteen-year-old in Paducah, Kentucky, who'd fired a dozen shots into his prayer group, killing three and wounding five others just after the assembly recited its final *Amen*. Like that looney-tunes in Salt Lake City killed by the police after he gunned down a woman and a security guard and wounded four others at the Mormon Family History Library.

Stevie bolted upright and called at Ari and Zev, "Try under the rug. Maybe that's where. How he did it."

I jammed the Ruger inside my belt, behind my back, and moved over to help Zev pull chairs out of the way and adjust the table, allowing Ari to throw back the rug. There was a button the size of a fifty-cent piece rising less than an inch inside the metal enclosure that was built flush with the parquet flooring.

Ari called out, "Bingo!"

Pushed down on the button with his sole.

Nothing happened.

He released the button and tried again.

Still nothing.

He banged the button hard with his heel. Once, twice. Again and again. Nothing.

It was my turn for a good idea.

I felt underneath the table for the doorbell Ari had mentioned, pushed and kept it depressed, and said to Ari, "Now try the button."

"What's to lose?" he said, and stepped on it.

Nothing at first, then—

The bookcase section swung open.

Zev raced inside behind his Glock, followed by Ari and his Glock.

I ordered Stevie, "Stay out here with Augie," and went in after them, ready to pull the trigger on Feather's Ruger.

Stevie, paying her usual attention to my demands, was on my heels.

The space was cramped, cold and dark except for a pale shaft of light entering through the doorway shelving. Three seemingly solid cement walls and nowhere to go except back into the library.

"Something's got to give in here," Ari said. "Another door somewhere. Feather didn't just vanish into thin air."

He ran his hand over one of the walls, then the others, crying out several times, when he encountered a nail or some other sharp protrusion.

The ceiling wasn't more than five or six inches higher than any of us.

Zev reached up and patted around.

Reported, "Not so much as a lightbulb."

His words clicked on a lightbulb in the *Think* balloon above my head.

I said, "Try the floor. A hatch. Like the tunnel hatch that got Augie, Aleta and me out of here."

"Make us some room," Ari said.

Stevie and I backed out and watched as they navigated the floor on all fours, their noses almost as close to the wood as their exploring fingers.

Maybe a minute later, Ari said, "Here. A latch."

Zev stepped back while Ari yanked up on it.

Nothing.

"Move away," Zev said and, when Ari was clear of the area, he shot twice into the wooden flooring. There was a springing noise and this time the hatch responded to Ari's pull.

He quickly jackknifed his body into the small opening headfirst, Zev securing his ankles, and advised in a voice coated with a hollow echo, "A ladder, but I can't see how far down it goes."

Zev helped him out.

Ari adjusted into a sitting position, his legs dangling over the side of the opening, and ordered, "Wait on us while we chase after this nutcase." Reading my expression correctly, he said, "The place could be full of secret doors, tunnels, who knows what else. He could show up back here, so you hold down the fort, Neil."

He gave a thumbs-up and dropped out of sight, followed by Zev.

Stevie and I settled at the table.

Augie draped Henri Godard's head with a delicate lace antimacassar he'd taken from an easy chair and joined us.

None of us spoke for several minutes.

I was taking mental stock of what we'd been through, what it all might mean, and imagined they were doing the same.

Augie spoke first.

"Zev is probably right," he said. "If the Homestead was part of the underground railway running slaves to safety, it stands to reason there'd be more than one hiding place and lots of passageways running through the walls."

Stevie nodded agreement, suggesting, "How the guy who clobbered Neil managed to get away. Turned into a ghost, like Feather."

I sensed something else turning wheels in her mind.

"What?" I said.

She unwound her face and ran a hand over the furrows that had formed on her forehead, then pushed loose strands of hair behind her ears.

"Honey, I think this room has another secret." Nodded agreement, this time with herself. "Before, Feather had me in a conference room where his buzzers were on a wall panel, in plain sight. Here everything is hidden. Buzzers under the table, under the rug to open doors. A gun. Extra protection, extra security . . . For what?"

I said, "Maybe also in the other room? All over? Making up for the lack of security outside the place? Maybe because of the art. In this room, the Picasso."

"Something," Stevie said.

She rose from the table.

Searched the room with her eyes.

I wasn't convinced, but I played along with her.

Got up and did some wandering.

When I arrived in front of the Picasso, I stepped back to admire it, then moved closer and began running a hand up and down the interior of the blue nude's immense, intricate and superbly hand-carved golden frame.

"I saw this once in a movie," I said, grinning over a shoulder. "A lot of movies."

I gave the frame a tug, and—

Life imitated art. The frame swung out, taking with it the lower portion of the wall to the floor. Revealing the solemn green steel door to a walk-in vault.

Stevie replaced her sarcastic *hah-hah-hah* with a simple declarative "Hah!" of triumph.

"I'd have given Feather credit for more originality," I said.

Stevie said, "Why? All he's ever been is a copycat."

I drew an invisible vertical line in the air.

"Score one for you," I said.

"You mean one more," Stevie said. "Now open it."

"Pressing our psychic phenomena, are we? Combination lock, notice?"

"Just try the handle, okay?"

I bowed obediently, gripped the door lever, turned it down and pulled.

The vault door glided open.

Augie guffawed and applauded.

Stevie smirked.

"I guess that's from a movie you missed," she said.

I stepped inside and felt for a light switch.

Unlike the hidden room, the vault had one.

The interior was seven or eight feet deep and about that wide across. Across one wall was a row of vertical storage bins full of framed and unframed oils, watercolors and drawings, suggesting the Feathers had run out of wall space but not their penchant for art thievery. Print cabinets stretched across the opposite wall, and I supposed the wide drawers were full of the authentic works on which Godard and Feather based their phonies.

I was about to open one for inspection when something sitting on top of the counter at the far end caught my eye. It looked like the black presentation box of the Warhol suite. The black lettering on the white label in the center of the cover said:

Andy Warhol
P O R t r a I T S

I walked out holding it in front of me like a serving tray and said, "Lookee, lookee. Even though you only brought the five, Feather thought enough of the silkscreens to get them stashed in a hurry."

Stevie shook her head vigorously.

"Can't be, honey. No. From the time I got here, Feather was never alone with them. They still have to be where he took me. His conference room."

Augie and I chased after her as she raced out the door to the central corridor.

Watched as she checked out one room after another until she found the room she was looking for.

"There," Stevie said, pointing at five silkscreens neatly spread out single file on the conference table, next to a black presentation box, twin to the one I was holding.

"Add one more question to the mix," I said. "If Feather already had a suite, why pay a ridiculous price for another one?"

Augie said, "I taught you better than to assume, amigo. Let's see what's in the box."

A voice behind us said, "An excellent idea."

We spun around.

It was the man who got away from me downstairs.

Standing just inside the door.

Aiming the 9mm automatic Zev had given me.

He said, "The gloves on the floor. One of you get them while Gulliver puts the box on the table. Then, open up the box and make sure what's inside."

"Who are you?" Augie said.

"Better you shouldn't know that, old man. Do what I ask or somebody'll be saying final rites over you."

"Is that a threat?"

"It can be more than that."

I said, "Augie, shut up and put on the gloves."

He bent over for them and worked his fingers into them like he was O.J. Simpson.

I settled the box on the table. Undid the cover tie-strings.

Moved to Stevie and put an arm around her. Pulled her closer.

She didn't resist.

Her hand moved behind me and patted the Ruger parked there inside my belt.

My pulse quickened and I flashed her a *Don't you dare* look.

Her flash back told me nothing.

Augie took off the top sheet of protective tissue and put it on the conference table. He alternated between tissues and silkscreens, making a fast inspection of each print before laying it facedown. When he was finished, he turned over the stack and carefully settled it back inside the black box. Closed and tied the cover and, looking back at the man, said, "All Warhols. All from the suite. Twelve of them."

The man said, "Twelve, yes?"

Like he already knew the answer.

Like he'd been quietly counting to himself, same as me.

Augie snapped back at him, "I said twelve."

I felt Stevie's fingers closing around the Ruger's fat grip and did a quick two-step away from her.

As quickly, the man snapped his gun on a direct path to my chest and said, "Please, Gulliver. Nothing foolish."

I raised my arms parallel to the floor.

"Thank you," he said; then, patiently, "The only reason any of you are still alive is because Miss Marriner helped me out earlier." He cracked a tight, brief smile. "Returning the favor, miss, but now we're even, so nobody, not Gulliver or anybody, press your luck. Not even you, Miss Marriner."

He stepped away from the door and said, "Old man, take the portfolio out to the hallway, put it down on the carpet and then go back."

Augie grumbled something unintelligible, but did as he was ordered.

The man told him, "Say a prayer for me sometime," and moved backward from the room.

He pulled the door closed.

I yanked out the Ruger and started after him, Augie on my heels.

The hallway was empty. The front door was open, the storm wind drumming it against the wall. The crystal chandelier dancing madly while foul swamp-smells and a dense curtain of rain poured inside.

I got there and pushed shoulder-hard against the wind. It wouldn't let me outside.

Augie cupped the side of his mouth and called over the cacophony of noise, "Write him off, kiddo. If he's out there he isn't going to get far, not in that storm."

Together we struggled to close the door. Headed back to the conference room.

Stevie was no longer alone.

Ari was with her.

I surveyed the room and asked, "Where's Zev?"

"Toilet," Ari said, pointing to an interior door.

"Feather?"

"Gone," Ari said, and shrugged it off.

Augie said, "He got away?"

"In a manner of speaking," Ari said, as Zev came into the room mopping his hands and his face with a bath towel.

He padded across the room and gave the towel and a sopping-wet washcloth to Ari, whose clothing was covered in muck; grime glued to his face with sweat.

"Door on the other side of the toilet leads into a room smaller than this one, like a private room," Zev announced, settling down in a half-sitting position on the conference table, near where Stevie sat. "Two leather easy chairs and some pieces of antique furniture. The mantel and walls full of photographs like the kind you see in a den. Mostly black-and-white. All old. Showing signs of aging."

Ari ran the cloth around his face, worked it around his hands, as he explained, "I was right about tunnels and trapdoors. One hell of a chase Feather gave us, believe you me. We took a few wrong turns down and around, including back to the atelier. Down one more level to a boat dock. A powerboat bouncing like crazy in rough waters pouring in from the marsh and farther out; I suppose, from the Intracoastal Waterway."

He folded the towels neatly and placed them on top of the table, then eased into the chair next to Stevie.

Zev said, "Next thing, we zig and zag and find we're at the place downstairs where you escaped from. The escape hole open. A body's floating heels-up in marsh water that's lapping at the floor."

"Feather," I said.

Zev shook his head.

"No idea. A young man. But right after that Ari and I see a body sprawled in a corner. This one Feather for sure. A bullet at close range. Split open his head like a melon."

"By the guy who got away from me?"

"Unless there's another shooter we don't know about."

Ari waved off the idea. "Stevie said you went chasing after him?"

"He beat Augie and me out the front door. We couldn't get past the storm."

"If he's out there, that takes care of him, too," Ari said.

"And Feather's Warhols and so much for us having the twelfth print," Stevie said.

Ari's face registered surprise. "What else did we miss going after Feather, before we found you here?"

She told him.

Ari clucked his tongue.

"A shame, then, us getting this close to having the twelfth print

> >
> }

finally and seeing what it is made it so special for Feather, for the shooter, for this Porter Havilland we heard about. For who knows who else or how many."

He looked across the room to Augie, who'd been sitting quietly all this time.

"Augie, maybe you had a good enough look when you were checking them for the shooter that later you'll be able to give us a description of the collector? His piece of art?"

"No," Augie said.

He got up and crossed to the conference table, his good eye sparkling like someone had sprinkled it with pixie dust. Gave a *Nice doggie* pat to the lid of the presentation box.

Announced, "I can do much better than that, Ari."

Augie waited for everyone's attention to shift back to him from the box before he sent a hitchhiker's thumb in my direction and said, "When my amigo made a foolish move that distracted the shooter, I put the time to good use."

My smile grew almost as expansive as his guessing, "You switched boxes."

"Twelve silkscreens for five, kiddo. Not a bad trade in any man's league."

The twelfth print was like the other eleven created in the style and name of Andy Warhol by Rudy Feather and Henri Godard, the portrait of a collector with a favored piece of stolen art from his secret collection.

I recognized the painting at once as the Gainsborough portrait of a young boy I had seen and admired in Feather's parlor.

The collector was an older version of Feather by about twenty-five or thirty years, the same face down to the Errol Flynn slash of a mustache and the lantern jaw. The body bent and shrunken by age.

Feather's father, all of us speculated.

Our guess was confirmed by a cracked and brown, decal-edged snapshot mounted in a sterling-silver frame that Zev went after from the next room. It showed Feather decked out in a U.S. Army uniform circa World War Two, his lieutenant's cap tilted at a rakish angle, posing in front of the Louvre like he owned the place.

"Nothing at all different or special about the print," Zev said, "so why would it be so important, so valuable to anyone but the son, and then only for sentimental reasons?"

We stayed congregated in front of the print, engaging in questions and speculation, until I realized something so obvious we'd all overlooked it up to now.

Henri Godard's embossed chop mark was missing from the lower right corner where it belonged.

"It's a fake," I said. "This silkscreen is a phony. We still don't have the real twelfth print."

30

Clegg spent the night nesting uncomfortably between the walls, rather than risk a room where he might be discovered by Gulliver, Marriner, one of the others. Like him, he supposed, the storm was keeping them from leaving, but the sound of their movements had stopped hours ago, whereas he couldn't sleep, kept awake by the hammering rain and his own anxieties.

His body ached from the cold and the dampness, hurt too much for him to believe he could get away again if they found him.

Hunger had also robbed him of strength.

Good thing he'd had a chance to explore the trapdoors and tunnels Godard told him about. Otherwise he would have been done for when he couldn't get out the front door to the cars in Feather's garage.

Hot-wire one.

Take off.

Maybe that was a good thing, too.

Clegg imagined what the roads looked like now, buried under impenetrable layers of mud or washed out altogether. Any wrong turn in the blinding downpour ending with a drop into one of the marshes.

He was resolved to get away safely. Nothing to do with the boss or the Warhols Porter Havilland coveted like the crown jewels, for reasons Havilland never shared with him, even after all this time and so much killing.

Everything to do with his son. The boy needed him.

There was no one else anymore.

Clegg had never been so close to being caught before. He didn't like the feeling that came with it. Not at all.

No Clegg anymore, and who knows what might become of his son.

Clegg picked up the box of Warhols and spoke to it.

"This is for my son, that's why," he said in a whisper that didn't have to rise above the winds, the loose-branches and whatever else might be trying to break through the walls of the mansion.

What he had to say was for his own ears. Nobody else's business.

"But this finishes it," he said. "I deliver the twelve. I get my last payment. I am gone. Finished. *Finito.* Through. Retired. Over and out. Gone with the wind."

Clegg paused and snorted what passed for a laugh at the joke: Gone with the wind.

Appropriate here and now, this place, this time, but a joke he knew he never would have made if he'd had to think about it.

He had never been the joking kind, not even growing up, when there was nothing to joke about except poverty, which was no laughing matter to him, only an excuse for street and school bullies to send him home bloodied. Or his father to rip into him, whenever the old man was drunk. Or sober, beating up on his mother first, Clegg unable to pull him off her, hard as he tried.

The only good that ever came out of that childhood was the childhood he was determined to create for his son. That the boy could still laugh and smile like a saint in spite of his late lousy rotten mother and the miserable—

Clegg snapped his eyes shut to that part.

He flashed back to Porter Havilland.

In the beginning, he'd agreed to join Havilland for the money. More than he'd ever made on his own, either off his studies in fine art or the expertise he came to without a degree, Murder 101 not on any college curriculum he'd ever come across. One of those providential learn-while-you-earn life experiences.

He banked most of what he made with Havilland, against future uncertainty. He made it his retirement fund, holding out only enough to live on and pay for whatever the doctors said his son needed. Cash up front. For them and for the hospitals and for—

He snapped his eyes shut again.

Yes, that, too.

Clegg brushed at his eyes.

God, I love you, son. Daddy loves you.

I know that, no matter what he makes of me, God loves you, too.

No medical insurance in his line of work, why he began filching art for himself. Retirement and security on the layaway plan. His bonus for a job well done, for Christmas, for the vacations he never had time to take.

Thank you, boss.

Oh, you don't know about that, do you, boss?

Fuck you, boss.

Fuck you very much, boss.

When he started taking pieces of art for himself from the collectors in the Warhol suite, he never knowingly took any work that had the taint of Nazi looting and plundering, or the unconscionable immorality of the pirates who followed after them caring more about satisfaction than the source, Porter Havilland included.

Clegg understood his hands were filthy enough without that sin, although some of it became his own sin anyway after he began reading about the Holocaust.

The Nazi bullies.

All the world their neighborhood.

Dachau, one of their playgrounds, where his emotions, his rage, were confirmed and the conflicts inside him grew.

Damn them, and—

Damned if he didn't get a special sense of contentment in ridding the planet of Von Harbou and his bully boys. The blood on his hands that time bore him great satisfaction—not guilt—exactly like the feeling he had when he administered a final goodbye to his old man before fleeing home.

Also, like an act of contrition.

Never again, old man.

Never again, Herr Doktor.

Never.

Arbeit Macht Frei, Herr Doktor.

Work Brings Freedom, Herr Havilland.
Soon, son. Soon. Soon, my dear little boy.

The silence woke him.

Clegg had no memory of falling asleep or for how long. Here in the dark, no sense, either, of the time. Only that it was quiet. No discernible noises inside the Homestead or from the storm. He was still in a sitting position, his back braced by the wall interior, his legs extended across the narrow space to the opposite wall.

He rose slowly and stretched the kinks out of his body, did a set of painful knee bends before picking up the Warhol presentation box and heading for the passageway he'd used in getting here from the boat dock.

He counted off the steps to the connecting door. Inched it open. The powerboat was steady, catching some reflection from the light bouncing off the marsh water. The light felt like the hours before dawn to him. Clegg held back another few minutes to be certain that nobody was around, then hurried across to the boat, ready to use the 9mm automatic, if it came to that.

Clegg checked out the open cockpit first. He inched up the corners of his mouth and said a respectful thank-you to Dame Fortune. The key was in the ignition.

He wrapped the Warhol box in plastic sheeting he found in the hull and securely strapped it to the passenger seat before he somehow managed to raise the boat anchor into its locker. He settled behind the wheel, powered up and headed into the marsh, pretending he was as good behind the wheel of a boat as he was a car, a notion dispelled at once when the boat leaped out of control and down the narrow channel.

The brake pedal resisted him.

He fought with the wheel, trying to slow the boat and at the same time keep it from leaping onto land.

Losing his grip several times and almost sending the boat into a spin.

Demanding more of his muscles than they had a right to give him.

Feeling excruciating pressure and pain explode onto his shoulders and somersault down his back.

Channels ahead running left and right.

Clegg needed to choose and fast, or crash into giant oaks lined across like a wall of telephone poles. The powerboat had developed a mind of its own.

He forced the wheel to the right, pulling strength from an image of his son, and screamed, "Turn, damn it, turn!"

The boat turned, but otherwise refused to cooperate.

The knot gauge reading at least the equivalent of a hundred miles an hour—

Scarcely slowed by marsh mud and garbage and a growing head-wind pushing the boggy water and stray debris over the wraparound windshield.

The storm's way of announcing it was on its way back.

The orange-tinted sky gone dark and gloomy, denying its earlier promise of a tranquil day.

Clegg forced the wheel steady with one hand, used his arm as a shield to keep from getting hit in the face.

He didn't know how much more of this he could endure.

He thought about jumping, taking a chance he wouldn't break his neck. Or drown. Or both.

The marsh became less of a jungle.

Clegg realized he'd guessed right on direction as the powerboat cleared the marshes and, after another moment, was racing into Murrells Inlet, past anchored fleets of deep-sea fishing boats dancing nervously to the approaching storm.

He pulled harder on the wheel to keeping from plowing into the last of them, crying out in pain when his muscles crunched into spasm, and—

Found himself bearing down on pleasure boats traversing the inlet, early-to-rise sailors who'd taken a chance on the weather and were now urgently honking their blow horns while dodging for safety and the shore through the choppy waters.

He barely avoided one.

Came within yards of colliding with another.

Missed a cabin cruiser twenty times his size.

Somehow managed to find a clear line and bounced past the inlet onto the Intracoastal Waterway.

The painted sign ahead said:

DETOUR 200 YARDS
DANGER
PROCEED WITH EXTREME CAUTION

Clegg saw he was heading straight for a wooden barrier that stretched across the Waterway. Slowing down wasn't an option, even if he could get the brake to work.

The cabin cruiser he'd missed was on his tail.

Pursuing him like some psychotic freeway driver.

Bearing down on him with its elephant horn blaring nonstop.

Bent, it appeared, on a revenge ramming.

Clegg stopped breathing again.

He used the adrenaline rush trying to work the steering wheel around and get out of the cruiser's way. The wheel was too much for him. He braced himself for the hit, positive it would send him into the barrier or the Waterway's cement-and-steel retaining wall.

The last minute, the cruiser swerved around Clegg's powerboat, honking a victory song as it pulled in front and increased speed.

The skipper must have been so intent on putting a scare into Clegg that he hadn't seen the detour warning.

The honking stopped at approximately the same instant he crashed through the barrier.

Creating an opening for Clegg.

The powerboat flew through it.

Skidded along the side of the cruiser.

Sent sparks flying as it angled off-center.

Appeared headed for the detour, but—

Missed it by a matter of yards and—

Sailed onto land.

Banged into a low brick retaining wall.

Bounced off and slid backward into the Waterway.

Began to sink.

Clegg sat motionless for a second, then shook his head clear and crossed himself. He sprang open his seat belt and leaned over for the Warhol portfolio. The buckle had been damaged and wouldn't give without a struggle. He put a mental picture of his son behind one last yank and managed to free the box. Leaped clear with scant seconds to spare before the powerboat went under.

The crash was attracting attention.

There was a wooded area about fifty feet ahead.

Clegg headed for it.

Demanding that his legs work.

He'd come too far to be caught now.

Work Brings Freedom.

Work Brings Freedom.

Work Brings Freedom.

Soon, son. Soon. Soon, my dear little boy.

Clegg worked his way through the woods in weather that had done another turn—the storm deferring to a sun breaking through the depressing cloud covering—and about a half mile later took a rutted three-lane road to a pedestrian crossing over the Waterway.

He found a gas station and cleaned himself off in the restroom, presentable enough not to raise questions at the motel down the road another quarter mile.

The room was typical tourist chic, overpriced for what it offered.

He slid the box of Warhols under the bed and was half asleep before his head hit the pillow.

Awoke almost six hours later, in the same position.

Sore and stiff.

Starving.

Fed himself from the service bar, waiting for the tub to fill.

Afterward, close to feeling alive again, Clegg pulled out the Warhols and settled on the mattress while he undid the plastic wrapping, smiled contentedly as he lifted open the lid and carefully removed the stack of prints, and—

Realized the old man back at the Homestead had pulled a switch on him.

Son of a bitch!

Next time he saw him he'd be a dead son of a bitch!

Gulliver, Marriner, the whole damn bunch!

Clegg waited until his rage was under control, his breathing back to normal, before tapping out Porter Havilland's special number.

The phone system noisily tracked through a series of relays before the first ring.

Havilland picked up on the second ring.

He wasted no time on greetings.

"I expected to hear from you before this, Clegg."

Clegg explained what had happened, but not about the switch, uncertain how he wanted to approach that news.

"I wondered where Marriner disappeared to after Everett messed up," Havilland said.

"Messed up?"

"Bungled his visit to Marriner. Came away empty-handed later, when I sent him to Gulliver's. Both of them disappeared after that. Now, of course, I can understand why."

"Nobody's perfect, boss."

Maybe it was in the way he said it, because a stretch of silence was followed by Havilland asking in a suspicious tone, "What don't I know yet, Clegg? Speak up."

Havilland's question was too direct for Clegg to dodge the answer. He told him about the switch. Waited out more silence on the other end of the call; longer this time.

Finally, Havilland coughed harshly in his ear, cleared his throat and said, "You plan to remedy that, of course." A statement, not a question.

"Of course, boss, but it may have to wait until they're out of that hellhole and—"

"I don't need or want details, Clegg. What I want as you well know is the complete set of Warhol portraits. You get them. You bring them to me."

"It could take awhile—"

"No details, Clegg. Just do it."

"Yes, I will. Meanwhile, I need a favor. I need you to wire money to—"

"No. I don't think so."

"Boss, you know why. It's nothing that can wait much longer. It's not there in the next couple of days, and—"

"Clegg, our accounts are current, correct? Up-to-date, correct? Everything due you has been paid, correct?"

"Yes, but—"

"Don't interrupt me . . . You bring me all the Warhols and I'll promptly remit all that you're due. COD, Clegg. That has always been our way of working together. Correct?"

"Boss, please, don't make me beg. Have I ever let you down?"

"Neither had Everett. Nobody's perfect, Clegg. You just said so, yourself. All the Warhols. All twelve of them. Then my word you'll be paid. In full. Like always."

Havilland hung up, leaving Clegg to stare despondently at the receiver.

31

Off and on, the storm had whacked out the electricity and the phones, land lines and cells, and it wasn't until morning that Ari was able to make contact with people he'd described for Stevie and me only as "some close associates of ours," after we had invaded Feather's kitchen and whomped up a breakfast of juice, scrambled eggs, pancakes, waffles and gallons of steaming coffee.

Ari said, "I told them about the dock, so they're coming by boat to get you back to civilization, see you safely off to Los Angeles. It would take forever otherwise, they said. Roads washed out by the lousy weather, where you can even find them."

"You and Zev?"

Zev said, "Ari and I will be staying behind with most of the others. We have our work cut out for us, you know?"

We were in the parlor, where we'd spent the night in front of the fireplace, like old friends at a slumber party. Stevie had caught some sleep angled in an armchair. I'd dozed briefly, a couple times, waking to find either Ari or Zev keeping cautious guard, always somewhere near the box of Warhols.

"If it were spring, you could call it spring cleaning," Zev continued, amused by his own cleverness. "After they get done you'll never know we were here or what went on."

"Feather and Godard. What happens with them? With the floater you found in the basement?"

Ari said, "People disappear all the time in this kind of weather, Neil."

Stevie showed she didn't like what she was hearing. "Who Neil so crudely called 'the floater.' " Striking me down with her stare. "Is probably a poor guy who happened to be in the wrong place the wrong time. With a family that'll be worried sick. How are you going to explain to them?"

"We're not, Stevie."

"Isn't he entitled to a proper burial?"

Her eyes pleaded for an answer she could live with.

Ari let a few seconds pass.

"Stevie, your heart's in the right place. You're full of compassion," he said, extending a smile teachers reserve for pet students. "I understand, but you should understand I have a mission to carry out that's stronger than any emotion I might be feeling personally.

"I know from tragedy. I live with tragedy every day of my life. I know tragedy doesn't recognize class distinction or right from wrong. We're here for the victims from another time, the ghosts of a greater tragedy. For their heirs. How it goes, but I'll include that young man in my prayers. Say kaddish for him like I do for others. That's the best I can do for him. For his family. For you."

He angled his head, turned up his palms, his expression a plea for understanding.

Stevie's mouth grew taut and her eyes began to glisten. She broke away from Ari's gentle stare. Seemed to leap from the armchair. Hurried to a far corner of the room and turned away from us. Shaking. Her head bowed. Her fists tight balls that moved up and down like she was exercising with weights.

Ari turned and looked at me. I sent him a signal that said she'd be fine, give her a few minutes.

Augie gave me a nod of agreement and, almost as an act of charity, changed the subject.

"Ari, what about the paintings?"

Ari looked up at the ceiling and rolled his eyes in obvious gratitude.

"We'll begin the inventory," he answered. "Pack and take what we can identify and what we're able to determine rightfully belongs to someone else."

"Which could be everything," Zev said.

Stevie wheeled around. I saw she was still on an emotional high wire.

She called to Zev, "And the paintings you're not sure about? What about them?"

"It may take us years to find out, but meanwhile better in our hands than left for the next vipers like Feather and Godard to horde and profit from."

"Someone is bound to start asking questions sooner or later," Stevie said. "Feather's staff. Who might be around, know what's been going on, or who'll be showing up when the storm ends. You plan on also saying kaddish for them?"

"Stevie, please. Try to give us more credit than that, okay?" Ari said. "Try to remember we didn't kill Feather or Godard or the young man. As far as anybody has to know, if we get challenged"—pointing to Zev and himself—"we are here supervising art appraisers going about their business while the master's away. The others? A building contractor and his crew. Fixing up after a storm of great magnitude. Not at all unusual."

Ari's cell phone rang before Stevie could respond.

He snatched it from his pocket, unable to disguise his relief for the interruption. He flipped it open and listened quietly, pressed the cell to his chest, and said, "Zev, watch after them."

With that he left the room.

When he came back after several minutes, he gave a look to Zev, passing glances at Augie and me, before settling an anxious face on Stevie.

"What?" she said.

Ari let Stevie's question hang in time, then, "Porter Havilland?"

"The link to Godard and Feather. What about him?"

"And Feather's father, don't forget about him. For all our years of work, Zev and I had never heard the name until Henri Godard revealed it to us. I promptly fed it into our network and just got a call. Of more than a dozen Porter Havillands unearthed around the world, our people located only one who deals in important works of art. In London. Buys and sells privately from a leasehold in the Mayfair area."

He seemed to be bartering for Stevie's goodwill back in asking, "Do you know the neighborhood?"

Stevie wasn't buying.

"Tell your people congratulations for me and go get the rat. And yes, I know the neighborhood."

"Very posh neighborhood indeed," Zev said. "Where you see more Rolls-Royces than anywhere—"

"Zev, you heard her. She knows the neighborhood." Ari studied Stevie for a few moments. I saw he was calculating how to approach her with whatever he wanted to say next.

So did Stevie. She said, "Why don't you just come out and say it, Ari. You couldn't possibly upset me more than you already have."

He acknowledged her judgment with a look and a gesture and said, "To go 'get the rat,' as you just put it, will take us more than going and getting him. For what happens next, we can use your help. What do you think?"

Stevie studied him hard from across the room, then came closer. Let her eyes drift from Augie to me before settling them again on Ari. Smothering him in what I used to call her silent close-up. Chin out, staring over the bridge of her nose. Open to interpretation.

Ari lobbed a smile at her.

"My people want to bring you to London, Stevie. You ring up Havilland. You tell him how several dealers you contacted about the Warhol suite said he might have interest. You suggest getting together to discuss it over dinner. Who could resist such an invitation, if only to experience the company of Stephanie Marriner? You go get a sense of him, learn what you can about the man, and afterward we take it from there."

"You want to set her up as a stalking horse?" I said.

"Yes, in a manner of speaking."

"Any way you say it, a stalking horse, and any way you say it I don't like it. She's been through enough already."

"She'll never be out of our sight, Neil." Turning back to Stevie: "If what we already heard is true, we'll be that much closer to locating more art for their rightful owners, maybe even more than we've come across here, and we'll owe it to you, Stevie Marriner. You'll be a real hero."

I said, "Not Stevie. I'll do it. Take the risk. After all, they're my Warhols that we're talking about."

"Too strange that you should suddenly show up in London unannounced knocking on his door, Neil. Not so, Stevie. She's a big gigantic star there. Her better than anyone else, once we make it so all of London knows Stevie Marriner is back in town."

Who could resist such an invitation, Stevie?

You'll be a real hero, Stevie.

You're a big gigantic star over there, Stevie.

All of London will know you're in town, Stevie.

Flattery, it'll get you everywhere, London included, especially flattery in the service of humanitarianism.

A smooth worker, that Ari.

He said, "So, okay, Stevie. What do you think?"

She studied Ari for a long time, like she was turning over the question in her mind, but I knew her answer was in place and there was nothing I could do or say to change her mind.

Two days later, Stevie was greeted at Heathrow Airport by Sir Albert Reville, her co-star in the West End play that a year and a half ago brought her reviews nobody would have believed possible for the former "Sex Queen of the Soaps," from even the most coldhearted of the critics.

She and Reville had been rumored to be an item during the run, and later, when they co-starred in a production at the National. They were constantly stalked by as many paparazzi as the heir apparent to the throne and his brother had inherited after the death of their mother.

This morning was no different. The media had massed for her arrival like a legion of Count Draculas and pandemonium erupted the instant Stevie swept through customs and leaped into the waiting arms of Sir Albert.

At once, even before their kiss-kiss, the area outside NOTHING TO DECLARE lit up like a minefield. The corridor echoed with cries of, "Now look this way, Stevie."

"Here, you lovebirds. Over here."

"Sir Albert, turn in this direction."

"Stevie, Sir Albert, straight into the lens this time."

"Big smiles, you two."

Stevie and Sir Albert sucked up the cameras and each other's lips for several minutes before they began racing to the exit doors, with four meaty bodyguards clearing the path for them. Elbows locked as tightly as their smiles. Shouting three- and four-word answers to barely intelligible questions screamed after them by reporters elbowing for priority with their mikes and mini-cassette recorders.

Me?

I was that guy over there, hanging back out of the way with our luggage.

Huffing and puffing behind the crowd.

Watching as Stevie and Reville dove into a waiting limo and weaved away through the traffic lanes ahead of a phalanx of paparazzi on wheels.

Ari Landau's hand settled on my shoulder.

"That went well," he said. "According to plan."

I didn't return his smile.

"She keeps telling me there was never anything between them, but just now she kissed him like she meant the goddamn kiss," I said, annoyed and unable to hide it.

"She's an actress. He's an actor. It's what they do."

"It's whatever else they do I'm thinking about."

"Neil, should I explain to you all over again that Sir Albert is doing her and us a favor, that's all? To hear you talk, one would come away with the idea that you and Stevie are still married."

"Old habits die hard," I said, surprised at the high-octane jealousy pumping through my veins. I thought that tank had emptied considerably, if not entirely, after I met Maryam Zokaei.

Apparently not. Apparently only until Maryam walked out on me. Was it that I needed Stevie, or that I needed someone? At least it was a question. Before, it was always an answer; the same one: Stevie.

Ari gave me an understanding look and said, "You didn't have to be here to see it, you know?"

True.

Except, I did.

Where Stevie had ignored me when I said she couldn't go to Myrtle Beach, this time, about London, it was my turn to be belligerent. Even without some acting hot-pants like Reville in the picture, I was not about to stand by and wave goodbye while Ari or anyone put my ex at risk.

Stevie heard back from Porter Havilland within hours of calling him from her suite at Claridge's.

She followed Ari's script, adding her own girlish charm and splashes of laughter straight out of a Noel Coward stage direction, a few times dropping her voice seductively, as if she were suggesting more than dinner for him.

"No, Mr. Havilland—thank you. Porter. Just the two of us," she cooed. "Sir Albert will be otherwise occupied this evening, clear through tomorrow afternoon, the earliest."

Another minute, she was calling Havilland "dah-ling" and showing off her equally lousy French acent. It used to be halfway decent, but that was before her lips were soiled by Sir Albert Reville.

"I thought here in the hotel, dah-ling. The *maître chef des cuisines* insists on serving us personally. A Scottish lobster salad with a lime-and-mango fondue as the main starter, followed by my personal favor-ite, *canard á la presse*, using the huge silver duck press like the one Escoffier used. The sauce to die for. Melon and wild strawberries for dessert, and wines appropriate to every course, but to know Claridge's dining room as I expect you do is to know that already."

However Havilland responded, Stevie's smile dropped to the lobby level.

She excused herself and covered the mouthpiece with her hand. Whisper-called across the sitting room to Ari, "He has a bad stomach that no longer tolerates rich foods and wants to meet in the morning. His place." Her expression begged, *Tell me what you want.*

Ari gestured affirmatively with both hands. He saw me seething with disagreement, put a silencing finger to his lips before I blurted out anything the phone might catch.

Stevie fell back into her act with Havilland.

"Sorry about that, dah-ling," she said. "Sir Albert on the other line. So possessive, that one. Where were we? Oh, yes. Your flat in the morning sounds splendid. Uh-huh. Uh-huh . . . Yes, all written down. Yes, I'll remember to bring the Warhol portfolio. Ten o'clock it is. Ta till then."

She replaced the receiver. Threw a finger-salute from her forehead. Followed by a look that begged our review of her performance.

" 'Ta till then'?" I said, mimicking her. "What happened to the 'Tally ho, old chap'?"

"Bugger off," she said.

"The last time you got up for a ten-o'clock anything—"

"You couldn't get it up at all," she said, and just as quickly, to Ari, "What now?"

Ari made like he hadn't heard her turn me back into a boy soprano and assured her, "Brilliant, Stevie. Brilliant. And you can sleep tonight knowing that long before tomorrow arrives you'll have nothing to worry about."

"How about me?" I said.

Stevie said, "Ignore him, Ari."

"You can worry for all of us, Neil," he said, making a joke of it.

Ari pulled out his cell, padded to one of the picture windows auto-dialing a number and, after a connection that seemed to take forever, said quietly, "A change in plans." He turned away from us and mostly listened while gazing at Brook Street down below.

32

Approximately fourteen minutes before ten o'clock the next morning, Stevie turned a corner onto Wemper Street in Mayfair and stared across the road at a well-kept residence not that far from the arches to Sheperd Market, taller than it was wide, like other buildings on the block painted a virginal white that took special radiance from an emerging sun.

The street was not yet alive with either locals or the tourists who'd shortly invade the Market's labyrinth of cobbled alleys packed full of shops, pubs and restaurants. Some upper-crust cars sailed by, some taxis. Foot traffic on the move in both directions. Women and men dressed for a day of upper-crust pleasure or some executive suite.

Others out for a blissful stroll or a brisk run in the reasonably fresh air.

Others controlling their dogs on tight leashes.

Others hugging grocery sacks to their chests.

Not so different from Westwood Village, Stevie thought, while she checked the time again. Except for the well-kept building whose two painted black numerals over the door said it was the place where Porter Havilland lived and conducted his business.

She studied the round face of her watch again, like the time controlled her life, which right now it certainly did.

Eleven minutes to ten.

She exercised care leaning the Warhol portfolio against the lamppost before rummaging for her compact in her handbag.

She studied her reflection in the mirror.

Not so bad in spite of the time difference between here and the States, the sleep she'd missed because of Ari and Zev. How much sleep? How many hours had they spent on the details, rehearsing for what was about to happen soon with the same exactness she'd experienced only with her stage directors? Never, certainly, during her years on *Bedrooms and Board Rooms*, where spending time to elicit the best performances from the cast was not a line item on the production budget.

A lot of hours.

Stevie fluffed her hair, adjusted her goggle shades, returned the compact to her handbag and relocked the box of Warhols between her arm and body. Wheeled around, away from Havilland's place, and used the chemist's shop window as a looking glass to check her outfit and tug a few places back into alignment.

Nothing fancy or elegant about the wardrobe she'd selected. A simple brown wool skirt and a persimmon-colored cotton turtleneck under a thigh-length duffle coat. Unstylish but comfortable rubber lug-soled mules. Even her cologne was subdued.

Seven minutes to ten and counting.

Ari and Zev had thought about her dressing in an outfit that was more stylish, classier, reeking of American Express Platinum Plus and impressive star power.

She persuaded them that less was more.

"I'd be out of the moment trying to impress him with a style show," Stevie said. "Havilland knows who's coming for breakfast and why. He wants to see the Warhols and that will be style enough for him."

"All of you talk like any of it matters," Neil grumbled from the couch, where he'd stretched out early to watch them go through the plan step by step, constantly criticizing and complaining, expressing concerns for Stevie's safety, before the hours caught up with him and he fell asleep.

He didn't wake up until minutes before she was ready to leave the suite. The worry lines owned his face as he hugged her and demanded she be careful, like anything less was ever even an option in her mind.

"You're packing, of course."

"It doesn't go with the outfit," she said. "Besides, I'd never be able to explain why if I were, especially in England."

Stevie turned and hurried out the door, heard him ranting at Ari and Zev before it eased shut.

Five minutes thirty seconds to ten.

Stevie started across Wemper Street diagonally, aiming for the sidewalk directly in front of Havilland's building. Were this some show-business take-a-meeting or press thing, she'd have opted for timing on the "fashionably late" side, but this morning's game had significance far beyond ego and status.

She walked at a steady but somewhat tentative clip and kept her head aimed at the front door, as if making certain she had the right number. She imagined Havilland hiding behind one of the drawn drapes, salivating with excitement while he tracked her and the Warhol portfolio, and—

Was halfway across the asphalt road when a taxi sped around the corner, charging straight for her like a Pamplona bull, its muffler belching shots of black-and-blue smoke.

Stevie froze.

She dropped the Warhol portfolio and thrust her arms forward, palms open, as if she'd be able to stop the taxi with her hands.

The cabbie hit the horn, hit the brakes, then—

Hit Stevie.

She slammed forward, hard, onto the vehicle's hood.

Pitched back in a twisting fall to the asphalt road.

Through half-shuttered eyes, Stevie saw the cabbie and his passenger leap out from and around the taxi.

The cabbie drop onto one knee and check her for a pulse.

The passenger bent over behind him, doing a panicky kind of dance and wondering, "She all right? She all right? She all right?"

The cabbie point to the warm trickle of blood spilling down a corner of her mouth.

"Something internal, by the looks," he said, in a voice not quite frantic. "Breathing, but barely."

He called across his shoulder, "Fetch us a doctor, someone. The lady here needs medical attention. Needs it bad."

Stevie was aware of a small crowd of pedestrians gathering, exchanging versions of what happened, mumbling concerns. Echoing the need for a doctor.

Someone volunteered to run fetch an ambulance.

She moaned. Half opened her eyes.

The light traffic was at a standstill. Vehicles behind the taxi were lining up, some complaining with their horns about the delay. Those in the opposite lane slowing to gawk.

She mumbled something about being okay and flashed her hands, directing people to back away.

The cabbie and his passenger helped her to her feet.

Propping her up by the elbows, arms around her waist, they led her to the sidewalk one slow step at a time.

She stalled them and made a gesture behind her.

"My things," she whispered. "My bag, my—"

"Right here, I have them," someone said.

"You doctor?" the cabbie said.

"No, I reside over there," the man said, moving around to where they could see him holding up a handbag and a black box. "The name's Havilland. Porter Havilland. The lady was coming to call on me."

The cabbie said, "We'll take her inside, then, while we wait out doctor."

Havilland's expression turned curious.

He seemed to struggle with the suggestion.

"Perhaps the front porch," he said. "It's covered and—"

Stevie's knees gave out and she sagged in their grip.

The cabbie said, "Lady looks to need more than that, guv'ner."

Havilland seemed to be debating with himself before he said with some reluctance, "Up there, then, follow me," indicating where.

A spectator joined them with an offer of assistance. The Good Samaritan who'd volunteered to fetch an ambulance returned, announcing, "Help on the way. I'll stay out here, point them in the right direction."

"Could cost me my living," the cabbie griped under his breath as he and the two men delicately led Stevie up three steps and into the residence.

Havilland directed them through the open archway to his immediate right, into a small, comfortably furnished sitting room. Well-worn sofas and stuffed armchairs covered in plastic, arranged in four conversational groupings, with empty wooden display easels on wheels bunched in the center of the room. Bare walls, except for hanging hooks and dust stains surrounding less faded wallpaper at various heights, suggesting where frames of various sizes once hung. Lots of track lighting in the high ceiling with nowhere special to aim. The lingering odor of disuse mixed with lemon-scented disinfectant.

Havilland walked over to the sofa nearest the entry and gave it several pats. "Here's probably best," he said in a flat American accent with traces of English. "Where doctor can get right at her."

"But back here for you," said the spectator who'd been assisting the cabbie and his passenger. He had quietly moved to the grouping deepest inside the sitting room and had an automatic trained on Havilland.

Havilland was too startled to move at first, but then turned as if to flee, only to find himself staring at a .22 aimed at his chest by the Good Samaritan.

"Wouldn't bloody try that, I was you, guv'," the Good Samaritan said.

Havilland looked away from the Good Samaritan to his hands, then raised them high, declaring, "Billfold's in my jacket pocket, in the entry-hall closet. Other'n that, you won't find much of value."

Sounding like someone who knew how to be robbed.

"Please take it and go," he urged. "You won't want to be here when the ambulance arrives and—"

Sent a look at the Good Samaritan, then put it into words—

"You didn't call for help, did you? This woman doesn't get proper medical attention quickly, you may have the law after you for murder."

"Your murder is more likely, we don't find what we're after," the Good Samaritan answered. "And not no bloody billfold. Now, do as me mate says, and move your bloody arse on down."

Havilland did as he was told.

The spectator took him by the shoulder, steered him into an easy chair and said, "That's being the good lad, now. You just be still a bit and mind your manners, Mr. Porter Havilland."

Stevie eased free of the cabbie and his passenger.

"I couldn't be sure at first, but I am now," she said. "That's not him. That's not Porter Havilland."

She pulled a handkerchief from a duffle coat pocket.

Toweled at the fake bloodstains on her face after taking from her mouth the pouch that, except for the colored dye, always reminded her of a used condom.

Wrapped the pouch in the hanky and deposited it back inside the pocket, mindful of Ari and Zev's repeated admonitions during their rehearsals, *Be careful not to leave anything behind to connect you.*

The cabbie, who was Ari Landau, said, "Meaning exactly what?"

The passenger, who was Zev Neumann, said, "You've never set eyes on Havilland."

The spectator, who was Neil, said, "You okay, babe?"

"Fine, honey, and definitely better than your accent," she said, still trying to come down from an atomic high, then to Ari and Zev, "I know voices. His isn't the one I heard on the phone last night. Whoever this guy is, he is not the Porter Havilland who returned my call."

The Good Samaritan, someone Stevie had never seen until this morning, one of the people Ari had kept referring to as "our locals," marched down to "Havilland."

Gentled Neil aside.

Pressed the barrel of his .22 underneath "Havilland" 's chin and in a hissing tone as ominous as the expression that suited his swarthy exterior, said, "Whoever you are, mate, I suggest you share with us, along with whatever else we think to ask. By the count of ten, mate, or I'll paint the ceiling with your brains. One . . . Two . . . Three . . . I hope yours isn't one of those minds full of speed bumps, mate . . . Four . . . Five . . ."

Eugene Barnstable could have been Porter Havilland.

He was the same age they'd figured Havilland for, give or take a year; the same age range as the father Rudy Feather had portrayed in the Warhol print he forged.

What Barnstable had even more in common with Feather's father was a partnership with Havilland that stretched back to World War Two. And like Feather's father, like Porter Havilland, he'd been un-known to the Mossad's treasure hunters until now.

"You know how it is," Barnstable said, leaning forward in his seat, hands laced in his lap, and nervously cracking his knuckles. "I was a kid back then, came in with the Sixth Armored. Buchenwald? Nothing you ever get out of your mind. Knew enough German to get kept around. Interrogating krauts. That sort of thing?"

"That sort of thing, yes, of course," Ari said. He was sitting across from Barnstable, also in a forward position, encouraging him with a soft smile and a soothing manner. "Go on. Please."

Barnstable glanced at Stevie and Neil, who were joined hips and hands on the sofa to his immediate right, and tried to ignore the Good Samaritan hovering behind him.

Stevie sensed he was relieved to be sharing his story, like some sinner revisiting the confessional of his youth.

Everything about him seemed average for a man somewhere in his late sixties or early seventies, from his appearance to his dress. His sallow complexion, which she had seen before on her unpublicized visits to terminally ill kids at Children's Hospital and the City of Hope, was an exception. His nicotine-stained fingers and teeth hinted why, as much as a rasp in his throat and his occasional shortness of breath.

"You hear stories. You have access to files. That sort of thing," Barnstable said.

"I know. I've heard before," Ari said.

"I'm doing Berlin with some buddies one night when I'm pulled aside by another Yank, who turns out to be Porter. He springs for a few brews before laying on me what he calls a golden opportunity to go home rich. Filthy rich, he says. I got no objection to filthy rich. Any kind of rich. Where I come from, we share the piss pot with our neighbors. How Porter knows from me and what I do, to this day I don't know how he learned, but he's got me down cold, like he's heard from someone."

"The names Frook or Feather mean something to you?" Zev asked from the piece of wall he was holding up with his back and one foot. Eyes steady out the archway. The automatic in his hand half hidden under the arm resting across his chest.

Barnstable gave the question thought before shaking his head. "Should they?"

Ari explained.

Barnstable shook his head again and said, "You have to understand something about Porter. 'Jack,' really, at least early on, before he had the need to learn how a Swiss bank account worked and what the Cayman Islands were for besides fun in the sun. John Porter Havilland. Jack to his friends, whoever they might be. After, it was like he was too good, too rich, actually, to be a Jack. He had to be Porter."

" 'Whoever they might be,' you said."

"Jack from the very first was the solitary man in the middle. However he worked, whoever he worked with, only he knew everything. We only knew where we fit with him. Me, I didn't care, so long as the bucks rolled in, and they sure did. Roll? It was more like rain. Like the sky just opened up and the manna fell from heaven."

"Where you fit. In your position after the war ended, you were his conduit to the artworks the Nazis looted."

"Yes, one of them, anyway. Never did learn how he found out about me. 'Friend of a friend,' he said. 'No names, please,' and I respected that. No skin off my nose. Jack told me what he needed from me. Names and places where some of the stolen stuff had wound up. Those 'Ali Baba and the Forty Thieves' caves the krauts and their partners in crime used to store their loot. Stuff our guys glommed on to and we were warehousing, waiting for their original owners to show up and make a valid claim, you know? Pretty soon, we were going like sixty beyond that, Jack and me. He'd hand over a list of what we should have. I'd sign off using names on the paperwork the department had verified already. Later, after the art was safely away, the paperwork would conveniently disappear, you know?"

"Of course," Ari said. "Please continue."

Barnstable started to say something.

Stopped and looked past Ari.

Three white-suited, stretcher-bearing men stood in the archway.

Stevie recognized them from the Homestead.

Ari lifted his arm above his head and made a circular motion with his index finger, then told Barnstable, "Go on, please. Just some of our friends here to have a look around while we talk."

"I can save you the trouble," Barnstable said. "Nothing to see here. Whatever you think you're going to find, you're going to find an empty building, that's all. Like this room here."

"Why is that?" Ari said, looking to Stevie like he knew already, but wanted to hear Barnstable's explanation.

"For years this was our European base of operation with me in charge, while Jack took care of the rest of the world from the States," Barnstable said, by now without a trace of English accent. A bare-bones American as flat as the Indiana landscape.

"Where in the States?"

A shrug.

"I wasn't in that compartment. We'd buy and sell from here, this room. A limited clientele, you know? Those we came to know and trust, you know? With their own secrets to keep. Two or three other ground-floor rooms we used for any art that wasn't suspect. For show. A front to legitimize the operation. For people who wandered in off the street. The rest of the place—mainly a warehouse. But not any-more."

"Because?"

"Age catches up with you, you know? Jack and me, we got our nest eggs, our screw-you money, a long time ago. The cream of our inventory was gone, too. So we settled our accounts and everything that was here Jack moved over to the States a couple years ago."

"To . . . ?"

"He worked all that."

"The files. Records of people you did business with?"

"That, too."

"Yet here you are."

"Jack over all the years never did me dirt, understand? As honorable a man as you could ever want for a partner. So I had no reason not to oblige whenever he'd ring me up with something needed doing, this part of the world. We kept this place for those special occasions."

"Like with Miss Marriner."

"Exactly. He rang me up last night, explained what was cooking. He told me she'd be bringing these Warhols and said to pay the freight, whatever it took. No question about him being jake for the money, of course. Jack even wanted me to add a little for myself, for my time and trouble. That's the kind of standup guy Jack is, see? Of course I shucked it off. What pals do for pals."

"How would he be paying you?"

"I'd let him know the amount. After a few days or so a letter of credit would arrive from somewhere. How it always worked between us."

"You have his phone number?"

"A phone number." Barnstable recited it.

Zev wrote it down.

Ari said, "What can you tell me about the Warhols? What did Porter Havilland say about them?"

"Only what you already heard. Anything else, you have to get from Jack, you ever find him." The sudden sparkle in Eugene Barnstable's gloomy eyes betrayed the grim set to his receded lips, like that possibility was up there with the Man of La Mancha's dream.

Stevie wasn't the only one who noticed.

Ari said, "You wouldn't be holding anything back?"

"Like what? Like my morning dump? I confess. That I'm holding back on you. You mind letting me hit the head?"

Ari signaled an okay to the Good Samaritan, who nudged Barnstable to his feet with the .22 and followed him out of the room.

Neil waited another minute before asking, "You believe him?"

"Mostly, yes, but he could be holding back."

"About the Warhols?"

"About everything. You heard all that misplaced loyalty from his mouth. No regret for anything the two of them ever pulled. Not one word of sympathy for the victims they helped keep victims." He made a despondent sigh. "What a world this still is."

One of the ambulance attendants appeared in the archway, calling Ari's name.

"Anything, Isaac?"

"Nothing top to bottom, Ari. This way for a long time, judging from all the signs."

"We'll leave the others to finish up, then," Ari said.

He used the armrests to lift out of the chair, put on his cabbie's cap and did some adjusting.

"Let's go," he said. "Zev with me, like before. Isaac here will help you into the ambulance, Stevie, and you can go with them, Neil. You're the doctor, for all anybody would remember or think. Anyone paying attention, it still makes sense what happened here this morning."

Stevie and Neil moved onto their feet, Stevie asking, "What about Barnstable?"

"He's finished in the crapper, Ran and the Miller boys will sit him down, ask more questions, some the same as already. See how much crap he might have been handing us. What else we can learn about Porter Havilland, and maybe we'll yet get answers about the Warhols. The collectors we don't know. What the twelfth print is all about."

Stevie said, "You're not going to harm him, are you?"

"Barnstable?" Ari made a *What kind of question is that to ask?* face, but his eyes broadcast indifference, the same look she'd seen at the Homestead, when they'd argued about the young man in the getaway hole.

"You saw what I saw," she said. "He's a sick old man."

"Yes," Ari agreed. "I can give you a long list of sick old men like that . . . Sick, but not harmless, Stevie."

"What's that supposed to mean?"

"You got invited here for breakfast. So—you smell any breakfast, anything at all that's cooking? Isaac, you found a kitchen in your explorations?"

"Clean as a whistle, Ari."

"So, whatever he had in mind for you after he got his hands on the Warhols, it doesn't sound like it included a meal, Stevie. I won't be surprised if the closet out there turns up more than Barnstable's billfold."

He aimed a finger-gun at Stevie.
Fired.
Blew the barrel clean.
Cracked a tolerant smile.

33

*S*tevie and I were dragging like test pilots for jet lag by the time we touched down at LAX, the twelve-hour flight marked mostly by bad movies, worse food, her snoring and, okay, mine too. We could have stayed for a few days of R&R, but both of us were bare-to-the-bone tired. Fully worn down and fed up with the whole Warhol business. Reconciled to the fact we might never learn the secret of the twelfth silkscreen in the portfolio, unless the answer surfaced during Ari and Zev's ongoing pursuit.

Better that way anyway.

Theirs was the greater, more significant mission.

This was their line of work, not ours.

I'd been through enough. I'd collected enough background material for a dozen columns without giving away anything that might tip Porter Havilland the Mossad was closing in on him. I'd get me home to the Heathcliffe, stow the portfolio and tackle Rip Van Winkle's record.

Wake up to a life that didn't include a daily dose of Andy Warhol.

The only prints I might consider: Those who spelled it p-r-i-n-c-e, and barked.

Yeah, sure, you bet. That'd be like spending Saturday matinees watching eleven chapters unfold in some Republic serial like *G-Men vs the Black Dragon* or *Government Agents vs the Phantom Legion*, then boycotting the twelfth and final chapter.

Shows you what stress and sleep deprivation can do to the mind.

It ain't over till it's over, right, Professor Berra?

A surprise was waiting for us outside the customs area of the Bradley Terminal.

Not Augie, who was expected.

I'd called ahead from the plane to let him know Stevie and I were on our way back, and he'd insisted on picking us up, although we weren't due until sometime after ten P.M.

The surprise was Tony B. Tony, beaming a smile bright enough to land a 747 as he parted the small group of others waiting for passengers, like Charlton Heston at the Red Sea, and called out Stevie's name loud enough for heads to turn.

"Ripped the information out of your service about when you were bumping down," he announced to the world. "I simply couldn't not shlep out here and share the news."

Tony B. Tony threw his arms around her and, with a wink for Augie and me, told her, "Deal's in the bag, babycakes. A firm go. Light as scaly-skin green as some *Star Trek* alien, based on Ossie Parkman's first draft. I set it up at Paramount and may have one of the Toms for the Freddie March role. Taking a meeting next week with their boys at CAA."

"Wonderful news," Stevie said, returning his air-kisses and taking two steps back. She seemed suddenly energized. "I almost didn't know it was you, Tony B. Tony. How much weight have you lost?"

"Thirty, thirty-five pounds. Was that switchblade diet you introduced me to." He smiled and slapped his body. "Nothing to worry your pretty head about. I'm good as new. The doctor says I'll live to be a hundred—if I don't die first."

Tony B. Tony laughed at his joke, steered her in the direction of a photographer lining up a shot and said, "You know Roger Karnbad. He's shooting exclusively for me tonight. The shots will be running all over the world faster'n you can say, 'Tony B. Tony, you've done it again.' "

A lot of snapping by Roger Karnbad.

Three cameras, no waiting.

Color.

Black-and-white.

Then some autographs and sweet, unhurried chat for several fans who approached her.

Then Tony B. Tony whisked Stevie away in one of those motor carts nominally for the exclusive use of the elderly and the handicapped. And, of course, celebrities, this being L.A., home of the HOLLYWOOD sign, where a golf handicap can be made to count in bending the rules.

I brought Augie up-to-date during the hour's drive to the Heathcliffe that should have taken a half hour, max, but for the aftermath of a freeway pursuit and showdown that had all the lanes bumper-to-bumper and choppers still hovering overhead. He parked the Rolls outside the entrance with the motor running. Refused an invitation I hadn't made, to come in for more chat over a nightcap. Popped open the trunk, so I could retrieve my carry-on and the Warhol portfolio. Was on his way before I'd figured out the right key and fumbled it into the thick plate-glass entrance door to the lobby.

I rambled flatfooted to the elevator and took it up to the third floor.

Lumbered into my apartment—at once trying to remember why I had left so many lights on as my answer to the state's energy crisis—to find I was facing a crisis of my own after I deposited the carry-on and the Warhol portfolio on the mail table in the entry hall.

Two men.

On opposite sides of the living room.

One slouched in my favorite easy chair.

One upright and uptight on a counter stool, answering the other guy's unyielding stare with one of his own.

Automatics casually pointing at each other.

The one on the stool, your basic workaday .38 Smith & Wesson revolver.

The one in my chair, a Glock of undetermined caliber.

The one on the stool I didn't know.

The one in my chair I hadn't seen since Myrtle Beach.

"Move in, over where we can see you," Stool Guy said.

"Do yourself a favor and listen to the man," Chair Guy said, oblivious to my flickering smile of recognition.

His spirit of cooperation was at odds with the way they stayed focused, like Edward G. Robinson staring down Bogart in an early Warner Bros. gangster flick, but still too soon for me to tell the bad gunsel from the badder gunsel.

Either way, I was the unhappy man in the middle.

"It thrills me to hear you guys agree on something," I said, heading across the room.

My broad laughter and Steve McQueen grin didn't fool either of them.

They ignored it, let me wind down, and then Stool Guy said, "Did you bring the Warhols back with you from London?"

I worked a grunt out of my tonsils, thinking, *Chapter twelve, here I come.*

"What makes you think I was in London?" I said, trying not to look like I didn't need a clue to guess the answer to the question. Stool Guy's withering glance said he was not fooled or amused.

"Much more of that and you'll be learning to piss with your dick cut off, I let you live that long," he said. "Now just answer my question."

He looked as mean as he sounded, like he had collected two or three dicks for every year he'd been around, which I put at thirty. There was something dirty about him, besides his mouth and the Heathcliffe maintenance-crew coveralls he was wearing.

"No, I didn't," I said, looking to buy some time while I psyched out my options, hoping it wouldn't dawn on either of them to check out the entry hall before some master plan sprang to mind.

So far, only my sweat was springing.

Enough to water Descanso Gardens.

"Why didn't you?" Chair Guy said, letting me see he was unconvinced.

He was calmer than Stool Guy, sportily dressed, but, going on past performance—actions louder than words—far more dangerous.

"An interested buyer over there," I said. "It was love at first sight. He gobbled up the Warhols quicker'n you can say, 'Everyone will be famous for fifteen minutes.' Maybe you know him? Porter Havilland. He runs an art gallery in Mayfair. I'll give you the address, if you'd like to head over there, take it up with him?"

"Yeah, right," Stool Guy said. "You trying to mind-fuck with us?" To Chair Guy: "Gulliver's saying that to mind-fuck with us, Clegg, that's all. Nothing like what I heard to get me here."

Clegg, formerly Chair Guy, stretched the tight set of his mouth and did a set of rapid eye-blinks, then inquired in a voice as cold as a cobra's kiss, "Exactly what was it Havilland told you, Everett?"

Everett, formerly Stool Guy, gave him a funny look and said, "Same as he told you, I suppose."

"He didn't tell me anything, Everett. First I'm hearing about London is now. From you. From Gulliver."

"Then tell me, what are you doing here? I slip in here not fifteen minutes ago and here you are camping out. I figured you got the same call I did from Havilland."

"I got nothing."

"Why I mentioned London in the first place, Clegg."

"More than Havilland bothered."

"Then what the fuck you doing here, anyway? Havilland sent me. What about you?"

"Maybe killing a little time on my own," Clegg said, his expression as empty as his answer.

"I hope that's all," I said, and tried a Cheshire-cat grin on him.

"Shut up," Clegg and Everett said in chorus, but their eyes stayed on one another.

Also their guns.

Their barely existent cooperation disintegrating by the word.

Could I make it work for me by feeding the furnace?

Divide and conquer?

I quickly considered my options.

Came up with none.

Just as quickly made a choice and said to Everett, "I was only kidding about not having the Warhols. Hope I haven't created any problems for you with your friend here."

"Didn't I tell you to shut up?"

Clegg said, "Let the man talk. Kidding about what?"

"Havilland loved the Warhols and bought them on the spot, I wasn't kidding about that. I said it had to be a cash deal. Dollars, not pounds. Havilland said he didn't keep those kinds of dollars around and he didn't want to lose on the exchange rate. He said someone'd be coming around when I got back. He said his name was Everett, that Everett would have my money. Do you, Mr. Everett, have my money? I have the Warhols for Mr. Havilland. Then maybe you and Mr. Clegg can go and resolve your differences, someplace else, while I catch forty?"

Trying to sound sincere, letting out enough anxiety to show I was scared by what I'd been hearing.

That part was no act, neither were my blasts of strained laughter.

How I've seen people behave in similar circumstances.

Clegg skimmed me with a look, then raised his brows at Everett, whose face had crinkled with distaste, like he'd just swallowed a glass of curdled something.

"Shit-for-brains is lying, Clegg. Only looking to make trouble between us."

That surprised me. I had underestimated the contents of Everett's brain.

Clegg silently appraised the situation, a cipher for an expression, his body language offering no hints to his mind, but always with his eyes locked on Everett.

Finally he said, "Gulliver, how much?"

"How much?"

"How much is due you from Havilland? What arrangement did you two arrive at?"

Clegg was buying it.

If he had turned to look at me, he might have seen the hope rays sailing behind my eyes.

"Two million," I said, improvising.

"Uh-huh." Clegg mulled the number while Everett ranted about what a lying prick motherfucking cocksucker I was, and some other things you never hear in a Disney movie.

Waving him quiet, Clegg said, "You in Havilland's debt for any reason, Everett?"

Everett him answered with a *What's this about?* look, and shook his head.

"Here's my thinking on it," Clegg said. "You and I, we split the two million between us, and fuck Havilland."

"I told you, this faggot's been lying. I didn't show up with any check; nothing. I got sent to do Gulliver after I got hold of the Warhol package. I get my standard payday after I deliver Havilland the goods. What is or isn't between you and Havilland is for the two of you to work out."

"So, Havilland did send you here?"

"Before. He was shipping you off somewhere and I got this deal. Havilland's last call, he told me Gulliver was due in from London with the Warhols, get back on the case. Only that. You know how close to the vest he plays things."

"I know. A million is more than the job is paying you, right?"

"I'd need to join the Teamsters to ever get a decent payday out of Havilland."

"So, we do Gulliver. We let Havilland know that we're the new owners of the Warhols and our price is two million, cash on the barrelhead. What's he going to do, put someone on to us? Havilland wants the Warhols too bad to stunt-fuck with us."

Everett took on the appearance of a butterfly collector working over a specimen without a magnifying glass.

Clegg relaxed his grip on the Glock.

I supposed that was meant as some gesture of good-faith negotiating.

Everett said, "We go that far, we might as well go all the way, Clegg. We take the bread like always. We bag Havilland, to protect our ass for certain, and we still have the Warhols for whatever serious buyers he had in mind."

"I think I know who some of them might be."

"Me too," Everett said, easing the .38 Smith & Wesson onto his lap. "We compare notes, who knows where it leads?" He tilted his head in my direction. "Him?"

" 'Pop goes the weasel,' " Clegg said. "I owe him big-time for a stunt he helped pull on me with the Warhols."

Oops.

Now it was sounding official.

My cunning and devious plan to divide and conquer them had turned into a *United we stand* for Everett and Clegg. And me? The man in the middle was near to becoming the corpse on the carpet.

"Okay, I lied," I said.

I had their attention again.

Now all I had to do was figure out what the lie was.

I never had the chance.

Before I could say anything, Maryam Zokaei rounded into the room from the entry hall.

Maryam was barefooted in a sheer babydoll that refused to be ignored, huge eyes bright beacons inside her night mask of white, humming a Persian tune I remembered as one of her favorites, by a favorite singer with an unpronounceable name.

She waltzed past us with an inordinately cheerful smile and chipper wave for me and an equally warm greeting for my unwelcome guests, both of whom already had their guns aimed at her.

"What the fuck?" Everett said.

I realized that in my tired state I'd neglected to shut the door behind me.

Something else I realized as she moved into the kitchen and got my Dust Buster and FloorPlow from the broom closet—

Returned to the living room—

Began FloorPlowing the carpet and busting dust from the couch and in and around Clegg's chair, telling him, "Excuse me, sir, it'll only take a few seconds."

Maryam was sleepwalking.

She tapped the barrel of Clegg's Glock, then headed to Everett and did it to his .38, followed up with a tap to the tip of his nose, wondering, "Aren't you boys a little old to be playing cops and robbers?"

She steered the FloorPlow out of the room and across the hallway to my bedroom, calling back to us, "Should only be a few minutes, then I'll put on a fresh pot of coffee for you and your friends, how's that? Cookies would be nice, but whipping up a fresh batch would take too long, I'm afraid."

Everett, tracking her with the .38, challenged me with his look and said again, "What the fuck?" Threw the look at Clegg, who appeared more curious than concerned.

"Neighbor down the hall," I said. "She's a sleepwalker. I must have left the door open. She can't do you any damage. Won't remember anything after she wakes up in the morning."

"Says who?"

"I've been through this before, Mr. Everett—"

"Just Everett. So what, you've been through it before?"

I appealed to Clegg.

"She has parasomnias," I said. "They're sleeping disorders, and one of them is sleepwalking. She may be doing the windows or something like that before she leaves. Anything's possible."

Clegg gave me a look like he was half asleep.

Everett said, "Sounds to me what you're talking's right there with 'The Mercedes is paid for' and 'The check is in the mail.' Like all the other shit you been dishing out." He told Clegg, "I think we'll have to take care of her along with Gulliver."

Clegg turned up a palm.

"A real shame about the cookies," Maryam said over the drone of the FloorPlow, which she was working backward out of the bedroom. "Give me a little warning next time you're planning on having guests, Neil. It'll be my pleasure." She made a clucking sound as she disappeared up the hallway. In another moment, the steady buzz of the FloorPlow quit.

Rising from the stool, Everett said, "I better go pull her back in here before she gets away."

He managed a step or two before Maryam reappeared. She had my carry-on on top of the Warhol box, which she was using like a serving tray.

Clegg and Everett exchanged looks.

"I'll say it again, Neil. You need a cleaning person to come in and tidy after you on a regular basis," Maryam said, then turned and re-entered the bedroom. She was out again before Everett could chase after her, this time carrying only the black box. "There a special place you want this?" she asked me.

"I'll take that," Everett said. He was on her immediately.

Maryam turned over the box.

"Thank you," she said. "Your friend's so helpful, Neil. I can manage the FloorPlow and the Dust Buster by myself." A minute later she was heading back to the kitchen with both.

And Everett was filling the doorway, the Warhols under his arm, his .38 pointing into the room. His smile on loan from the man in the moon.

"Wouldn't you say me getting and keeping the whole two million from Havilland is a better idea than sharing it with you, Clegg?"

Clegg answered, "You should leave the good ideas to General Electric is what I think, Everett." Dispassionately, as if the double-cross Everett seemed ready to pull was coming as no surprise.

Everett said, "If I'm going to leave two bodies behind, I don't see a reason why it can't be three just as easily."

"At least your arithmetic works," Clegg said.

A popping sound.

It turned Everett's chest red and lifted him off the ground, then down, still holding the Warhols and the .38, his face frozen in amazement.

Clegg had his Glock on me now.

I saw he'd somehow managed to slip on a silencer during the distractions Maryam had created.

"You had this planned all along?"

He said quietly, "Everett's always been as easy to read as the *E* on an eye doctor's chart."

"And now?"

"If the old man hadn't switched boxes, none of this would have had to happen between you and me, Gulliver."

"There'd still have been Everett."

"You'd have figured something out. A whole new set of lies. Something would've worked."

"With you?"

"No, and no time now for you to try anything."

"The Warhol portfolio's what you came for. Why not just leave with it?"

"Yes, I will. Afterward."

"But you'll let my neighbor go. I swear it's the truth. She's walking in a world of her own. She won't remember this happened. You. Anything."

Legitimate panic filling my voice.

What I said—

Nothing Clegg had to think about.

No charity in his eyes.

Clegg shook his head. "Let's say I like to be as neat in my business as your lady friend. Wherever I go, I do my own housecleaning."

"Then why would you possibly think about leaving behind a dead man staining the carpet with his blood, much less two other dead persons?" Maryam asked from the kitchen.

She was leaning over the service counter, using it as a base for her elbows. A firm two-handed shooter's grip on the Beretta I keep stashed in my bedroom closet. Aiming it steady and straight at Clegg, a sitting duck, hard to miss at that range.

Maryam also had put her distraction to good use.

"Were you ever asleep?" I said.

"What, and miss all the fun?" she said.

34

Gulliver hurried to Everett and retrieved the .38 while he and the woman traded nervous, tension-relieving chatter about what to do next, 911-ing the cops, that sort of thing, while keeping Clegg targeted in their crosshairs.

They were so caught up in the moment they didn't understand they only knew what they had done, where he knew what he was doing. Their lives were still in his hands, even after he did as Gulliver ordered and slowly leaned over, placed the Glock on the floor, and push-kicked it away.

Gulliver looked comfortable with a gun in his grip and that made him more dangerous than the woman. Pop him first, on the roll to the floor, Clegg decided, then catch the woman. The shot would be tougher.

At that angle, she would have extra cover from the service counter, could get off a shot, maybe two, but he'd be traveling, a moving target, and she didn't have the eyes of a shooter. He saw the doubt there. He saw the lack of commitment to killing. Even if she did pull the trigger, she was bound to miss.

Clegg told himself, *Take your time, like always, while their over-confidence grows. Catch them at high tide, before they go for the telephone.*

The looks passing between them announced loud and clear they were more than neighbors. Lovers, more likely. That was the message he was getting from her voice and Gulliver's.

He envied Gulliver. She was a beautiful young woman. Sounded intelligent. The kind of woman he'd thought he had, and maybe for a time did. But that time was long past *Maryam*. Nice name. Pretty. Like she was. Like his wife had been.

Gulliver saying to her, "You should've just kept walking."

"The door open like that, I couldn't pass up the chance to say hello. See how you are. You haven't been around and I found I was missing you. Can you believe that? I can't."

Yes. Lovers.

"Instead of your stupid stunt, you should have gone to the phone and dialed nine-one-one," Gulliver said.

"I heard enough to know there might not be time for me to call and the police to get here. You should be thankful, seeing as how my stupid stunt helped save your life."

"It could have cost you yours. How would anybody be able to ex-plain that to your kids? Not the kind of guilt I'd want to carry around the rest of my life."

Her kids?

Clegg interrupted them with the question.

Maryam hesitated before responding, "Two, not that it's any busi-ness of yours."

"Boys?"

A deep sigh. "A boy and a girl. In that order."

Spoken proudly, with unquestionable devotion, but Clegg also heard certain regret.

"How old is your son?"

She told him.

"I have a son who's the same age . . . Does your son like to visit the zoo?"

"He, the children, they don't live with me. They're not in this coun-try. They . . ." Her voice faltering.

Clegg hadn't meant to cause the pain he saw engulfing her, not this way.

Gulliver, sensitive to her emotions, said, "Time for us to call the cops. Can you manage the wall phone from there?"

The woman shook her head.

Gulliver took his time pondering how to handle the situation.

Clegg knew, if their positions were reversed, he'd have capped both of Gulliver's knees before going for a phone.

Finally Gulliver said, "Keep Clegg in your sights while I come around. Okay?"

"Okay."

Gulliver moved slowly and cautiously. Sidestepping. The .38 trained on Clegg. Showing some smarts in taking a route that wouldn't put him between his girlfriend and Clegg.

Clegg counted off the steps in his mind.

When he lost Gulliver in his peripheral vision, heard Gulliver's labored breath behind the easy chair, Clegg made his move.

He pitched forward onto the floor.

Connected with the Glock.

Rolled onto his back.

Fired a random shot into the ceiling to confuse Gulliver and the woman, who fired a reflex shot that sank into the back of the easy chair.

It was all the time Clegg needed to shift onto his feet and dash behind her.

He ran one forearm around her neck, pressed the Glock under her chin and ordered her to release her hold on the Beretta.

The Beretta hit the counter and bounced onto the floor.

"That's a smart girl," Clegg told her, then called to Gulliver, who was frozen behind the easy chair, "No chair and her bullet would be in your belly. Drop the thirty-eight or my bullet'll catch her in the head." Gulliver dropped the .38. "Wise decision. Now, sit in the chair, your hands on the armrests where I can see them." Gulliver went around the chair and sat.

Clegg indicated his approval and said to the woman, out of Gulliver's hearing, "Did you ever take your son and daughter to Disney World?"

"I never had the chance," she said.

"When you do, they'd like it. My son, he loved it. I hope to take him there again one day."

Gulliver said, "You know there's no way you'll get away with this."

"Of course there is," Clegg said. "Tell me, what's in the black box? This time the right Warhols?"

"Yes," Gulliver said, gripping the armrests like he was on a jet bouncing through rough skies, his eyes moving from the Glock pressed against the woman's neck, to various parts of the room, like he might stumble over some escape route from the situation.

"All twelve silkscreens?"

"Yes."

"Describe the last one for me, the twelfth print."

Clegg listened to Gulliver explain away the collector as Rudy Feather's father and how the Gainsborough portrait of a young boy he proudly exhibited was the one Feather had hanging prominently on his parlor wall.

Afterward Gulliver asked, "What is it that makes that print so special that people are killing and being killed?"

Clegg considered answering him, then changed his mind.

The way Gulliver talked, he had left something out.

It didn't matter now.

He said to the woman, loud enough for Gulliver to hear, "I want you to be as good walking when you're awake as you were when you were sleepwalking. We're going to get the Warhols."

Gulliver was unarmed, but it was never worth taking any unnecessary risks, so Clegg used her as a shield in working around the counter and across the room. Once or twice Gulliver looked like he might try for the .38, but wisely stayed settled in the easy chair, tapping a nervous drumbeat with his fingers.

Clegg ran the Glock down the woman's spine while he sank to his haunches and swept up the black box.

He asked her, "Are you a good mother to your son and daughter?"

Low, so the question remained just between the two of them.

"Yes," she said without hesitation.

"Then I'm sure you'll have the opportunity again. When you do, remember about Disney World. Buy them the cap with the Mickey Mouse ears and the little propeller on top. They'll love that."

Louder now, so Gulliver could hear him, "She's saved your life twice in one day," he said—

And moved swiftly out of the apartment.

Within hours he had used a set of his fake credentials to book his flight and was waiting out the departure time at a motel less than twenty minutes from the Hertz dump at LAX under an altogether different assumed name. He sank into a deep sleep while waiting for Porter

Havilland to return his call. The phone, when it finally rang, startled Clegg from a dream that was almost entirely erased from his memory by the time he remembered where he was and found the instrument.

The lingering part had to do with Lucy, the woman from Billy Bob's in Fort Worth. She was on his mind again. This time maybe a substitute for Gulliver's woman, Maryam, who had so many of the same admirable qualities.

If Havilland sounded surprised to be speaking with him, not Everett, he covered it well with his exuberance at Clegg's opening comment: "I have them, boss. All twelve."

"When can you get them here?"

Clegg spelled out his terms.

When he finished, Havilland said unhappily, "Highly unusual, Clegg. Not the way we usually do business."

"It is this time," Clegg said. "My price for the suite is two million and I'll be on my way to you with the Warhol suite the minute I confirm one million of it has been wired and received. No COD this time, boss. My son's too precious for that."

"This time, then, is the last time, Clegg. No next time. We shake hands and go our separate ways after you make your delivery."

"Sure, boss," he said. "Never again. Works for me."

Clegg racked the receiver knowing Havilland well enough to know he wasn't going to hand over the second million like that.

Havilland was sure to have some nasty plan in place by the time Clegg arrived.

That was okay by him.

Clegg had his own nasty plan for Havilland.

That night, he was at the same bar at Billy Bob's where he'd first met Lucy. Unable to shake her from his mind, he'd rerouted himself via a stop in Dallas–Fort Worth. The honky-tonk was as crowded and noisy as the last time, lots of good-looking women roaming loose or at the bar playing eye-games with the cowboys over their long-necked beers.

"Juicy Lucy," she'd called herself, but that was part of her façade.

Lucy was far more real than she let on at first.

Clegg wondered how her bumlets were, if maybe he'd get the chance to meet them sometime. Maybe sometime with his son, once the boy was better.

He asked the barkeep for the time.

Late, and he was feeling it.

He'd give Lucy another half hour, resigning himself to the likelihood they weren't going to connect tonight. Maybe he'd have better luck running into her the next time, after he finished his business with Havilland.

"What's this?" Clegg asked as the bartender set a fresh club soda in front of him.

"Compliments of the lady three stools over. Said to say you look like somebody can't find his way out of the Dumpster and might need a little cheering up."

"A pro?"

"Could be, I suppose. She's new to me."

Clegg leaned forward and checked her out.

A pretty woman in her forties. Large, hungry black eyes on a sweet face under a black Stetson, the kind that Hoppy always wore on television. A motherly softness falling out of a low-necked blouse that fit like a tightly laced corset over snug bluejeans.

She caught him studying her and sent him back the kind of smile he always found irresistible.

Clegg raised the soda glass and she answered his toast, then eased off the stool and hip-swung her way over. "I hope I wasn't being too forward just now," she said, her silken voice ruffled every few words by what was either a whiskey or cigarette scratch.

Clegg shook his head no, got up, and insisted she take his place.

She settled onto the stool and crossed one leg over the other, raised her glass and offered, "Cheers!"

"Cheers!" he said, touching his glass to hers.

"I'm Porter," Clegg said, only because it was the first name that came to mind.

"Hello, Porter," she said, her smile growing larger. "A pleasure. I'm Aleta."

35

Maybe six minutes after Clegg fled, Maryam and me still in the middle of some serious hugging, four people spilled into the apartment, four men, two women, all of them armed and aiming. In the lead was one of Ari and Zev's associates from Myrtle Beach. The others resembled exchange students at UCLA.

The leader, tall, athletic, looking like he belonged in a military uniform, snapped out search instructions to them, grunting as he stepped over Everett to confirm we were okay.

"That one slipped by us," he said, apologetically, his voice heavily accented. "The other one must have been inside and waiting before we got here, but we're on to him now."

"What about Stevie?" I said.

"Fine, so don't you alarm yourself," he said, sizing up Maryam at the same time, curiosity riddling his face. "We're there now at her place and we'll be looking after her for as long as necessary. You as well."

Maryam threw an arm across her half-exposed breasts and excused herself, heading for the bedroom to get a robe.

"What got you here?"

"An urgent call from Ari Landau. Information our people picked up after you left England," the leader said. I started to ask another question, but he staved me off with his palms. "Nothing you have to know, Mr. Gulliver. Now, is there someplace you and your lady friend can go while we clean up? You give us a few hours, it'll be good as new here, like none of this ever happened."

"We have to call the police," I said.

The leader gave me a stern look.

"Mr. Gulliver, I don't think so. Neither should you. We got ourselves bigger fish to fry than that dead mackerel on the floor. This gets out, it could get in the way of all we've been on the verge of accomplishing for years."

"Havilland? The Warhols? The lost artworks?"

"Possibly more, based on what's coming from London, but it could end at another brick wall if word got out. Why no police, you understand? No television or newspapers. Our little secret."

"Like Myrtle Beach?"

No answer.

"Like London?"

No answer.

Maryam, who had returned, took my hand and said, "Come on, Neil. Let them do their work."

A week later we were still questioning why Clegg, when he fled with the Warhols, had left Maryam and me alive. She and I had theories that seemed to make sense, but not after we threw in the fact that Clegg was too practiced at killing to be an amateur and even had hinted at leaving no witnesses behind. *Housecleaning*, he'd called it.

Maybe we'd never know Clegg's reasons.

Maybe just as well.

Both of us were realists willing to accept our blessings in any form of arrival, a concept reinforced by Ari Landau when he phoned to arrange a meeting with Stevie and me.

"Stay away from it now," Ari said. "Better all the way around, my friend. You'll hear when I see you."

———

We met two days later at Stevie's place.

Ari's arrival, with Zev in tow as usual, happily cut short an argument inspired by my ex, although Stevie would claim otherwise.

We were sitting on the balcony, sipping iced tea and enjoying a cloudless afternoon skyline, too dazzling to be anything but computer-generated. I was describing how Maryam knew about the Beretta stashed in my bedroom closet.

I said, innocently, "Maryam and I got to talking one morning about how secure the Heathcliffe is from burglars and break-ins. I got up and got the Beretta to show Maryam I took some precautions, and how she should think about doing the same. I volunteered to arrange with Jimmy Steiger to take her out on the police range for some lessons, like I did with you in the long ago, and—"

Stevie cut me off.

" 'One morning,' you said? You had the conversation with her 'one morning'?"

She gave me a look you'd never see on a happy camper. Settled her glass on the railing and averted her eyes.

"Curious, Neil. You never were the one for *conversation* in the morning with me."

"You and I, we never had that much to talk about," I said. "Except about you, of course."

She must not have heard the good-natured tease in my voice, and not because of the heavy street noise below, the hum of motors and the jazz riffs from horns in traffic thick with commuters.

"I don't think so, Neil," she said, using my name like a doomsday signal. "What's the real attraction? You can tell me. You talk a lot about yourself, is that it? And finally you've found someone who doesn't mind *listening*? Tell me, how does she manage to keep that conversation from putting her back to sleep?"

"That was never our problem and you know it."

Arching backward, she pitched a look of disbelief at me. "It was so low on the list we never got to it before I ran screaming."

"Oh, I always wondered what that noise was. Up to now I thought it was your Jolly Green Giant of an ego in need of a lube."

The intercom buzzed.

Stevie smacked me with disdain and charged off to answer it while I headed inside giving silent thanks that rescue doesn't always call for firearms or a Saint Bernard.

It was Ari and Zev.

Pretending not to notice the iceberg atmosphere, Ari added two more sugar packets to his coffee before pushing aside the small talk.

"First off, you should know Eugene Barnstable turned into a most agreeable chap after he was presented with his options," he said. "So, Zev?"

"So. Arafat and the Palestinians should be smart enough to cooperate like that."

"We got from him the names of more collectors with art to hide. Names we never knew. Names to go with faces we had already come to despise. Their secret locations. The underground collections where you wouldn't think to look, you didn't know already. More. Buried in museums, including some of the big ones that might not know they have looted art on their walls or stored which the rightful owners still hunger after."

"The Warhols?"

"Yes, names there, also. Not all of them. There are many we're still missing."

"And the twelfth print? Rudy Feather's father with his Gainsborough?"

"Not real like the others," Ari said. "When the prints were being made by Henri Godard and Andy Warhol's stand-in, Frankie Freddie Frook—"

"You mean Rudy Feather."

"By any name, Neil. Frankie Freddie, Feather, recognized what the suite he and Henri Godard were creating in Warhol's name for Porter Havilland was all about. From love or pride or simple stupidity, Feather was inspired to include his father. It was all done from memory. Havilland went crazy when he heard this from Godard, maybe only because he had unwittingly come this close to finding the partner who double-crossed him.

"He ordered Godard to destroy all copies of the Feather print before the portraits suites were assembled and delivered for the collectors who had paid through the nose for them. Godard did as he was told by Havilland, except for the one silkscreen in the bootleg suite he secretly made for himself."

I shook my head. Not that the puzzle wasn't coming together, but—

There was still a big piece missing.

"If Havilland wanted them all destroyed to begin with, why did he become so dedicated to finding the twelfth print when he learned one still existed? I don't think so, Ari. I think there's more to it."

"If and when we ever learn that, it could be our key to learning much more, my friend. As the saying goes, 'The truth is in the details.' "

"Get your hands on Havilland, get the details?"

"Too late for that, I'm afraid."

"What's that mean?" Stevie said.

"We found him, Havilland. Thanks to Eugene Barnstable, who turned us on to the man Everett. We wasted no time. Everett led us to Clegg and through Clegg we were able to track Havilland to his lair. To Missoula, Montana, of all the places in the world. Who'd ever think to look there? Except for slate mining, nothing at all ever happens in Missoula, Montana."

He stopped.

I sensed a punch line coming and told him so.

Ari exchanged a knowing glance with Zev.

"We chose to stay two steps behind Clegg, and they were two steps too many," Zev said. "Dead, both of them, before we could do anything."

He zipped his finger across his throat, then a second time.

"I want to think they saved us the trouble," he said.

Ari signaled him to be quiet.

"No way of explaining the why of it or how it happened, only that both were shot dead," Ari said. "Close range. Hard to tell who shot first. From all signs, it was some kind of lovers' quarrel. Before cleaning up we checked and found the house was empty. Every file, empty. A storage vault, empty." A shrug and a smile of acceptance.

"So where does that put us?"

"Us-us, Neil, not you-and-we us," Ari said quickly. "I don't think you'll have to worry anymore about anything, while our job isn't over yet. Maybe not for a long time. But I promise you this much: When the time is right, you, Neil Gulliver, will get the story first. The entire story. One as big as the dreams so many of our people have held dear for all these years."

"If I get tired of waiting?"

"Neil, don't even think it," Zev said ominously.

What followed was one of those silent minutes that seem to stretch into hours, when nobody wants to say anything that could be taken the wrong way—

Or the right way.

Finally Ari kicked off a hearty laugh with a smile.

He said, "Zev, a joke's a joke, but stop with your kidding already. You'll have our friends thinking you might be serious."

Zev took the cue and shook his head hard enough to rip something loose inside. He began laughing louder than Ari. Slapped his knee at the funniest joke never told. "Forgive me," he said. "I apologize."

I didn't believe him, but smiled an acceptance.

The way Stevie dropped her lids told me she also knew better.

"Anything else you want us to know?" she said.

Ari acted out a broad *How could I have forgotten?*

"Yes, so much conversation to start, it got in the way of a very happy reason to have this visit with you . . . Zev, go ahead . . ."

"A very happy reason," Zev agreed. He leaned over for one of two burlap bags that had been resting by the side of his seat and offered it to Stevie.

She cleared room on the table for it, undid the simple knot with a tug, and in another moment had slipped it off the Warhol presentation box.

"That's right," Ari said. "It's back where it belongs. The one thing we found beside Havilland and Clegg."

"The five I brought to Myrtle Beach, or Feather's set?"

"The five. Our people came across them in going through the Homestead. Feather's set?" A shrug. "So far, no idea what Clegg did with it."

Zev had taken the larger of the bags and set it against a wall.

"Come, Neil. You'll appreciate this one especially," he said. "It turned up in London, when our people were cleaning out the Barnstable place."

Maryam and I made the drive the following weekend, a Saturday that promised only intermittent clouds to interfere with a shimmering turquoise sky and a temperature predicted to hover in the glowing eighties. I'd proposed to Stevie that she join us, use the opportunity to get to know Maryam.

Not surprisingly, she declined.

She had a good enough excuse to mask her irritation, if you didn't know better: Paramount was passing on the Lombard project because Tony B. Tony could not get a commitment from either of the Toms, both of whom were "dying to do it" but, alas, had prior commitments that would take them through the year 2050.

Consequently Stevie was spending the weekend with Tony B. Tony and Ossie Parkman, retooling scenes to suit Russell Crowe, who might be available, and otherwise preparing for a pitch meeting on Tuesday with Jeffie Katzenberg and, if he's back from wherever wasn't here, Stevie Spielberg.

"Still not too shabby, huh, honey?" she wondered into the phone.

"When'll I know I've made it into the A-group?" I said. "When Tony B. Tony starts calling me 'Neilie'?"

Stevie hung up on me, leaving me to continue wondering how hung up I still was on her.

Maurice Kline lived within walking distance of Balboa Park and the Globe Theatre, in a settled neighborhood lined on both sides of the street with the style of duplexes and garden apartments popular in the twenties and thirties, in a one-bedroom at the back of a twelve-unit court overgrown with two-story-tall trees and shrubbery.

He welcomed Maryam and me at the door like old friends, glasses propped up on his forehead, a script folded under his arm. His potbelly sneaking out from his shirt and overhanging a pair of shorts that revealed spindly legs full of blue veins and bumps.

"Getting a leg up on the new season," Maurice explained enthusiastically as he ushered us inside. "Jack O'Brien back from his two Tony nominations on Broadway and has me in mind for one of the leads in Simon's *The Sunshine Boys*, if that's what opens the new season." He patted the script like he was burping an infant. "The Jack Albertson part, if you saw the original production. George Burns in the movie, of course."

The apartment was small, clean and comfortable, filled with plastic-covered furniture and a lifetime of memorabilia on the walls and every surface.

Framed posters from shows he'd been in.

Photographs autographed by stars and forgotten faces, Maurice in some of them.

Family photos assigned spots of greater prominence.

"Help yourself," he said, pointing to a tall pitcher of lemonade and an open box of sugar wafers on the dining-room table. "Get comfortable anywhere, relax, and tell me to what I owe the pleasure of your company."

He settled cautiously in a well-worn chair and watched with curiosity as Maryam circled the room, stopping finally in front of a medium-size poster prominently featuring a teenaged Maurice Kline. All the text in Yiddish.

"The woman with her arms around me is Stella," he said. "Stella Adler. It says above the title, next to my name, 'A rising star in the tradition of the Adler *menchen*.' I should only live so long."

Maryam asked, "Would you mind if I take it down for a minute?"

Maurice exaggerated his look of curiosity before giving her a generous *Go ahead* wave of the hand.

"As long as you don't run off with it," he said.

She removed the poster from the wall.

Found a safe place for it on the floor.

Turned around and said, "Neil, I think you should do the honors."

She walked around behind Maurice and covered his eyes with her hands while I pulled the wrapped package from the burlap bag Ari and Zev had delivered earlier in the week. I carefully removed the interior wrapping and walked the oil painting to the open spot on the wall.

A perfect fit.

I adjusted the frame and stepped aside so Maurice would have an unrestricted view.

I nodded at Maryam.

She removed her hands.

Maurice stared silently at the Berthe Morisot painting of the woman in the white dressing gown that the Nazis had stolen more than a half century ago from the collection of his parents, Dr. and Mrs. Josef Kleinschmick.

Then, Maurice cried.

36

My subconscious kicked in just when I thought I'd managed to put the Warhol suite out of my mind.

In a dream.

Something Henri Godard had said to Stevie and me in Rudy Feather's atelier before Godard attacked Clegg and Feather began blasting away with the Uzi and unintentionally dropped Godard.

In my dream the cast of characters was dressed as pirates, wielded swords and flintlocks and looked like I'd borrowed them from a Warner Bros. movie.

Errol Flynn kindly standing in for me.

The delectable Olivia De Havilland, in a blonde wig, for Stevie.

Olivia/Stevie asking Basil Rathbone, as Godard, "What about the twelfth print in the suite?" after Rathbone/Godard confesses he's "Mr. France" and having lost the Warhol silkscreens to Aaron Lodger (J. Carroll Naish) in a card game.

Rathbone/Godard answering her in an acceptable French accent, "Ask your friend Monsieur Lodger that question. It was there when I turned over the portfolio."

That jarred me awake.

I leaped out of bed and punched in Stevie's number.

"You have a clue what time it is?" she said.

"Just listen to me for a minute."

Instead she hung up. I punched in her number again. There's no service on her private line and the phone rang a few hundred times before she surrendered.

"This better be good," she said.

I told her about the dream.

"Olivia, huh? I'm flattered. She went on to win two Oscars, you know?"

"I know," I said.

A few hours later, she'd postponed a meeting with Tony B. Tony and some honchos at Fox and we were on the road to Aaron Lodger's place in Palm Springs.

It had been a long time since we were at the crafty old crime boss's heavily gated and guarded fortresslike Italian villa, about a mile above the invisible border between Palm Springs and Palm Desert, at the top of Gilbert Roland Road.

His watchmen knew to expect Stevie's emerald-green BMW.

We breezed through and followed hand commands to a parking space close to the home's main entrance.

Were permitted inside without more than an eyeball inspection for weapons.

"The soap still stinks without you," Aaron Lodger told Stevie as we were ushered into his presence by some kid whose choirboy visage was undermined by the gun bulge under his jacket. "I don't know why I even bother watching anymore."

Lodger was rearranging some of the Betty Boop dolls and bronze figurines from his vast collection that dominated the oak-paneled, supersized McDen. He quit and shambled over to a hard, flat-backed chair positioned like a throne.

"I got my regular card game waiting for me at the club, so tell me fast what's this all about. Time's money. I ain't getting any younger, besides."

Lodger gripped his hands in his lap and rolled his thumbs while Stevie repeated what Godard had told us.

"So?"

"So is it true, Mr. Lodger?"

"I don't know why it should make any difference to you anyway. I brought them to you as a gift and you didn't even want to take them." Turning to me he said, "You did right by them and by me, Neil. Tell me what's the big *tsimmis* all of a sudden with your wife."

"My ex."

"She's here with you, you with her. Ex marks the spot. Just answer me."

I told him as much as I thought he should know.

If Lodger sensed I was holding back, he didn't let on. He let the information sink in, slowly, like some old Univac not ready to step aside.

"You know something about the Jews, you two?" He got up and cautiously crossed over to the bookshelf wall, where he inched some of the leather-bound volumes in and out until he was satisfied with their alignment, then turned back to us. "Us Jews never give up. That's why we're still around, like it or not." Heading back for his seat, he called to the choirboy, "Dennis, go to the jukebox and press-twenty-two." In a minute, the sound system was pumping out "Rhapsody in Blue." "George Gershwin was a Jew," Lodger said. "Did you know that, Dennis?"

"Yes sir, Mr. L."

"And don't you ever forget it."

"Yes sir."

Lodger's head descended and he closed his eyes. It was impossible to tell if he was thinking about something or had fallen asleep. Almost as quickly, his cold eyes were back on us. I was ready to swear his taut white skin made a noise as he cracked what was meant to be a smile.

"You got me, dead to rights," Lodger said, "so it's a good thing you're not the IRS. I'm gonna tell you something what happened. I get those pictures from Mr. France and I'm curious enough to have a look. They're people who mean nothing to me and paintings I can live without. Except for one. One of the pictures, there's a painting I always been partial to, one of my favorites. Don't ask me why, except maybe she looks a lot like my *mamala*, God rest her soul. Something I always saw in it from the first time I set eyes . . . Dennis, from my bedroom, on the wall that's right next to Richie, may he rest in peace. Go get it and bring it here. On the two, Dennis."

Dennis hurried off like he was late out of the starting gate.

"So, I kept that one for myself, before I came to your welcome-back party, Stevie, with my unwelcome gift." He let the words sink in. "Didn't figure any reason for you to ever miss it. Had it framed the same as Richie, seeing as how it was by the same artist."

Dennis was back.

Lodger screamed at him, "Dennis, damn it all to hell! They don't have X-ray vision. Turn it around, so they can see what the picture looks like."

"Yes sir, Mr. L."

I don't know which of us made the louder sound, Stevie or me.

We moved on the print for a closer inspection.

"Yeah, a beauty. You can look, you can touch, but you don't get to take it away from here," Lodger said.

Godard's chop mark was where it belonged.

The collector was still Rudy Feather's father, exactly as he'd appeared on the Feather forgery, but—

In this print—

The real twelfth print—

It was not a Gainsborough on proud display from Daddy's illicit collection.

It was *La Gioconda*—

Da Vinci's *Mona Lisa*.

I called Ari and Zev's 800 number the instant we hit the road back to Los Angeles.

The mechanical operator reported it had been disconnected.

I kept trying to reach them over the next few weeks, at numbers I had and a few I had no business having, slipped to me by contacts who owed me a favor. Links inside the Mossad and all the highly positioned others answered me the same way.

Always the same response.

Nobody had ever heard of Ari Landau or Zev Neumann.

Almost six months later, Maryam phoned me, then rushed over. She gave me a kiss on the neck and slid into the chair she pulled up next to mine by the computer terminal. "I knew you'd want to see this," she said. "It came about ten minutes ago. In today's mail."

Maryam handed over a postcard.

The picture side announced, *Greetings from Disney World*.

The photograph showed Mickey Mouse posing with his arm around a small boy, both waving at the camera lens.

The boy had a smile on his face almost as big as he was.

On his head was a skullcap with Mickey Mouse ears and a little propeller on top.

The message on the reverse side, hand-printed in block letters, said, DON'T GIVE UP HOPE. YOUR TURN WILL COME.

It was unsigned.

Some Author's Notes
and Acknowledgments

Andy Warhol's greatest work of art may have been Andy himself.

Early in his career he became aware that celebrity was often more important in today's society than most degrees of talent—genius, even.

He mined that concept to his own fruitful advantage, in the process winning for himself more than the fifteen minutes of fame he predicted for everyone else in the world.

Andy was already notorious when I met him for the first time.

His soup cans had made him the object of public ridicule and few critics in the art community were taking him as seriously as others who'd spiraled to reputation in the leap forward generally lumped together as "Pop Art" in the reportage and criticism of the time, the late 1950s and early 1960s.

He was a filmmaker, whose movies were built on notions defying viewers to view, not only out of the mainstream but nowhere close to a tributary. These films were reviled by the public and the critics, ex-

> >
> >
> >

362 cept those who understood, appreciated and accepted the Marcel Duchamp dictum *Art is everything.*

Andy was guru to a gang of acolytes who hung around his never-
never land of a studio, The Factory, and on to his coattails, like Andy
was their ride away from obscurity.

For several of them he was, in art, in movies, in publishing, even
in music, where he helped to put brand-identification on the likes of
Lou Reed and the Velvet Underground, even among the dead, who
cling to life in documentaries and tell-all autobiographies that owe their
existence to Andy Warhol.

For the others, wherever they are today, they can at least fall asleep
to memories of a time when Andy let them treat his rainbow as their
own.

That first encounter with Andy is assigned in *Hot Paint* to Augie Fowler,
as is the *Coast* magazine feature story, "However Measured or Far
Away." Except for injection of one fictional character important to sub-
sequent events in *Hot Paint*, the piece runs almost in its entirety and
almost as it did in 1969.

It was Andy's increasing notoriety and the commercial sensibility
of the magazine's editor, Digby Diehl—who would go on to a career
that included a stint as book editor of the *Los Angeles Times*, publisher
of Abrams Art Books, and author of numerous bestselling biographies—
that caused him to suggest I tackle the assignment.

Who more obvious, given I was writing a monthly art column for
Coast in addition to running an international public-relations firm?

Besides, the calculating Digby observed with his infectious grin, I
could link the visit to a business trip from L.A. to my New York office
instead of tapping into *Coast's* limited expense budget.

Arrangements easily fell into place over a few phone calls to the
offices of Andy's *Interview* magazine, the details worked out by his
right-hand man and key strategist of the time, Bob Colacello, whose
enthusiasm soared when he learned mine would be the cover story in
an issue devoted almost entirely to Warhol.

I was joined on that eventful visit to Andy's Factory by my wife
and co-adventurer, Sandra, and a client and pal, Melissa Hart, who at
the time was starring on Broadway as Sally Bowles in Hal Prince's original production of *Cabaret* and a year later, in 1970, would pick up a
Tony nomination as Best Supporting Actress in a Musical, *Georgy*.

(I acknowledge them here out of guilt for omitting any reference to their presence in "However Measured or Far Away." Suffice it to say at this late date, their amazement and amusement at the Factory carryings-on equaled and may have outdistanced my own.)

The *Coast* cover story was the first for Warhol in a key consumer publication.

More than that, it exposed the fact that Andy alone was not responsible for making his art, that Brigid Polk (in fact, Brigid Berlin, daughter of Richard Berlin, the late Hearst publishing-empire executive) had a hand in executing and signing Warhol limited editions, news that was quickly picked up by *Time* magazine and carried worldwide.

And somewhere in one of my art cabinets, framed, is the sheet of paper on which Brigid showed off her signature-forging skills, which Augie later shoves at Andy for a signature.

The Warhol encounter built around rock idol Richie Savage that climaxes with Neil Gulliver leading Andy onto the stage at Madison Square Garden to observe Richie's SRO concert from behind the amps, happened a lot like it's presented, except the rock idol was Shaun Cassidy and the author substitutes Neil Gulliver for himself.

Shaun, a PR client at the time, as was brother David before him, bears absolutely no resemblance to Richie, except for my borrowing from my clear memories of Cassidy fans who crowded outside the Plaza Hotel praying for sight of him, his photo session with the late Barry McKinley for an *Interview* cover, and the avalanche of murmured recognition and applause as I led Andy through the house of young girls with raging hormones to his spot downstage-right from Shaun's keyboard player, Michael Lloyd, then, as now, a major hitmaking record producer with rooms in his Beverly Hills home decorated wall-to-wall in gold and platinum records.

During that session in Barry's studio, I asked Andy if I might borrow his Polaroid to take a souvenir photo. When I turned the camera on him, not Shaun, the surprise registered at once on his face:

It's been my sense ever since that Andy recognized his place among the rich and famous, but was never quite as comfortable with it as he was associating with the celebrities whose company he quietly basked in, like some shy hero-worshiping kid who somehow had managed to slip into the playground of his wishful fantasies and expected to be caught and evicted at any moment.

Preparing for *Hot Paint*, when I dug out *Coast* from my files and reread the piece for the first time in all these years, I was surprised at how early and accurately I'd sensed and summarized Andy's importance to art history, and now—

To this novel—

However measured or far away.

At the time the monthly column for *Coast* was offered to me, Sandra and I already were making regular excursions to the galleries lining both sides of La Cienega Boulevard in the 1960s, as well as the County Museum of Art and the Pasadena Art Museum, shows of student work at the old Otis Art Institute campus behind MacArthur Park, the one where Jimmy Webb noticed that someone had left a cake out in the rain.

The column and feature stories I subsequently contributed to *Coast* and elsewhere, like the *Los Angeles Times Magazine* and *Rolling Stone*, made it possible for me to hang out with artists of reputation or just coming into their own, and to get acquainted with some of the great private collectors.

Visit their homes and tour their collections.

Get a sense of the history behind their grand obsessions.

It became an eye-popping experience, entering the home of someone like a Bernard Solomon and finding a Monet water-lilies over his fireplace and, nearby, a van Gogh *Pietà* the color-blind collector would one day quietly allow the Vatican to buy from him.

Or a special thrill, being invited by the movies' legendary "Little Caesar," Edward G. Robinson, to tour his second great collection—the first one a victim of divorce—gasping and gaping open-jawed at a Picasso masterpiece that dominated the staircase landing. The oil was never loaned for public viewing by Eddie, who m'yawed side-of-the-mouth dialogue he'd probably used hundreds of times before: "Picasso was the greatest bull artist in the world, you know? . . . Sometimes, the greatest artist in the world."

The column provided welcome relief from the insanities of rock and roll, played into my passion for art and gave me an education in the finer points of lithography and limited-edition prints that play a major role in *Hot Paint*.

The renaissance in lithography in America was in its infancy at the time, artists drawn to it by Tatyana Grossman's Universal Limited Art Editions in New York, and in Los Angeles by June Wayne at the Tamarind Workshop.

Among June's master printers was Ken Tyler, who would one day strike out on his own and come to form Gemini G.E.L. with Sidney Felsen and Stanley Grinstein, later heading east to continue pioneering new techniques and methodology at Tyler Graphics in upstate New York.

Gemini's spirit of adventure and advancement brought numerous major artists to Los Angeles, and it's where I spent many an hour watching master printers like Ken and Serge Lozingot at work, lunching with Sid across the street at Ma Maison, or spending time with artists in residence, including Jasper Johns, Frank Stella, Robert Rauschenberg, Roy Lichtenstein, James Rosenquist, Sam Francis and David Hockney.

I'm grateful to them and to others, such as Arthur Secunda, William Crutchfield, Shiro Ikegawa, Raphael Soyer, Larry Rivers, H. C. Westerman, Billy Al Bengston and James Strombotne for these fine, fondly remembered days.

Elements of *Hot Paint* dealing with the Nazis' systematic plunder of the great art collections of Europe and the disappearance of hundreds upon hundreds of masterpieces into private hands and secret collections are based on historical fact and contemporary news reports, as works continue to be rediscovered and the heirs of looted owners battle governments, dealers, auction houses and private collectors in the courts for return of plundered property.

For anyone interested in learning more about those dreadful times and events, I strongly recommend the definitive study by Hector Feliciano, *The Lost Museum: The Nazi Conspiracy to Steal the World's Greatest Works of Art*. It proved extremely helpful to me in blending elements of historical truth into my fictional events and characters.

Clegg's memory of the Dachau death camp, meanwhile, is based solely on my own visit with Sandra, Suzanne Somers and her husband, Alan Hamel, following production of Suzanne's network TV special for servicemen stationed at the Ramstein Air Force Base in Germany.

It was something the four of us felt we had to do, as painful as it might be—

And it was—

As an obligation to history.

I still have those cold stones Clegg took away with him as a souvenir.

They are as cold as ever, an unnecessary reminder to *Never forget*.

Some thanks now to people who helped me help Neil and Stevie make it to this fourth adventure, leading off as usual with Tom Doherty and his great team of pros at Forge, especially my editor, Natalia Aponte-Burns, whose always-on-point, gentle words of suggestion and direction invariably inspire the best work possible out of me.

Sandra Levinson read and reread (and reread again) *Hot Paint*, first as pages-in-progress and then in its various stages en route to "The End," catching errors of fact and keyboard and waving the red flag whenever something didn't track to her satisfaction. No holds barred with this kid, who was backstopped in blue-ribbon fashion by Deborah Levinson and Sandra Roberts.

And, I add appreciation here for reasons professional or personal or both to:

David and Janine Levinson, Erin Levinson, Therese Jansen, Daniel Jansen, Judith Arfin, Bertha Skolnik, Ida Nislow, Janet and Jack Sigman, Paul Jacobson, Sondra and Irv Palmeri, Jay and Brenda Lowy, Harvey Geller, Ron and Janet Tepper, Macey and Ruthie Lipman, Stan and Norma Layton, Michael Duberchin, Barbara Shore, Patty Ravalgi, Stu and Micki Bernstein, Henry and Ilene Miller, Liam and Aleta Campbell, Cary and Deborah Johnston, Gayle and Brett Ash, Terri Hirschfield, Beth Moore, Patti Morrill, Jan Burke, Gayle Lynds, Gregg Main, Gar Anthony Haywood, Jo Fluke, Nathan and Andrea Walpow, Kent Braithwaite, Malvin Wald, Frank and Margie Barron, Jerry Buck, Donnie Coleman, Don Whittemore, Steve Hoffman, Lew Weitzman, Susan Crawford, Julie Alley, Jay Bernstein, Joe, Michael and Robby Sutton, ever and always Grelun Landon, Saul Burakoff, Dr. Edgar A. Lueg, Dr. Michael P. McNicoll, and the Honorable William Jefferson Clinton.

—Robert S. Levinson
Los Angeles, California
January 2002
www.robertslevinson.com